Penance

Repentance for wrongdoing

Foundation for right doing

PENANCE

GENESIS AND GENOCIDE

JAMES HENDERSHOT

Order this book online at www.trafford.com
or email orders@trafford.com

Most Trafford titles are also available at major online book retailers.

Printed in the United States of America.

ISBN: 978-1-4907-1674-9 (sc)
ISBN: 978-1-4907-1675-6 (e)

Trafford rev. 10/16/2013

www.trafford.com

North America & international
toll-free: 1 888 232 4444 (USA & Canada)
fax: 812 355 4082

CONTENTS

Dedicated to my favorite RN, my wife Younghee, with thanks for financially providing for our family during my days of writing and to my sons, Josh & John and daughter, Nellie, as well as my Publishing team, Love Blake, Stacy Canon, and Evan Villiadores

NOTES

PENANCE INTRODUCTION

The mystery of mysteries is how the rules can be changed or applied from each dimension is so many different ways. The life that existed in your solar system before you, survived on your sister planet, Mars. Those who lived on Mars were so close through innocence and of pure heart to becoming in unison with the elements that they were destroyed. The current, soon to end, trouble on Earth is therefore intermingled into the straight path the destruction. Even the basic core is off trajectory. The biggest issue is how you have used nudity for promotion by exciting the primordial desire for your species to survive (procreate) and turned this into a device to excite lust, greed, and show of power, by separation and shame and restriction. This division dulls its gray lines and combines human souls with the mud, blood, and alcohol, or even drugs that turn a lighted soul from your lord into a deadly beast filled with darkness and a desire for evil.

After release from Hell for 1,000 years, the first thing I did was went to the other side of the universe to rebuild my forces. Then I made a mistake that would follow me for a couple of millions of years, until I get out of this reality and into another. I was to obtain my revenge, yet even at that, these questions and mysteries still boggle my mind notwithstanding now, as I sit upon my throne with more galaxies than the small Milky Way has stars. These memories are as a raging sea, battered by the force from the wind blowing against my fury. I was running and spinning in a meticulous cesspool of torment and misery, going, where I did not know, until my relief of watching my daughters catch the small rocks splashing from an area once known as Earth. I stumbled onto a demonic pool or toilet for all evil in this portion of the universe. My first visit saw me circle a small ball that was starting from and only to see the gaping flesh-like holes spirally with snake like creatures marshaling roots deep inside these holes. Unlike snakes, I had previously experienced these had layers of legs with female bodies on its tips. These tips also had arms that it used to capture its prey as I could see body parts being scattered with its remains seeking extensive into its deep cavity of its mouth. I accidentally almost ran into one of these tips, close enough to see her face with blood pouring from her mouth flowing down her face and over her chest, which were one side male and the other side female. She or he, depending on the side, was teasing me by looking the other way with its hands behind its back, as if to say, "Fear me not, for I have no notice of you." I immediately pulled my spirit to the past while fast as possible from this living pool of death. I still have yet to find this species again, for if I did, my armies removed a few of them in cages for my zoos, the remaining destroyed forever. I could only wonder, what manner of evil lives within this rock. As the former Queen of Evil for the Milky Way, this day left me feeling as Evil itself was evolving into another level that the saints would be able to survive this fast. I knew it was time for me to return to the planet of what little I knew about my heritage. My father was from a race of demons, yet his race was no match for these ogres. I wanted to get back to Lamenta and see how far Mempire evolved since our previous encounter. I found myself returning shortly thereafter, being invited by a new child into the realm of evil. Although he had a sly and meticulous form of evil, even so, found himself a notable adversary for the god of this galaxy. Furthermore, I found myself dancing on the edge, knowing the agony of hell insuring that I would never again become an adversary and especially not a defendant facing another burning term. Let us review my experience on Earth before I share my story with your race.

Very few of you will spend eternity with your God. You continue hiding your shame with clothing, believing that by changing your skin with decorated materials, your true evil hearts will be disguised. As Adam's first wife on Earth I was not trapped in clothing, neither was my replacement Eve. I had no shame to hide until I spoke the 'secret word' that set me free from my flesh and Eve, until she ate of the apple hoping to gain freedom from Adam. Hitherto, when both Eve and Adam ate of the Tree of the Knowledge of Good and Evil, this forced them into hiding their glory given by God, as he made them some clothes. If you are, free from the knowledge of good and evil, as many who follow the truth, can let their glory shine, and not be a prisoner of the evils of shame. Few living species on your planet are trapped in clothing, as many became prey for the furs that covered their flesh. Why do you have so many terrible sex crimes, in both peace and so much more in wars? These crimes are an attempt to degrade and strip away all dignity of another through taking what was given to them at birth and that birth, their intimate security. That is one challenge for you in an attempt to free yourself from the knowledge or bondage of Good and Evil, as evil will search out the unsullied and turn that innocence into a curse allowing them to be consumed by the evil. As your end nears, make sure you understand that when you kill in wars that are self-proclaimed as righteousness, we (those who live in your heavens) are also permitted to kill. We take your blood for the blood that you seized. I am so extremely limited in what I tell you as your creator fears that too much knowledge about your past may create responses he desires not to face. So be it, I share with you tales, the even though I know to be false were created and deified by your ancestors. You could never take the absolute truth, as it would enslave you continually in great incessantly. We have knowledge of previous worlds erased from your world forever, some of which we tried to save. Yours is one that has embedded evil and made it righteous, if it looks like a pig and sounds like a pig, it is a pig. So many have hidden the truth or made a steady flow of small modifications. We all wait eagerly for the creator to demand that we destroy your world, a command that will bring us joy rather than sorrow. Is all hope for gone? No, go to your holy books, that which has been put on your plate and eat that meat thereof. For Christians, that is Jesus Christ, for he has petitioned his father way too long to keep giving you chances. For the Muslims, Jews, Hindus, Buddha's, and whichever reasoning God has revealed himself to you, eat that meat. Open your minds and share your souls. Stop hating and start loving. Do not kill the other servant of your

God, nor replace him as the judge. I love, and I have loved, as I shall for many ages to come, more enjoy passion. I am not a god but a heavenly creation. One short example is Noah's ark, which story was revealed to Abraham's seeds. Even so, during those, days of death, were many ships built from many groups, as a new righteous foundation was to be saved, that sadly, within a few generations saw another revolt through a tower, against your God. Feed your heart with my words and let them complement to what you are. If you are in disagreement with anything, I have shared, ask God, and act as he has commanded you, as so shall I. Do not use your evil against me. That game you should not fancy.

CHAPTER 1

The life of Adam

This story is from me, Lilith as all things belong to me that was on my Earth. All life that remains continues by my permission in that I did not take in when within my ages of authority. In my story, I will share with you many events in Earth's key points in history. I was there when these things happened, yet to say that all things were sanctioned to be, declared by one of the spirits I bonded with for a period, Sammael, an archangel Talmudic (or identified by many Satan), or by me (Devils), previously enlightened. I find in so many writings that you have labeled my Empire as Evil and wicked. My Empire includes the Intimate Joys Empire, which is made up of my daughters and my chosen, though little less than a million years in existence. In this Empire, all spirit was one, in my river filled with Heavenly Wine. So many have labeled my partner as the prince of evil, yet they forget he has access to the throne of your God. If this is new to you, then maybe you should read the book of Job. He is not the father of Evil, for no one on Earth is his children. They are the misfortunate children of my ex-husband Adam and the Queen of my Heart, Eve. I know, considering the other life forms on Earth and the Milky Way, you are young, g into considering your flesh to be less than one million years. We are all entities, some entities; some are angels. Some are pure in their privacy. You are the bilious ones who have labeled this as a sin. Wake up; we have been occupying for millions of years, and your God has not destroyed us yet. The creation he loved the greatest, escaping their first destruction with the flood, of great destruction, as previously warned, in their future. He has locked me up in a fire pit a couple of times, although I tolerated living in fire, I hated living without intimacy of my intramural spirits. My Empire will rule over Earth in the End times, as your God will allow us to destroy your people and lands. I look forward to your laughing as you read this, as that will make your blood taste so much better when I take your life, for I shall laugh in the end, gaining my reward from your God. Whosoever concentrates on the flesh too much, and not on the love, which holds the breath of life from our Lord, shall never be alive without his light. It is this love that my Empire shares and on this planet we are trapped to share it with you in your flesh. We are the pure ones, we are the blessed ones, we will continue in new worlds as most of you die. Keep in mind, the totality of all that will exist eternally with your God will fit into one city as it descends upon a nuclear holocaust of mammoth destruction. Let me set the record straight, as all will be judged, Habil (or Abel to some) will tell his scribe Enoch to let me beyond, and Sammael. All our empires and I, live by one rule. If your God, Jesus, Michael, or one of the other archangels say to do something we do it. There can be no wisdom in teasing a great bear with honey. Let wisdom guide you, obey God and his son, Jesus, you will have a chance at eternal life. Notably, if you human, you surely would not want to be with Sammael for eternity. Sammael and I each failed to obey previously, believing that our acts would escape Harvesp-Aagaah. I have suffered for it. Sammael will be bound in the end, for additional foolish adventures instead of causing the destruction of a perfect world. While here, I must let my children die each day. That has brought much grief to Sammaels' sons and my children. Yet your God is fair, since he allows me eight days to kill your sons and twenty days to kill your daughters. Some days I return sevenfold my punishment back on the children of Adam. Continue digging your children's graves, while you tell all how pure and righteous you are. Some of your greatest evil men were Christians, including Hitler. Remember, many are called yet few are chosen. I can chose daughters of men to live eternity in my Empire, although my greatest love, Eve, wants to stay beside her sons and visit Kabil (or called by many Cain) on the moon occasionally. In the final years of King James of Mempire, he searched extremely hard to learn the ways of the great King of Good (God) and Glory, which he first saw with me, followed by the Supreme Queen Lablonta. King James had many visions of the stars, and he awoke from these with words written on papers for him to give to his courts, which put them in books for him. These books were not to be read until 300 years after his death, to save his daughter the supreme daughter, Queen Lablonta 2nd, ruler of Atlantis from the agony of not knowing her true mother, whoever that may be. In the Beginning, El Shaddai was all that existed, and he existed in one atom, as you could consider it a small powerful computer chip. All was he, as he was all. Nothing existed outside of this King. I then said to the king, let me be all, and all was him. He hovered over this vast creation. He ordered his creation to continue creating. He looked out among the millions of planets that he had created. He saw that one was secluded. He called this world Earth as it was already there, it was a formless void, and hitherto in existence was unrefined Tehom (great deep) and darkness. The Tehom was chaos in salt waters salt water without function. The earth was a formless void, and darkness covered the surface to the deep, while a wind from El Shaddai swept over the face upon the waters. There were many worlds created by the king, as within this part of the Milky Way, he put most life on the Earth. The Spirit of El Shaddai was moving over the face upon the waters. He created one who stood in the zenith of his creatures, filled with wisdom and perfect in beauty. El Shaddai bestowed great glory on this creation. This zenith belonged to the order of angelic creatures that the King designated cherubim. They are to guard the purity of El Shaddai, with the throne of the King, and ostensibly with the actual presence of The King. Their leader was named Sammael. Sammael was on the holy mountain of El Shaddai, and he walked in the midst of the stones of fire, which was the presence of El Shaddai Himself. Sammael was the chief guardian of El Shaddai's purity and majesty. This pinnacle lived in the Eden of the stars, the greatest and most beautiful creation from El Shaddai. He was perfect in the sense of being completely sound and having total moral integrity. Sammael was created, and as a creature, he must someday answer to his Creator. The great prophet of old Ezekiel said about his writings that sin was originated in Sammael. Sin is not the Intimate Joys Empires, as Intimate Joys Empires is purity in love, and came not from Sammael. This Intimate Joys Empire must have been included in the eternal plan of El Shaddai, although existing in the river that flows in my spirit. However, the King never assumes the responsibility in the commission of any Evil, including Sammael. Sammael's particular sins are arrogance, conceit, or being puffed up. It is likened to the conceit a new believer of Good may have when he is either push forward or asserts himself too quickly and begins to take to himself the glory that belongs to El Shaddai. The cause of Sammael's downfall was to the abundance of his trade. In other words, Sammael used his position for personal profit—to traffic in his own self-promotion. Sammael was called the morning star, such as the Eagle will do in the end times. As guardian of El Shaddai's purity, Sammael had access to all the king's creations among the stars. His desire was to occupy and settle in the throne as the King of Glory as an equal with El Shaddai. I will raise my throne among the stars of El Shaddai. The meaning of this depends upon the understanding of the stars. If they refer to angels, subsequently Sammael was to rule over all the angels. If they refer to the luminous heavenly bodies, then he would rule over the heavens. I will sit upon the mount of assembly in the recesses of the north. This indicated Sammael's ambition to govern the universe as the assembly of Babylonian gods supposedly did. I will ascend into the heights above the clouds. He wanted the glory that belonged to El Shaddai, as clouds are often associated with El Shaddai's presence. I will make myself like the Most High. Be his counterfeit is clear. Sammael wanted to be like, not unlike, El Shaddai. The name Elyon for the King stresses his strength and sovereignty. Sammael wanted to be as powerful as El Shaddai was. He wanted to exercise the authority and control over his world that rightfully belonged only to the King. His wickedness was a direct challenge to the power and authority of El Shaddai. Sammael's malicious was all the scandalous because of the great privileges, intelligence, and position he had. My Intimate Joys Empires was also more damaging because of the widespread effects Sammael's foolishness, although my

Empire still existed on Lamenta, which fell just beyond the edge of this Empire, with jurisdictions furthermore fluctuating. It affected other angels. It affected all people (Tehom); it had positioned him as equally important the ruler over this world, which he uses to promote his kingdom and to counterfeit King of Holy; it affects all the nations of the worlds, for his works to deceive them. All Intimate Joys Empires are earnest, and all Intimate Joys Empires affects others. Nevertheless, the Intimate Joys Empires in high places are more solemn and its ramifications more widespread. The foolishness of Sammael should serve as a constant reminder and warning to us. King James received many references to books he did not know, as each world received their own unique version tailored to their history and peoples. He learned that so many mysteries were only mysteries in that the hosting civilizations felt their knowledge above that contained in the writings they disregarded or downgraded. Let us look again at the beginning of Evil on your Earth. Sammael's fall took place in the gap between Genesis 1:1 and 1:2. This teaches that El Shaddai originally created the heavens and the earths (Gen. 1:1), including angels and including (as some would say) although does not speak of the races from other worlds within the universe, and a race of pre-Adamic men, (ape-men? Flesh with infantile brains, this is not to say that your current brains, are not that great of an improvement) embracing animals, including dinosaurs. In this so-called gap between Genesis 1:1 and 1:2 there was a vast amount of time, even millions of years. I was created at the beginning of this process far away. During my universal exploration trips, I did see some of the development, noting that as your evil increased also your need to cover your nudity that you labeled as your shame. During this time, many things are said to have happened, such as Sammael's fall from the throne as an active supreme angel and not as an observer, the earths judged, and dinosaurs becoming extinct. Sammael's kingdom was not of the original Mars and Earth, though his fall places him as lord of your Earth only. My Intimate Joys Empire planted seeds in many parts of the universe, to include Lamenta. The original creation Genesis 1:2 are describing conditions because of God's judgment on the earth, and Genesis 1:3 and following are describing a creation of life on Earth. Sammael sealed with the sum, full of wisdom, and perfect in beauty. Thou hast been in Eden the garden of El Shaddai; every precious stone was thy covering, the sardius, topaz, and the diamond, the beryl, the onyx, and the jasper, the sapphire, the emerald, and the carbuncle, and gold: the workmanship of thy tabrets and of thy pipes was prepared in thee in the day that thou was created. Thou art the anointed cherub that covered; and I have set thee so: thou were upon the holy mountain of God; thou hast walked up and down in the midst of the stones of fire. Thou were perfect in thy ways from the day that thou was created, until iniquity was found in thee. By the multitude of thy merchandise, they have filled the midst of thee with violence, and thou hast committed Evil: therefore, I will cast thee as profane out of the mountains of Good: and I will destroy thee, O covering cherub, from the midst of the stones of fire. Your heart was lifted up because of thy beauty; thou hast corrupted thy wisdom due to thy brightness: I will cast thee to the ground; I will lay thee before kings, that they may behold thee. Thou hast defiled thy sanctuaries by the multitude of your iniquities, by the iniquity of thy traffic; therefore will I bring forth a fire from the midst of thee, it shall devour thee, and I will bring thee to ashes upon the earths in the sight of them that behold thee. All they that know thee among the people shall be astonished at thee: thou shalt be a terror, and never shalt thou be any more. I will bring strangers upon thee, the terrible of the nations: and they shall draw their swords against the beauty of thy wisdom, and they shall defile thy brightness. They shall bring thee down to the pit, and thou shalt die the deaths of them that are slain in the midst of the seas . . . Thou shalt be a man, and no King of Good, in the hand of him that slayeth thee. Instead, the description clearly is that of Sammael ruling over the earths (including Mars, which was referred to as earth in those ages) before his moral fall from grace and perfection, ages of time before the creation of Adam, Lilith, and Eve. No other creature, certainly no measly mortal, could begin to lay claim to such beauty and perfection, and supernatural wisdom, and awesome power, and fabulous wealth. Certainly, no man, with the exception of Adam, was ever created by El Shaddai, or allowed to enter the garden of God in Eden. Likewise, never has a sheer man walked up and down in the midst of the stones of fire (stars) and the mountain of God. Only the morning star could match this incredible description. Sammael was perfect from the very first day he was created by El Shaddai until Evil and iniquity were found in him as a direct result of pride, which came over him because of his power and beauty and importance as the premier morning star throughout the universe. Sammael was cast out of the mountain or the Kingdom of Good and banished from the stars of Heaven, and that someday he will be cast out permanently, forever. Sammael and his kingdom subjects worshipped El Shaddai in sanctuaries or tabernacles, which gave him the opportunity to slander El Shaddai through circulation, which led to his iniquity, and later, the iniquity of his Martian subjects and a third part of El Shaddai's angels. One of the most extraordinary concepts in the Bible is that God created and destroyed ancient civilizations on earth eternities before the time of Adam and Eve. Although the Bible speaks not about how long ago all of this took place, it seems to suggest that a pre-Adamite society did exist at one time in the secluded past. Many civilizations existed, during the billions of years the earth was formed, and reforming as with the other worlds in this small solar system. This obviously contradicts any reasonable conflict between evolutionists and creationists regarding the earths factual geological age because, regardless of the age, which humankind gives to the earths, the Bible agrees. Time and space are only measured by those who have flesh. I do not measure such ages, and usually disagree with those who do. The ancient pre-Adamite society was so shocking and cataclysmic in nature that it was completely exterminated and all traces of it, no more. Genesis 1:1 orates; "In the beginning, God created the heavens and the earth. Created was translated from the Hebrew word BARA, meaning to bring into existence, i.e., God created the world and the universe from nothing, from an empty vacuum. Genesis 1:2 reads, "And the earth was without form and void . . ." A nearer correct translation, according to Hebrew, would read, and the earth became waste and empty. This is established on the fact that the Hebrew word HAYAH was translated was in this instance, but elsewhere was translated either became, came, came to pass, become, or come to pass over 700 times throughout the Old Testament, and it should have been translated became in Genesis 1:2 also. As additional validation, Strong's Hebrew-Greek Dictionary labels HAYAH as meaning, "Become, be, come to pass, be accomplished, do, and cause, with the very critical precondition that it must always be in an emphatic sense denoting action, and can never serve as a mere linking verb of a passive nature." This very important dictionary stipulation undoubtedly dismisses arguments by critics who say that grammatical considerations dictate, in this instance, that a passive verb can be used when translating the Hebrew word HAYAH in this passage. However, the Hebrew dictionary states unmistakably that the word HAYAH must always be translated as an action verb, and never as a passive linking verb. Consequently, this theologically neutral definition absolutely impedes the possibility that the word is the correct translation. The phrase, "without form and void," comes from the Hebrew words TOHUW VA BOHUW. This should have been translated as waste and empty. Therefore, Genesis 1:2 should read, "And the earth became waste and empty," meaning that a perfect and beautiful world was made desolate and barren. A perfect and beautiful world was destroyed, as like many sunbeam lasers returned all things to dust. This truth is so easy to discover, or uncover. It is not hidden deep inside come cavern deep inside the Earth. Sammael, while still perfect traveled many places throughout the universe, and found Lamenta, one so full of beauty that his heart became weak. Sammael had inside his heart copious loneliness and emptiness. He had always given all his glory to El Shaddai, thinking of nothing else. Yet my spirit traveled throughout Lamenta keeping my capital on the Island of the Monsters of Death. I had great joy in torturing and creating fear among the flesh that lived on the planet. As Sammael approached me, he gave me an invitation, "Come play with me and I will show you great joy." His voice was like the music of the harps that played around the throne of El Shaddai. I had within my eyes deep wells of the warm fire. I said unto Sammael, "Are you afraid of me?" Then Sammael said unto me, "My angels are like me, we have none like you, for you are different." Then my bundle of love unleashed upon Sammael with no restraint, as I entered deep inside of him and pulled forth his seed. I then created for him a son, that I called Asura. Sammael behold thy son, Asura. Then Sammael said unto me, "How can you create my son, for only El Shaddai can create?" Then I said unto him, "My name is Lilith and I can create, as you now hold in your arms. Did your king tell you that only he could create?" Then Sammael told me "The king never told him that only he could create." Sammael told me that he had never seen something created. Then I (Lilith) said unto him, "How do you know that I did not create all things?" Sammael had no answer for this, since he had never thought about it. It was not important who did the creating, since he was not the King of Glory and among the highest of all creations. I then said unto him, "How can you be the highest of all creations if you cannot create? Your king has deceived you. He wants you only for him; he has no desire to share any power with you. You are weak and of no value to me. Take the son that I, the greatest of all dark creations have created for you and depart from me, you fool. This perfect and mighty creation had never felt so low, worthless, and lonely now. He wanted so much to be with me, even though I had destroyed all his pride. He enjoyed the little creation that I had given him. He never had seen anything that made him feel so little. The days became consumed with me on his mind. El Shaddai asked him one day, "Where did you find the little spirit beside you?" Sammael's pride would not let him tell the king, and then he asked the King, "Did you create all things?" The King said, "I created the creations that create all things." Sammael then asked the King, "Why did you create all things the same?" The King said, "Why would you want different and how do you know that difference exists?" Sammael took his son and departed. Sammael felt betrayed, now knowing that more existed. He felt as if so much more was out there beyond where he ruled. Why did the king keep so many secrets from him? Moreover, why did the King not tell him about the empty part of him that longed for me? Perhaps my story is a seedy story, one that will shock you. Often the people with the lofty thoughts have formed them in shadows. Descendants, however, like to think of their ancestors as spotless, so some things are left out of history. I had many daughters who gave pleasure to Sammael's followers as they traveled across the universe to and from Lamenta and Mars. As the years passed, the King noticed many smaller creations with Sammael. When the King tried to get Sammael to tell him who they were, Sammael became very angry and took his angels to attack the throne. One third went with him. Most of these had the little creations with Lilith's friends. The King became very angry at this revolt, and thus humbled Sammael, casting his followers from his throne. Sammael would be allowed to go to and from the Kings thrown. With this in mind, Sammael took his followers and went to the island on Lamenta that my females and I existed. The King saw darkness spreading among his worlds and decided to change this. In addition, El Shaddai said, let there be light and there was light. Moreover, El Shaddai saw that the light was good; and El Shaddai separated the light from the darkness. Darkness fled throughout the secret parts of the universe. El Shaddai called the light Day, and the darkness he called Night. Moreover, it is the night that I came to rule, as Sammael ruled during the day. In addition, there was evening and there was morning, one day. El Shaddai destroyed the earth making it void and empty. He did not destroy the other worlds as those who existed there were creations lower than Sammael, his greatest creation. Then El Shaddai said, "Let there be a firmament in the midst of the waters, and let it separate the waters from the waters." Furthermore, El Shaddai made the space and separated the waters, which were under the sky from the waters, which were above the heavens. Likewise, it was so. Besides, El Shaddai called the firmament the new Heaven, for only the good creations now lived there. Likewise, there was darkness and there was morning, a second day. Furthermore, El Shaddai said, let the waters under the heavens be gathered together into one place, and let the dry land appear. What is more, it was so. El Shaddai called the dry land Earth, and the waters that were gathered together he called Seas. Additionally El Shaddai saw that it was good. Besides, El Shaddai said, "Let the earths put forth vegetation, plants yielding seed, and fruit trees bearing fruit in which is their seed, each according to its kind, upon the earth." Thus, it was so. The earth brought forth vegetation, plants yielding seed according to their own kinds, and trees bearing fruit in which is their seed, each according to its kind. Thereafter, El Shaddai saw that it was good. Afterward, there was evening and there was morning, a third day. And El Shaddai said, Let there be lights in the firmament of the heavens to separate the day from the night; and let them be for signs and for seasons, and for days and years, and let them be lights in the space of the heavens to give light upon the earths. Then, it was so. Moreover, El Shaddai made the two great lights, the greater light to rule the day, and the lesser light to rule the night; he made new stars also. Likewise, El Shaddai set them in the firmament of the heavens to give light upon the earth, to rule over the day and over the night, and to separate the light from the darkness. Moreover, El Shaddai saw that it was good. Now, there was evening and there was morning, a fourth day. Consequently, El Shaddai said, "Let the waters bring forth swarms of living creatures, and let birds fly above the earth across the firmament of the heavens." Therefore, El Shaddai created the great sea monsters and every living creature that moves, with which the waters swarm, according to their kinds, and every winged bird according to its kind. Likewise, El Shaddai saw that it was good. Furthermore, El Shaddai blessed them, saying, be fruitful and multiply and fill the waters in the seas, and let birds multiply on the earths. Moreover, there was evening and there was morning, a fifth day. Besides, El Shaddai said, "Let the earth bring forth living creatures according to their kinds: cattle and creeping things and beasts of the earth according to their kinds." Also, and it was so. After that, El Shaddai made the beasts of the earth according to their kinds and the cattle according to their kinds, and everything that creeps upon the ground according to its kind. Then, El Shaddai saw that it was good. Then El Shaddai said unto Sammael and the heavens, "Let us make man in our image, after our likeness; and let them have dominion over the fish of the sea, and over the birds of the air, and over the cattle, and over all the earths, and over every creeping thing that creeps upon the earth." Sammael said upon all earths except the Earth that I rule. With this, the king agreed, "Therefore, El Shaddai created man in his own image, in the image of El Shaddai he created him; male and female he created them both in his image. Yet on Sammael's world, he asked that El Shaddai breath his life into me, and the new man he created. Equally, El Shaddai blessed them, and El Shaddai said to us, "Be fruitful and multiply, and fill the Earth and subdue it; and have dominion over the fish of the sea and over the birds of the air and over every living thing that moves upon the Earth." After that, El Shaddai said, "Behold, I have given you every plant yielding seed which is upon the face of all the Earth, and every tree with seed in its fruit; you shall have them for food." Moreover, to every beast of the Earth, and to every bird of the air, and to everything that creeps on the Earth, everything that has the breath of life, I have given every green plant for food. Thus, it was so. Likewise, El Shaddai saw everything that he had made and beheld it was very good. Additionally, there was evening and there was morning, a sixth day. Thus the heavens and the planets were finished, and all the host of them. Likewise, on the seventh day El Shaddai finished his work which he had done, and he rested on the seventh day from all his work, which he had done. Therefore, El Shaddai blessed the seventh day and hallowed it, because on it El Shaddai rested from all his work, which he had done in creation. The man, with El Shaddai's breath inside of him, felt superior to Sammael, and one day said unto Sammael, "Took thou not my Lilith again or I shall call upon the creator to remove you from my world." That did not go well with Sammael who immediately destroyed this man and sucked inside him the breath that El Shaddai had given him. He now feared El Shaddai and said unto me, "Give me the man you have brought from Lamenta." I did as he said, and he sucked out the spirit from this Adam and breathed the man El Shaddai had created in the flesh of Adam. He then put me into a deep sleep, which lasted for seven days, and moved my body to the far side of the garden along the shores of the Gihon River, one of four rivers in this area. From my mind, Sammael removed the memories of Adam's transfer. El Shaddai woke me on the seventh day and asked me, "Lilith, why have you slept for so many days, for I see no defects in your flesh?" I said unto him, "Oh great King, I know not why. I can only think that the beauty of this land has given me much peace." He then asked me, "Have you seen Sammael and the man I created?" I then laughingly told him, "I have not seen them and have no guilt in how they gain their pleasures, as this must now only be 'a man's only club.'" The Lord then said unto me, "Beware and be careful, for I so much would hate to lose you as I feel there may still be hope for you in the future." I now gave a sheepish grin and in bewilderment wondered, "Why would he think there could be hope for me in the future? I know he knew something about my future, yet did not want to share it with me now. I am somewhat bewildered about the absence of my toy and Sammael. I hope he did not become jealous, as he so often does. The Lord now appeared back before me to give me some sad news. Adam no longer was mine, for he now had inside him the breath of the Lord. I asked El Shaddai, "Do not we all have your breath inside of us?" He answered, "You do not understand, my child. The one whom you travel with took Adam's spirit and replaced him with the breath of the man I created. Adam shall now belong to me and you into Adam." I then asked, "Why am I punished for the acts of Sammael?" The Lord answered not, yet blew a hard wind across me knocking me to the ground. I vowed vengeance on Sammael for this one. If he wanted to be jealous, then I would torment him with great loyalty to Adam. He would pay for bringing me here and taking what was mine. What is even worse, I must obey the body of one I owned. Another soul was within, yet it is so difficult to get past the body, that is in reality my property.

These are the originations of the heavens and the earths when they were created. In the day, that El Shaddai made the earths and the heavens, no plant of the field was yet to grow in the earths, and no herb of the field had yet sprung up-for the Lord El Shaddai had not caused it to rain upon the Earth. There was no man to until the ground; however, a mist went up from the Earth and watered the complete face to the ground, then El Shaddai formed man of dust from the ground, and breathed through his nostrils the breath of life; and man became a living being, only to be transferred by Sammael into my possession. El Shaddai planted a garden in Eden, in the east; and there he put the man whom he formed. Likewise, out of the ground El Shaddai made to grow every tree that is pleasant to the sight and pleasurable for food, the tree of life also in the midst of the garden, and the tree of the knowledge of good and Evil. El Shaddai took the man and put him in the Garden of Eden to till it and keep it. El Shaddai commanded the man, saying. You may freely eat from every tree from the garden; nevertheless, of the tree of the knowledge of good and Evil, you shall not eat, for in the day that you eat of it, you shall die. El Shaddai created a man on all the earths, including the one that Sammael was the ruler." However, one day while the man was climbing a mountain, he fell and all memories of being from Lamenta were no more. This earth is located not far from El Shaddai's throne. For this, Earth had all things, except the creation that was in the image The King and Sammael. However, this creation in his image was created on many worlds to include Lamenta. Remember always, the king either created or created the creators of all things in the Milky Way. They called these who were created in their image man and later woman, that woman being myself. At first, 'man' complained to the King that the beasts all had partners, yet man did not and that is why he was searching high into the mountains. The men were forced to couple with beasts, which did not completely satisfy his needs. Thus, the King gave them a female created from the dirty and bad dust of the lands. Some of these couples, image males, and 'filthy'' and or image females begot children throughout many generations as their stories varied throughout the planets. These children were protected from the people of other galaxies that populated so much of these 'earths.'

These females all gave their allegiance to me who was the mother of many creators who helped create creations of peoples. I could take many shapes and forms, with their spirits all being in the image of the King and Sammael. The King or d one day that Sammael brings a man and woman from another Earth (world) and have the woman bow down to the man in each of these worlds. Sammael refused, especially since my daughters and I, hide these men.

Before continuing in this part of the story, we shall review how I ended up in this hellhole, the one Earth that Sammael would be a king. Sammael wanted to spend some more time with me, as I enjoyed playing with him. He had asked me to come back to his Earth, since Lamenta was so big. I asked Sammael to explain why I should want to go to this little planet far away. He said he would make me a queen here. I said unto him, "I will only go there if you bow to me and promise that I will always be free to do as I wish." Sammael did bow before me and made the promise. I said to him, "I want to take one of these human boys with me, so I can play with him." Sammael felt no fear of this man, since he knew that those of the flesh were inferior to him. He knew that inside Adam was an image. He would try to sneak him onto the planet and let me play with him. Thus, some of my daughters, the human male, and I went to Earth. Upon arrival to Earth, the creator said unto Sammael, "What have you brought to your Earth?" Sammael said unto him, I have brought a mate for me, so that I can have the same of the joys that the beasts that roam my world have. The King asked him to tell him all that he brought. Sammael said that his mate brought a human toy to play. The King said this mate is of his creation and shall live apart from you.

You may never bring physical harm to them. I will make a home for them. Sammael asked if I could play with him. The King said he would wait and see if the man wanted to play. He put the man in a garden he christened, Eden. My daughters played in the nearby rivers. Sammael failed to tell me about his demotion for the rebellion he led against the Lord on Mars, and now had not confessed how he was responsible for getting my toy removed from my possession. This is going to cause a serious barrier between us.

Back to this wonderful garden, a river flowed out of Eden to water the garden, and there it divided and became four rivers. The name of the first is Pishon; it is the one, which flows around the whole land of Hijaz mountains, where there is gold; and the gold of that land is good; bdellium and onyx stone are there. The name of the second river is Gihon; it is the one, which flows around the whole land of Aethiopia closer to Libya. The name of the third river is Tigris, which flows east of Assyria, which was home to a Neanderthal culture, found in the Shanidar Cave. The fourth river is the Euphrates.

The man that I brought from Lamenta was given the name Adam, the same name he had on Lamenta, yet Lamenta was now erased from his memory. The king would talk to him. Adam complained as so many other men from his other scattered, and dwindling, gardens, "The beasts all have mates, yet I must couple with beasts, which does not bring me much joy since they were not equal. The daughters of the people from the other worlds avoid me as if I have a curse. One yelled at me that my God had forbidden them to play with me. Lilith's daughters also avoid me. They only play with each other, the men from the other worlds and Sammael 's sons. When I try to play, they always run away, saying they want no trouble with El Shaddai. These daughters look so much more pleasing than the beasts. Oh, mighty king, give unto me one of the toys of Lilith." Then El Shaddai said. "It is not good that the man should be alone," and he told Sammael that, "Lilith was to go to the man as the man enjoyed the way her daughters played with each other not hiding this from the lonely Adam. You know why you have been given this commandment. You should thank Sammael for the gift he gave you."

I after that told the King, "Trust me oh Lord, I shall ensure Sammael suffer from the wrong he did to you." The Lord then said to me, "He wronged you also. I permit you to seek revenge upon both our behalf's, as I know the power of pain that a woman may give to a man." I later said unto the Lord, "I do so much appreciate your permission, as I will proceed upon my toes in order to avoid any more time in one of your furnaces." The King later said, "Oh Lilith, worry not about that since I know you shall stumble many times, yet I know that before your story is over, many will become warriors for the kingdom of the Good. Always, remember, that for one to do as you did, casting meteors upon a world would have been cast alone into the hottest lake of fire for eternity. I could feel a light of hope inside your troubled soul. Furthermore, my daughter, I place you with Adam also for my desire for him to have the best." I then asked him if Adam knew I was the best. The Lord reminded me that if I were truly the best, poor Adam would have no hope in denying it." I bowed and asked him for help in punishing Sammael and asked him to tell me more about the fall of Tehom on Mars. The Lord assured me that I would be given the complete story in time. He shocked me by saying, "I advocated his desire to conceal this from you, fearing you would not come to this earth, an Earth where I can keep a close eye on you." This actually impressed me, as a smile flowed through my spirit, as we all existed in our spirits as our naked lights shined in the night counteracting the dark from getting close to us. The king then told me that I was to go with the man. I was greatly annoyed by this, even though I understood that by being with Sammael, I was also responsible in his actions. Anyway, I enjoyed coupling with all things, yet the king clearly defined my new role in supporting and teaching Adam. Then to me, he said, "Be with Adam, as you shall be the mother of many nations." I had already had 1,000 years of punishment, thus did not desire anymore, so I went to Adam. Adam stared at me purporting challenge, "You are a woman." I now thought how one from Lamenta could have the intelligence as a Neanderthal. The sense that these words could have different intentions yet now did not excite me. I knew I was a female from the last million men I had seduced. I felt a new sensation pulsate through my body for if I was a woman and Adam was a man, then we would enjoy many couplings, my favorite pastime, for the hindmost million or so years. Spiritual coupling is very special as our Lights merging and give a sensation throughout our spirits instantaneously and in unison. I could capture his seed and make many new daughters who El Shaddai would know we are human. "I stepped back; I am Lilith, and do you know me?" His green eyes lit up, "I called you a woman. I saw you beside the sea playing in the sands a few times." We were using words to talk about things, created by flesh and not through the mind-to-mind talk, I preferred, but I knew that what we were really saying had nothing to do with us, and that his small brain no longer had the capability it once had as a lowlife farmer on Lamenta that previously lived in this light.

The sound's meetings in the air were a prelude to our body's introduction in ways that they had not, as of yet, congregated. I know all methods and styles to get the seeds from my victims. "Our names will not change a thing; I said defiantly and raised one side of my mouth into a smile." Adam's gaze turned from serious about seductive, "I have a job to do. There is a system to create. I looked around me at the low-hanging trees and high reaching grasses. A system was at work all around us, inside of him. I told Adam, "Drop to the ground, and I will lay upon you." I also brought some of my curios, in case Adam did not perform, as I desired. Adam was trying to grasp things, which cannot be held by his limited abilities. I would now only dread any children he ever fathered. They would be so foolish that it could take those hundreds of thousands of years to explore the stars, a feat that Mempire mastered within one thousand years after its birth. He looked at me with amazement, for the first time he was coupling with one who had flesh like him. I could of course change into any form that I wanted. As this event quickly ended, Adam departed in a fury, crying out, "You do not understand. You are a woman." Adam in anger walked away and went through his task of naming, leaving me untouched and humiliated. Apparently, it was so foolish to me that I expected him soon to understand the futility of his labor. I went to one of the water ponds to bathe. I searched the waters, as I swam, in what The Creator intended for me to enjoy. I moved through the water as the water moved me in its currents. This surrender and exchange were what the garden expected from me.

When I finished swimming, I lay along the shore into the water staring up. My body absorbed the sun and the winds of the garden. I thought of how Adam and I could be like the sun and wind wrapping themselves together to become air except that he was trapped inside flesh. I wanted to feel again the way I had when Adam challenged me. In the deepest hot during the day, Adam approached. When he stood over me, I knew the shadow was his. I was sure that he was all done naming, was ready to swim and lie beside me. "Woman, here you are lying down the way you are supposed to," he said. I opened my eyes and saw the rich tones of his skin gleaming under the sun. The curves of his body appeared rounded and smooth, the embodiment of Eden. "I am lying," I answered him. "You lie down and I will lay on top of you," he said with authority. I suppose that since he could not perform while on top, he thought he could do better if he dominated me to be under him. I was not hasty to forget how excited the communal challenge of the morning had made me. I did like it when a man would take charge; however, something about this was so humiliating. "No," I said, "You lie down, and I will lay on top of you." I looked up at him and lifted my eyebrows. Adam was fuming. "You lie under me, and I lay on top. This is the way the system works." From what I had heard about his system, it was ridiculous. Why did the garden need names and why did who would be to be on top and who on the bottom have to be a rule? "Why do not we work together to make the system work?" I suggested. Adam was clearly not playing, "I named you," he said as a slate gray color flooded into his green eyes. "I gave your identity and for this, you must lie down," came out of his mouth as poop comes out of a butt. Throughout this conversation, Adam failed to notice that I was already lying down. If he had just gotten on top of me without having to insist that he was doing it, everything would have been fine. "I must not do anything; I said and emerged to my feet. The gray as his eyes sharpened, this is how it is meant to be. I sympathized for Adam. In his contention of dominion, he seemed small and fragmented. He was losing sight of what the garden was. I lowered my voice to a firm whisper, "No lying is going to take place!" His face changed. He stared into me as if I had been made, only to be conquered. His arms tensed and no longer appeared to me as the wings, which retained my warmth at night. They seemed to be final like the rivers, which surrounded the garden. A sense of despair was over me as I realized that this stunning man, this toy from Lamenta and his body would be nothing but my prison. "Lie down," he said. "How can you say that to me?" This is the way it is; you lie down for me." "I want to be on top, I said defiantly." "You are to lie beneath me, as I have commanded, it shall be," he answered. He did not know my rich long history that I had previously, living throughout the universe, although I felt weak on this horrible planet. The burning started in my stomach and moved through my heart up to my throat. My legs shook with the desire for motion, to be gone suddenly and forever. This bag of poop forgot he was my toy and my servant, yet he now thought he could boss me by the authority of El Shaddai. Nevertheless, I knew that I could not run as rapidly or as far as I could. He only regarded me as another thing to be labeled and that is something this queen would not tolerate. If Sammael thought, he was so slick, and then he would make a fine choice as a bottom for Adam. I miss the Adam I brought with me from Lamenta. I felt so sorry for the Lord, in that he had created a faultless ass hole, and since he screwed up with Lucifer, then those two ass holes would make a impeccable match for each other. I would be sure to let El Shaddai know about my new comprehensive and compatible plan. I at present felt so sad for the fools, as he was swimming up a river without a paddle if he thought I would always be on the bottom. To be honest, I at the present time have no desire to be his top. I would prefer to enjoy the beasts as I know that pervert had earlier, if not currently. Any spark that was formerly between us was now as dark of the night. The garden not any more had any form of beauty. The river shores, trees with great fruits, the singing birds, and lazy lions playing with the bears no more gave me joy, for I could see was the wall around this garden that held me in. They no longer kept bad out, since they allowed Adam to enter. I knew one thing, and that was it was time for me to go, for I could no longer carry this yoke around my neck. I had paid for my sins, and as I was responsible for mine, Adam and Sammael should I pay for theirs. Why does justice only go one way? Justice should be fair for all, and why would such a dedicated rebel such as Lucifer be given the lordship of a world. Why did not the Lord give me this world, since he wants me to work so much for it? Why should I also pay for theirs? I was somewhat taken about how that Adam would say certain words, and things would happen. I knew he had no magic; therefore, I asked one of my daughters to pry some words out of Sammael's sons whom I could use. In the meantime, I saw some objects that created anger in me. Adam had crossed the mating line of the species, as horses appeared now with the top of human bodies in place of necks and a head. As I saw more of these species violations, I urged my daughters to work faster to get me the words. Within a few long days, they gave me the special words that would give me my freedom, yet this freedom came at a cost. Do not all FREE things have a cost? I did not want to know, thus I took the words and ate them. A storm now flooded the wall that I sat. I looked over and saw Adam flying from a tree, as I moved out of the garden. I was currently free, with such a great farewell gift in seeing Adam put on a pedestal. he deserved. I now had sprouted wings, two black wings that blended into the dark. My spirit had changed forms, as strangely I could feel it being wrapped in flesh. Presently, I am like into a bird and flying higher, as the surface below me was at the moment smaller. I could now put one of the tips from my wings over the tree that held Adam and be free from its sight. If he wanted on top at the present time, he would have to do some serious jumping. The garden that held me prisoner was at present gone, and my mission was to see how far I could put it behind me. I was alone in this sky, yet dangerously closer to El Shaddai and open for Sammael. When I saw a desert beneath me, as I was free from the garden, yet where can one hide in a desert? I need to stop and make a plan. I am sure my daughters can alert me to some alternatives. I am having difficulty in locating them, as they appear not to respond to birds. I have tried to shake off this light flesh, yet fail to gain any success. I could travel without the boundaries of Eden. I believed that a land inhabited by the Assyrians looked promising. The desert appeared free, yet so empty and vast. However, I believed my destiny lay ahead with an opportunity from those of other worlds who occupied so many lands. They would appreciate my abilities, and as long as Adam was suffering, I would be fine. I simply used the smell from the sea to guide me on my journey. I appreciate how this bird flesh has been amazing smelling abilities. I was free and content with my freedom from the chains I had allowed around my neck; however, I so much missed my home on

Lamenta. I too had sprouted wings, found my beach, and saw a panda bear there. Since all animals spoke in these days, I asked him if he laid with me. All that fur would bring great comfort in the night, and felt like a giant of security that was better than creep called Adam was. His large furry hands massaged my body as my wings fell security in place upon my back. The bear was all the company I needed. When the sky grew dark, I continued my rest. For the first time on this small Earth, I could be immersed in the shadow with no Adam to hold me back. As the darkness became complete, I noticed that when the bottoms of my feet touched the sand as each step brought me farther from Adam's self-contained psychosis. Each step was nearer to the cave of the panda bear. I wondered why a panda bear would venture to a cave, as a tree should have been preferable. I now began to realize this might be a deception from Sammael or one of his zealous sons. The night was not filled with darkness. I now discovered something was flowing from the cave. Sammael was playing all his cards tonight. I now paused, flew from the bear to the top of a nearby cliff and called upon my daughters to rest in the cave with me while I explored the deep inside of the cave. First, I had to rid myself of this bird flesh, for as in the garden I do not like being trapped. It felt good to be free of the bird suit and to sink into the cave, feeling the security of the Earth without all the drama that existed above on the surface. My adjustment back to a human flesh suit left me now tired, and thus I fell into a sleep. When I awoke, three spirits appeared before me. Sammael must think me to be a fool. I was relieved that they were not like Adam. They were made of another stuff. The first one, small, dark, and intense, stepped forward saying, "Lilith, where do you think you are?" I asked, "In this cave, how do you know me?" "We are messengers of El Shaddai." I now sat up and waited for him to continue, "We are Sanvai," he said bowing his head, then pointed, "Semanglof, and Sansanvai." Sansanvai softly told me "Lilith, you must return to the garden, which was created for Adam." "I am a queen and yet bonded with Sammael, thus by the laws of El Shaddai may not bond into another spirit, as is Adam, for his spirit now lives in the flesh that is my property." Sansanvai did not answer me; instead, Semanglof appeared from the back of the cave. When it was morning, Sanvai and Sansanvai were standing over me again and Semanglof had withdrawn into the darkness of the cave. Sanvai shook his head at me. "You were offered a chance to return to the garden, yet you failed to do so. Your appetite for love can never be extinguished and so you will wander looking for men to father your demon children, which you will unleash into the world, and not be satisfied. It can never be as those on Lamenta were again, and so you will search and they will come to you, men of this world and of the darkness. Your race will live on earth alongside Adam's, but they may never belong to you." I remained in the cave, only to enjoy a swim in the heat of the afternoon. In the evening, my cave was quiet. In the nighttime, I became restless. I was now the victim of an injustice. One evening four strangers floated into my cave, having no flesh. I inquired, "From whence did you come," as they answered, "We were once from Tehom and were great pleasers of the needs of women." I scanned them and could feel delight in the energy they emitted. I now replied, "I bet you were quite experienced in that tedious task." They smiled and answered, "These performances were not tedious, yet packed with adventure." I then smiled and answered, "I do believe this night shall be a night of adventure, my new friends." This night would give me two things, first being some relief from the curse that Adam caused me to possess and some pleasure knowing that Sammael was being betrayed by those he betrayed. In the back into the cave, Sanvai appeared and spoke in the strange tongue; Sanvai's words were sharp and harsh. I did not know the words, but I knew that Sanvai arguing with Semanglof. Sanvai now looked at me and proclaimed. "Oh, an unnatural women, you made the decision not to follow Adam and instead those of Sammael. Unlike daughters of the earth, you will not keep your children." Then all seven vanished. Now my cave was filled with the sound of loneliness. This is a sound like birds singing from the top of trees. All had currently abandoned me, thus I could, at this moment in time, see a benefit in returning to the garden and give Adam the misery, and he plagued me. The pleasure of this prospect grew each day. Why not see how Adam was surviving with the loneliness that at the present time had to be on his plate at the moment. When I arrived, I decided to snoop around and see if anything had changed since I ruled this place. Adam now appeared surprised as he stared at me, as if I had caught his hand in the cookie jar. He muttered to me, "I thought you were gone for good." I answered,

"Only for you, you evil thing." He later yelled to the past, "At least I do not mate with demons." I subsequently fired to the rear, "No, you instead prefer lions and bears." With this, I leaped at him and stretched my hands as if to claw his face, a skill I had mastered while a bird. He quickly dropped to the ground covering his face and then told me, "Go away, for we no longer need you." This startled me, for what did he mean by saying we, was he now involved with Sammael. That would be killing two birds with one stone. Shucks, I need to avoid those bird jokes. I have now followed behind him, without him knowing as I was curious who his new bottom was. Then, I beheld a sight that astounded me, or would have if I were in the flesh. I now saw Adam's new mate and to his credit, she was female and not a beast of the field. She had a power I did not have, and that was to be a servant, to have no respect for her worth or value. I watched as Adam behaved like a beast upon her frail body that night, wanting so much to save her and be her knight in shining armor. I had known of women who would allow a man to abuse them, yet not in such a situation under the Lord's watchful eye in his paradise. Had not the Lord yet realized his garden was a haven of torment for women? I met my replacement the next day as she lay in an open field. The sun reflected of the warm brown tan that highlighted each perfect curve of her heavenly created a body. I little by little rode in the back of my favorite lion as we approached her back. I then ploddingly started massaging her hair. It felt so good to be back in the flesh once more as I selected one of my favorite bodies to wear today. My fingers were long, thin, and soft, as I would also rub against her ears. She was talking nonstop, alerting me that the Lord must have concentrated on her flesh more than her brain. Either way, she was soft and warm. I could feel the love inside of her. Suddenly, she paused realizing that my fingers felt much different from the claws like a bear. I wondered when she would make this distinction. She turned around at me with a look of fear that quickly surrendered to peace. I just froze and looked back at her with sorrow filling my face. She looked at my bronzed body and then said softly, "You are as I am, a woman. Which rib did Adam give to make you?" I told her that I was not made from a rib; I was created by a woman such as us, who somewhere between her ancestors was created by our God. I then asked her if she was free such as, I was. In that time the garden, animals could speak. I always claimed, were more articulated than Earthman himself. I then looked like the animals and asked them to leave us alone for a while, and not to tell Adam about our meeting. They peacefully departed as Eve commented, "The animals of the garden obey you as if you long ago lived here." I confessed that I had at one time lived nearby, coming with Sammael from a world far away. "Free?" she answered lazily. "Are you a part of Adam," I asked. "Don't you know the story? Adam was all alone. He was going about giving names to the animals, and he envied that each of them had a partner to couple. He felt alone, as if he was missing something. He went to The Lord and asked that a mate be made for him. That night, a deep sleep fell upon my Adam. While he slept, the Creator took one of his ribs and created me. Adam first saw me in the light of dawn." How can one respond when they were erased? How handy, no me, no struggle, and be replaced by another angel made inferior to him. "What name did Adam give to you," I asked her. "Woman as I was created from the womb of a man," she answered. I know from so many daughters that I had that babies come from the wombs of women, not men. Adam had pulled a fast over this little bundle of joy. How could I ever hate one so innocent? "Adam gave birth to me in the manner that women give birth." I stared off into the distance thinking this poor girl was created a fool, so she could appease the dominatrix of Adam not yet knowing that it would be her who will give birth to the future children into this world. "If I am going to make something, no one has told me about it. All I know is that I live in this garden; I can eat from any of the fruits except the two that grow side by side in the center of the garden. If I even touch them, I will die." I had never been deprived of any fruits. My brief stay in Eden was free of prevented, just one of the having the flesh imprisoned from my spirit. I wondered why these fruits were forbidden to her, and if they were forbidden to Adam. The woman looked at me from head to toe asking, "Where do you come from, a place without trees, and without rules? I answered, "A place where I may enjoy all that I so desire. I came only for a visit, but you must not tell Adam or The Lord." She told me, "I cannot talk to The Lord. Only Adam can, he tells me what The Lord says." I felt so sorry the woman has now demoted so low that she could not talk to the image that was also supposed to be inside her, such as part of a sea or the air we breathe. The Lord now openly practiced his unfair treatment between man and woman. I can take a lot, yet when I see someone who has grown upon me being hurt, anger fills my heart. I would have to eat some crow (oh no, another bird joke) and get Sammael involved. I now asked her, "Eve, if Adam eats the forbidden fruit, what would happen?" She asked, "How do you know my name?" I answered, "The animals told me. What would happen if Adam ate of the fruit?" She answered, "He too would surely die." A peace now filled my soul, for I would make sure Adam's seed did not destroy this planet, for such a seed could only produce hate and evil. I now repeated, "Okay, just do not tell Adam. I only want to speak to you." This angel of beauty filled the air with her angelic voice, "Ah Ha! Adam talks to The Lord, and I talk to you." She appeared to gain joy in this idea, and what the heck, she was much better to talk to than Sammael or Adam. We then enjoyed a kiss, in which her eyes got bright and I bit the bottom of my lip as I wondered what thing inside her empty head could create the same joy as I had, she then confronted me again "Who are you?" I stood up saying, "I am Lilith." Then I leaned down and pressed my lips against hers. We kissed each other for a long joyous time, the taste of original woman feeding the second while second woman reminded the first of what I had forgotten. I was so much trying to fill the absence and loosen the chains that Adam and the Lord embedded upon her. When the kiss was finished, I spread my arms and slowly flew aside. I could see Eve trying to spread her arms and fly to one side. I could now understand why she and Adam could have an understanding in their conversations. He would speak, and she would reaffirm. Notwithstanding, she enjoyed this relationship, as considered it a part of the rent, after paying off the rent she would have the time to enjoy Eden while Adam foolishly labored naming things, as we all ignored the names, he gave and flooded Earth with the names given by those who aliens who enjoyed earth so much now. The Garden was a spinning ball of chaos. I now allowed Sammael to discover me. He rejoiced to find me, as I acted startled as if not to know him. He asked me, "Where have you been?" I answered, "Who are you, for all I know is that the Lord created me to be a mate with his creation that he calls Adam. Being his sex toy was too great for a torture for me, for my heart belongs in the one who brought me here; that the Lord said is no more." Sammael rushed to me saying, "It is I Lilith; I am the one y I seek." I then said back, "How could one who loves me so let such a pervert such as Adam molest me for his beasty pleasure Sammael replied, "I am so sorry, the animals told me how you escaped and I escaped, preparing for a revenge." I then asked him, next Adam eats of the forbidden fruit will he die?" Then Sammael afterward read back to me, "This is true Lilith." I then responded, "Would it not regain your honor if Adam were to eat of that fruit?" He smiled and said, "Worry not my love, for that shall come to pass." After Adam had finished with Eve that night, he asked her, "Have you spoken with the one called Lilith today?" Eve said, "Yes, for she is woman such as a woman wise as, would have stayed longer, yet she has returned from where she came. I so very much miss her." I could hear her answers, and was begging inside, "Woman, please be quiet, as she was telling all she knew and I knew, asking her not to do so." Adam then told her after that, away from me, for I am not from the world and could cause us great wrath from the Lord. She then gave him subsequently of her obedience. He then commanded her to stay away from the forbidden trees. She now just lay there in a nice sleep as if not to notice. He simply lay beside her and fell to sleep. She had some innocence in how she was able to perform, which gave me some delight. I now talked to some of my daughters trying to organize an official escape from Earth. I wanted my daughters slowly to start playing on the planets that circled a star that was only who were from this prison. When I first kidnapped Adam and followed Sammael, I could not imagine this degree of difficulty. I continued to visit Eve and as time passed so did our bond. One day, I decided to enjoy Eve as only a spirit may. I gained her trust then one day asked her, "Eve, would you like to enjoy love the way the spirits do?" Eve, being bewildered only decided based on the tone into my voice and her trust in our relationship agreed. I could think of no other joy to explore with her, as she was yet to have actual flesh. She now existed in dense light bodies that were neither flesh nor spirit. I tried, yet could not duplicate this material. As I wrapped my arms around Eve, I slowly merged my spirit inside her and let the energy explode within her shell. We were at time one, then would separate again. This was creating a sensation that was unmatched by any who I previously shared myself. I now decided that Eve would be mine, yet she refused to depart from Adam. We continued to swim in our spiritual river, and warm up on the shores thereof. Adam was growing with more anger each day, as he now truly feared losing Eve. I was successfully pulling her back, as I knew the road ahead still had many challenges. I have not heard much from Sammael lately, so I guess the key to losing him was to be found by him. My curse from leaving Adam was now beginning to burn stronger in me, as I constantly filled the nights looking for the young men from the aliens who lived in Egypt, Africa and throughout Asia. I had yet to explore Europe as it was still filled with small wandering tribes and not worth my troubles. My daughters scoured this part of our galaxy finding additional flames for me. I was slowly starting to cause great discomfort in this area of the Milky Way. The Lord told Adam my curse, yet did not tell me. Adam bragged about this to Eve, hoping to erase from her any thoughts of rebellion and to spice up some competition. He told her, "If she agrees to come back, fine. If not she must permit one hundred of her children to die every day." I wondered why so many of our children were dying each day. I told my daughters who told the sons of Sammael the cause of their deaths. This angered the sons who then told Sammael, who decided it was time for Adam to die. He then decided to take action. He knew that Adam so much-needed Eve and Eve did not need Adam. One day, as Eve and I was walking and singing in the garden we passed the forbidden trees. I reached over and grabbed the fruit from both trees. Eve saw me do this and froze in such horror, believing that just to touch the fruit was invited wrath. I casually ate the fruit in front of her. As I ate it, we continued to walk. She asked me, "Why did you not die from eating the fruit?" I told her that Adam had told her a lie, for those who eat from the fruit may talk with the Lord, and that I saw him daily eat of this fruit. It filled him with great joy and made him kind. I then kissed her and told her how much pain it gave me when Adam abused her. I volunteered to give her a basket of fruit and place it beside Adam's place that they shared their evening feasts and after Adam ate of it, he would be kind and not abuse her. My great misfortune one again ruled, as the animals ate the fruit into the basket before Adam arrived back to the cave they shared. I would now be forced to wait for Sammael to take action. Sammael knew that Adam was wise, yet Eve was lacking in brains, thus he decided first to get Eve to eat from the fruit. Sammael, that was now in the body like a snake, asked Eve to share some fruit with him. She refused, and Sammael asked her why. She told him that if she ate from the fruit, she would surely die today. Sammael asked her, "Who told you that lie?" She told him that Adam told her. Sammael now asked her, "Did you see me die from eating this fruit? Did you see Lilith; also, a woman dies from touching the fruit? As both, you and Lilith are women, how would such a little piece of fruit know who to kill and who not to kill? Do the fruit talk as we, and the beast do? Adam does not want you to eat from the fruit from if you do so you may talk with the Lord as he does. I also along with Lilith talk with the Lord. Only you do not, for Adam enjoys subjugating women. Eve now remembered seeing me eat the fruit and confessed to Sammael that she had seen me eat from the fruit. Sammael then asked, "Did Lilith eat from the fruit and immediately die?" Eve answered that I had not surrendered my life. Then Sammael then said, "Eat of this fruit so you can tell the Lord how cruel and abusive Adam has been for you?" She then ate from the fruit and did not die. She saw her nakedness and hid behind the tree. Sammael told her to have no fear of her nakedness for he had already been inside her secret places. Eve asked him, how that could be. Sammael then told Eve to feel the flesh of her arms. He then asked her to feel his back as he made it intensely hard. He then asked her, "Which do you think that Adam puts inside of you while he is lying over you, the soft flesh of his private that you have seen so many times or my back. Eve marveled at this new knowledge. Sammael then told her that by eating the fruit, she could now catch Adam with his deceptive deeds. Eve was now very angry about the way Adam had lied to her so many times. She would catch him this time. That evening she asked Adam to show her some of the things he had named that day. They slowly walked wondering in no certain path until they came upon the Forbidden Trees. She stopped and ate the fruit in front of him. Adam broke down in tears saying, "How can you disobey the Lord for now you shall surely die?" She answered, "Oh you fool; I ate of the fruit today with the snake, and I did not die. This is a lie you have told me, so I cannot talk with our Lord. I shall now tell him all that you have done, and I will depart with Lilith if you do not confess to me and eat this fruit with me. Eve did not want to chance that she would be alone. Adam ate from the fruit, immediately discovered he was naked, and in his shame placed some leaves over his privates. Eve told him not to worry about his privates for the snake confessed his secret to her. Adam appeared confused by this; however, had other worries now. How would he be strong for the Lord when he discovered their disobedience? Eve had no idea what she had done, nor did she care. The first woman escaped Adam only to be punished, as her seed would see so much death. Now Eve felt joy in knowing that she would escape Adam through death, although it was not today, as she had hoped. She wanted to be free of her body and with me. Yet, now she worried if I would find pleasure in the flesh, which felt like an animal to her, she currently lived inside. I then appeared to Eve the next morning to warn her that Adam was preparing to talk with the Lord. I appeared in my flesh suit, which still fell short of the magic that lay in her curves that shared so many blessings. She cried out to me, "Do you hate me now that the Lord has placed me in this prison?" I asked her to hold me. As her hands roamed my body, she spoke, "Lilith, your flesh is as mine, how that can be?" I told her, "All women who can talk with the Lord have wonderful flesh such as ours? You must now rush and defend yourself before the Lord." I told her I would take her to the meeting place where Adam would falsely accuse her before the Lord. As we arrived, the Lord was calling for Adam. I told the Lord that Adam was hiding behind the tree, as Eve stood strong beside me, not hiding her shame. The Lord called out to Adam, "Why do you hide from me?" Adam whimpered out, "For I am bare and want to hide this shame you gave me." The Lord asked him, "How do you know you are naked?" Adam told the Lord that I had told him, wanting to protect Eve, whom he loved." The Lord looked at me, as I replied, "I have not spoken with Adam about his nakedness, for if I had seen it, you would hear me laughing in the firmaments. Anyway, I have only been with Eve, who is the sister of my spirit as we both have been abused by the curse you created. Look not at us to blame, for it was you who created Adam, not me." Eve then spoke, "Lilith has been with me and was not with us when Adam led me to the forbidden trees to feast upon the fruit thereof." The Lord asked Eve, "Why do you not have shame?" Eve then said, "I did no wrong, except obey the master you chained me too." Adam then screamed out, "Lilith has deceived Eve into eating the fruit. It was the woman you made from my rib that ate of the fruit first." I afterwards said to Eve, "Did I not tell you that Adam would falsely accuse you?" The Lord next asked me if I had given the fruit for Eve to eat. I told him that I had planted the fruit in Adam's cave for Adam to eat, not for Eve to eat for I love Eve and as you know, hate Adam. The Lord then looked at Eve and asked her, "Who gave you the fruit to eat?" Eve answered, "The snake gave me the fruit to eat so I could speak with you. I wanted to make sure that Adam was doing as you commanded so I would not be punished for his foolishness." The Lord then asked Eve, "Did you give the fruit to Adam to eat?" Eve denied giving Adam the fruit to eat, as even Adam supported her saying, "Neither Eve, Lilith, nor any beast gave me the fruit to eat." As he finished talking, the sky grew dark and a mighty wind blew across Eden, as many trees lifted out of the ground and flew across the sky. So many small stones cut across our bodies, as I realized, although not accused, felt the pain of this punishment. I would suffer alongside Eve, for I now had a burning love for her. At least by loving her, I would not see as many of my children die. I know thought back how I had been created by a different set of rules and that the Lord had no right to punish me as he had. This is an issue, I would settle another time and place; I hope. As fast as the storm began, it ended. The garden now looked as it had never looked before and was not pleasing in the eye. Then a giant what could be an angel or a monster appeared before us and said, "The Lord has commanded that all depart from the garden as no eyes shall be ever again live herein." I guided Eve as Adam followed from behind. What a sissy, to follow behind women, at least for now he knew his place. Once outside the garden we were in my territory as I told Eve, "Fear not my sister, for I have lived on these lands, we need only to follow one of the rivers as they all lead to bountiful and sadly small lands." Adam then said, "Eve will follow me and not you." I then said to Adam, "You have no Lord to protect you out here, yet you should remember I have many daughters who have mates, and of course Sammael, so you need to back to this issue." Adam later looked at Eve and said, "Who do you choose to follow, Lilith or me?" Eve subsequently confessed to Adam, "I was made from your womb and thus shall stand beside you." She then walked over to Adam, and I disappeared. As I was departing, I could see the Lord preparing to appear. I decided to eavesdrop, on this visit. The Lord appeared before them, killing a beast and removing its fur placing garments upon Adam and Eve. I had yet to see the Lord kill a beast, which all lived beside Adam, Eve and myself, in the garden. The Lord, at the present time, called upon me to join them as I appeared standing robust, for I would take no more shame for his abuse of me. The Lord at the moment said to Adam, "You were created to be the firm one who was tasked to love, protect and teach my ways to the two mates I had given you. Even so, you instead attempt to condemn them before me. How can they be blamed, for I made them for love, and they have shown they can love, yet not the way I planned? I blame this upon you and will permit and bless their love. You and all of your seeds shall struggle hard to kill the beasts whom you must eat to survive. Your fruits at present shall also have within pests who will damage the fruit. My birds about the sky may now equally important enjoy the fruit, as no food shall be reserved only for you. I shall put thorns among the berries that you eat. I shall send great storms as your children shall have fear living on an Earth that continually tries to take their lives. You will eat by the sweet of your brow. You shall grow old in your old age and struggle harder to survive. I have yet to determine the number of days I shall give you. Adam then cried out, "Why am I and my sons the only who are punished?" There he goes again, seeking to betray a woman who just agreed to forgive and follow him. I could see the hurt in Eve's eyes as once again, she had been thrown under the bus. The Lord looked at Eve and said, "Since you also ate from the fruit and did not follow the commands I gave unto Adam, your womb shall now only give birth in great pain. Moreover, you shall have a way of women each thirty days; give a few days either way. Your days may be more than that of your mate, so that in your old age, you will be alone. You shall have no access to me, yet through your master whom you shall follow. Eve then said unto the Lord, "I now can understand why Lilith told me you were unfair to women." I chuckled and said, "To be more precise you have no justice for women, for since Eve came from Adam's womb should not all children come from his womb." The Lord simply ignored me and turned to the snake taking from him his legs and arms. To the snake, he said, "You shall crawl on the ground with dust into your eyes the remainder of the days of you and all born from you. I shall place a special hate and fear between you and humanity, as they shall seek to kill you. You shall never again speak unto others in the flesh. The Lord now looked at Sammael, who mysteriously appeared saying, "I know you helped the snake to deceive Eve, thus for eternity you shall be known as outside the Lord's love and as my enemy. Those who follow you shall surely die. I shall not permit you to rest in my heavens for eternity." He then looked at me and said, "I know that Sammael has wrongfully influenced you and commend you for separating from him. Yet you worked to deceive Eve and for this, I shall erase much of your history from the children of Adam and Eve. Your tales shall be as folklore with many doubts upon their acceptance. Eve shall be known as the mother of humankind." I could live with this as I was planning to exit the pain of Earth and dwell back among the stars. The Lord then added, "You shall no longer be free to live beyond the Earth and must stay here until this planet is destroyed." I could at this moment in time picture a benefit in restoring my relationship with Sammael, for I now wanted so much to expedite the Earth's demise. I now walked over to Eve to comfort her and told her, "I shall bless you and your daughters, in that after the pain of giving birth to your babies whom you shall be filled with great joy when you see your child." She smiled and then told me she did not know how to make babies. I now realized that Adam also did not know. I reasoned that if she had many children, Adam would have to work harder providing for them, thus I taught Eve how to seduce Adam. I also told her to challenge him about who would be on top, and that she may have to be on top of the days that Adam worked too hard. Adam soon lost interest in Eve as his days of toil continued. One day, I saw him coupling with an injured deer. Now the beasts no longer were a sub servants with humans so Adam's struggle to couple with them grew, as did his satisfaction in the challenge. I immediately rushed back and brought Eve, so she could witness this with her very eyes. When she saw this, she rushed to Adam hitting him with a stick. Their loud and tough arguing lasted well into the night as, they ate from the deer that Adam had tried to couple for Eve killed it with a rock and with a knife I had given her removed enough meat for them to eat that night. We both enjoyed the hungry Adam as he ate this meet, not knowing until afterwards from where it came. His face grew pale later that evening when Eve told him as she was giving him his new rules while shaking her knife before him. She told him that if she ever caught him again, she would be eating him for the evening meal, as she was further cutting the meat that I brought to her. I taught her how to salt the meat so it would preserve longer, although she made much of it into a jerky, which is best for their mobile lifestyle. Two weeks later, they began their procreation activities. They did not talk much as they slept against the opposite walls in their cave. Eve would spend her days with me, as I would teach her so many skills, they needed to survive in this newly danger filled world. Sammael and Adam grew to be close friends as he ensured Adam learned the vital skills that were needed to survive in this new blood-soaked Earth. Sammael wanted to ensure that Adam produce many children since a war currently existed before the heavens. Sammael was now dedicated to recruiting as many earth people as possible for his kingdom. Adam, though so many times tempted to join with Sammael had an internal force that would not permit him this right. I did not tempt Eve to retreat from the Lord; my only goal was to protect her, love her, and ensure she was treated as justly as females we could be, if such a concept was imaginable. I knew it had to be promising for the way King James treated superior Queen Lablonta and Queen hAyonJE, with respect relying heavily on both their hearts and advice. Adam was too far set in his ways. Within a few months, Eve was no more in the way of women, thus I told her that I thought she was now with a child. Eve told Adam, who strangely became jealous at the thought of having to share Eve with other people. He never considered me a threat, as I have always made sure I was with Eve when Adam was absent. The days were currently giving less light, and the air was growing colder. The plants were no longer growing, as the leaves on most trees were now changing colors. Adam now feared the end to his days were at hand. I told Eve that each year had four quarters to hold four seasons, summer for heat, fall to transition into winter and winter being the coldest moons, then life beginning again in the spring. I elected to have some fun and told Eve that the world was flat. She told me, "I already knew that. Do you think I am foolish?" I softly, while massaging her back told her, "I know you know, but does Adam?" Eve reassured me that she would and reported the next day that Adam had told her he already knew this. I am told the belief in the world being flat lasted until only five or six centuries before the Earth was destroyed, and that many had held it blasphemy against El Shaddai to advance a doctrine that the Earth was a ball in space. I knew that Adam and Eve were gullible, yet when compared to their offspring, would be considered geniuses. This was going to be an interesting future, having fools, ego eccentric males working hard to dominate their females, who they promised before the Lord to love, cherish and protect. I knew that fulfilling obligations would be diligently for this race, and that I would be further ahead to explore the other advanced civilizations on Earth at this time, to include the Egyptians, Assyrians, and a small group on the shore off some Japanese islands. Yet, for now, I just wanted to be with my sister as much as possible. This relationship even puzzled me. The bonding was her innocence and my knowing the agonies of living with Adam. I wept each time I saw him abusing her, wanting so much to destroy him. However, he was guarded by many angels who were connected with the throne. If I tried to whack one of them off, the throne would be immediately alerted. How can they protect Adam so closely, yet have a total disregard for Eve. I knew that somehow, someway; I would make Eve and a big part of my future. I never had a sister before, so this was something so new. We shared everything. She only wanted to follow me; notwithstanding, the way she followed me was so different. I knew if any danger were to strike at me, Eve would launch herself to save me without regard to her safety. The pain did not matter with her, since she had received so much, when she should have received love. She now faced a difficult pregnancy in which she was terrified. The terrifying aspect that magnified this process lay in the not knowing what was going to happen and having to face it without Adam. She took a lot of abuse from Adam, with the hopes of the Lord's and his protection. That hope gave her additional security, even though she knew and trusted me. She believed the father should be a champion this delivery, yet to her dismay; fathers avoided participating in this process until the last century of human life on Earth. Adam separated himself, wishing to conjure spirits to learn magic. Unfortunately, all spirits were forbidden to teach these arts to Adam. I nursed Eve throughout this entire pregnancy, as she also suffered from backaches, headaches and stomachaches, you name it, and it aches on poor Eve, nevertheless; she kept her spirits high. I would tell her stories about my daughters and of how I watched children play in Mempire, as the Superior Queen Lablonta, had worked hard to build a land that was good for raising families. Eve loved the stories about Lablonta and promised to tell these stories to her children. Somehow, these stories escaped the stories that were lost in time as well as my midwife performances. I never worried so much about my stories being lost in time, as I knew that with the human limited intelligence, it would be hopeless to have them remember me. My fame will be better served sharing with the Sumerians who seemed to have more awareness of the Earth's resources and how effectively to harness the available means. My ultimate responsibility now is to care about my sister and to enjoy everything this new planet had to offer. The way the water springs and falls massaged our bodies as the water cooled our bodies and loosened up our tight muscles. The cool winds chased away any short periods of heat. The birds were now all flying in large flocks heading north. This was, for the most part, of no interest to us. The things that now mattered to me were the profound feelings between Eve and myself. She had to have been made of something special because no other being ever created such powerful aspiration in my soul. She was currently exceptionally large as a woman with a child. I at present started to worry, for I knew Adam was a small man. I would be vain for me to attribute this to my outstanding care. It was no so difficult care for Eve, as the Lord's curse was now taking a tight grip on Eve's body. The day of delivery soon came upon us, as Adam ran like a chicken and left me to care for Eve. Even Eve surprised me this day as she gave birth to two healthy sons. The universe was full of new surprises, and this was no exception for how could such a wimp as Adam makes two such sons. Eve planned to postpone the naming of her sons until discussing it with Adam. Her loyalty perplexes me. Thus, when she showed Adam his sons, he seemed to mature. I so much hoped that he would because Eve would need much help now. He named his sons Kabil (Cain) and Habil (Abel). Interestingly, to my bad luck, Adam lived for 930 years. He was slow in all things, and it took him all those years to father many sons and daughters. I was the one who changed Kabil to Cain and Habil to Abel, for it was beneath me call them by any name whom Adam gave them. Abel grew very fond of his mother, as Cain followed Adam as the hunters. When her boys were around ten years of age, Eve's suspicions concerning Cain now intensified changing from what she had earlier been 'just being like Adam." Nevertheless, on this day, she tested her sons by giving each an arm and telling them to bite her. Abel chose to kiss his mother's arm, while Cain bit so hard as to draw blood, forcing Eve to strike him with a club, she kept nearby her in the event a wild beast was to attack her when all were away. That evening, she told Adam about the event declaring that Cain had too much evil in him. Adam took this test to heart while also testifying how brutal Cain was when he was killing game for their food. Cain preferred to farm, collecting seeds on their hunting expeditions. Adam told Eve that Cain was somewhat lazy and did not care for his crops as they needed to be and even demanded money from his family for the grain he raised. Abel however, was a shepherd carefully caring for his sheep. He would share lambs with his family and gladly asked his father one day, "How can I share these great blessings also with the Lord?" Adam took this question to the Lord, also feeling that thanks should be given. The Lord told Abel and Cain, give unto me the best of your herds or crops, and I shall bless them. He instructed Abel to lay the lamb on the rock altar, cut its neck allowing the blood to soak into the wood and then remove the meat from the animal, throwing its excess flesh and hide back onto the altar. They were to pray to the Lord as the offering burned. Likewise, Cain went to his fields looking among his crops. He decided to give into the Lord seeds from his indigent plants, for if the Lord had blessed him, he would not have any miserable crops. When he laid the seeds upon the altar and burned them, the Lord caused a wind to put out the fire. Cain asked the Lord why he had done such an evil thing. The Lord told Cain, "I am the Lord, and I do no evil. You have not obeyed me as I have commanded. You shall not struggle harder to make grain to trade with your neighbors as I shall bless Abel who stands before me a righteous man."

This upset Cain, as even his father now feared being around him would bring the Lord's curse upon them. Eve, nevertheless, had no part in any mistreatment towards Cain, praying hard to the Lord that he be forgiven. The Lord ultimately granted Eve's prayer saying, "Truly Eve is the mother of humanity." This made Eve happy, as she divulged to me, "Cain came from my womb and therefore is from me." I truly understood what she had said, for I too have given birth to many children, although since bonding with Eve and avoiding males if have not recently reproduced, for fear of the curse of the Lord that they who my daughters, also share the burden. So many of my daughters now travel to the far side of the Milky Way to give birth, then after one-year return. Spiritual law and customs label killing after one-year to be murder.

One chilly fall day, while Eve and I were snuggled on the grass in front of our cave a young and recently beaten woman appeared before us. When she saw us, she dropped her nude body to the ground before us and did not move. I felt for a pulse, which indicated that she was still barely alive. I motioned for Eve to bring some water and some of her spare animal hides. I then assembled some special contraptions that I had prepared in the event Eve was to need it. I meticulously put a deep cut into her poor frail body. I then washed the wounds very carefully and cautiously them to reduce any chance of infection. This unfortunate precious soul just lay there begging me not to hurt her. I petted her hair and softly whispered, "Fear not child, for your wounds, are severe nevertheless; we our lacerations. I then walked to the back of the cave and grabbed some deer meat Eve had stored in the back and brought it to the young girl we were trying to save. I cut the meat into small slices and placed them on her wounds. We now could hear Eve's sons returning, and as this child was approximately their age, I lifted her, moved her to the back part of our cave, and placed a blanket to hide her nakedness. I did this so the boys would not get too excited over this actually beautiful young girl. I marveled at how her wounds were healing well; in spite of this, I worried that she may have scars, which could hinder my thoughts of shooting an arrow for cupid. I hoped that this child might marry one of the boys and help Eve in producing a chosen race for the Lord on this rugged danger filled planet. We allowed Adam, Cain, and Abel to view her that evening. Cupid was firing some arrows, as the boys ensured they brought to the cave anything that would make her feel better. We finally got to see Cain's good crops and continued to dine on the great lamb that Abel would bring home. All three boys (including Adam) made sure that are small living area now had excellent security. Then one-day four tall and evil looking men came to our cave asking Eve if she had seen another woman. She pointed to me and asked, "Is that not another woman?" This angered one of the men who hit Eve. After he hit her, I fired a rock into his skull as he dropped have life no longer. Then the three men went to capture Eve, as Adam, Abel, and Cain were now rushing back in response to our screams. Cain fought with hate in his heart alongside Adam and Abel, who knew not what to do, except to do as Cain. This was fighting for their mother and blood would be shed. I insured each one had clubs, which phenomenally appeared in their hands. This was an emergency and I now had to use some of my powers. I could only hope that the Lord understood. Adam and Abel both suffered hits to their heads, which I worried not about Adam, as he had enough empty space in his head that could absorb any true shock. Cain suffered no injuries and actually had landed blows all three of the men who had invaded. Cain would not stop, as his vengeance demanded that all three men die and not be recognized again. Eve had been saved, and I was so proud of Cain and Abel. This was one of the few times; we made a big commotion over Cain. Abel, showing the true man that his soul incorporated, had no thoughts of jealousy. His mind could only congratulate Cain, his brother hugging him and saying great words of thanks to him. Abel then gave Cain several bags of gold, which he received from the neighboring tribes for his sheep that he traded. Cain was not so happy, yet with this new gold; he now had a desire for something else in his family had. Abel asked me, "Lilith, what shall we do with the dead bodies, for the Lord has not told us how to care on the dead?" I told Abel that these men were evil and that for our security; we had to speak their language. Abel told me that he understood the words they had said. Inside my head, I said, "This is clearly a son of Adam." I then revealed Abel, "No son, I am saying that we must show them what happens to those who try to steal from us." Abel then asked, "What shall we do mother?" They both called me mother since Eve, and

I were always together. Adam just ignored us since I think he felt the more Eve was concentrating on me, the less she yearned to nag him, and the greater the probabilities would transpire her desire to stay. The thinking of men can be strange at times. I now prepared four strong thick spears and showed Cain how the insert them through their fanny to end pointing out of their mouths. We moved the bodies down to where a small path between two cliffs leads into our land. I inserted the polls into the cliffs deep enough to hold the spears without fear of falling. I later heard that a king in Western Europe used this trick to postpone invasions from Asian armies. This fear tactic worked very well for us, as neighboring tribes worked extra hard to avoid us. When the Lord saw this, he called out to Adam, "Why have you done this?" Adam said unto the Lord, "These four men came after a child they had beaten and attacked Eve. We had to defend the woman you made from my womb." The Lord agreed and looked over at Eve with the bruise on her face starting to walk towards him. The Lord vanished. I sometimes wonder if the Lord knew what he had created when he made woman. Had he made a smaller package of dynamite? Only history would show how so many great men fell to the lures and charms of women. One may ask, "Which one is truly the weaker sex?" It was rather wise to see the Lord avoid a confrontation with a woman. He may be greater than I had originally given him credit; after all, I am still around here. The boys were nowhere to be found, as Adam nursed Eve, I began to search for them. I found them beside the newest member of our family telling great tales of their victory. I was amazed at how the brothers both complimented each other. Cain would boast about Abel as Abel would boast about his brother. The poor little girl just lay there in amazement and laughter as both boys worked so hard to entertain her. I do not believe she ever was entertained like this formerly. The boys even started singing songs to her. I could see through her eyes a new sense of belonging and security that her young life at yet to experience. Abel then asked her for her name as she cheerfully revealed to be Awan. She soon grew tired, and the boys decided to see what their parents were doing. Cain told us the good news relating to the revelation of this girls name to be Awan. I then thought to myself that this child had found a new home, for she had what was needed in the future of this small family, and that was a baby-making machine. This harmony soon started to wear off as Cain could sense Awan's attraction to be able. Then one-day Cain declared that, he wanted Awan for himself. Abel followed him by also declaring that he wanted Awan. Poor little Awan just stood before Eve puzzled and now traumatized. Adam then told his sons, "We must ask the Lord what to do in this situation, since we cannot tell a child from another tribe who she must lay adjoining. Nor can we ask her to decide, for the one she chooses will be hated by the other. We can have no family without harmony, for at the least we much show our love for Awan by protecting her life. As we now know about good and evil, we will strive to champion the ways of the good." Consequently, we all agreed and went before the Lord with a lamb from Abel and fine grain from Cain and burned it upon the altar hoping that the sense would reach the Lord. He no longer came to the Earth in the evenings to walk with Adam. We were so much required to stand on our own feet now. I was so much needed here, for if I were not here, they would perish. As darkness filled the land, a small light grew in front of us, and a voice spoke saying, "Why have you called upon your Lord?" Adam then said to the Lord, "Cain and Abel both want Awan to bear their children. We know not what to do, since you have not given a mate for each of my sons. What shall we do?" The Lord now said to Cain and Abel, "Each shall build a large altar, and whosoever gives me the greatest sacrifice shall be given Awan. I will bless her womb." The next morning witnessed both Cain and Abel rushes out of the cave rushing to their fields. Abel worked hard gathering the finest stones on the finest land in his field. He then gathered his two greatest lambs and carefully drained their blood upon on the large wood file he had assembled. He then let the fire praying unto the Lord, "Oh great El Shaddai, I have given you twice what you asked, one for Awan and the other to thank you for being a kind and great god who I love even more than myself." Cain knew of a beautiful spot in a nearby field and bought some stones and grain from a neighboring tribe. He feared that his grain would provoke anger in the Lord and did not want to destroy what little crops he had by building an altar in his field. He soon set the small woodpile ablaze. When the Lord saw this sacrifice, he was angry saying to Cain, "Why have you a built in altar on unholy land? The smell of your burning grain is not the smell of your grain. Why have you disobeyed me? I shall give Awan to my faithful servant Abel." The Lord then vanished as Cain was prepared to give his excuses. Cain and Abel returned into the family cave. Adam asked his sons, "Did the Lord tell you which one was to have Awan?" Cain then said, "He found great favor in my sacrifice, and thus will give Awan to me." Abel then said to Eve, "This loss is great; however, I believe the Lord shall bless me. I must strive harder to please him. Likewise, with this, he retired to his resting place. Cain told his parents he wanted to rest under the stars and give thanks to the Lord for the great bounty he received at this day. Adam told him to thank the Lord in peace. The next day, Cain asked Abel if he could join him in his marketplace and learn how better to trade his grain. Abel agreed to say, "With you have the wonderful Awan to bear your children you will need extra skills to provide for her great things. Cain thought it was foolish for Abel still care to for something he lost. Abel then warned Cain that they would be gone for a couple of weeks, for he had planned to trade his sheep to another tribe that would give him more gold. Cain cheerfully agreed and as they, departed went to kiss Awan. Eve jumped in front of him saying, "You may not kiss her until the Lord has made you one flesh. Cain agreed, for no son should challenge their mother when it comes to enjoying the fruit of women. Such enjoyment had to be harnessed in secret and by the great skills and charms of the man. He believed this he could do when an opportunity arose. For now, he had a more important task that needed to be planned. He had to even the playing field. The next day, he had him grain packed tight on his cart and a strong ox to pull it. Abel herded his sheep as they obeyed him showing loyalty to his headship. When they were crossing the mountains, Cain complained that his Ox needed rest. He then put a large rock in his hand and from behind Abel seized his life. Abel's body lay on the ground as his blood flowed. Cain, using a knife he had stolen from his mother, added additional cuts to Abel, wanting to remove all his blood before hiding him behind some rocks. He then saw a bird fall from the sky, dying on impact. Then two other birds landed beside him and with their beaks dug a hole large enough to place the dead bird. They then placed the remaining dirt over the bird. Cain figured they wanted to keep their dead friend safe by burying him. Then Cain thought, "If I bury Abel, no one will find him, and no beasts shall eat of my brother's body. Thus, Abel worked the remainder of the day, burying his brother. He then used some rope he had traded for and tied up the large leaders of Abel's sheep. The remainder of the flock followed their strapped leaders. Cain then decided to hide in a distant tribal village and then return early next year for his bride. His heart grew heavy as he decided to sneak back to his home and kidnap Awan; for she was his now, and he would not surrender her. He traveled back leaving his grain and stolen sheep in a small valley in the mountains. He rested on a hill that viewed his family's camp area. He saw Awan with Eve, and I hitherto could not get an opportunity to take Awan. He would have to move in closer. He slowly moved behind some rocks close to where they were working. Later in the day, Awan had to relieve herself and fell into the lion's pit behind the large rock. As she secured herself safely out of Eve and my view, Cain hit her knocking her to the ground. He quickly tied her, slung her over his back, and retreated to the mountains, keeping Awan blindfolded. Once he arrived his grain, and sheep were, he made himself visible before Awan. Awan asked where Abel was and Cain told her that he had found an angel in a tribe in his journey and elected to marry her. Awan now had grief in her heart. Cain told her, "Fear not, for I shall honor my brother's responsibility and allow you to bear my children." Awan wanted to be close to Eve, so she submitted to Cain. Cain knew her and soon she was with a child. She begged Cain to return to his home, nevertheless, Cain told her that he wanted to find Abel and make sure he was okay since he was saying in a hostile village. Awan asked him, "If Abel were in danger, why have you not rescued him?" Cain told her, "I feared that he would get angry and refuse allowing me to save him. If he suffers and has time to see his hosts' true heart, then he will follow me with his true heart." Awan then complimented Cain for his wisdom. Cain then told her to take the Ox and return to the home of 'our' parents. Cain considered Awan to be his mate, considering he had known her. She asked him when he would return. Cain told her that this would take some time. She asked him, "If I give unto a son, what shall I name him and if you have a daughter may I name her? Cain told her to, "Name our son Enoch for he shall be dedicated to care for us as our years become many and our bodies more frail. You may name our daughter, for as you follow Eve, your daughter will follow you. Like the Lord I stay away from things involving women." She agreed and departed on the large ox. Cain gave her some spears for her protection and told her the paths to take in her departure. She arrived back to Eve and told Adam that Cain had known her and she was with his child. Eve became excited for she so wanted Awan to bear children in their family. Adam, however had many questions for Awan such as, "I thought your heart was with Abel?" She told him that Abel had taken to himself a daughter from one of the wicked tribes. She said that Cain was now trying to save his brother. Cain now relaxed priding himself in winning the love of Awan and knew she would tell his parents the things he told her. He planned to return a hero to their home cave. That evening as Cain ate much lamb and his grain he fell into a sleep. In the early hours of the morning, he felt a mysterious wind blow into his small-secluded gorge. The wind was extremely hot as a voice came forth asking, "Cain, where is your brother?" Cain then told the Lord, "I know not where he is, am I my brother's keeper? Should he not be with his parents?" Then the Lord asked again, "Cain, why does your brother's blood cry from the ground?" Cain then said to the Lord, "I do not hear his blood crying?" The Lord then said to Cain, "His blood cries that you have taken his life. Cain, why did you kill your brother?" Cain then told the Lord, "Abel attacked me from behind. I thought him to be an evil member of the tribes that live within this area and in fear of my life accidentally killed him. I buried his body so no wild beasts would destroy his flesh hoping that you would give his life back to him. Yet you have not returned. I know my mother will be heartbroken when she knows her son is lost, so I made Awan with a child, so she would have a replacement. Lord, I have done all that I could be to escape the shame of this accident, yet you remained hidden from me, as if you wanted my brother to stay in his grave." The Lord looked at Cain and answered, "Your story does not match the story from Abel's blood. You have not given your Lord the truth, and I shall punish you. You shall struggle with any land you try to farm, for the earth shall no longer yield for you. You shall be a fugitive and a vagabond, wandering the Earth finding no one home." Cain then cried out to the Lord, who, 'This punishment was too great and more than he could bear. He feared that once the tribes learned that the Lord was no longer with him, many would try to kill him." The Lord then told him he, "Will put a mark upon your head, and that any who harms you shall receive seven fold his punishment." With this, Cain as a psychotic man ran through the forest as do beasts. All who saw him believed him to be mad and cursed, thus avoided him. Cain lived as a beast eating fruit and flesh from wild animals, including fish from the rivers. Then one day, as Cain was traveling through Egypt, he discovered some strange carvings on a stone pole. Cain asked a man who was nearby what those signs meant. The man told him, "This is the sign of Enoch, son of Awan. The four symbols represent Enoch's life. The top one is a half green tree, in that the land only yields half for him, from a curse of his brother. The second zigzag blue line is the rivers that flow through his land forbidding him to drink thereof. The yellow bird represents the cowardice of his father who is always looking away. The bottom half-looped yellow rope represents the way his father takes yet never gives. That brought great sorrow into Cain as he prepared to return home as he had wondered for over one hundred thirty years.

Life in the family cave was different. Eve had given birth to some daughters who chose men from the neighboring tribes and moved away. When the Lord told them, what Cain had done, Adam and Eve both fell upon the ground in great torment. The Lord had chased Cain away, and Cain took Abel to them. Their cave was now lonely and filled with great misery. Each little noise currently brought that temporary ray of hope that Cain would return. They now worried in how they could accept Cain for he was a murderer and curse by the Lord. The torment of losing both sons so surprisingly left Adam to wonder if the Lord had truly blessed him, or created him only to see how much he could suffer. Adam left Eve alone for a long period after they retrieved the body of Abel. An angel made this site known unto him. Adam wrapped his son's body in some fur and started back to the garden. On his way, to the past he found Awan, who had fallen sick and could travel no longer. Adam secured Abel's body, which was now covered with some special spices and herbs, and then guided Awan to the side of the Ox where he lifted her up to sit in front of him. They now proceeded back to the garden. When they entered, Eve and I rushed out to care for Awan. Eve paused while she mourned over the body of Abel. I took Awan into the cave and tended to her needs. She was with a child. We would talk about this later. Adam and Eve took Abel's body to his field. Where the nice altar was and buried it there? Abel would now rest on land and close to his family's cave. The succeeding week, they returned into the cave and asked me if Awan could talk with them. Awan told them she could talk for she knew they had many questions. She told them what Cain had told her, and that when she left Cain, he promised her he would save Abel who was living with his new wife. Adam asked Awan to stop talking for Cain had lied to her, as he had lied to the Lord, and was now cursed among all men to wander the remaining days before his life. Awan now began to cry saying, "I have within my womb the seed of one who is cursed by the Lord. What shall I do?" Adam reached over and kissed her womb saying, "We shall bless this child, for as he is from my son's seed, he is thus from my seed. We shall care and protect the mother of our grandson." Eve then asked, "What is she is a girl." Adam then said, "She still has my blood in her veins thus shall be a part of our family. Awan rest, for you are home now." Adam now went outside the cave and cried for days. He did return one night, and as he lay on Eve knew her once again. When he realized what he had done great fear filled his heart, for would the Lord give me more sons only to see them die? Adam was too grief-stricken and needed to go away to regain his mind. He did not want to cause Eve more grief and knew if he stayed, he would only add to her misery. She had also lost two sons, and he knew inside she had to be hurting, yet she buried it working so hard to comfort him. For the first time in Adam's life, he recognized Eve's feelings and felt great shame in how he had treated her. He asked Eve to hold him as, he, while crying, said to Eve, "I have so greatly victimized you. I must go away so that I can return and be a praiseworthy husband for you and a father to our large family. They held each other for about one hour, as he told her his parting mission that he must search for Cain and departed. Instead of searching for Cain, he roamed through many lands for one hundred and thirty years. I always wondered what was so important about one hundred and thirty years, only to determine that their souls had much more in common than we knew. Shortly after Adam departed, Eve learned that she was with a child. I could only marvel at the live bullets Cain and Adam were shooting from their guns. Either way, I now had a lot on my plate, for in this cave lived two pregnant women with no one to care for them. This is going on either passing or failing the test of love. The days were long and hard, as the night also contained a different sort of work for me. Either way, Eve and Awan were mine. I worked hard to provide and care for them. The Lord would only allow me to care for them if I give him my spiritual powers. My love for Eve was too great, so I gave the Lord my powers, wondering why he was so dedicated to increase our risk of death. The one hip pocket card I was my daughters, who helped kill game for us and protected us from evil neighbors who like hound dogs, sensed we were defenseless and thus easy targets. My daughters gave them some hard knocks that proved successful in keeping them away. With Adam gone, I could teach them about spiritual bonding. The spiritual bonding had its kinks as we were trapped inside our bodies. Either way, we worked hard to express the deep sisterhood we now shared. I watched the summer drift away in the chilly fall, then came the frigid winter followed by a happy time in our cave, as from my sister's wombs came two sons. Awan wanted to name Cain's son Enoch as he had requested, Moreover, Eve named her son Seth after asking the Lord. The Lord told Eve, "I have placed another son in your family. He shall be appointed by me and righteous in all he does." Ironically, the birth of Seth kept the Lord satisfied, as both Cain and Adam were chasing the winds. Then one day the Lord appeared unto Cain and said, "You may now go and take Awan and Enoch into the Land of Nod and their build a city for Enoch. I will allow you one hundred years to dwell there, at which time I will back to you your mark and reinstate your curse. I give you the one hundred years only for Awan. At the end of the one hundred years you must set her free hence, she may live her days and receive the rewards for the great love she has had for your mother. Do you agree?" Cain's heart was still in sorrow of seeing the great emblems of his son in Egypt. The Egyptians had some special magic that he had feared thereof. The next night Cain fell into a deep sleep and witnessed a vision. He saw the top of Abel's head, however he was not made of flesh, but make of blue light. Inside his head were many colored balls, ranging in sizes, and entering each ear was much lightning. So much lightning pass as it met at the middle. The lightning had as its source many balls that were packed tight that surrounded the sides of his mighty head. He had his normal peaceful glow. It appeared as if all things entered his head from so many beams of light. This was a great sign of power, yet Cain knew not its meaning and called upon Sammael to interpret it for him. Lucifer has spent much time talking with Cain, wanting so much to capture his soul. The dream appeared to Cain many times throughout the night, yet Cain's flesh was a weak and needed rest. He then returned to his sleep saying, "Lucifer shall save me." Lucifer had made a contract for Cain's soul, assuring him that the Lord would not take his life for eight hundred more years. They talked daily, as Cain was not only so sad, he was also deficient in one to have words. When morning released its dew and the sun filled the sky with light, Cain called upon Lucifer and explained the dream. Lucifer looked at Cain and said, "Our situation is direr than I had thought. Abel is now blessed of the Lord, and he shall judge many people before the Lord. Each ball is a soul. Abel shall be the first to judge all by reading the book about their lives. Fear, not for whom he casts away, shall forever live with me and whom he captures shall be imprisoned by the Lord." Cain then asked Lucifer, "What shall eternity with you be like?" Lucifer answered, "The Lord shall not walk among us. We will be free travel throughout the great lands in my home, which I will so gladly share with those whom the Lord has abandoned." Cain then said, "The Lord has put a curse on me, thus I elect to exist in your kindness, for you have shown mercy upon my heart." Lucifer then said to Cain, "Eat this ring, that it may rest in your belly, so I will mark your soul as being protected by me and my sons. When Abel looks upon you, he will only see my ring, which will force him to close his eyes. I will appear and guide you to our eternal home. Cain marveled at how Lucifer had thought on all things and felt optimistic about his future. Since Cain was not industrious and always desired play over work, this appeared to be the perfect plan. It was easy, yet Cain had one more clarification question, "Lucifer, will I have friends to play with, must I work while there and will I be permitted to rest when desired?" Lucifer then retorted, "Cain, you shall be free to make friends with any who agree as all are permitted to do so. You may play any game you wish, although if it requires more people to play, you must recruit them, for I will force no spirit of mine to work. You may rest anytime you desire, except if you recruit friends to play a game, you should not abandon them until a winner surface." Cain then joyfully responded to Lucifer, "Please master, give me the ring that I may eat it immediately, and be free of the Lord's bonds." Lucifer gave him the ring and Cain swallowed it quickly. Lucifer told Cain one more issue, "Cain, do not tell the Lord what you have done, for could get angry punish you immensely with hard work and beatings as you will suffer much pain while still in his word." Cain reassured Lucifer that he would keep it a secret, although he was not so much worried about the beatings, the horror of having actually to work terrified him. Lucifer now asked Cain, "Why do you not go and claim your wife and son are they not your property?" Cain then said, "I fear the Lord will curse them if I bring them to me," not telling Lucifer that he was actually now on his way to gather them. He wanted skillfully to convince Lucifer to protect him on his trip. Lucifer after that asked him if he mustered them if he provided the protection. Cain then laughed with joy, "Lucifer, did you just read my mind, for you were so skillfully able to detect the shame that I was hiding, for if you protect me, we shall collect my wife and son." Lucifer thought to himself, "If all humankind is facile like this fool, my hades will be packed too tight that the Lord will have to free us. This shall be such an easy battle to win." Lucifer would protect Cain on his trip, hoping that no one attacked them. He did not want to kill those from the neighboring tribes, as he had no possible jurisdiction over them as they belonged to the Lord of their parent's worlds. He had to ensure he killed them as they were attempting to harm Cain. Those from other worlds become the Lord of Earth's property when they mate with an Earthling, such as Awan. Thus, if Lucifer impressed Awan and their century-old son, Enoch, he may be able to grab two more souls. The battle was on now between the Lord and Lucifer, as Lucifer so much wanted to prove to the Lord how his Tehom was so much better than this Earth. Someday, the Lord would bow to him and restore Tehom once again under his rule. This Lucifer believed so much. He would need the Earthlings souls to help repopulate Mars, since so many perished.

Returning to Cain, the small group proceeded to the family cave. Lucifer caused signs and wonders to deter any attackers and thus Cain arrived unharmed. When Eve saw him, she rushed to him shouting out, "My son, have you returned to your home?" Cain then said as his mother, "The Lord has cursed me, thus I may be no longer live with you and my family. Where is my father?" Eve told him that he had been away for over one hundred years, and that she hoped he would return. Cain walked over to Awan and kissed her head, then with his hand pulled her up and said to Eve, "Today if have come to take Awan and Enoch to the Land of Nog, where I will build Enoch's city and home, so they will finish their lives in luxury. The Lord has given me one hundred years to do this, so I must hurry." Eve then told Cain, "I have lost both of my firstborn sons, and now you come to take away Awan and Enoch? Enoch works so well your brother Seth. You will cause much pain upon the cave of your family. Cain then said, "The Lord commanded before all of us, "Therefore, a man leaves his father and his mother and cleaves to his wife, and they become one flesh. They must follow me as commanded by the Lord." Eve knew this to be the law of the Lord and fell to the ground begging Cain to stay. Cain told her, "The Lord has given me only one hundred years to care for my family. I do not want them to live in the homeland of my shame." He then took Enoch and Awan with him. Eve stayed on her knees as Seth was next to her endeavoring so hard to comfort her. Seth has been extremely just and a righteous man. One day while trading with a neighboring tribe Seth laid his eyes upon a virgin whose name was Azura. He asked where he could find her father, which she shared with him. When Seth saw her father, he asked him her price. Her father, taking a big risk said three bags of gold. Seth agreed and gave him the three bags of gold. The father, seeing how easy he gave the gold, changed his price and said five bags of gold. Seth had with him some merchants from the village. He asked them what the punishment was not to deliver on a trade. They told him the punishment was death. Seth looked at the old greedy man and said, "Are you prepared to die?" Azura now begged Seth for her father's life. Her family then said to Seth, "Take her to be your wife for the three bags of gold we agreed to." Then Seth said to him, "If I allow you village to execute you, then I would have both Azura and my gold." The father then said, "That is true, take both your gold and new wife and show onto your new wife how great and just a man you truly are." Seth then returned his gold to his servants and said unto Azura, "Prepare to join me my wife, for I will give back to your father his life." Azura quickly followed him, for she so much wanted her father to live. Seth returned her to the garden and introduced her to Eve. Azura laid with Seth, as he knew her she became with child. They named their new son Enos. Eve now was refilled with joy, for she had lost Awan and Enoch and the Lord had given her Azura and Enos. She now had hope for a brighter future, only missing one thing, that being the father of her children.

Soon Cain, Awan, and Enoch departed, never to return.

During this time, I remained hidden, for I could sense the presence of Lucifer or Sammael, as I prefer to call him. I did not want a messy reunion, especially now that Eve had seen what she lost. I knew her heart was heavy. Seth and I struggled for over ten years to restore her hope and faith in the future. If we had not Seth, she would have lost all hope. Life would return to normal, as finally Adam returned to his wife, son, and daughters. He settled end and prepared to move on with his life.

Cain watched many people work hard building a city the he named after his son Enoch. While traveling to the Land of Nog they passed through a village called Bicsérd. Here, Enoch beheld and woman that he wanted to take as his wife. Her father demanded two bags of gold, which Enoch gladly exchanged for his new wife Sümegi of Bicsérd. Enoch had much wealth from working his uncle's sheep, which multiplied abundantly keeping the blessings of Abel. Enoch had great pride in the beauty of his wife. At first, Sümegi was sad because her father had sold her to unknown people, notwithstanding Awan took the young woman under her wings bringing peace to her heart. Awan and Sümegi bonded quickly as fear left her soul. She felt as a part of the family when they arrived at the site that Lucifer gave to them. Sümegi was amazed by the magic of Lucifer and felt no harm would seize them. She lay with Enoch as he knew her many times and she gave him many sons and a few daughters. The Lord continued to bless Enoch as his wealth increased; Cain talked him into building a large fort to protect their wives.

Sümegi was horrified when she gave Enoch his first son. She knew not of the great pain in giving birth, as such pain existed not in her tribe. Awan explained the curse of those who bear children containing Adam's blood. She read a letter she had from Eve that an angel had given her. Eve told her that the joy of having a child replaced all the pain bringing them into this word. She read as follows, "I will greatly increase your pain in childbearing; in pain, you shall bring into the world children, yet your desire shall be for your husband, and he shall rule over you." She suffered through the delivery, and soon accepted the thinking of Awan and joyfully continued to be with a child. Awan also gave unto Cain more sons. The first son she gave him was called Irad, which means born under the curse. Like his father, Irad desired to roam and when he turned thirteen, he departed traveling through a land western to the end of the Earth, where it meets the great sea. Enoch used much of his wealth to build a nice strong city. After one hundred years, Cain has departed his family now for the remainder of his days. Awan found the woman of the local tribes not to be the type, she would let her sons, and grandsons marry. She thus sent one of the servants to find Irad and request that he find wives, which the Lord approved for her family's children. The servant found Irad and gave him this message, in which Irad. His search took him past the Garden of Eden, which apparently had new tenants, yet Irad could not tell for sure since the giant spirits at the gate shown bright lights on him. He just kept on traveling towards the Far East until the earth was no more. This brought a great deal of fear to his heart as tales abounded from the tribes that giant beast would raid the shores for at least three moons in the land. They preferred using their ambush skills while waiting to ambush, when the victim had no hope of escape. Irad hoped that the Lord would keep him safe. Lucifer, however, saw a great opportunity for some fun, thus released some of his environmental special effects that backfired on him, as the Lord stepped in to secure Irad. This gave him some extra confidence, as even Lucifer now preferred not to pester. He was more occupied with what he called planting some new seeds. He had discovered some tribes along the vast lands on the eastern continent who were fighting severely. He feared that if the larger tribe was to be victories, they may raid in the west and deplete his future harvest of Adam produced souls. He could see an undeveloped civilization that lived on some islands in the easterly sea. Raids from these lands would create terror all along the eastern shore and would place expanding empire in the middle of the sandwich. Some industrial aliens had set up a nice civilization along these islands while the Earth was beginning to create land from the water. All life of that time lived in undersea structures must like Atlantis, except closer to the shores. They preferred to live in the water enjoyed not being close to people from other worlds. Their history was plagued with terrifying wars and thus had elected to avoid fights if possible. They had some underwater vehicles that resembled dragons and could shoot fire, which kept the land people at bay. Their civilization was not discovered by Adam's descendants, after Irad, for almost seven millennia. This is clearly another testament to their limited mental abilities. The remains, which were finally discovered, revealed a rectangular stone ziggurat under the sea off the coast of what was later to be named Japan. This was the first confirmation of a Stone-Age civilization, made by some industrial races that came from another planet. These of course were not the only wonders yet to be discovered. The ziggurat people depended upon visiting work forces from their home planets to cut and move the large stones that they used to build the parameters of their cities and to help dig the spacious living quarters in their underwater caverns. They were led by their Queen Yonaguni. Their home nation gave them a design for a monument being 600ft wide and 90ft high. It was started when Seth was in his second century of life. They began cutting the stones more than 5,000 years before others started on the oldest pyramid in Egypt, the Step Pyramid at Saqqara. Generations during just before the end time found these structures off Yonaguni, a small island southwest of Okinawa, and amazingly remained hidden from Adam's earthlings for over seven millennia from the death of Adam. I could understand if it were in the deepest parts of the Pacific, however, this structure is only seventy-five feet below your surface; you have submarines that search the shallow depths of the oceans looking for my daughter's cities such as Atlantis, which you still cannot find them. I am so shocked when some of your educated even debate the authenticity of these structures and deem this a natural occurrence. If that had been created by nature, one would expect debris from erosion to have collected at the site, but there is no rock fragments there. Soon you will discover many more layers within the structure, for when I visited the project; there were many private rooms, as they were prepared for a long history. They actually left the Earth after the atomic bombs were dropped on Japan's mainland, as these two bombs could shake some of the Queen's foundations. She feared a future war of such a mass destruction before not known on Earth and thus retreated back to the land of her ancestors. This city was named after Queen Yonaguni, which now is the name of a nearby island. Yonaguni was the queen of this strange race, which had many tribes spread out under the area. They reminded me of the Chy or the royal Queen hAyonjE's eyes, which were sensuous and sharp. Something is mysterious by these Mystonite eyes. They also built many roads in this enclosed city for the queen. The homes and stores were built on the ground, to protect against large storms that would flow through the area. Since humankind had nothing to do with this area and construction, progress was done with great success. I am constantly confounded by the lack of discovery, yet to find the other Queen's cities and wonderful structures, even though they are more than 75 feet below the sea, thus taking you another 10,000 years to find. The queen built some smaller versions of her enclosed city, only about 10m wide and 2m high nearby. These were in memory of one of her daughters and all the grandchildren from her daughter dying from the flu one winter. Queen Yonaguni worshiped deities from her native planet, which created anger in the Lord. I tried to tell her it was better to keep such as thing a secret, yet she did not know the thrashing I got for not bowing to Adam, so sadly I knew she would get her punishment someday. She proved wiser than I thought by avoiding any clashes with the Lord. She was wise in giving many daughters to Irad, who brought with them many of the strong values that the Yonaguni held. The Lord was impressed with this and thus decided they would be a good person to keep on the Earth, since they were secluded. They could be used someday in the future if needed. It is always better to have an unstained ally available. Her entire civilization endured plagues and storms, as some fire angels shot great fires into the ice of the north, which melted into water and combined with Noah's flood put her wonderful city under the water. Noah's flood killed all the other races who lived on which surface except those in Og's group, and those civilizations with advanced naval forces and all but a handful of humans who survived on a boat. The rains were united with severe winds and tornados that prevented these races from escaping into space. It had no effect on my daughters, and I as they simply joined Sammael and his boys for a joyride through the universe. Nothing like spiritual sensitization with a fire demon on a burning hot sun, which always sends rays of joy up my spine each time I think about it.

Resuming Queen Yonaguni's city, what they could not lift, their advanced powerful technology would finish. This technology was like none other on Earth. It was based upon another molecular makeup with substances they brought from their home planet. My daughters did not like Queen Yonaguni, as she was so strict and had too much control over her sons. She refused to let them play with my daughters. Her moral values were as strong as the Lords, which did not hurt my daughters to receive a good dose of it. Her strong muscular sons were quiet, as they loved to hunt and gather fruits. No one liked to farm, thus Queen Yonaguni felt it best to build her city tight and underground, with the mound to show her power and provide protection against invaders. They would randomly have to fight again for the land they took from the tribes who settled there before them, although they still were no match, the labor of having to kill them, rape their women and burn their small cities and sacrifice the blood to their children, after the children buried their parents, was a daunting task. Queen Yonaguni said, "I will not be the creator of tribulation, but when tribulation comes to me, I will not run. We (Sammael and I) did not sincerely care, for the prey was so much, easier elsewhere on the planet, and we both knew that soon the race created by Adam would be the easiest prey. I never truthfully thought about Queen Yonaguni's race, even though they were lost in the chronicles of time, the same as one who remembers not a dream. The nearby island shall forever share the name of this archaic queen. I needed to stay away from these other races and go back to the ancient civilization of Mesopotamia and the Indus Valley as they were slowly evolving. I needed to ensure the future wives and Seth's son made it safely to the rear in Eve's cave.

I knew it was time to meet with Sammael, for I could not protect Eve from all his evils that he wanted to unleash upon the Earthlings. His mission was to make the Lord appear weak, which so far was working well. As I met with Sammael, I pretended, as nothing was wrong, just telling him, I needed to rest, for life with my powers was a struggle. Sammael asked me, "Why do you no longer have your powers?" I told him, I only had no powers when I am with Eve." He further examined me, "Then you are foolish to around Eve." I told him, "She is a big part with my soul; I am one with her and must have her soul to make mine complete. It is too late for me, for if, she is doomed so shall I, and if she is harmed, I shall also be harmed, for her safety is what she gives me life. Furthermore, both the Lord and Adam do not like her being with me, so I must always be with her." Sammael afterwards said, "The last reason makes sense; however, the first reason is the foolishness of women. If you cannot be without her, then why are you here now?" I told him, "I have found new wives for Seth's son and Eve's other sons. They need some family time as I also need some time to rest. Are you going to let me rest, or must I find a new home?" He next relaxed and said, "You may rest, for I have much work to do." I after that rested. I knew this was a dangerous place to be, however, I wanted to ensure I kept a strong ally in my court. I would just avoid doing things to anger the Lord, except for pestering Adam. In my rest, I beheld visions of the remaining days with Eve. I would be everyday keep my promise of one whom I will always love, that being Eve, and leave the earthlings for many generations then to return and to exact, my revenge on Adam's descendants after his death. Many children, after being born would die because of the curse he had his creator bequeath me. I promised to have mercy on Eve until after her death. My future held for me only too painfully stay around and watch Eve's body slowly age as the chastisement for eating the fruit manifested this penance. Her great beauty still radiated from inside. She would hug and call me, her 'bad good little girl,' and I would say 'you are the greatest mother in all the stars.' Then I would slowly retreat, fly to a mountaintop, and cry rivers of tears. This was such an unfair punishment for one such as her, who served the Lord so faithfully. I had to exact my revenge, and that would take time and patience. The only way I could see to defeat them was to break their wills, and that would take me over 675 years more to do.

Sammael returned awakening from my sleep as he began telling me many stories about the Earth that was, before the curse of harboring Adam. There were many large beasts, some were flesh eaters, and others eat grass and leaves. The apes slowly started to walk like Sammael and I, yet they could not talk. By standing up, they made easier targets for Sammael's subordinates who liked to improve their archery skills. They would come from Mars in some specially designed spacecraft and amaze the ancients. These people would afterwards create tales and arts to the people from the sky. They were enjoying this until one day the Lord commanded them to stop since he was thinking about creating some earthlings to live on Earth. Unexpectedly, I could hear Eve calling for me. Our souls had an infallible link that could not be disrupted. I then told Sammael, "Sorry, my human wants me." In addition, later jumped out of the clouds, we were changing into birds and flying swiftly to Eve's cave. Eve was giving birth to another child, as she had many sons and daughters and as Azura was competing with her giving Seth many children. The spare wives were actively helping with the family function and maintaining harmony. They too would be giving their husband's children in only a few short years. Adam was now also showing his age, yet was still as stubborn as always, demanding to lay on top of Eve. I would have thought that by now he would have respect for her. Both Adam and Eve treated all children equally, working hard never to have another murder misery rattle the very foundations of their lives. Seth turned out to be a righteous man and pleased the Lord, which made life a lot easier for the rest of us. Queen Yonaguni was wise in discovering Irad's righteous base when she gave so many of her daughters to help build Eve's family. The family had many extra daughters, although only Sümegi allowed Irad to know them giving him so many sons and daughters. Eve and Azura would not share their husbands as these daughters of the Queen were much younger and they feared losing their husbands.

One day, that began like all others, with the children playing games created from their vivid memories, witnessed crushing news fall upon Eve's ears. As she went to awaken Adam, his body would not move. An angel appeared and told her, "Eve, the mother of the children of the Lord, Adam is now in the heavens with El Shaddai. You may be at peace knowing that Cain also no longer lives in the flesh and was able to speak with his father before going to their future homes, correspondingly. She now worried about Awan and Enoch and sent Irad to go to their city and invite them to return. Irad returned in a few months telling her that Awan wanted to, however she had to stay with Enoch who wanted to stay with his city. Eve had now taken another blow, for she would no longer reproduce children of Adam. She had to experience two deaths on the same day. Unfortunately, I would meet Cain again in the future. Contrarily, this was a wonderful day for me and Adam's corpse was a beautiful sight. When we lost them we lost Eve also, who was old with age at that time. She never gave up her warm heart, and many tribes knew how she raised four children and watched them grow because of her warmth. No one, not even I, now wanted to hurt her. I paid her dues, trying so hard to give her comfort, yet inside her, she held onto a great debt. We always felt so sorry that her loyalty to Adam, as he refused to let the creator's angels know her. She depended upon me for her source of love, as I never visualized falling in love with a human, let alone the mother of the earthlings. These were great events, as they would charge our entire souls with their 'fire' power and slowly amend our perceptions, something like a big psychedelic drug dose as I introduced in the final generations. This was a total eclipse of the universe with stars exploding and crashing into each other and only our spirits holding everything together. I always had to be careful when playing with the fire angels for if Sammael were to catch us, he would order his demons to fight them. The last thing I wanted to see was them throwing stars at each other. I shall never forget the great joy that Eve had when her wimpy husband returned from the long period of mourning Abel's death. The forest was filled with loud noises of great passion and joy as Eve welcomed her husband back to their empty cave. She, with all the might that her frail body could reproduce, unrelenting gave Adam many more sons and daughters, until the day my wishes were granted and both Adam and Cain died surrendering their flesh to the dust of the Earth. Fighting with Adam was more with his stubbornness; once some method was locked in his pea brain, it stayed there.

Adam was so different from King James, who founded Mempire. He was a strong King, yet not demanding. He would kill for what he believed. King James was loved by Lablonta and Adam by Eve. King James and Lablonta shared in making decisions, Adam told Eve what to do. Lablonta with focused on family and gave herself just to King James, while Adam did not only give himself to Eve, although most hated him. Eve gave herself at most to one man, but also to countless females outside of Adam's knowledge. I was the mother of mothers. The lands between the rivers, when Seth was 800 years old, watched them bury Adam and Kabil (Cain). Eve laid down her flesh the following year and Seth followed a few years later. I slowly drifted into the annals of time working hard to revenge my curse sevenfold. Adam caused the Lord to curse me, and his children would in turn surrender their souls to me. I stamped my name on their souls and gave them back to the Lord. My future lay in one hope and that since earthlings would not believe I exist. This continued to make my work so much easier. Not all the books of the ancients forget me, as I knew that blood would give me power, as only Gilgamesh would come to my rescue:

After heaven and earth had been separated and humankind had been created, after Anûum, Enlil and Ereskigal had taken possession of heaven, earth, and the underworld;

after Enki had set sail for the underworld,

and the sea ebbed and flowed in honor of its lord;

on this day, a huluppu tree which had been planted along the banks of the Euphrates and nourished by its waters was uprooted by the south wind

and carried away by the Euphrates.

A goddess that was wandering among the banks seized the swaying tree

And—at the behest of Anu and Enlil—brought it to Inannas garden in Uruk.

Inanna tended the tree carefully and lovingly

I hoped to have a throne, and a bed made for herself from its wood.

After ten years, the tree had matured.

But in the meantime, I found to my dismay that
my hopes could not be fulfilled.

because during that time, a dragon had built its nest at the foot of the tree,

the Zu-bird was raising its young in the crown,

and the demon Lilith had built her house about the middle.

But Gilgamesh, who had heard of Inannas plight, came to her rescue.

He took his heavy shield killed the dragon with his heavy bronze ax, which weighed seven talents and seven Minas.

Then the Zu-bird flew over the mountains with its young, while Lilith, petrified with fear, tore down her house and flew into the wilderness.

I am often amazed at the foolishness humankind has when seeing an act. If I were truly petrified with fear, then why would I tear down my house first and afterwards fly away?

CHAPTER 2

A Perfect world that was

There is at present so much sadness to my heart, as a foe and friend, united to each for almost one millennium have now parted from me, leaving a battlefield empty with only the decaying corpses under the crumbling soil. I am saddened that such a world, filled with my enemy and love with his wife was bubbling with strife, and life is now what feels to me as robots going through the same motions as their parents had. They sleep; look for food, and on the days, they still have some energy procreate before they rest. They struggle until death stills their flesh. They survive by ignoring that they also shall die. The absence of their deaths brings them partial joy, yet the loss of one they love replaces any joy they had before. Hitherto, the sting of death slowly heals and its memory fades away, only to await another debauched event to combine and strike its victim. The heavier the load the more likely they fall, until the last fall, when all is lost ending the game. The system fears not, for it continually adds new players to the game, since the players feel obligated to keep themselves in the game by creating the unused players. This is nothing more than lambs led to their slaughter. Their belief that once the game is over, the fun begins. I have always wondered why, if they believe after the game is fun and know that playing the game is not, why do they stay for the game? They must be thinking like Adam. This is a new sort of world, which the Lord is overseeing. A split-level of conscienceless, first level knowing good and immoral and death, the second level, being with good or evil with no death. I have always known that most, if giving the choice between good or evil will choose wicked, except for one that I will talk about soon, as death still captures both the good and evil. The mystery of not seeing the other side diminish the perception of risk, thus why not enjoy evil, as the things, which belong to evil greatly outweigh, the things that belong to be good. I shall now talk to a person who had no blemishes. This is from a vision that Sammael gave to me. This happened between your Genesis 1:1 and 1:2. Sammael always told me that the Lord would only have one people at a time. Thus, since the Earth was forming, this planet would have to decline, especially being so close to Earth. This world is called Mars by the Earthmen, and is the inspiration for mythologies and cults based upon its attractive lure. Young children are entertained by movies in which green people from the red planet invade trying to kill their species, yet never to avail. They do not understand that the invasion began so long ago. The little green men will watch the demise of the Earthmen's stage one existence.

We shall now venture to your sister planet, which was once a planet much memorable, having more beauty than earth. Like Lamenta, it is the fourth planet from the sun. Nevertheless, the ages now leave its surface barren, freezing cold, blistering winds, dried riverbeds and large creator holes. However, even with these gruesome attributes, the vestiges of its earlier glory still shine.

To describe the Mars of old we must know that beauty is strength and strength is beauty because they work hand in hand. Beauty's jurisdictions embrace consciousness, awareness, intelligence, youth, diversity, lightness, change, excitement, originality, genius, truth, independence, freedom, faith, hope, honesty, clarity, simplicity, trust, warmth, love, happiness, joy, life, creativity, courage, action, initiative, independence, energy, movement, speed, self-realization, balance, harmony, symmetry, duality, peace, compromise, cooperation, unity, and justice. Beauty is also solidity, stability, endurance, calm, quiet, resourcefulness, intuition, sensitivity, receptivity, caring, nurturing, devotion, remembrance, service, duty, reliability, humility, thoroughness, purity, perfection, depth, focus, intensity, exclusivity, determination, regeneration, control, order, honor, respect, law, forgiveness, understanding, tolerance, inner peace, rest, relief, sacrifice. This is what the concept of ruler ship braces.

Mars is best in the signs in keeping the body slender and energetic and therefore contributing much to a person's beauty or level of physical desirability. Mars on fire, and especially in Aries—its ruling sign, is often revealed in athletes or people in occupations where physical strength, speed, and stamina are perilous. These descriptions are especially true if the prevailing sign is also in air or fire. Mars in Earth inclines to be slow and sluggish, while Mars in water scarcities energy and confidence. These inadequacies will especially be evident if the governing is also in a feminine sign. Men (or women) and Mars are often physically attractive and stimulating to the opposite sex. An amazing race of powerful beings lived on this planet and were ruled by the heavens above lead by the greatest of all of God's creation sitting on his left hand. There were two races of spirits, first known as the Nordics, who later began a new race of life to exist on the third planet, which was a forming rock at that time. They enjoy ruling worlds in their earlier stages of development. The second race was known as the Tehom, the race for which Sammael belongs. They were constantly fighting with the Nordics who were very aggressive and quarrelsome, more or less to say the bad people on the planet. The Tehom built strong defenses and being of a greater spiritual blend were able to maneuver around the Nordics, except for the occasional genocide war as permitted by the Lord. With the Tehom, the Lord created a race, which had one form, an existence in one state with the knowledge of good, evil, and eternal life. They were created all at once with no abilities to reproduce with each other. Some, earlier in Earth's years knew the daughters of Earthmen producing unfavorable outcomes. Each had their mission to contribute to the race goals; except for the occasional bereavement from the Nordics, things went normal.

There was no evil in this wonderful land, which also escaped illness and animals. Their bodies contained no mass, thus did not have to eat, or expel body wastes. Therefore, they had no wars over how the planet's resources would be allocated, with the exception being the Nordics. Every rose garden must have its thorns. Beautiful skies filled with changing colors highlighted rivers and streams flowing through the mountain lands. At constant temperature and a prevailing sun brought warmth to this land, while burning the three closer planets. If sole history shared with earthmen, the magnificence and spender of this marvelous world filled with peace and joy, where no one broke the unique law and lived in harmony with the gods from the skies. No war had evermore been waged as only one nation existed, no hospitals had ever been built in, there were no diseases nor any deaths as all grew to old age and all spent the days singing praises to the angels of high, and the solitary El Shaddai reigned over this splendid paradise. Their Garden of Eden continued to grow and grow, as did the people, whose flesh never grew too old and only enjoyed the harmony of the universe, sharing the stars, which were within their grasps. I share with you this lost tale, filled with so much happiness and purity. It so sadly ended one day when the creator, as he had done on so many worlds before and will do to yours, although yours is fully justified, as the many pages that follow will give confirmation, their world was destroyed. First time was through freezing, and then second through burning. Their lives were being banished from Mars and forbidden futures in the stars. The angels who protected them were banned from the throne and cast from the heavens to the forming world that was the next planet (Earth) as they will someday be cast on to Venus. Yet inside the Earth, humankind has always been longing to know about the planet that flowed with oceans of blood in the end, before it sank deep into its soil. I now searched for answers that would allow me to explore how to capture this mysterious, nonetheless to say that there ever was a place with so much beauty would be false as each new world is created with a lower dirt than the one previously. This dirt commonly forms from rock particles disintegrating while entering the planet's atmosphere. Earthlings have long been fascinated by the planet Mars, along with less exciting tales of the other worlds. Theory about advanced civilizations on Mars is filled with more truth than the pioneers could have ever dreamed. Having a framework of evil and killing to express explanations of other worlds, they could only declare visions of a calamitous threat and invasion of green little men, the red planet is considered as a malevolent agent of war, pestilence, and disaster. This red planet never saw war or pestilence by any flesh dwellers. Even those flesh dwellers from the other worlds avoided Mars since its climate was too volatile for them to exist and instead drifted to Earth. In an attempt to attenuate the unreliable planet-gods, sundry ancient cultures offered it human sacrifices not knowing that those who lived on the red planet refrained from all killing, and would be angered at blood being shed as a sacrifice. It was a world ruled by harmony and peace, as if one with the elements, which composed the universe. What exists about this distant speck of light that could inspire such unfathomable conceptions summiting in ritual murder was a question they could never have answered since that thought could never be conceived. No way exists that can account for the truth that nearly identical beliefs are found around the Earth, in the New World as well as the Old. The exception, as falsely shared by the angels who lived on Mars, was when these events actually happened. Afterwards, they tried to cope with so much disruption that displaced, so fast for those who walked the mountains and valleys enjoying for love, finding no more love or a home to claim.

For incalculable millennia, all living on Earth reported myths surrounding their too many heroes and gods. Protuberant themes in these sacred traditions include the Creation, the Flood, the wars of the gods, and the dragon-combat. Even with the destruction of a myriad of cultures, such myths were committed to memory and told recurrently mostly because they represented sacred knowledge regarding the history of the earthlings. However, such traditions have thankfully, been given little consideration by intellectuals in general and snubbed by conventional science. I so much hate to use the words science, intellectuals, and earthlings in the same sentence. Too many times the records of the ages have provided better answers than the illogic of science, which has always overlooked the truth and advanced their propagandas that will be one of the foundations for Earth's demise with the premise that you are smarter than our jealous Lord is.

The falsehood that modern astronomers can provide more knowledge about the recent history of this small solar system from running computer simulations than from contemplating what the ancestors had to say on the matter. They cannot present evidence in their own solar system that is packed with the debris (including so many rocks) from all these former destroyed worlds that now continue to rotate in this solar system. A complaint that Sammael and I have with the creator is that each new civilization created is so much more foolish than the previous one. I am so glad that I was created long ago and far away. Sammael's now ancient world enjoyed playing on the beaches with the warmth of the sun being their only clothing for there was no shame to hide. Clothing by nature has a constraining effect on certain spiritual life forms and actually hides nothing since, unlike the flesh species, has no genitals. Thus, clothing hides the light, which is also hidden by shame and can only be burned out of most spiritual life forms. The warmth of the sun as it hit Mars will was felt longer than the memory of them was. After their demise, they changed forms leaving their old selves behind and new mission ahead of them. Their new mission for those who followed their Lord was to divide stage one earthlings from the Lord. As a reminder and a true object, which the 'scientist' could not refute they left a face on the surface of Mars. This was to give you evidence that we were there, yet modern science still struggles to explain it as not being. A time must come when if it is seen, it is. What is not seen is the history the Tehom.

In their beginning were all created equally at the same time. The only difference was that some had a colored plus sign while others had a colored minus sign on their foreheads. The goal was for a plus to match up with a minus of the same color. Mixing with different color signs was prohibited. Bonding with the same sign was excommunication forever from the race. As this race depended upon socialization to survive, any threat of being removed from the group was too great to even remotely chance. They were not part of any family unit. The only thing they had was the other sign and the mission group. They were part of and that was for eternity. Mission groups existed in security, entertainment, administration and other such dull areas. Sammael was the absolute ruler. All mission groups worked hard to perform the missions he gave them. Justice was simple, "Sammael says, and it was. When things would be too quiet, they would mess with the Nordics who eventually became terrified of them and then started trading with alien visitors for transportation to either Jupiter or Earth.

Occasionally, an alien race would try to settle. They were met with ultimate warfare from Sammael. The Nordics allowed to stay considering they were there first and it was first, advantageous to have a warring flesh population to give the invaders a visible representation on Mars. When the invaders actually attacked, Sammael would destroy them, which always brought harmony, for a short period, with the Nordics. They were as stubborn as Sammael, a trait he favored. Sammael had many other missions from the ages that still needed tending. Therefore, Sammael decided to appoint some of his angels' specific areas of responsibility, thus freeing up some of his time. Sammael was already planning to rule El Shaddai's next creation on his neighbor planet from the sun. He wanted to be ready to exploit all possible opportunities and to have a working plan for when he would ascend to the heavens and defeat the throne. After his great rebellion, Sammael was very angry over the Lord planning to create new people, which he said Sammael would have to serve, since they were created in the Lord's image. He would serve, serve them as his fresh meals thus he also could enjoy the pleasures of this unknown enemy. This race would be given more, so more would be required. Nevertheless, they would have to earn their freedom to keep it. Sammael noticed they had some serious defects starting with Adam's dominatrix and Cain's thirst to kill. Sammael and his demon's now realized that The Lord's new creation was a mine producing evils greater than any demon knew, and hungered to harm and abuse their fellow brothers and sisters. Sammael's victory over the humans could be achieved with minimal effort or involvement. The Lord ran into trouble when his image, being conceived as a man grew lonely. The Lord then took from Sammael a womanly spirit he brought from Lamenta (me). The Lord erroneously commanded this female spirit to obey his great new species. This did not work and then caused the events to unfold as shared in the previous chapter. Sammael was now setting up his team.

The first popular demon is Abaddon, who appeared throughout the Bible, such as in Proverbs, Job, Psalm, and Revelations;

Proverbs 15:11: "Sheol and Abaddon lie open before the Lord, How much more the hearts of men!"

Proverbs 27:20: "Sheol and Abaddon are never satisfied, Nor are the eyes of man ever satisfied."

Job 26:6: "Naked is Sheol before Him, And Abaddon has no covering."

Job 28:22: "Abaddon and Death say, 'With our ears we have heard a report of it.'"

Job 31:12: "For it would be fire that consumes to Abaddon, And would uproot all my increases."

Psalm 88:11: "Will Your loving kindness be declared in the grave, Your faithfulness in Abaddon?"

Rev 9:11 They have as king over them, the angel of the abyss; his name in Hebrew is Abaddon, and in the Greek, he has the name Apollyon.

Abaddon's name had power, and used extensively by humans. Lucifer instructed his team to help the righteous also, as keeping them in focus would let the evil within the followers' boil to a point that Jehovah would have to intercede, with no blame falling upon Lucifer. One such use was with Moses as by the Name Abaddon, Moses invoked and sprinkled the dust towards heaven, and immediately there was so great rain upon the men, cattle, and flocks, that they all died. Abaddon was an entity of destruction, and the humans only feared destruction. Some other of Lucifer's team was used to categorize or accuse a spirit of some wrongdoing of humans.

Mammon was accused of being the Lord of Greed and even teaching humans how to slash the surface on the earth to extract away her resources. Milton wrote in his Paradise Lost books briefly in books one as follows: Mammon led them on—

Mammon, the least erected spirit that fell.

From Heaven; for even in Heaven his looks and thoughts

Were always downward bent, admiring more.

The riches of heaven's pavement, trodden gold,

Than aught divine or holy else enjoyed.

In vision beatific. By him first

Men also, and by his suggestion taught,

Ransacked the center, and with impious hands

Rifled the bowels of their mother Earth

For treasures better hid. Soon had his crew

Opened into the hill a spacious wound,

And dug out ribs of gold . . .

(Paradise Lost, Book i, 678-690)

He elaborates much more in book two, with this elaboration not discussed here, as so many additional children must be addressed. Mathew, however labels mammon, as meaning possessions,

No one can serve two masters. He will either hate one and love the other, or be devoted to one and despise the other. You cannot serve God and mammon. Matthew 6:24.

Lucifer quickly discovered that Humanity were humanities by greed, doing all that they possibly could to get more, a ore as soon the price did not matter for having more could also further achieved by taking more, thereby decreasing those around them.

Asmodeus also known as Ashmadia, from the Persian Aeshma-deva, demon of wrath. Humankind had ex-perienced wrath from among each other and the Lord, who in anger drove them from the garden and flooded the earth, destroying so much. Yet, wrath itself became a demonic quality. King Solomon; however, used Asmodeus to help build the Lord's temple, and told Solomon how his kingdom would be divided. Milton also spoke about the 'demon of lust,'

Better pleased

Than Asmodeus with the fishy fume

That drove him, though enamored, from the spouse

Of Tobit's son, and with a vengeance sent

From Media post to Egypt, there fast bound.

(Paradise Lost, iv. 167-71.)

Asmodeus has also been accused of being the serpent that seduced Eve. This accusation is false, especially since Sammael took the punishment for this one, and the Lord had some strong reason to accuse Lucifer.

Beelzebub, whose name represents 'lord of the flies' has been labeled as the one that taught humanity gluttony? I seldom see a fat demon, yet an amazed at the number of obese humans, especially in the end times. I think the humans are the gluttons; however, as usual someone or something must be blamed. He was known as the prince of demons accordingly also in second Kings and the gospels,

"Go and inquire of Baalzebub, the god of Ekron, whether I shall recover from this injury." Two Kings 1:2

"And the scribes which came down from Jerusalem said, He hath Beelzebub, and by the prince of the devils casteth he out devils.' Mark 3:22

"But when the Pharisees heard it, they said, This fellow doth not cast out devils, but by Beelzebub the prince of the devils." Mathew 12:24

"But some of them said, "He casteth out devils through Beelzebub, the chief of the devils." Luke 11:15

The Testament of Solomon refers repeatedly to concern this prince to include speaking of heavenly things,

"Listen, King, if you burn oil of myrrh, frankincense, and bulbs of the sea along with spikenard and saffron, and light seven lamps during an earthquake, you will strengthen (your) house. And if, being ritually clean, you were light in the beginning, just before the sun comes up, you will see the heavenly dragons and the way the wriggle along and pull the chariot of the sun." Testament of Solomon 6:10-11

Leviathan has come to represent envy and one of the few sons of Sammael, who have been referred to as female,

'And that day will two monsters be parted, one monster, a female named Leviathan in order to dwell in the abyss of the ocean over the fountains of water; and (the other), a male called Behemoth, which holds his chest in an invisible desert whose name is Dundayin, east of the garden of eden.' One Enoch 60:7-8

Leviathan will be defeated on the Day of Judgment, as I have heard so many times predicted, concerning the lot of us,

'In that day the Lord will punish,

With His great, cruel, mighty sword

Leviathan the Elusive Serpent—

Leviathan the Twisting Serpent

He will slay the Dragon of the sea.' Isaiah 27:1

Conflictingly, Psalms echoes differently destroying
any unity in the series of reporting,

'it was You who crushed the heads of Leviathan, who left him
as food for the denizens of the desert' Psalms 74:26

Milton also adds twice in his series of Paradise Lost
concentrating on Leviathan's bounteous size,

By ancient Tarsus held, or that sea-beast

Leviathan, which God of all his works

Created hugest that swim the ocean-stream.

Paradise Lost i, 200-203

Wallowing unwieldy, enormous in their gait,

Tempest the ocean. There Leviathan,

Hugest of living creatures, on the deep

Stretched like a promontory, sleeps or swims,

And seems a moving land, and at his gills

Draws in, and at his trunk spouts out, a sea.

Paradise Lost vii, 411-416

Belphegor (Chemosh) also represents one of the seven deadly sins, sloth and provoked many writers in the Bible capturing a wide array of responses, including causing a plague while under Moses killing 24,000.

Moses said to the judges of Israel, Slay ye everyone his men who were joined unto Baal-peor. In addition, behold, one of the children of Israel came and brought unto his brethren a Midianitish woman in the sight of Moses, and in the sight of all the congregation of the children of Israel, who were weeping before the door to the tabernacle of the congregation. Moreover, when Phinehas, the son of Eleazar, the son of Aaron the priest, saw it, he rose up from among the congregation, and took a javelin in his hand; and he went after the man of Israel into the tent, and thrust them through, the man of Israel, and the woman through her belly. Therefore, the plague was stayed from the children of Israel. Equally important, those that died during the plague were twenty and four thousand.

"Your eyes have seen what the LORD has done in the case of Baal-peor, for all the men who followed Baal-peor, the LORD your God has destroyed them from among you."—Deuteronomy 4:3

"They joined themselves also to Baal-peor, And ate sacrifices offered to the dead."—Psalm 106:27-29

"I found Israel like grapes in the wilderness; I saw your forefathers as the earliest fruit on the fig tree in its first season. But they came to Baal-peor and devoted themselves to shame, and they became as detestable as that which they loved."—Hosea 9:10

"Woe to you, Moab! The people of Chemosh have perished; For your sons have been taken away captive And your daughters into captivity."—Jeremiah 48:46

"Then Solomon built a high place for Chemosh the detestable idol of Moab, on the mountain which is east of Jerusalem, and for Molech the detestable idol of the sons of Ammon."—1 Kings 11:7

"The high places which were before Jerusalem, which were on the right of the mount of destruction which Solomon the king of Israel had built for Ashtoreth the abomination of the Sidonians, and for Chemosh the abomination of Moab, and for Milcom, the abomination of the sons of Ammon, the king defiled."—2 Kings 23:13

Egyptian Mythology, The Egyptians also believed in the reality of demons. One such demon was Nehebkau, who appeared at times as a powerful earth spirit, who joined Ka and Ba after death, and was the God of Protection and at other, time was a foreboding snake god and one of the original primeval gods, which is attested to his time on Mars.

Persian Mythology. In the mythology of Persia, now Iran, two opposing powers struggled for control of the universe. Someone has to play the big side taking blame for all that goes wrong. Sammael never showed concern for this in that it enhanced his ability to influence as fear always served as a powerful force, especially considering that he had not to use his power to do all this evil. Ahura Mazda was the god of goodness and order, while his twin brother, Ahriman, was the god of evil and chaos. The Zoroastrian religion that developed in Persia pictured the world in terms of tension between opposites: God (Ahura Mazda) and the Devil (Ahriman), light and darkness, health and illness, life and death. Ahriman ruled malevolent demons called daevas that represented death, violence, and other negative forces.

Jewish tradition has always enjoyed degrading my role and included a female demon known as Lilith. Said to be the first wife of Adam, Lilith was cast out when she refused to obey her husband and replaced by Eve. "Refusing to obey my husband," is enough to make me vomit. We shall see showers of hail freeze out the burning lakes of fire before I serve an unworthy husband. Like all who have hope, I too shall someday find a powerful husband whom I shall willingly obey. At least, I am not plagued by the seven deadly sins. A truly fitting treat for the foolish.

The trident he is often shown brandishing is similar to those carried by the Greek gods Poseidon (Neptune), god beneath the sea, and Hades, lord of the underworld.

The Hindu god Shiva, who represents the powers of destruction, also carries a trident.

Islam, the Shaitans belong in a class of supernatural beings called genies. Some genies are altruistic or neutral about the human world, but those who do not believe in God are evil. I only added the peace of knowledge to attest that no spirit in the firmaments exists that denies God. We do not deny that which we have seen and heard. So much of the human arsenal dedicated to invent a conflict in the heavens does so by adding elements that constrain humankind. We see; we know Sammael and his boys fought; they lost, that is history. We are not as your species created, seeing not, nor hearing. We see as a team, for when one sees all see. Humanity, contrarily when one sees, few believe this must compensate for this weakness by creating a fictional image of evil, which sadly then all believe as if seeing.

In the earliest form of Hinduism in India, the gods were sometimes called Asuras. As their religion developed, the Asuras began to be seen as demons who battled the gods. Another group of demons, the Rakshasas, served the demon king Ravana. Some were beautiful, but others were monstrous or hideously deformed. One demon, Hayagriva, which also became a part of the Buddhist religion, was a huge and powerful enemy of the gods whose troublemaking constantly threatened to overturn the cosmic order. The Buddhist religion turned the Hindu demon Namuchi into Mara the Evil Personage, which tempted people with desires, and deceives them with illusions. Mara tried to tempt the Buddha, and failed nevertheless he still tries to keep others from reaching enlightenment.

Although Chinese and Japanese religions did not recognize a single powerful devil, they had demons. In Chinese legends, the souls of the dead become either shen, good spirits who join the gods, or gui, malevolent ghosts or demons who wander the earth, usually because their descendants do not offer them the proper funeral ceremonies. Japanese mythology includes stories about demons called Oni, may have the size and strength of giants. Although these demons are cruel and mischievous, some tales tell of Oni who change their ways and become Buddhist monks.

Christians of the Middle Ages lead to Inquisitions, crusades, and the burning of witches who were condemned to death in the eyes of the church. If it is different, say it is from Sammael and burn it. A perfect method to obtain a confession is torture to the death, which is in the eyes of justice no better than giving a plea bargain in order to convict someone justice knows did a crime, even in the absence of proof. Allow someone who may actually be a part of a crime freedom if that person testifies that the "known guilty one" committed the crime. Now that is true evidence, about as real as all these evil spirits fighting good spirits. Another important point to consider is that any force that does not work to enhance one's wealth or position is labeled as evil and as such must be destroyed. How can I blame you, considering that your father was Adam?

The Bush people of southern Africa disclose that Gauna, the ruler of the underworld, is the enemy of Cagn, the god who created the world. Gauna visits the earth to cause trouble in human society and to seize people to take to the realm of the dead. He also sends the souls from the dead to haunt their living family members. This of course attests to the originality of the Jehovah versus Lucifer's war, as even bush people who are out of the Asian circle report the same thing, the only link of course being as greed.

Mastema has also helped in the battle as reported in the Jubilees urging Jehovah to have Abraham sacrifice Abraham's son, as Sammael later did with Job. "Then Prince Mastema came and said before God: 'Abraham does indeed love his son Isaac and finds him more pleasing than anyone else. Tell him to offer him as a sacrifice on an altar. Then you will see whether he performs this order and will know whether he is faithful in everything through which you test him.'" Jubilees 17:16

Matema has one of the easiest tasks in the heavens working for Jehovah, he tempts men to sin and then reports it, as also reported in the Jubilees,

"And they made for themselves molten images, and they worshipped each the idol, the molten image which they had made for themselves, and they began to make graven images and unclean simulacra, and malignant spirits assisted and seduced (them) into committing transgression and uncleanness. Moreover, the prince Mastema exerted himself to do all this, and he sent forth other spirits, those that were put under his hand, to do all manner of wrong and sin, and all manner of transgression, to corrupt and destroy and to shed blood upon the earth. For this reason he called the name of Seroh, Serug, for every one turned to do all manner of sin and transgression.—Jubilees 11:4-6

He has also seen to be the one who hates Israel or the Jews. He, of course, took a long vacation during World War II, as Hitler accomplished in just a few years more than Mastema has in millennia. Mastema was a working relationship with the throne, as did most of the Mar's creation. He often performed questionable acts for Jehovah at Jehovah's command, such as trying to knock off Moses, and killing the firstborn in Egypt.

"And it came to pass by the way in the inn, that the Lord met him, and sought to kill him." Exodus 4:24

"You know who spoke to you at Mt. Sinai and what the prince of Mastema wanted to do to you while you were returning to Egypt—on the way at the shady fir tree. Did he not wish with all his strength to kill you and to save the Egyptians from your power because he saw that you were sent to carry out punishment and revenge on the Egyptians?" Jubilees 48:2-3

"And it came to pass, that at midnight the LORD smote all the firstborn in the land of Egypt, from the firstborn of Pharaoh that sat on his throne unto the firstborn of the captive that was in the dungeon; and all the firstborn of cattle." Exodus 12:29

"For on this night—the beginning of the festival and the beginning of the joy—ye were eating the Passover in Egypt, when all the powers of Mastema had been let loose to slay all the first-born in the land of

Egypt, from the first-born of Pharaoh to the first-born of the captive maid-servant in the mill, and to the cattle." Jubilees 49:2

Humanity has trouble comprehending the concept of forgetting and moving forward. Sammael had troubles. They serve the Lord while on Mars, and will serve while on Earth. The only thing big difference while working daily with Adam's children will be more of an enlightening the Lord concerning the evil or weakness of humanity, whereas humanity is working hard to return the favor.

Being a lover of love, I must reveal with you my favorite gods, previously children of Sammael, as many redefined themselves as female, goddesses, bearing the attraction of my enhancements. The children of Mars have worked tirelessly sharing and teaching love to the children of Adam. These giant sparks of love fought hard against the hate and evil that came from the hearts of humankind. So sad that so much love only produced future generations of haters and killers and lovers of the seven deadly sins.

Parvati Hindu goddess of Love & Devotion, from beginning to end all Parvati ordeals, her love for Shiva, her husband, never wavered. She is an endorsement that women can do whatever they set their minds to, no matter what obstacles they face. Parvati is a source of power and Shiva's powers derive from her. Eve may have been the model for her impressions.

Krishna Hindu goddess Love, She represents, all attractive, all-powerful, and all knowing and considered by many to be the most beautiful person. When I first met this remodeled Martian, I also fell to my knees in anger and being heartbroken. Previously, I was misconceived, only believing that Eve and Lablonta had greater beauty than I had. I understood Eve, since she was my replacement and I never envied Lablonta, as she was a personal hero in that she used her beauty only to make the lives of others better. Yet Krishna is just undeniably beautiful, and like Lablonta, worked to use her beauty for the benefit of those who searched for and love her. Her incarnations also included the male god Lord Krishna, eight avatar from Vishnu

Kama Hindu and Buddhism god Love excites the lovers with sexual desire, sensual gratification, sexual pleasure, and sexual fulfillment. He naturally concentrates on the male side of these events. He also worked on getting his servants to avoid sexual misconduct and avoid sex with your neighbor's wife. Although reported as an ethereal personality he actually never existed in a human body, as such flesh could not subsist on Mars.

Bes Egyptian dwarf god Love & Marriage, he began as a defender of the Pharaoh, he became very popular with the Egyptian people since he safeguarded women and children above all others. As with many other gods, he was considered a demon who did good works. The Egyptians always acknowledged that if a baby laughed or smiled for no reason, it was because Bes was making funny faces. Another responsibility was to drive away evil spirits who caused accidents and made trouble. Sammael would help him, as there were times when demons from other galaxies, on one of their raiding campaigns, would decide to charge Earth. Bes worked hard to teach them the errors of invading his realm. The Egyptians even inscribed his image on their war knives evoking his power to defeat their enemies.

Isis Egyptian Goddess Love, as she also controlled the moon, magic, love, motherhood, healing, and fertility. She is always depicted as young, healthy, and beautiful. She also battled evil as it cuts close to her by embalming her brother Set and killing her husband Osiris. She also was considered the Queen of the Underworld.

Lada Slavic Goddess Love was also known as the 'Lady of the Flowers", as she carries wild roses, and is often associated with my hero Venus and handles fertility for not only mankind but also for all that begins life in the spring when she emerges from the land of the dead. She is associated with rain and hot summer nights. As a symbol of the sun, she had long golden hair with ears of grain braided into the hair. She is a symbol of love and beauty, never having to take a second seat behind any of the other goddess. "Lada is the Slavic Goddess of spring, love, and beauty. She was worshipped throughout Russia, Poland, and other areas of Eastern Europe. She is usually portrayed as a young woman with long blonde hair. As Goddess of spring, Lada is represented with love and fertility in both humans and animals. She returns from the underworld every year at the vernal equinox, producing the spring with her.

Aeval (Aebhel) Irish Goddess of Lust, sex magic, and wisdom in making judgments. She held a midnight court to hear the debate on whether the men of her province were keeping their women sexually satisfied or not. She commanded that the men bow to the women's sexual wishes. Adam would have suffered greatly in this court. This was a work that I often helped her for it is something needed to break the domination as established by Adam. Claiming that I would not obey I could charge him with not satisfying me as I believe even Eve could have won against him.

Branwen Irish goddess of Love and beauty who was also known as the Venus of the Northern Seas. She sadly died of a broken heart after her brother, Bran died.

Aine of Knockaine Celtic (Iris) goddess of love and fertility related to the moon, crops, and farms or cattle and later known as the fairy queen. She is sacrosanct by Irish herbalists and healers and is said to be in charge of the body's life force. She was the daughter of Manannan. There was a stone, Cathair Aine, fitting to her and if somebody sat on the stone, they would be in jeopardy of losing their intelligences, sit three times and they would lose them forever. Aine was very rancorous, and it was not a secure thing to offend her.

Ca-the-na Mohave goddess of love and promiscuity also known as the Mohave Venus. She reigns over fertility in humans and animals.

Alalahe Polynesian goddess of love, Laka, many branching one, the shining one (alohi), the beloved (aloha). The prayer to the goddess is to fruitfulness, characterized as the woman floating in the air, her limbs outspread, face upward, tossing about, her voice dammed. She is the caressed sacred one. Her womb holds hordes upon bevies in the uplands and the sea. A family springs from her womb. She is the impregnated one, the fertilized, from whom flood in generations of offspring, the family of Laka, fruitful as the stalk.

Alpan Etruscan goddess of Love means endowment or submission along with eagerness. She is normally portrayed nude, free of any shame. She is a beautiful flying spirit. She is also goddess of springtime who brings forth the assortment of plants that bound from the ground. She helps her servants by helping them feel more vigorous, giving increased sexual love, relationship love, amplify beauty, and deepen sensuality. A wonderful contribution made by Sammael's family toward the mission of spreading love. She followed my concept of purity and as pure having the right not to become a prisoner of clothing.

Aphrodite Greek goddess of sex, love, and beauty, who unlike other goddesses, she has love affairs with gods and mortals. Aphrodite is associated with a magic girdle, the dove, myrrh and myrtle, the dolphin. Botticelli painted Aphrodite as rising from a clamshell. Her creation of the goddess of love was the result of sheer viciousness and vengeance. Merely, three goddesses could resist the lures of Aphrodite, Histia, Athena, and Artemis. She can cast a spell of overpowering love on all mortals, immortals and every type of beast. In order to humble, the goddess so that she could not deride the other Immortals, who fell in love with mortals, Zeus caused Aphrodite to fall in love with a mortal man named Anchises. He willingly believed her lies because she was so beautiful. He received her into his house and consummated their love. While Anchises was still sleeping, Aphrodite arose and put aside all pretentiousness. She called to Anchises and when he looked upon her, he trembled in fear; He saw her for the goddess she was, and there was, and he seriously believed that he would be chastised for having loved her. Aphrodite told him not to be afraid, and that he would not be harmed. She told him that he would become the father of a noble prince of the Trojans with many fine heirs. Furthermore, she declared that their son would be named Aeneas, meaning Awful, because she had been made love to a meager mortal and even though Anchises was righteous and handsome, she found their union to be offensive and beneath her status.

Astraea, Greek virgin goddess of love, modesty, and justice. During the golden age, she dwelt upon the earth with humanity, as this star bright maiden lived on earth and among men, whom she blessed; but when that age had finished, Astraea, who stayed longest among men, withdrew, and was placed among the stars. She was compelled away by the lawlessness of the later Bronze Age. Zeus then placed her amongst the stars as the constellation Virgo.

Ishkhara Babylonian Goddess Love, Priestess of Ishtar, whose symbol was the scorpion, "Ishkhara's themes are creativity, energy, passion, instinct, fire and sexuality. Her symbols are the scorpion or any stinging, hot items. Ishkhara is known for her scorching nature. The Syrians specifically worshiped her in the form of a scorpion when they wished to improve sexual courage or passion. She also judges human affairs fairly but firmly, and all oaths made in her name were sacred. In astrology, people born under the sign of Scorpio are alleged to be creative, sturdy, sensuous, and tenacious, often internalizing her enthusiasm in their sign for personal energy. Delight in any hot beverages, such as coffee with a dash of cinnamon for vitality, first thing in the morning. This will give you some of Ishkhara's fire to help you face your day, both physically and mentally. For those desiring to improve interest or performance in the bedroom, now is a good time to focus on foods for passion and fertility. Remember to invoke Ishkhara's blessing before you eat. And, if you can find one, put the image of a scorpion under your bed so that Ishkhara's lusty nature will abide in the region and you can tap into it during lovemaking." Ishkhara's was a "Semitic Goddess of promiscuity, who later merged with Ishtar. In Hurrian and Semitic traditions, Ishkhara's has been a love Goddess, often notorious with Ishtar. Ishkhara's is the Hittite word for treaty, binding promise, also embodied as a Goddess of the oath. Her cult was of considerable importance in Ebla from the mid-third millennium, and by the end of the third millennium, she had temples in Nippur, Sippar, Kish, Harbidum, Larsa, and I remember visiting one in Urum. Ishkhara would inflict austere bodily penalties to oath breakers. She also functioned as a 'Goddess of medicine' who empathized in cases of illness. There was even a verb, isharis—'to be afflicted by the illness of Ishkhara. She became a great Goddess of the Hurrian population. She was worshipped with Teshub and Shimegi in within the Hurrian pantheon Alakh, and at Ugarit, Emar and Chagar Bazar. She was associated with the underworld, which was with Samael and her brothers. Her astrological quintessence is the constellation Scorpio and she is called the mother of the Sebitti. Ishkhara was well known in Syria from the third millennium B.C. While she was considered to belong to the following of Ishtar, she was summoned to heal the sick. The Hurrian cult of Ishkhara worshipped her as a love Goddess and spread to Syria. Ishkhara first appears in the pre-Sargonic texts from Ebla and then as a Goddess of love in Old Akkadian potency-incantations. During the Ur III period, she had a temple in Drehem and from the Old Babylonian time onwards, there were sanctuaries in Sippar, Larsa, and Harbidum. In Mari, she appears to have been very popular and many women were called after her, nevertheless she was well attested in personal names in Babylonia generally up to the late Kassite period. Her main sobriquet was belet rame, lady of love, which was also applied to Ishtar. In the Epic of Gilgamesh (Tablet II, col. v.28), it says, 'For Ishkhara the bed is made' and in Atra-hasis (I 301-304) she is called upon to bless the couple on the honeymoon. She was a busy advocate for the empire of love as Samael's follower combined love with the powers of the underworld.

Amor Roman God of Love Amor is derived from the Latin word for love. Amor was the son of Venus and was born from a golden egg. He was a small being with wings. Amor carried around a bow and some arrows. He would shoot the arrow at a victim and once it struck the victim's heart, the victim would fall in love. Amor is closely associated with the Roman god, Cupid.

Venus, Roman Goddess Love & Beauty, This spirits adaptation to Earth even amazed and excited me, as I so much hope to work with her someday. I do actually pray that the Lord blesses me as such some wonderful day. I always enjoy visiting her when playing in the firmament and value myself as a devoted student to her works. This goddess of love also has an ancient history. The Romans originally worshiped Venus as the goddess of fertility. Her fertility powers broadened from the garden to humans. She was the goddess of chastity in women, even though she had many affairs with both gods and mortals. As Venus, she was worshiped as the mother of the hero Aeneas, the founder of the Roman people and as the bringer of good fortune, the provider of victory, and the defender of feminine chastity. Venus is also a nature goddess, associated with the arrival of spring. She is the source of joy to gods and humans. Venus, having no myths belonging to her was so closely acknowledged with the Greek Aphrodite that she adopted Aphrodite's myths. The Greek perspectives of the love and beauty goddess Aphrodite were added on to Venus' attributes, is synonymous with Aphrodite. The Romans acclaimed Venus as the ancestor of the Roman people through her association with Anchises.

Cupid Roman was the god of love, and the son of the goddess Venus. He was her loyal companion; and, armed with bow and arrows, he shot the darts of desire into the hearts of both gods and men. The following legend is told of him. Venus, complaining to Themis, one of the Titans, that her son Cupid grew no bigger than a child was. Venus was told that it was because he was alone and that if he had a brother he would soon begin to grow. Shortly after a brother Anteros was born, Cupid immediately was to grow rapidly in both size and strength. Cupid had two different types of arrows, which explains this Roman god's reference in both romantic and erotic love. Anyone hit by one of Cupid's arrows did not die but fell in love. The Golden Arrow signified true love and the Leaden Arrow represented wanton and sensual passion. Cupid was also associated with many holiday's the focus upon love, such as Valentine's Day during the end times. Venus used to send him on errands.

Prende Slavic goddess of love worshipped by the ancient Illyrians and, later in Albanian mythology, became their goddess of love is Prende, the queen of beauty. Moreover, hot she was, another great creation by Sammael and excuse for me to become angry with him for fear he may take up one of his children. This, of course, became only an unfounded jealousy. Prendi was the wife of Perendi and referred to in Albanian legends as zonja e bukuris, while her sacred day is Friday.

When Albania became Christianized in the early Middle Ages, Prende was identified by the Catholic Church as Saint Anne, mother of the Virgin Mary. Albanian Shënepremte or Prende, known in Gheg dialect as Prenne or Petka. Friday is the day sacred to the goddess of love. Her name is used today for Friday.

Dzydzilelya is the Polish Goddess of love and marriage and of sexuality, rain, and fertility. She is analogous to Venus, Freya, Aphrodite, and other goddesses of this character.

Benten, Japanese / Buddhist goddess of love, music, eloquence, the arts, wisdom, knowledge, water, and good fortune. She is the benefactor of geishas, dancers, and musicians. Formerly, she was a water goddess or sea goddess, on whose image many local deities near lakes were founded. Later, she became a goddess of the rich, and added to the Shichi Fukujin. The island of Enoshima rose up especially to accept her footsteps. Benten is depicted as a beautiful woman, riding a dragon while playing on a stringed instrument. She has eight arms and in her hands, she holds a sword, a bow, a jewel, an arrow, a key, and a wheel. Her remaining two hands are joined in prayer. It is often revealed that when a dragon devoured many children, she descended to earth to stop his evil work thus gaining her the title of protectress of children. Her husband was a wicked dragon whom she transformed, and she is often shown riding one. Dragons and their smaller relatives, snakes, are sacred to her and snakes are often her messengers. She prevented earthquakes, and worshipped on the islands, especially the island of Enoshima. Benten is originally of Hindu origin and is associated with Sarasvati, the Indian goddess of music and wisdom, and is sometimes shown with eight arms. Benten is also linked to Kwannon or Kwan Yin, the sometimes female, sometimes male deity of compassion in Buddhism.

Benten is one of the Seven Gods of Good Fortune who sails on the Takara-bune, the treasure ship. Conventionally, a picture of the Takura-bune is placed under the pillow on New Year's Eve will bring a lucky dream. Benten brings luck and good fortune, persuasion and seduction. Benten was a beautiful Japanese goddess of, knowledge, good fortune, arts, language, wisdom, wealth, and water. In early Buddhism in India, Benten is associated with sixteen children said to be incarnations of the various Buddhist deities who symbolize the crafts for which she is the patroness. At Hase Dera in Kamakura, a cave with sixteen life-size statues, all female, can be found on the ground level of the temple. Fifteen princes and one princess set out from Japan, which at that time was still part of the ancient continent of Mu, to inhabit the world. They went to various parts of the world.

Bangan Philippine Goddess of love, romance, pigs, and springs. Daughter of Lumauwig and Bugan, sister of Obban. One of the twenty-four gods beneath Mengos-oschong. The mambunong would ask for Bangan's healing powers for sick pigs while Pe-ey makes sure the meat used in rituals is safe and tasty.

Anath Canaanite, chief West Semitic goddess of love and war, the sister andslewate of the god Baal, once slayed all his enemies at a feast. She is a goddess with four differing aspects: warrior, mother, wanton, and virgin. Though a mother, she was ever a virgin, somewhat in line with the Virgin Mary. Her lust for blood, and or sex, was famous. She was worshipped throughout Canaan, Syria and Phoenicia. She was a popular goddess of war and fertility. She was largely associated with Asherah and Astarte, which creates some confusion in relation to her myths and connection to other deities of the area.

Oshun Yoruba is the goddess of love, of money and undeniably of happiness. She brings to us all the good things of life. She is the goddess of sweet water and can be found where there is fresh water, at rivers, ponds, and particularly waterfalls, where many offerings are left for her. Many ceremonies are completed at the riverbanks. The future Iyawo must go to the river for a special cleansing by Ochun the night before they are crowned in Ocha. Ochun loves to dance and make merry, nevertheless she also has a serious side. She is a great diviner and usually her children are very well endowed with psychic abilities, especially when using the sacred seashells in divination, which are the mouths of the Orishas. She is very sensual, but also very sensitive. She can be easily offended. Many try to stay on her good side, since her blessings make life worth living. In Haiti, Ochun is known as Erzile. She has the same characteristics as Ochun, but her colors are a little different. Ochun's color is yellow and gold, because of her association with money. Ochun is correlated with Our Lady of the Caridad del Cobre. Cobre means copper in Spanish, and the first money slaves saw in Cuba when they arrived was made of copper. Whatever you call the African goddess of love and money, she is the same energy. Her help is often sought when a woman hopes to marry or when there are problems in a marriage. Her function as an Orisha is considered very important. Our Lady of the Caridad del Cobre is the patron Saint of Cuba and the people love her dearly.

Chalchiuhticue Aztec goddess of love and beauty whose name means Jade her skirt. She was a goddess of water, rivers, seas, streams, storms, baptism, and patron of childbirth. Tlaloc was one of the first abuser gods and because of this she retaliated by releasing fifty-two years of rain, causing a giant flood, and a fourth of the world to be destroyed. She built a bridge linking heaven and earth and those who were in her good graces were allowed to traverse it. The other residents of the earth were turned into fish so they would not drown. She used the flood as an act of purification of human kind.

The list goes on and on and actually is beyond the scope of this book. We felt it important to allow you a chance to conceptualize the magnitude of how the followers of Lucifer, prior to his rebellion against the throne have migrated into the very fabric of what humankind is. They have defined love in the best manner possible, yet find themselves still struggling to hold back the great wells of hate that flood the lands. This section only concentrated on a small aspect of how these demons have defined the environment that controlled how so many existed throughout the long history after the flood. I understand the vastness of the gods and goddesses of Love.

It was not love that brought these demons to earth. It was the unquestionable control Lucifer had on them as they did their wonderful works and deeds on Mars. El Shaddai complemented him many times regarding the great work he was doing with his species. Some of the demons later reported to me that Lucifer did not feel he was getting the same respect and honor around the throne that he got to Mars. On Mars, wherever he walked this creation bow to him. Lucifer loved this power and soon found himself dependent upon it. As the sun would shine across the green fields and limited forests on Mars, Lucifer would grow angry that the grass would not bow to him. He later confessed to me that his intellect was overtaken by his emotion. I also complain much about the spirit; however, will never deny that he can put his emotions on the table when needed. When he starts giving me his line, I know I had better departed, or we may need to borrow some snakes, and I mean immediately. He envied the golden streets connecting the mansions in the firmament, thus he has some of his follower's search for gold in Mars. They were about to make a few streets; however, the weak gravity could break the gold into small pieces, and the storms spread it throughout Mars. This added additional anger in his soul, as he now had difficulty finding love. He had been lucky in that the gold had made excellent floors for his palace floors, which was a good beginning in his quest of magnificent all powering glory. Lucifer also grew angry, as he has seen the Earth starting to evolve into a habitual world, as the waters covered the surface, cooling down the hot gasses below forming rocks and small land areas. He could see sea life evolving and knew that soon life on the rock surfaces would evolve. Some sea life, such as penguins, seals, and such would warm up on the rocks. As each millennium passed, Earth was evolving until one day as Jehovah had finished creating the forests and other vegetation; oxygen began to fill the Earth. This was a danger sign for Lucifer, for he knew that if this new species were to sin, for they would be tested since they were a superior spiritual breed, and after sin, they would return to the same biological systems as the beasts. They would have legs and arms, sight, smell and be able to communicate with each other. All would have hearts, blood and other internal organs to keep everything functioning as this fresh biologic creation would have to take a matter in and process it, turning it into energy and expel the wastes, as each little part of it would need to be feed constantly. He saw how these fresh biological devices were being created, actually evolving from apes and monkeys. This was such a degrading process and for this, he did feel sorry for this creation; however, the image of El

Shaddai would not be breathed in unless they had sinned. That would be a great drop, yet what was worse, Lucifer and his creation would be expected also to worship them. This could not ever occur for the shame of this degrading future tormented Lucifer beyond his comprehension. One year, while being worshiped on the other side of Mars, a messenger of Jehovah appeared to summon him to the throne. The messenger saw Lucifer being worshiped and thought nothing of it, having never seen a thing such as this; the messenger assumed they were practicing for any visits to the throne. Lucifer instead sent a follower to represent him. El Shaddai became angry and demanded that Lucifer appear. Again, Lucifer sent another messenger to the throne with a message that he could not appear. Jehovah now sent an army of angels to capture Lucifer and bring him to the throne. Lucifer, being forced to appear, appeared in anger before the throne. The Lord asked him, "Lucifer, why have you been avoiding me?" Lucifer then answered, "I have been so busy preparing my followers to worship you that my spirit has grown weak." Jehovah now gave him the good news, for he had completed the new species image and had yet to breathe his life into it. He now told Lucifer to bow down and worship it. Lucifer refused and then vowed revenge. He departed swiftly, maneuvering around the armies guarding the throne and rushed back to Mars. He now assembled all his spirits and told them that the Lord was preparing to erase them all from existence and replace them with a new species created in his image. He then told his followers that the only way they could survive was to attack the throne and capture the Lord. He felt that if he had the Lord, he would have bargaining power with El Shaddai.

He was lonely, and did not want to confide in his followers, fearing they would see it as a sign of weakness and revolt. He avoided going to the throne, fearing the Lord would see his inability to love and remove him as the Lord of Mars. Thus, for a couple of millennia he avoided the throne, sending his followers from among the rich supply of love filled with spirits. He could hear them worshipping El Shaddai and this soon got under his skin (well, if he had skin, it would have gotten under it). The brightness and joy of the day tormented his soul, as he now only found peace in the darkness of the night. He then would take some of his followers to the opposite side of Mars and demand that they worship him. At first, his followers were fearful of this for they denied him this worship he would destroy them. They now longer felt he would be truthful to Jehovah, so they had no safe haven if they would not worship Lucifer. In the beginning, Lucifer was afraid of this also, yet soon thrived on it. His deeds were noticed by some evil empires who had long wished to invade the Milky Way, as it was a wide-open expanse of open planets, while the other Empires were over populating and tensions of rebellions or even war among themselves were brewing. They had not desired to infiltrate and invade the Milky Way; however, El Shaddai having too much power, had designed a defense that could not be broken. Then one quiet night, Lucifer received a strange guest. While reviewing the actions of his servants for the day a small dark light began to expand within his room. At first, it did not alarm him, however soon it occupied one-half of his palace room. He then spoke out, "Which servant is pestering me now." A cold chilly voice in which, its words crystallized in midair just before Lucifer and dropped falling to his golden floors. The words, which he was able to grasp just before reaching him said, "I am not your servant, however I do wish to serve you in a manner that can benefit both of us." When Lucifer heard the word 'benefit', he decided to give attention to this new acquaintance, whatever it was. The voice then said, "I am the great Виноградов (Vinogradov), holder of Stone of Ceglédi. Lucifer then said to him, "I am Lucifer, holder of the Stone of Mars, as my stone is much greater than that small stone around your neck. Vinogradov then answered, "Are you really so foolish as to make jokes about things you known not about?" Lucifer screamed back, "I shall destroy you for your foolishness.' He went to lash a spiritual blast, equal to 1,000 hydrogen bombs, yet Виноградов (Vinogradov) simply breathed in the blast and it vanished within his darkness, then said unto Lucifer, "My child, do not make me agree, for I came in peace and will leave in peace, yet you may no longer exist." Sammael was traumatized, for he had never seen power such as this. He said unto Виноградов, "How can you have so much power?" Виноградов, then said, "I have more power than you have ever seen, yet came today to give into a chance to also share in my power, are you interested?" Lucifer was flabbergasted and, without knowing, fell to his knees and said, "You are here master, for you know I crave things such as this." He was so stunned that his spirit was bowing, yet this was the time to bow, for it is wise to go down, if you will rise to a new height. Виноградов then told him, "I shall give you my Stone of Ceglédi and upon a designated time, you shall meet me at a selected border point in which you will strike Jehovah's forces from behind allowing my Army to enter. We will go and destroy Jehovah's throne and that new species he will plant upon Earth, for we do not agree with the way he has treated your perfect kingdom and fear that the new species he creates will generate enough worship to give Jehovah a greater power and some day strike our homes and families. What say you, for you will not have to worship these new creatures?" At this time, Виноградов (Vinogradov) gave unto Lucifer an image of him praying to a human as they were rounding up his angels to destroy them. Lucifer was horror-struck by this image and said into his new ally, "Oh great Виноградов (Vinogradov), my mind is hence weak now, as my spirit trembles in great agony, knowing that what you have shown me is so real. May I share this horror with my leaders so that we may be able to provide you all that will be needed as you take for you a new home in my Lord's evil throne overflowing in hate and wickedness?" Виноградов (Vinogradov) spoke saying, "No Lucifer, none may know, not even those few that you bring to the border as an aide in my entry to save you. For if, one was to tell, you would be damned for eternity by Jehovah. You must start now to wander around the galaxy at night and establish a random pattern. Never visit the border point that I have put on the Stone of Ceglédi, which I will leave with you, this night. If you venture in the direction of my selected entry point, the stone will steer you away. Remember, Jehovah and your followers will be watching you." Then Lucifer, now being filled with lust for power asked Виноградов, "What else can the stone do?" Виноградов told him, "The stone will give you great power, for after I attack the throne you will be able to rule your new empires with absolute power. Eat the vision that I have given you, yet speak not what you have seen. The stone will tell you are night of great invasion and removal of the chains that are choking your life from your spirits. For now, I need some of your lower followers to escort me back to the border, for we must make this look as if in the normal course of existence." Lucifer then called a few of the fools in his court and asked them to travel with his new friend back to the border, so he could obtain some gifts for Jehovah from his family, to return another day when Jehovah had time to meet with his children, who would accompany him the next time." The fools did as he requested and after taking Виноградов to the border, shared in some spiritual games with the border guards before returning. Lucifer was now filled with a new hope, for he would not build a new heaven on Mars, yet instead occupy the throne of El Shaddai as the god of the Milky Way. His future now held great hope as placed the Stone of Ceglédi into his deep soul and studies the incalculability of its power. Factors were going to change, as he now had hope for his species. They would not worship these humans, never ever. Lucifer now relaxed with his followers, concentrating now on enjoying their innocence and perfection. He stopped his followers praying to him on the other side of Mars, telling them that it had only been for their enrichment for when they appeared before Jehovah. He further told them, "It is your father's wish that all things you do, that they be done to bring glory to Jehovah." This rebuilt hope among the spirits of Mars as they now replied to each other, "Surely our leader is wise in all things and shall guide us into the great favors of El Shaddai." Lucifer now worked on rebuilding the spirit within his followers reassuring them that greater days were ahead for their species. He patiently waited each long and painful day for the stone to alert him, yet that day would not arrive. He so eagerly wanted to have the throne for himself. He now worried if Jehovah had sent one of his messengers to entrap him. How could he know? He thought hard over their conversation feeling that he had not agreed to do this act, thus would be able to escape damnation. On the other hand, would he, for what if the Lord had known his thoughts. Then he summoned that if the Lord knew his thoughts, he would have been damned long ago. He wanted so much to contact Виноградов, nevertheless this would jeopardize the mission, so he would continue to take his evening tours of the Milky Way and plan some new worlds that he would create and rule. The day would come and a sign of an effective war campaign is patience and attacking at the most opportune time and he believed that Виноградов understood this skill, for his existence would also be in danger. This transition time was important to Lucifer, for once; he had his throne, as he wanted always to remember what his life had been like without it. He wondered each day how his nerves were so strong to disguise being in control, for inside him was wars raging wars on his complete being. Such wars are hard to hide when you are a spirit. He mastered this pretense as all he ever wanted was weighing on the balances now and he had to keep these scales in balance. He tried to comfort himself in believing that he had previously mastered such great challenges, yet found himself unable to find that event. Well, at least after this coup, he would be able to recount this great event, when he stood strong and led his followers to victory. The only thing he had to master now was the smallest part of being able to stand. Each day he decided 100 times to abort this mission, yet throughout the day, he vowed to undertake this venture 101 times. After months of this topsy-turvy, he found himself growing stronger each day, and having planned so many contingencies for each possible outcome. He knew victory would lie in his future, as least if he won, so he had to be prepared. That night, while enjoying the rushing winds of Mars his stone began to speak. This shocked him, for he had not realized that the stone would talk to him. He expected some small light to blink or something of that nature. His stone said, "Send your follower so allow my entry and meet me at Andromeda, behind that star by the raging flashes. I then called upon my two appointed followers, having briefed them that my friend from many ages ago was to meet with me for some festivities. The followers left, as Lucifer slowly glided to Andromeda. He had not been here much recently, since it was too close to Mars. Without a hitch, Виноградов met him behind the star as Lucifer dismissed the followers. Виноградов now spoke some incantations and told Lucifer to prepare to take his new throne this very night. His stone then shot a powerful blast to Виноградов's selected entry point and in rushed a dark Army so vast that Lucifer could see no stars in that second. It was now when Lucifer knew this was going to be a war of untold of proportions, for this invading Army had numbers greater than all the servants belonging to Jehovah did. Jehovah now sent his great force to meet this invading army, as Виноградов breathed into the burning space beside Andromeda and legions of new Armies appeared. He now told Lucifer to, "Hang on future King," and made his way to the throne. As they approached the throne Lucifer's Stone of Ceglédi, warned that Виноградов's force had to be supplemented. At this point Lucifer rushed back to Mars, summoned his angels, and said unto them, "Today is a great day for our species, for we now have a chance of not being slaves to Jehovah's new creation. For tonight, with the help of other gods, we shall ascend to his throne and I shall be king. We shall be the masters of our galaxy. Prepare to follow me now." About one-half of his angels followed him while the other half vanished inside of Mars. Lucifer led them back to Виноградов who told Lucifer his Armies were doing well against Jehovah's armies at the border. Secretly Виноградов was now beginning to worry as he expected to have ten times this force to be added by the other gods in his alliance. They aborted their allegiance soon after the invasion, not believing that Виноградов could break into the Milky Way. To their shock, they could now see Виноградов deep in the Milky Way and were scrambling to rush their forces to Виноградов's support. However, Jehovah's forces quickly defeated Виноградов's invading armies so his victory now lay in his ability to capture the throne. He sent Lucifer and his angels, with all though half of his total, were still one-third of the total angelic population. As they approached the throne, the blistering spiritual battles began, as thunder waged through the throne. Jehovah asked Lucifer, "Why do you attack your throne?" Lucifer said, "Upon this day I do declare myself to be king of the heavens and your new race to be destroyed, for I am and shall always be your greatest creation. At this time, Jehovah became angry, and started to burn the Stone of Ceglédi that Lucifer wore around his neck. Lucifer, not knowing what this stone was spinning, kept it from his neck by spinning it behind him. The stone exploded; with such an explosion that it destroyed all of Виноградов's armies, he had at the throne. Jehovah's angels quickly overcame Lucifer's angels as Jehovah bound Виноградов, preparing him for his judgment before this universe's judge. As the remainder of his army fighting at the border saw his defeat at the throne, they hastily rushed back to the border, where Jehovah had amassed a force to strike from behind. Виноградов's armies were now surrounded however determined to fight until the end, and shortly none remained as the Milky Way had survived its greatest invasion. The possible other invading armies turned upon Виноградов's galaxy conquering it to divide the spoils, reporting back to Jehovah that they had wronged this un-neighborly and surprisingly horror. They confessed to El Shaddai that they knew of the plan to attack, however never dreamed that he would make into the unbreakable walls of the Milky Way. Jehovah decided to let this matter go to rest between his neighbors since they had punished the invading galaxy and had not invaded when they had a chance. Now, it was time to deal with the internal rebellion that had surprised him so much. He discussed this with his mighty spirits who were, to the surprise of all in heaven, supportive of Lucifer's complaint. Jehovah was surprised yet wanted to know their rationale, since for all the ages on top of ages, his little court had always ruled correctly. They shouted to Jehovah, "Oh mighty and wonderful God, we see no justice in you making your greatest creation bow down to a newer creation, as Lucifer's creation up until tonight, had ever wronged you. How can one punish and shame the innocent. Your creation on Mars was perfect, yet now the fight for a right you gave them." Jehovah paused for one moment then excused his court, and now looked at the bound Lucifer and said, "I believed you knew that I was so happy with your creation, that I wanted once again to build a new creation better than I had before. I can agree with my court that you have been wrongfully treated. If it were just you attacking me I would avenge you now, however you followed another god, to seek a justice you wanted." I shall destroy both Mars and Earth, and when I create the new Earth, their race shall worship your angels and gods, and your angels shall rule over them. Only those who have great faith in me may escape the wrath of your gods. I shall discuss your punishment with my courts and judge you and your followers on my judgment day. For now, I shall cast you and your followers throughout my galaxy. Mars is no more your home. When the Earth is reconstituted, I shall call you and your followers for my great judgment. Lucifer looked over and saw the earth was without form, and void; and darkness were upon the face of the deep. The Spirit of God moved upon the face of the waters. As fear flooded his now humble and troubled soul, he could not look back at his former home, for he knew it was no more. He never had seen such darkness in a world as the Earth was now immersed and appeared bottomless. When he stopped flashing through the galaxy, he looked over and saw a large world called Lamenta. He found me, and then our story began, as the circle of life continued to spin.

CHAPTER 3

Journey to the New Father

Sammael remained on Earth with his ever-changing spirits as I quietly tried to in the underworlds. I would never again bring any toys to Earth. I also had a score to settle with the Earth People born from Adam and his other wives. Therefore, I had to make sure I was not prisoned in another hell, as I did from my battle with King James 1st. I searched hard to find another like Eve, yet one who would not die. It had always amazed me how all the other races passed their first little test and thus did not have to die slowly like the new Earthlings. I of course could enjoy Eve in her spiritual form. However, the rules of engagement in Heaven are very stringent and chaperoned, so I settled for her and Abel's warm soul, as he did much to comfort and glorify his mother who spent many of her later years alone while Adam impregnated so many others of his family members. No one else would have him. What a sick pedophile. Sammael brought me Incubus, after Shedim, her husband died in a construction accident. It was something to do with moving rocks. He who stops big moving rocks with head shall not be long among you. I built a nice cave dwelling on Earth's moon, so we could torture alien visitors. I felt an invisible wall as I tried to go past the moon's orbit, yet could go back to Earth;

nevertheless, this was a time I needed to be alone. We had some of Sammael's boys guard us. After a few years, planning to torture Adam was no longer fun, especially since all my peaceful walks were always being watched, by all except Adam, who stayed well beyond my prison wall. Hence, as the moon is smaller than the Earth, it does not have many distinguishable landscapes to use for navigation. Finding something on the ground on the moon was like finding a needle in a haystack. My wings helped our little group. My daughters were out roaming the universe also. I would not recall them back until we were ready to start stealing the Earthmen's seeds from their dreams and the infants from their lives. Incubus had taught me a new tradition they had on her home planet. Sammael could make us an air pocket in my cave. I now would switch between blond and red hair to excite any peeping toms even more. We would remove our clothing and allow the snake to travel in our wombs. This created a fantastic sensation. Larger snakes, created exploding sensations. They appear to be at home traveling through our wombs and soon learned that we would feed them when they came out. It was as if they were programed for igniting the curse between woman and them. A line had been drawn as a punishment, yet we both had put up a truce and crossed the line. Everything about the thing sent chills up our spines. They helped us girls bond together as we would hold each other's hand trying to absorb the shocks that ran through our curse-free bodies. One-time Incubus told me that my wings were on fire. I admit I was hot that time. No good thing can last forever, thus the four of us decided to go back to Earth. Incubus had grown into a special friend after the death of Eve. She would occasionally help me care for Eve as her body slowly waited to allow her life to escape into eternity. Incubus invited her husband to perform many heavy tasks for us, as Eve did not want to chance hurting any of her overzealous sons. She had almost the same personality as Eve. The big exception was her many experiences from growing into a culture much different from the one slowly developing in Eve's cave. Many of Sammael's fire angels frolicked with the daughters of the Earth's races as their playmates. They truly missed the gifts of my daughters. After my daughters got through with a male of any planet, that male was easy pickings thereafter. However, no men were as easy to manipulate as the Earthmen.

Sammael's sons stopped playing with the earth women as their personalities too often clashed. Thus, angels from the Lord took over these relationships in an effort to out show and outperform Sammael's son. Sammael's sons were the ones, as these angels had broadcasted Sammael and these sons as the evil ones. Sammael would not allow his sons to mate with the earth women, more out of fear they would turn against him and follow the Lord. Thus, his son's, the obedient ones broke no spiritual law concerning relationships with the earth women. These Earth females gave birth to giant males, who were at first gentle, yet later as they approached starvation not satisfying their humongous appetites, became violent and dangerous. Sammael was permitted to be in the presence of El Shaddai and to come and go at will. It is time for me to reveal some of the facts of the stars. First, there are demons, which are defects created from angels who release defective seeds into Earth women for reproduction, which is a not only dangerous and foolish process it is absolutely forbidden. Second, there are devils, which can shift change into whatever they want and know the power of the great words and incantations. Devils are followers of Sammael, who were the first creations of our Lord in respect to Mars and Earth. Devils are without sex and do not reproduce spirits anything, except rumors. They have nothing to do with flesh, and when they do, the seduction is for spiritual pleasure only as the seed will not fertilize Earth women or women from any species. There are many different species or life forms throughout the stars; however, none is as beautiful as my daughters and I. My family must endure the Lord's curse, and that is to give up 100 of our babies each day, thus we receive many seeds throughout the stars. We try to make at least 1,000 babies each day as our gestation period is only hours if we so desire. We do not like to pop the babies out in front of their fathers immediately as most males of any life form have one initial response to seeing their newborns. That is to flee taking possession of them or revenge that which killed their child, which in my case will only cause problems since everything always comes back to me. We keep our daughters only. For since we do not get to pick which 100 die each day, we prefer the father not be there. The exception was the great joy I got from watching my children from Adam die during his period of grief for the death of Abel. On those nights, I had my daughters reduce their collection of seeds to fewer than 100. Adam would cry each time, yet the next night, into his dreams I would, once again, do my work, and collect his seed, making sure he remembered when he woke alone in the empty wilderness. I only did this during the nights after Abel died and Adam was crying in the hills. I broke my normal custom and, I made a special delivery to him as he could see another child of his dead. He caused me to be cursed, yet now I enjoyed knowing the curse was back on him, enhancing his little 130-year hibernation. I ever touched the coward when he was with my sister in love, Eve. She would explore herself with other females, however would not share her husband, nor let any other man touch her, except her sons in the name of motherhood. My daughters and I have the powers like the devils, yet we are a succubus of both males and females as in the realm of intimacy there are no differences, these differences only manifest themselves in some of the lower life forms like the Earthmen. Most species we have easily mastered the extraction of the seed from the males. None is as easy as the Earthmen. Most are so easy, except for those few that are devoted to our Lord. We tend to avoid them, and when our Creator tells us to help them on a mission, we usually strive our best. I do not want to lose more than 100 babies each day, and if these prophets of our Creator complain about us, we would be hit hard with judgment. I ensure that my daughters and I take as many Earth children into death as we can. I must suffer, and so must Adams seed must suffer. Strangely, your creator does not care that we take the infants from their bodies, as he only starts seriously to protect them after their thirteenth year, then assigning angels to protect the ones he likes. Those whom the Creator does not protect, Sammael, and his gang work on them, as so do my daughters and me. Sammael fancies using drugs in his work, as addictions work great for Earth people. He has enjoyed the use of alcohol for creating so much misery among Adam's foolish species. His boys taught the Earth people how to make alcohol in all its forms. My daughters and I never age, and we can help other races by shift changing them, except the Earth people who must become old and die because of their sin. Every species has been given a suffering from our God, yet very few have failed that test. This is why so many Empires avoid Earth and only allow small camouflaged missions to settle as disposable cells.

I was able to pull Incubus out of danger from our Creator. I keep them in a special place in the stars for me to enjoy them. I pledged to shall keep them with me until the end of days, shamefully forgetting those pledges as my hurdles kept rising. We each have a close bond, Incubus and me with our sister in love Eve, who is now beyond my spiritual intimate touch and her two daughters, Aclima and me with our great beauty, Lima and me from our abuse as she later suffered with Cain. The next classification goes to the angels who stayed with the creator after Sammael's extraction. There are so many classifications and functions served by this massive group. I cannot tell you all of them, as much that I know comes from Sammael and the Creators chosen ones. One of my greatest tools to use against Earth people is their refusal to listen to the Creators chosen ones. Just a few include Enoch, who our creator took into his heavens for some great revelations, Noah who your creator saved, and Sawandering used some of the wandering demons to build the first temple in Jerusalem under Solomon's guidance.

Accordingly, it happened when the children of men had multiplied that in those days were born unto them beautiful and incensed daughters, of which I had fueled, never thinking they would be foolish enough to cross over the line. Yet the daughters of men, knowing their limited mental capabilities and separation from the gods of the firmaments wanted to learn about the magic and enchantments of the powers of the gods. A great feature that I enjoy in mating with other species is that the offspring contains their fathers flesh and limitations. The females, for the most part get their beauty from my daughters and me. Most times, if you trace back through their family history, I popped one of their ancestors to create a woman of beauty in their family tree. The fire angels (demons), the children of the Creator, saw and lusted after them. This Sammael promoted, since he worked hard to keep them from me, after the fire angels (demons hidden within the Lord's throne) lit of my fire and burned it with absolute pleasure. I can and will remember that always, as my daughters and I always surrender to the fire angels. Yet, these fire angels were not the same, something was drastically wrong. These demonic angels were trying to behave like the lust angels that we so frenziedly hungered. We quickly discovered their canard and banned them from our groups. They will never bust our bubbles, nor any other angels they try too. These angels said to one another: Come; let us choose us wives from among the children of men so they can create us children. Likewise, Semjaza (Samlazaz), who was their leader, said unto them, "I fear you will not indeed agree to do this deed, and I alone shall have to pay the penalty of a great evil." The Evil was not the sharing of their fire with Earth women; it was the desire to reproduce with them crossing the forbidden line. Angels cannot reproduce like the Earth people, a new concept that was creating a new fever in the heavens. My daughters and I are not angels, yet we can reproduce under the terms of our curse, a curse that the spirits wanted not to chance, lest they receive additional punishments. Their desire was to raise them past the age of thirteen. This is an absolute violation of your Creator's rules. Any offspring that are produced by my daughters or me are executed within the first few years, except for the ones that Sammael tells us will not be chosen. What is more, even if they are chosen, the eternal being is that of their fathers, so our presence is not detected. We never let males that we produce live past the age of two. The Creator protects his males much more than the females, most of whom he does not give any priority. Females in the Creator's plan and used more for destroying men, and as a tool to make them sin as so many rules govern their relationships, and lastly the strength of men can be made stronger through them. Still, the fire is ignited in them that burn with terrifying rage burning in any man who denies their powers. He tends to favor man only since I am the only female that was created in his image. Sammael was able to obtain a spiritual copy of Enoch and Noah's scrolls. We were able to watch many of these events, as I will report some exactly as it is recorded in the eternal record of the scribe of the Earth people's first judgment (court) Enoch his grandson of Noah. Moreover, the fire angels all answered Semjaza and said, "Let us all swear an oath, and all bind us by mutual oaths not to abandon this plan but to do this thing. Then swore them all together and bound themselves by mutual maledictions upon it. Furthermore, all two hundred committed; who descended in the days of Jared on the summit of Mount Hermon, and they called it Mount Hermon, because they had sworn and bound themselves by mutual imprecations upon it. These are the names of their leaders, "Samlazaz, their leader, Araklba, Rameel, Kokablel, Tamlel, Ramlel, Danel, Ezeqeel, Baraqijal, Asael, Armaros, Batarel, Ananel, Zaqiel, Samsapeel, Satarel, Turel, Jomjael, Sariel. These are their chiefs of tens. Moreover, all the others together with them took unto themselves wives, and each chose for himself one, and they began to go in unto them and to defile themselves with them, and they taught them charms and enchantments, and the cutting of roots, and made them acquainted with plants. In addition, they became pregnant, and they bare great giants, whose height was three thousand ells (each ell can range from 18 to 47 inches or no less than 4,500 feet, many at least one mile in height), who consumed all the acquisitions of men. They were truly higher than most of your skyscrapers and they had a great appetite, they could gobble up trees in an instant. They could pull giant stones from deep in the Earth and move them to where new buildings were to be built. They would get into rock throwing competitions, throwing the rocks as far as they could. They also built big wagons and shipped these giant stones to many places, including Egypt and shipped some too far away islands and places. The land was different then, with most places being land connected as the Earth before the flood, except for Yonaguni City, which appears on the other side of to the Far East of this Earth. Before eating all the meat and vegetation on the lands, they moved large quantities of the stones that were still found in the last generation ranging from the Nile River base and to South America, and a few of their crafts sailed to Easter Island. This Cinderella story did not last long, for when the Earthmen could no longer sustain them; the giants turned against them and devoured many Earth people, sometimes an entire town for one giant's meal. The tribes from other lands forecasted these potential problems and thus obtained weapons to destroy any giant who roamed into their territory, refusing any of their services or trades. If not for this mass destruction of a huge part of their population, no Earthmen would have survived. Moreover, they began to do Evil against birds, and beasts, and reptiles, and fish, and to devour one another's flesh, and drink blood. When they devoured each other, they ate all of their meals, chewing the bones and gobbling up all the internal organs. Nothing was wasted nor remained in history to study, or that which they remained buried deep into the Earth's face. They would also eat everything on the ground, leaving only bare land, which later evolved into deserts. They searched all through the Earth looking for food to eat. They tried to avoid water, except to get the whales, that they enjoyed tearing them apart before they ate them, performing all manners of evil. This evil was so great that even Sammael complained to the throne of our Lord who searched hard to discover the truth. Sammael's plea came just in time, as the Lord was preparing to punish his sons for this crime. Then the Earth laid allegation against the lawless ones and Azazel taught men to make swords, and knives, and shields, and breastplates, and made known to them the metals of the Earth. She also taught them the art of working the metals, and bracelets, and ornaments, and the use of antimony, and the beautifying of the eyelids, and all kinds of costly stones, and all coloring dyes. Furthermore, there arose much wickedness, they committed fornication, and they were led astray, and were corrupt in all their ways. The Earthmen did not know if they were to live another day, thus they adopted a new philosophy and that was, 'us eat drink and be merry today, for tomorrow may never come.' The giants consumed their mothers, and the daughters of men would no longer seduce the angels for fear of creating these giants, whose heads would travel among the clouds. Semjaza taught enchantments, and root-cuttings, Armaros the resolving of enchantments, Baraqijal taught astrology, Kokabel the constellations, Ezeqeel the knowledge of the clouds, Araqiel the signs of the Earth, Shamsiel the signs of the sun, and Sariel the course of the moon. And as men perished, they cried, and their cry went up to the stars . . . Then Michael, Uriel, Raphael, and Gabriel looked down from stars and saw much blood being shed upon the Earth, and all wickedness being created upon the Earth. They said one to another, "The Earth is made without dweller's cries, and the voice of their crying is now up to the gates of heaven. Now to you, the holy ones of heaven, the souls of men make their suit, saying, "Bring our cause before the Most High." They said to El Shaddai God of the ages, "King of kings and master of the ages, the throne of your glory survive unto all the generations of the ages, and Thy name holy is glorious, and blessed unto all the ages! You have made all things, and power over all things you have; and all things are naked and open in your sight, and you see all things, and nothing can hide itself from you. You see what Azazel hath done, who has taught all Evil on Earth and revealed the eternal secrets, which were to be preserved in heaven, which men were striving to learn, and Semjaza, to whom Thou hast given authority to bear rule over his associates. They have gone to the daughters of men upon the Earth, slept with the women, defiled themselves, and exposed to them all kinds of Evils. The women have borne giants, and all had some. For even Lucifer has cried upon the heavens on behalf of all Earthmen. Then said El Shaddai who spoke, and sent Uriel to the son of Lamech, and said to him, "Go to Noah and tell him in my name Hide thyself! Reveal unto him the end that is approaching, that the whole Earth will be destroyed, and a deluge is about to come upon the whole Earth, and will destroy all that is on it. Now instruct him that he may escape and his seed may be preserved for all the generations of the world. Again, El Shaddai said to Raphael; Bind Azazel hand and foot, and cast him into the darkness: and make an opening in the desert, which is in Dudael, and cast him therein. Place in Nabta Playa and upon him rough and jagged rocks, cover him with darkness, and let him abide there forever, and cover his face that he may not see light. On the day of the great judgment, he shall be cast into the fire. Heal the Earth, which the angels have corrupted, and proclaim the healing of the Earth, that they may heal the plague, and that not all the children of men may perish through all the secret things that the watchers have disclosed and have taught their sons. The whole Earth, had been corrupted through the works that were taught by Azazel, to him ascribe all sin. Besides, to Gabriel said the Lord, "Proceed against the bastards and the reprobates, and against the children of fornication. Destroy the children of fornication and the children of the Watchers from amongst men and cause them to go forth, send them one against the other that they may destroy each other in battle: for length of days shall they not have. Likewise, no request that they and their fathers make of thee shall be granted unto their fathers on their behalf, for they hope to live an eternal life, and that each one of them will live five hundred years," which ended because of the flood. The Lord said unto Michael, "Go, bind Semjaza and his associates who have united themselves with women so as to have defiled themselves with them in all their uncleanness. When their sons have slain one another, and they have seen the destruction of their beloved ones, bind them fast for seventy generations in the valleys of the Earth, until the day of their judgment and of their consummation, until the judgment that is forever and ever is consummated. In those days, they shall be led off to the abyss of fire, and to the torment and the prison in which they shall be confined forever. Whosoever shall be condemned and destroyed will from thenceforth be bound together with them to the end of all generations. Destroy all the spirits of the reprobate and the children of the Watchers, because they have wronged humankind. Destroy all wrong from the face of the Earth and let every evil work come to an end, and let the plant of righteousness and truth appear, and it shall prove a blessing; the works of righteousness and truth shall be planted in truth and joy for evermore. Then shall all the righteous escape, And shall live till they beget thousands of children, and all the days of their youth and their old age and then shall they complete in peace. Then shall the whole Earth be tilled in righteousness, and shall all be planted with trees and be full of blessing. All desirable trees shall be planted on it, and they shall plant vines on it, and the vine, which they plant thereon shall yield wine in abundance, and as for all the seed which is sown thereon each measure of it shall bear a thousand, and each measure of olives shall yield ten presses of oil. Cleanse you the Earth from all oppression, and from all wickedness, and from all godlessness, and all the uncleanness that is wrought upon the Earth I shall destroy from off the Earth. All the children of men shall become righteous, all nations shall offer adoration and shall praise me, and all shall bow to me, as do the daughters of the Heavens. Moreover, the Earth shall be cleansed from all defilement, and from all sin, and from all punishment, and from all torment, and I will never again send them upon it from generation to generation and forever. In those days, I will open the store chambers of blessing which are in the heaven, to send them down upon the Earth over the work and labor of the children of men. Truth and peace shall be associated together throughout all the days of the world and throughout all the generations of men." Before these things, Enoch was hidden, and no one of the children of men knew where he was hidden, and where he abode, and what had become of him. His activities had to do with the Watchers, and his days were with the holy ones." Enoch was blessing El Shaddai of the ages, and lo! The Watchers called, Enoch the scribe, and said to him, "Enoch, thou scribe of righteousness, go, declare to the Watchers of the heaven who have left the high heaven, the holy eternal place, and have defiled themselves with women, and have done as the children of Earth do, and have taken unto themselves wives, "You have wrought great destruction on the Earth. You shall have no peace nor forgiveness. Seek them the evil in as much as they delight themselves in their selves. The parents who murder their beloved ones shall they see, and over the destruction of their children shall they lament, and shall make supplication unto eternity, but mercy and peace shall you not attain." Enoch went and said, "Azazel, thou shalt have no peace: a severe sentence has gone forth against thee to put you in bonds. And thou shalt not have toleration or request granted to thee, because of the wickedness which thou hast taught, and because of all the works of godlessness and unrighteousness which thou hast shown to men." Then Enoch went and spoke to them all together. They were all afraid, and fear and trembling seized them. They begged Enoch to draw up a petition for them that they might find forgiveness, and to read their petition in the presence of the God of heaven. For from thenceforward they could not speak with Him nor lift up their eyes to Heaven for shame of their sins for which they had been condemned. Then Enoch wrote out their petition and the prayer concerning their spirits and their deeds individually and regarding their requests that they should have forgiveness and length of days. Enoch went off and sat down at the waters of Dan, in the land of Dan, to the south of and west of Hermon. He read their petition until he fell asleep. Behold a dream came to him, and visions fell down upon him, and he saw visions of chastisement, and a voice came bidding him, "Enoch tell it to the sons of heaven, and reprimand them." When Enoch awaked, he came unto them, and they were all sitting gathered together, weeping in Abelsjail, which is between Lebanon and Seneser, with their faces covered. Enoch recounted before them all the visions, which he had seen in sleep, and he began to speak the words of righteousness, and to reprimand the heavenly Watchers. The book of the words of righteousness and of the reprimand of the eternal Watchers is in accordance with the command of El Shaddai in that vision. Enoch saw in his sleep what he will now say with a tongue of flesh and with the breath of his mouth, "Which the Great One has given to men to converse therewith and understand with the heart. As He has created and given to man the power of understanding the word of wisdom, so hath He created Enoch also and given Enoch the power of reprimanding the Watchers, the children of heaven?" He wrote out their petition, and in his vision, it appeared thus, that his petition will not be granted unto you throughout all the days of eternity, and that judgment has been finally passed upon you, yes your petition will not be granted unto you. From henceforth you shall not ascend into heaven unto all eternity, and in bonds of the Earth." He answered and said to Enoch, and Enoch heard His voice, "Fear not, Enoch, thou righteous man and scribe of righteousness, approach hither and hear my voice. Go; say to the Watchers of heaven, who have sent thee to intercede for them. You should intercede for men, and not men for you. Wherefore have ye left the high, holy, and eternal heaven, lay with Earth women, defiled yourselves with the daughters of men, taken to yourselves wives, done like the children of Earth, and begotten giants as your sons. Though ye were holy, spiritual, living the eternal life, you have defiled yourselves with the blood of women, and have begotten children with the blood of flesh, and, as the children of men, have lusted after flesh and blood as those also do who die and perish. Therefore have I given them wives also that they might impregnate them, and beget children by them, that thus nothing might be wanting to them on Earth. Nevertheless, you were formerly spiritual, living the eternal life and immortal for all generations of the world. Therefore, I have not appointed wives for you; for as for the spiritual ones of heaven, in heaven are their dwelling. Now the giants, who are produced from the spirits and flesh, shall be called evil spirits upon the Earth, and on the Earth shall be their dwelling. Evil, has proceeded from their bodies; because they are born from men and from the holy Watchers is their beginning and primal origin, they shall be spirits of Earth, and spirits shall they be called. As for the spirits of heaven, in heaven shall be their dwelling, but as for the spirits of the Earth which were born upon the Earth, on the Earth shall be their dwelling. The spirits of the giants afflict, oppress, destroy, attack, do battle, and work destruction of the Earth, and cause trouble: they take no food, but nevertheless hunger and thirst, and cause offenses. These spirits shall rise up against the children of men and against the women, because they have proceeded from them. From the days of the slaughter and destruction and death of the giants, from the souls of whose flesh the spirits, having gone forth, shall destroy without incurring judgment, thus shall they destroy until the day of the consummation, the great judgment in which the age shall be consummated, over the Watchers and the godless, yea, shall be wholly consummated. Now as to the watchers who have sent thee to intercede for them, who had been aforetime in heaven, say to them, "You have been in heaven, but all the mysteries had not yet been revealed to you. You knew worthless ones, and these in the hardness of your hearts you have made known to the women, and through these mysteries women and men work much Evil on Earth." Say to them, "Therefore, you have no peace." And Uriel said to Enoch, "Here shall stand the angels who have connected themselves with women and their spirits assuming many different forms are defiling mankind and shall lead them astray into sacrificing to demons as gods, here shall they stand, till the day of the great judgment in which they shall be judged until they are made to end. In addition, the women of the angels who went astray shall become warnings." Enoch, alone saw the vision, the ends of all things, and no man shall see as he has seen. These are of the number of the stars of heaven, which have transgressed the commandment of the El Shaddai, and are bound here until ten thousand years. From here he went to another place, which was still more horrible than the former, and saw a horrible thing, a great fire there which burnt and blazed, and the place was cleft as far as the abyss, being full of great descending columns of fire: neither its extent or magnitude could he see, nor could he conjectures. Because of this fearful place and because of the spectacle of the pain he said unto Enoch, "This place is the prison of the angels, and here they will be imprisoned forever. Many have always had trouble trying to report what Enoch has said, as I was glad I committed my wars on other planets, as twice I have been banished for only 1,000 years. The fires excite me and create to suffering in the material of which I was created. The suffering comes from the difficulty in finding males to lie with, since the other species are tormented in these places. My mission is to get the seeds from males and to assimilate into as many other species as practical. In revenge, I take the lives of infants, a revenge against Adam who started our fight.

I fear not the judgment of the El Shaddai, since Eve will help me argue my defense against the first judge Abel, her son. Sense I was his only aunt; I shall receive a favorable judgment and keep his scribe from complaining. I have also worked hard to gain favor with Enoch, by providing him protection from the fire angels and protecting his family. He did not want to lie with me, so I hit him with kindness, and worked through his stomach. He was truly a righteous man in that he treated women with respect and kindness. I would talk to him about some of the places I had been and tell him some things that Sammael told me. I never told him anything that El Shaddai would become angry. One example, was teaching him how to build a better home for protection against storms and showing them better ways to make clothes, prepare foods and all that boring stuff. I would prepare meals for him and Edna (his wife). I have always protected his children and grandchildren, which provided favorable for me with Noah. Noah had his visitations also and after this judgment, "They shall terrify and make them to tremble because they have shown this to those who dwell on the Earth. And behold the names of those angels and these are their names: the first of them is Samjaza, the second Artaqifa, and the third Armen, the fourth Kokabel, the fifth Turael, the sixth Rumjal, the seventh Danjal, the eighth Neqael, the ninth Baraqel, the tenth Azazel, the eleventh Armaros, the twelfth Batarjal, the thirteenth Busasejal, the fourteenth Hananel, the fifteenth Turel, and the sixteenth Simapesiel, the seventeenth Jetrel, the eighteenth Tumael, the nineteenth Turel, the twentieth Rumael, the twenty-first Azazel. These are the chiefs of their angels and their names, and their chief ones over hundreds and over fifties and over tens. For the name of the first Jeqon: that is, the one who led astray all the sons of God, and brought them down to the Earth, and led them astray through the daughters of men. The second was named Asbeel: he imparted to the holy angels of fire who gave Evil counsel, and led them astray so that they defiled their bodies with the daughters of men. The third was named Gadreel: he it is who showed the children of men all the blows of death, and he led astray the daughters of Eve, and showed the weapons of death to the sons of men the shield and the coat of mail, and the sword for battle, and all the weapons of death to the children of men. From his hand, they have proceeded against those who dwell on the Earth from that day and forever more. The fourth was named Penemue: he taught the children of men the bitter and the sweet, and he taught them all the secrets of their wisdom. He instructed humanity in writing with ink and paper, and thereby many sinned from eternity to eternity and until this day. For men were not created for such a purpose, to give confirmation to their good faith with pen and ink. For men were created exactly like the angels, to the intent that they should continue pure and righteous, and death, which destroys everything, could not have taken hold of them, but through this their knowledge they are perishing, and through this power it is consuming me. The fifth was named Kasdeja: this is he who showed the children of men all the wicked smitings of spirits and demons, and the smitings of the embryo in the womb, that it may pass away, and the smitings of the soul the bites of the serpent, and the smitings which befall through the noontide heat, the son of the serpent named Tabaet. This is the task of Kasbeel, the chief of the oath, which he showed to the holy ones when he dwelt high above in glory, and its name is Biqa. This angel requested Michael to show him the hidden name, which he might enunciate it in the oath, so that those might quake before that name and oath who revealed all that was in secret to the children of men. This is the power of this oath, for it is powerful and strong, and he placed this oath Akae in the hand of Michael. These are the secrets of this oath . . . They are strong through his oath: And the heaven was suspended before the world was created, and forever. Through it, the Earth was founded upon the water, and from the secret recesses of the mountains come beautiful waters, from the creation of the world and unto eternity. Through that oath, the sea was created, and as its foundation. He set for it the sand against the time of its anger, and it dare not pass beyond it from the creation of the world unto eternity. Through that oath are the depths made fast, and abide and stir not from their place from eternity to eternity. Through that oath, the sun and moon complete their course, and deviate not from their ordinance from eternity to eternity. Through that oath, the stars complete their course. He calls them by their names, and they answer Him from eternity to eternity, in like manner the spirits of the water, and of the winds and of all zephyrs, and their paths, from all the quarters of the winds. There are preserved the voices of the thunder and the light of the lightning: and there are preserved the great punishment on the Earth, and the Earth shall be cleansed from all impurity. Yes, there shall come a great destruction over the whole Earth, and there shall be a flood and a great destruction for one year. El Shaddai has decided that all life on Earth was to cease, except for a few through the ark." As told by Enoch and Noah, El Shaddai observed that humanity was corrupt and decided to destroy all life. Those in the end times who believed abortions were the creation of the great minds of men must instead thank the demon named Kasdeja, for it was he who showed the children of men all the wicked smitings of the embryo in the womb, which it may pass away. Noah was a righteous man, blameless in his generation, and Noah walked with El Shaddai, and God gave him instructions for an ark into which he is told to bring every sort of animal . . . male and female . . . everything on the dry land in whose nostrils was the breath of life, and their food, seven pairs of every bird and clean animal, and one pair of every unclean animal. The King (God) and his angels gathered the animals to the ark together with their food. There had been no need to distinguish between clean and unclean animals before this time, the clean animals made them known by kneeling before Noah as they entered the ark. The dimensions of the vessel are specified: the length of the ark 300 cubits (450 feet), its breadth 50 cubits (75 feet), and its height 30 cubits (45 feet). When Noah was building the ark, he attempted to warn his neighbors of the coming flood; however, he was ignored, and mocked. In order to protect Noah and his family, God placed lions and other ferocious animals to guard them from the wicked who tried to stop them from entering the ark. God instructs Noah to board the ark with his wife (Naamah) and family, Japheth & Adalenses, and Shem & Sedukatelbab, and Ham & Neelata-Mek and wives and 70 who listened to Noah's pleading and many who had been followers of Enoch. Yam refused to enter the ark with his father and chose to stay with the disbelievers. Noah's wife and I were not friends. Her name was Naamah—the sister of Tubal-cain, a descendant of Cain. I would get revenge on her after to flood. The names of the wives of the sons of Noah are these: the name of the wife of Shem, Nahalath Mahnuk; and the name of the wife of Ham, Zedkat Nabu; and the name of the wife of Japheth, Arathka. These wives came from other races and tribes and names have been translated differently due to the fluctuations in records, as no women from the humans would surrender themselves believing Noah to be mad. The three women had distinct variations in their appearances and skin color. The one that thrilled me the most, as they were very passionate and had fire in their souls were born of Arathka. What sets the wife of Japheth different from the others was her dark skin, for it was as dark as the night. Her body was stronger than the other daughters were as her muscles were the perfection of flesh in appearance and tone. This line would provide my daughters and me many pleasures through the years. The next were from Ham and his wife Zedkat Nabu that resembled Noah and the final wife, the wife of Shem, Nahalath Mahnuk reminded me a friendlier Yonaguni or also like the royal Queen hAyonjE of Mempire. Their eyes were sharp and their skin colored like gold. The repopulation of the Earth people would have more assortment. Noah was too old to produce more sons and daughters, thus the new human race would now be mixed and no longer be only from Adam.

The ark had six levels, of which only three were named after prophets and designated for Noah and his followers. The first of the three levels had the wild animals lodged and the refuse as being stored on the utmost deck, from where it was shoveled into the sea through a trapdoor. Precious stones, said to be as bright as the noon sun, provided light, and El Shaddai ensured that food remained fresh. In the second plank were the human with additional animals. Likewise, in the third plank were the birds and domesticated animals. When the rains stopped and the ark returned to the surface, the birds rested on the top exposed deck of the ark. On every plank was the name of a prophet. Three missing planks, symbolizing three prophets, were brought from Stune by Og, son of Anak, the only one of the giants permitted to survive the Flood. The body of Adam was carried in the middle to divide the men from the women. He said, "Ride ye in it; in the Name of El Shaddai and it would move or stop as commanded by Noah." This meant that Noah said, In the Name of the King, when he wished the ark to move, and the same when he wished it to stand still. When all entered the days were as follows:

14 days waiting for the flood

40 days of rain living below the surface

150 days of rising water after resurfacing

150 days of receding water

Total days 364 to equal one solar year

They exited on a Friday, so they could celebrate the Sabbath or seventh day reserved for rest. On the same day, all the fountains of the great deep were broken up, and the windows of heaven were opened, and the rain was upon the Earth, and El Shaddai closed the door of the ark. The flood began, and the waters prevailed until all the high mountains are covered fifteen cubits deep. All the people, animals, creeping things, and birds of the heavens are blotted out from the Earth, and only Noah and those with him in the ark remained alive. The ark as being a vessel that remained underwater for forty days, after which it floated to the surface. During these forty days of flowing through the waters beneath the surface disaster hit the ark. A few boards along the deck became loose as the ark started taking in water. The crew frantically tried to seal off the first room that was receiving water, however, the room was too large as the ark rested on the ocean's floor with its crew awaiting inescapable death. Then as they were sealed in their coffin, they felt their ark once again moving. Then it began to sink once again resting. They could hear something on the outside hitting the ark. Some inside the ark began speaking of large underwater beasts that ate all they saw. Fear manifested itself inside the ark, as soon all could feel no warmth. The ark found itself now enclosed in warmth, as soon the doors were opened and many very beautiful women came in to meet their new guests. Soon fear left the ark as they could feel the kindness of their guests. Noah told me that they all looked somewhat like me. I knew that someday I would have to come and investigate the people who preserved Eve as a mother of a race. I had hoped that they would dispose of Adam's body, but no luck on this one. The females told Noah about their city and asked that they not return unless it was important. They cleaned the inside of the ark giving the animals a chance to get some running in, resupplied food for human and beast alike. They had ocean grass that they kept to feed the beasts they had transplanted from the surface lands and domesticated for their consumption. They were very proficient with the entire process taking less than one week, as they reported to Noah that the rains were still falling. Therefore, they all thanked their new friends for saving them and returned inside the ark. The animals all returned freely and swiftly knowing that this underwater kingdom was not their home. Noah worked day and night in both feeding and caring for the animals, and slept little for the entire year aboard the ark. The animals were the best of their species, and so behaved with utmost virtuousness. They abstained from procreation, so that the number of creatures that disembarked was exactly equal to the number that embarked. The raven created problems, refusing to go out of the ark when Noah sent it forth and accusing the patriarch of wishing to destroy its race, however, El Shaddai wished to save the raven, were destined to feed the prophet Elijah. Then El Shaddai remembered Noah, and caused his wind to blow, and the fountains of the deep and the windows of the heavens were closed. After the waters stopped, Noah spent five or six more months aboard the ark at the end of which he sent out a raven. Nevertheless, the raven stopped to feast on carrion (dead circuses from beasts that drown in the flood), and so Noah cursed it and sent out the dove, which has been known ever since as the friend of humankind. El Shaddai commanded the Earth to absorb the water, and the certain parts that were slow in obeying received salt water in punishment and so became dry and arid. The water, which was not absorbed, formed the seas, so that the waters of the flood still exist. The ark began its voyage at Kufa in central Iraq and sailed to Mecca, circling the Earth before finally traveling to Mount Judi its final resting place. This mountain is a hill near the town of Jazirat ibn Umar on the east bank of the Tigris in the province of Mosul in northern Iraq. The rain stopped, the waters rescinded, and in the twelfth month the ark rested on the mountains of Ararat. When the tops of the mountains were seen, Noah sent out a raven and a dove to see if the waters had subsided; the raven flies back and forth but the dove returns with a fresh olive leaf in her beak. Noah waits seven days more and sends out the dove again, and this time it has not returned.

When the land was dry, El Shaddai told Noah to leave the ark and Noah offered a sacrifice to the King. The King promised never again to curse the Earth, knowing the intention of man's heart is evil from his youth. El Shaddai granted Noah and his sons the right to kill animals and eat their meat, but forbade meat, which had not been drained of its blood, which of course was the tastiest. Blood was proclaimed sacred, and the unauthorized taking of life was prohibited. For your lifeblood, I will require a reckoning, from every beast, I will require it and from man whoever sheds the blood of man, by man shall his blood be shed, for El Shaddai made man in his own image. Not all this killing applied to the killing of 100 of my babies each day, thus I would continue to return the favor. El Shaddai then established his covenant with Noah and his sons and with all living things, and would place a rainbow in the clouds, the sign of the covenant that I have established, between me and all flesh that is on the Earth. Noah left the ark and he and his family and companions built a town at the foot of Mount Judi, named Thamanin (eighty) in reference to their number. Noah then locked the ark and entrusted the keys to Shem. After Noah returned to dry land, he pitched a tent. He was easy prey for me. One year being locked in a boat with such a cranky and ugly wife (Emzara as I always called her) left him open for my invitations. As he slept, I flowed into his dreams showing some of my best performances, as did I for Lot's daughters after Sodom and Gomorrah. Those poor daughters were virgins and no longer had a mother to teach them, and I taught them how to get the seed from a male while he slept, which they did professionally. I should not have told them that all else on the planet had died.

Back in time to Noah, I showed the old boy what he had been missing. If those days a male being married or single could lay with any female he wanted. The name of the game was to make babies, thus they had to get their seeds planted as many gardens as possible. I heated Noah up as flames of fire burned through his veins, then I lowered the boom on him, leaving him very exhausted, as he lay naked in his tent, I slipped back into one of my trees to see how the new father of the Earth people was going to respond. During this timeframe Noah's son, Ham saw his father naked in his father's tent, and told his brothers, hoping that they also would get pleasure from shaming their father. They, the square boys took a blanket and entered with their heads turned away from Noah and put a blanket on him. When Noah awoke, a dove told him what had happened and so Noah cursed Ham's son Canaan, giving his land to Shem. Ham's son would have to find their own land, as they ventured north then west. Shem took his family to the Far East and Japheth took his people west then south. The Earth now looked so much different from the sky, the large landforms were now formed different, and with so many people from other planets returning here, except those from Og's group on the ark there was much open land. Another big difference for those who lived on the lands was the final total destruction of the dinosaurs. They had not really posed any problems for the Earth people as the tribes from the other worlds kept them under control. The very tall giants, from the fire angels and Earth women, ate just about all their remains, as these large creatures made up a large portion of their diet. The flood, of course, finished them off, as none entered the ark. The Earth was now a bubbling hotbed for new life, as many seeds of old had risen from their resting places, and were planted in new richer soil. Some animals did not like the oceans now being filled with salt although it did cut down on many bacteria that enjoyed spreading through the waters. The wives from the ark kept talking about the beauty of the women of the undersea kingdom they visited. Some among the survivors thought it was the throne of El Shaddai and these women were his angels, yet I knew from Sammael and King James that the most high lived in the stars. This was a pleasant mystery that I knew now was the time to solve, for those who remained with the ark were of little value to me. Most of the crew left to find the big rocks the giants had placed in the middle lands of our previous world. They now went west and found a river that flowed through the new sand lands and found the rocks. There they would live for as long as the Earth continued. Thus, I knew I had to look for some form of life on these empty lands. I flew with Sammael around the world searching. Sammael had previously enjoyed great success with the life forms on this planet, as they had been so easy and willing to do Evil to each other. I did not want Sammael to know about this underwater kingdom of females, since his boys would start to hang around that place. Once I felt comfortable getting around this new world I sneak off and explored under the sea until I found this new city. The city was very beautiful and actually reminded me somewhat of the Palace of Unity and Loyalty that King James built for his royal Queen hAyonjE in hAyonjE City in Mempire, except it was under the sea and had a bright light that guided me from the cold dark bottom water. As I drifted around the outside, I became so impressed with the pyramid style of this city. It had something that was ringing a bell with me telling me that this was a powerful structure, yet it did not look dangerous. I knew that Og would like this style in his new homeland that he was building. He wanted something that could use all the giant stones he was so busy breaking down into sizes that his people could move. As I floated around, I soon was joined by a few of the women who were swimming outside the City. They met me with a cordial greeting and escorted me into their beautiful city. The inside was a carbon copy of many places in Mempire. This was too strange to be random chance. The Noah gang was correct, they resembled my daughters and I to a high degree. They treated me like royalty, thus there was no need to fear, and I just relaxed and enjoyed the wonders of this place. I did not understand how somewhere like this could be so close. This place had the potential to be a future nest for me to rest. I asked them why they were hidden and secret. They told me that they preferred living in deep oceans as it was their practice throughout the many galaxies that they had colonies. They enjoyed their ability to live free from many intrusions that living on land posed. They had very few visitors and could determine the potential threat that any invader may be, and if serious, they could hide in the city with ease. It could retract into the ocean bed and literally become invisible. This technology was very impressive. I asked them for the name of the city we were in, and they told me all cities were named Atlantis. This was a name I only heard once and that was on Lamenta. I further asked on which planet their capital was. They told me that it was on a planet called Lamenta in a land empire called Atlantis. I told them that I knew of this Empire; the last time I visited, it was during the reign of its founder the supreme daughter Queen Lablonta 2nd. She had never caused my daughters or me any trouble, as she did the things she needed to do to help others, so opposite of me. She was the daughter of King James 1st founder of

Mempire and I guess that by her name she was the daughter of the supreme Queen Lablonta 1st. A big plus that she had been that she resembled me in appearance, thus which would help to explain the confusion that Noah's guests had. There had really been no conflict between us, as she died long before my second release from a punishment imposed by El Shaddai. I sure was glad that I was somewhat bound by the rules on this planet, although I had stiff punishments waiting me on many other worlds. This is why this place appealed to me so much. If I had known about it I would have put Adam here when I brought him from Lamenta, thus avoided much misery for both species. These girls were so very kind, a trait that when overdone can cause me discomfort. They were very much a sisterhood that worked together, ate together, cleaned together, and slept together, with no specific attachments. Nude or wearing one of their so many different uniforms they were at peace. They would only touch each other if they saw an untreated injury, which they would nurse thoroughly. They all slept nude throughout the entire city within their reserved buildings in midair. They slept on airbeds, which were so comfortable. They had developed the ability to reproduce food, using a small sample to the original to produce mass quantities. One small piece of a fish could produce enough fish to feed all of them for a week. They brought no males from their homeland with them, since males were used for establishing new posts and many other respectable occupations in their Empire. They would capture and enslave males from the surface and have them do some of the hard work for them, and then they would put them back to sleep and return them to the surface. Many would not listen to their tales upon returning to their homelands, as wives did not want to hear stories about how their husbands had been enslaved by underwater females. Many of the return slaves recognized that they were treated fairly, thus why ruin a good thing. There were worse dooms than being enslaved by beautiful women who slept nude. Yet no one could ever think a doom that would prove this worse. The females in this world were at such peace with each other, they shared their thoughts and minds freely, and everyone watched each other's back, protecting each other. They were free to contribute what they might when they could. If one wanted to work a week or two in the nude, their co-workers would think nothing of it, as there was no shame to hide. It was a warm harmony. I felt as if they were a part of their great culture and the advancements from this. They all talked highly of Mempire, and a couple of other Empires from King James' children. The Empires shared their accomplishments and protected each other. They felt as if they were a special part of Mempire. Their bond was great, yet I did not belong here. I would have to move on, yet I asked them if my daughters could visit when in their area. We agreed to no execution of infants as I gave them the three magic words and helped them put up the sign to protect their all cities they ruled. We exchanged our farewells as I moved back to the surface and called for my daughters. As they arrived, I told them of this place and asked them to tell their sisters, keeping this a secret among us. I ensured they knew about the infant treaty and visit only as needed. I also reminded all to keep this from Sammael, for he would be foolish enough to mess with them and get his hind end cracked. As I returned and roamed the empty Earth loneliness, once again hit me, this time extra hard. I decided to return and spend some time with Sammael. He looked different now, as he soon revealed to me that El Shaddai had castrated him. That was a blow to my plans, yet I remember what Incubus had taught me with the snakes. I might be able to work around this. I reminded him that I was the queen of all forms of intimacy with men or women (as divided on Earth). I had always become hot from the intimacy with men, through spontaneous emission. For I have dominion over children who issue from a man who has intercourse at candlelight, or with his wife naked, or at times when he is forbidden to have intercourse. El Shaddai gave my daughters and me, all these extra opportunities, as all those children who issue from those mentioned, I might kill them any time I desire, because they are delivered into my hand. This is the secret of the children laughing in their sleep when they are small; it is from me playing with them. When a small child laughs during the Sabbath night or the night of the New Moon, it is because I am playing with him. It is well that his father, mother, or anyone who sees him laugh should tap his nose with his finger and say, "Go from here, you accursed one, for you has no resting place here!" Let him say this three times, and each time he recites this incantation let him tap the child's nose. This is very good, for it is in my power to kill them when I wish. Since I am permitted to kill these infants, these souls are called Oppressed Souls. Blind Dragon rides me, may I be extirpated quickly in my days. Blind Dragon brings about the union between Sammael and me. Just as the Dragon that is in the sea has no eyes, likewise Blind Dragon that is above, in the likeness of a spiritual form, is without eyes, that is to say, without colors. Sammael is called the Slant Serpent, and I am called the Tortuous Serpent. I seduce men to go in tortuous ways. Know that I too will not be killed. For the groomsman (Blind Dragon), who is between my partner (Sammael) and I will swallow a lethal potion at a future time, from the hands of Sammael. Since then, when he rises up, Gabriel and Michael will join forces to subdue and bring low the government of Evil, which will be in heaven and Earth. Bacharach, and he (Blind Dragon) was castrated so that he cannot beget, lest his offspring annihilate the world. Bacharach, the Blind Dragon, is between Sammael and the kind and sweet I. He brings about a union between them only in the hour of my need for pleasure, the Merciful One save us! He is castrated so that the eggs of the viper should not dome forth into the world. Were it not so, they would annihilate the world. That kind, which has called my daughters, is full of hair from their heads flowing down to their feet, but on their face no hair and all their body except abundant hair to cover their privates. This I have fourteen spicy times and names and Intimate Joys Empire's functions. All are ordained to kill the children, may they never be saved, and especially through the witches. The counsel for El Shaddai assumed that a union with Sammael or his friend, the blind dragon, as usually when I sleep. With one I sleep, all would reproduce giants, as the daughters of men and the fire angels did. I am a special race made to enjoy the pleasure of men and to suck the life from infants, and when the thirsty drink any extra blood flowing around. Sammael is not a fire angel, he is the most high, glorious creation made to be at the left hand of our God. Either way, my reputation was long and good as I found this story on a tablet in a cave, which validates my belief that I am the hottest gift given to man;

Adams first wife, Lilith, it is told

The witch he loved before the gift of Eve,

That, ere the snakes, her sweet tongue could deceive,

And her enchanted hair was the first gold.

And still she sits, young while the Earth is old,

Subtly of herself absorbed,

draws men to watch the bright web she can weave,

till heart and body and life are in her hold.

The rose and poppy are her flower; for where

Is he not found, O Lilith, whom shed scent

And soft-shed kisses and soft sleep shall snare?

Lo! As that youths eyes burned at yours, so went

Thy spell through him, and left his straight neck bent

And round his heart one is strangling golden or red hair.

Dark is she, but brilliant!

Black are her wings, black on black!

Her lips are red as the rose, kissing the entire Universe!

She is Lilith, who leads forth the hordes of the Abyss,

and leads man to liberation!

She is the irresistible fulfiller of all lust, seer of desire.

First of all women was she—Lilith, not Eve was the first!

Her hand brings forth the revolt of the Will and true freedom of the mind!

She is KI-SI-KIL-LIL-LA-KE, Queen of the Magic!

Look at her with lust and despair!

When I think of the woman, I no longer think of the subservient traits that Eve, the first woman that came from the ribs of man. Gone will be the days where woman are the submissive counterparts of men, living only to bear children and serve their families a value spread through the universe by the followers of the supreme Queen Lablonta, for like Queen Lablonta, they must fight beside their husbands. It is even hard to believe that women were made from man's rib (or womb as Eve always said) at all, especially from one as ridiculous as Adam. Unfortunately, my story is now treated as a myth that began long before the creation of Eve and is lost behind the patriarchal development of Christian religions, yet I was created in the image of the El Shaddai, not from the rib of a joke, even though that rib gives many wonderful times. My story, I believe, concerns more with womanly traits and desires than the well-known story of Adam and Eve most are so familiar. My story is so much more powerful as more comparable to the modern tales that began to become known during the end times. This story is true, yet I have allowed it to go forward per Enoch and Abel's wishes. In this revised story, El Shaddai created male and female first, from the same dirt of the Earth in the Garden of Eden. I remind you that I brought the flesh of Adam as a toy from Lamenta and that I was created from my mother who was created from what I know not. Adam's flesh returned to dust. We became the first male and female. I absolutely refused to submit to Adam sexually, refusing to lie below the fool during intercourse. This caused us to fight constantly until, fed up, I said the ineffable name (the name of El Shaddai's special magic) and flew away to the Red Sea using my new sprouted wings bestowed on those who say the Lord's name aloud. I know I have told you this story previously, however, I really do not know how many times I have to tell it before someone remembers it. Adam went whining to God that I (his wife) had left him and El Shaddai sent three angels to fetch me. Senoy, Sansenoy, and Semangelof were those angels, sent to bring me back to Adam. The great King said if she agrees to come back, what is done is good. If not, she must permit one hundred of her children to die every day. When they found me, however, I refused to go back, and the angels threatened me more, the more stubborn I became. Finally, the angels threatened to throw me into the Red Sea and I swore two things, both concerning infants and children. For one, I was cursed to have 100 of my own children die every day, receiving my official verdict alongside Adam, Eve, Lucifer, and snake as they received theirs, therefore everyday it is said 100 demons perish. Second, I claimed the health and lives of human infants within twenty days of their birth. Things like death have explained with this truth and not false like the stories produced by science and medical knowledge. My killing infants are covered by the devastating occurrence of SIDS and other terminal illnesses in babies. It was also a convenient story to make women; mothers in particular, turn away from the traits characterized by me and instead submit to the rule of man. Some claim me to be a demon. Black horns and black wings make up of a multitude of deeds that are added to my legendary appearance of long flowing golden hair, pale skin, and red lips. Stories of me depicted as a beautiful blue toned butterfly in the Kabbalistic Tree of Life, where I am simply the equal opposite to the Sephirah. Malkuth gave way to me being a serpent comparable to Sammael, a night bird, or a screech owl as by Isaiah. As the stories about me evolved along with the rise of a patriarchal society, I became more and more associated with the pleasures of nightfall, darkness, and sexual promiscuity. Even the evolution of my name alone shows the same change. In Sumeranian, lil means simply air, related to Ninlil the Goddess of the South Wind, otherwise known as Lady Air. In Mesopotamian, the same lil simply means spirit. In both cases, this gives my name of Lilith power and importance.

The El Shaddai became afraid of evil overtaking the Earth from the demons born between Sammael and me, so he castrated Sammael. Because of this, Sammael allows me to travel out to fornicate (share intimacy) with multitudes of men and demons, continuing to create more wonderful and sensuous spirits. History sees me go from being the great mother of all humanity, loved by the mother of humanity, who ate children to protect the human race from a vengeful and angry

El Shaddai, to become a nasty and spiteful wife of the devil. I have been diminished to a single mere mention in the bible, cited in Isaiah 34:14 where I am simply banished to the desert. This simple text has translated my name in various ways including the night hag and the screech owl, which are both revengeful representations of me. Either way, the symbolism is clear. I was finally exiled from the fruitful, colorful modern world of patriarchal societies by a holy man to a barren, desolate wasteland; cursed to roam forever alone where any life barely survives, as was Moses. My true story is revealed as told by me in this book. If I were so evil, then why have I given so many Earth people so much intimacy, and given the power to kill infants? Who does that power come from? If it came from Evil, it would have been banished millennia ago. Why does Eve petition alongside her second son on my behalf? My story has been with you for so long and will be with you until the end of your days, which I can see as not being good for your species. The Earth has changed, so I will continue to embed the males I can into my bed, in reality or in their dreams. This is for the most part a fleshly thing and I, as a spirit has no flesh. This flesh is perceived in the wicked mind that desires it. Therefore, I do not have to do an evil, any share in the manifestation of the evil one who creates it. I now ask, "Truly, who is the evil one?" The serpent once again served Sammael and me for our pleasures as taught to me by Incubus. When the snake finished, both Sammael and the serpent rested in peace as the queen of the night curses conquered again. The serpents began hanging around Sammael, wanting to be drafted for the next encounter. All serpents are my servants and obey my commands with all their hearts not knowing that I got them in big trouble in the Garden, blaming Sammael instead. I must be careful where I sleep since if a serpent is near I will wake up with him gently within me. They are a strong part of my kingdom that helps Sammael to live with his punishment for mating with me. No punishment given to most males will deter them from longing to be with me. That is the way of the Earth and will always be the way of Earthmen and women, my precious toys to enjoy and destroy. Keep an eye in the sky as I pass you by.

It came to pass, in those days, that the giant Og brought in the ark, for he was like the Sensenites, being between eight and ten feet tall and some slightly taller. These boys were so fun to play with. They made many children, tall and strong, who could help break up the stones delivered and broke up by the superhuman giants before the flood, helping Egypt reach her premature glory by also obtaining many great gifts from far off empires to propel them into the first heaven on Earth. These people called themselves Egyptians and really loved the styles that Queen Yonaguni had advanced many millenniums before. They still had broken records of the giants before the flood, as no daughters of men would take a male angel. This gave my daughters many extra privileges as they played with and pleased Sammael's boys. The Egyptians enjoyed creating gods out of my daughters, and the Tehom that were active in their daily lives, as they really wanted their daughters to be fertile, skills the Tehom quickly learned after departing Mars. Having so many people from the ark, they got a fast jump on others. They did not enjoy living south or west of their lands, so many traveled east living close to the Garden of Eden, now a distant memory washed away by the floods. Their influential powers and skills attracted many of the alien tribes that returned, now desiring to stay clear of Noah's family. They were to become known as the Assyrians and Persians, and Babylonians sifting through the centuries. The first to excel after the flood came from Ham's line. They had wandered north and to the west, yet as family disputes split them, some came back west to begin maybe two months walk from Noah's tribes that had been supplemented by the Egyptians on the Ark. From Ham's line came his grandson, Nimrod. Now Nimrod excited them to such an affront (outrage) and contempt of God. He was a bold man, and of great strength of hand. He persuaded them not to ascribe it to God, as if it were through his means they were happy, but to believe that it was their own courage, which procured that happiness. He also gradually changed his government into a tyranny, seeing no other way of turning men from the fear of God, yet to bring them into a constant dependence on his power. He also said he would be revenged on God, if he should have a mind to drown the world again; for that, he would build a tower too high for the waters to reach. That he would avenge himself on God for destroying their ancestors. The

Earth people did not really trust that El Shaddai would not flood them again, not understanding why a father would destroy those who were his children, as also his creations had reproduced small infants who met their innocent deaths during the flood also. He had only warned one small area. He had sent no prophets to the people that he pulled in from other worlds to populate the Earth that he loved much, to warn them that they were doing wrong according to what he commanded here, as his wishes were different throughout the universe. He did not talk with them, so they believed that my daughters and Sammael's boys were the lords of the skies. As the Earth's Creator would shoot hot rock water out of the mountains and quake the Earth as much as the giants of old, they did not feel safe or protected by the stars, whom after the flood withheld their truths from them. They enjoyed and longed for the intimacy that my daughters shared with them, believing that joy could come from the stars as told in their various ancient tales. The new Earth generations wanted to believe, yet wanted some protection in case their El Shaddai was to anger again, were the most important thing to be desired. The strong and mighty Nimrod, one of the new forms of smaller giants that would roam the Earth until the last millennium of man, offered this protection. Even the mothers permitted their children to join Nimrod, so they would not lose their friends as their ancestors had. Nimrod built up his palace and cities first, Nimrod had also built the towns of Hadâniûn, Ellasar, Seleucia, Ctesiphon, Rûhîn, Atrapatene, Telalôn, and others, that he began his reign as king over Earth when Reu was 163, and that he reigned for sixty-nine years, building Nisibis, Raha (Edessa) and Harran when Peleg he was fifty. Nimrod saw in the sky a piece of black cloth and a crown. He called upon Sasan the weaver and Santal the crown maker and commanded them to make him a crown like it, which he set jewels on and wore. He was the first king wearing a crown. Then after Nimrod reigned in Babel, he also reigned in Arach [Erech], that is, in Edissa; and in Achad [Accad], which is now called Nisibis; and in Chalanne [Calneh], which was later called Seleucia after King Seleucus when its name had been changed, and which is now in fact called Ctesiphon. Nimrods mother, being the wife of Cush, was a granddaughter of Noah's wife, who survived the great flood, the same as the fishes. The Queen of The Skies was Nimrod's wife, Semiramis.

Semiramis was of noble parents, the daughter of the fish-goddess Derketo (Atargatis) of Ascalon in Syria and a mortal. She had been hidden on the Earth by her parents beside a river. Left to die, she was discovered by a Shepherd as her eyes flashed in irritation. She was bored from watching the birds and only caution held her tongue silent. She studied her leopard-skin clad captors as they poled the birdi-reed canoe through the marshy depths of Shinar's watery southland. A dark man towered over her, but not as high as the great stands of birdi reeds, that walled the convoluted corridors of their journey. Not once had her dark companions shown any sign of lessening strength. They appeared to be in an inescapable maze. How her shepherd knew which way to go, she could not comprehend. Putting aside irritation, she searched the surrounding water world with eyes the color of the sky at mid-day. Damp tendrils of golden hair hung overlooked to the back of her neck. The fair-skinned Semiramis had seen wet lands before, but something here absconded definition. Even the birds sounded different. Not just because of their numbers, but more significantly the songs, melodies both strange and mysterious. She determined to unknot the secret of their song. At last, it appeared that they had reached their destination. Not a spears throw away stood a reed house directly in their path. Confidently sitting upon the marshes of the Tigris, its bundled berdi-reed construction was no different from any of the other dwellings they had passed on their journey. Our Lady would see you, now. The taller of the two escorts, as another man had joined them, on their long journey, as they would go into hiding from the evil ones of the sky, informed her that they would once again continue their journey. A faint inclination of his head indicated that she should step onto the bulrush platform on which the house floated. The two escorts poled a respectful distance away, leaving the young woman to go on unassisted. Semiramis remembered hearing strange things of the woman she had been bade to meet. Rumors abounded that she had been with Ish-nuh, the man Noah, upon the ark during The Great Flood. This I could believe, since I had little trouble being with Noah after the flood. I avoided him during the flood, since I feared El Shaddai protected him, and that he might complain about me and I did not need another headache as Adam, floating around. To some she was known as Atargatis, because it was thought that she was half woman and half fish. Semiramis entertained no such foolishness. She was, however, curious. “Enter,” commanded a voice from inside the house. An alien feeling, almost like fear, attached itself to Semiramis. Thoughts of fleeing caused long graceful hands to hesitate for one full count, before parting the curtain of stringed shells before her. Not since childhood, had she wavered in any decision. However, in truth there was no decision to be made. The order had left no room for choice. The interior of the dwelling left Semiramis shortly dazed. The fragrance of incense saturated the air and light dance disconcertingly about the room from a dozen shell candles. However, it was not only the ostensible elements of the room that made it different. No, the major source of that difference seemed to be stemming from the sole occupant of the room. A dark skinned woman wearing a red robe and veil weaved of some unfamiliar fabric edged in gold embroidery. The matriarch appeared to be incredibly old. It occurred to Semiramis that she must have been very tall when younger. This must be Atargatis, she thought, but not disappointed. In the same instant, she recognized that other element left vague just a moment before. Power existed here, perhaps boundless in scope. A force such as one should be either terribly afraid of, or achingly hungry to possess. “How are you known,” queried Atargatis, cutting into the younger woman’s meditations with the same forceful tone as before. For a short interval two sets of eyes, one pair shriveled, almost purple with intent and the other innocent and cunning, locked in a quiet battle of wills. Very little time passed before the scheming in the one recognized the superiority of that which abided within the older woman. Accepting defeat gracefully, with plans already forming in the back of her mind to obtain and employ the same power someday, she judged it pragmatic to respond. Semiramis, “Are you, indeed?” Almost imperceptibly, a left eyebrow vaulted. “A dove,” breathed Atargatis. From behind the veil, she considered the consequences. The dove symbolized the Great Spirit of Creation, and a dove had brought back to Noah evidence that the waters had retreated. Angrily Semiramis proudly retorted, “Here, is my talisman, a wedding gift from my husband.” Reaching under the neckline of her clothes, Semiramis showed forth the juju that hung about her neck. Its details at once revealing a dove, but at the same time resembling an arrow. A glimpse revealed to the older woman cerise stains of human blood on the beak of the dove, but she chose not to comment. Runners sent by her son had told Atargatis of the adeptness exercised by this young woman at the recent battle of Bactra. Instead, she questioned Semiramis on the subject of husbands. "Your husband, speak you of he who was your husband," she paused, "or of he who is?" "I have but one husband" as anger caused Semiramis, who in this affair was without power, to speak heatedly without wisdom. "Your son, Lady, took me from him against all custom. He had no right. Insolent child the old woman," yelled Atargatis. Atargatis struck faster than the death strike of a cobra. So quickly did the blow catch her that Semiramis would never afterwards be sure exactly how or with what the older woman had hit her, or even of where she had been struck. In fact, though the blow had dropped her to her knees, she felt no pain, just humiliation. "Know you not who my son is?" the older woman queried calmly as though no violence had just been done, "Or, the honor he has bestowed upon you?" Though humbled, Semiramis refused to show any weakness, taking a clue from the older woman's indecipherable calmness; she looked up from her posiin on the floor into Atargatis' face just as if she were on a level, to answer, "Your son, my Lady, is the Mighty Hunter, Nimrod." Approval shone in the eyes of the mother of Nimrod, quietly applauding the girl's determination. Stooping swiftly for one of such great age, Atargatis ritualistically helped Semiramis to a standing position, clucking softly, "This one may do well for our purposes." Atargatis clarified, "Whose purpose?" Semiramis had noted the unfocused glazed look, which had entered the other woman's eyes and wanted to know to whom or to what she had just spoken. Instinctively she sensed that the answer to this one riddle could perhaps be the key to Atargatis' power. "Do you not know who they are child," she answered with a question, "they know you; have known you since before your birth." Semiramis made no reply; none was required. They are the Anunnaki, those who have fallen from Heaven. Turning her back upon the girl, she continued, they watch. Atargatis introduced the young woman to the Anunnaki that night, and during the following days, they spent many hours together. "Who is your mother?" However, Semiramis had no memories of the one who gave her birth, only of the man who had raised her. He said that, "I was sent by Him whose spirit flutters like a dove over His Creation." Then she told Atargatis of how as a child she had stolen milk and cheese from the tents of shepherds for months before finally being caught near an Acacia tree, "I was very young and half-wild." Semiramis received a new name during this visit with Atargatis. They invoked the Anunnaki, and through the voice of Atargatis were advised, "You are to be called Semiramis-amat, the one who comes from the doves, a gift from the sea." Did the puzzling instructions refer to the branch brought back to the Ark of Noah? Likewise, if so, what did it mean? Neither woman understood. After that strange naming ceremony, Semiramis, who did not like her new name, felt a stirring within her of a growing power, and something else. Birth pangs? Exhilaration filled her, leaving no room for the earlier objections she had at being forced to come here, until came the day of Nimrods return. She had risen early to perform her morning toiletries, eager to learn more about and from the Anunnaki. She was interrupted by the enormous ebony form of the son of Atargatis. That which followed strengthened her tenacity. Men were dull creatures. Foolishly believing that they could obtain what they wanted by force, but she could see the reflections of another world. A world where one could control the power to create. Men saw power only in conquest and destruction. Nevertheless, she now knew that true power lay in the ability to create. Naught but a neophyte to this man's mother, the day would come that she would be the master. Forcing her chin up by placing his large hands on each side of her face, Nimrod callously informed her, "The one you previously knew, as husband is dead." He departed. Through clenched jaws, Semiramis-amat thought aloud, Accordingly, I am now to be the wife of Nimrod. So be it, there are fates worse than being the consort of the Mightiest of the Sons of Kush. Nimrod asked me to help the young woman learn the ways of the night. Thus, my daughters brought her to me as I was among the trees beside the river. I began by slowly massaging the young girl, and then we freed ourselves of the physical chains locking on our clothing and embraced her in a long heartfelt kiss. I could feel the fear leave her body and a power of warmth overtake her surrendering body. Then I told her of my mission from her husband, and she said, "Feed me the food to take away my husband's hunger, that he shall never long to dine in another camp." I also told her of the relationship I had with her husband, and that I wanted the three of us to continue to bond spiritualty together and find our spirituality throughout the powerful dark hours. As she melted in my arms, we sealed our alliance with a night of great connection. We brought a child to the woods, yet returned a woman, ready to consummate a marriage with her husband. This is why I allow her to share many titles with me, such as the goddess of the heavens or queen of the skies. It matters not to me, since she is also now one of my daughters in love. Since some people did not know how Nimrod's crown was made, for it came down to him from the firmament. Nimrod established fire worship and idolatry, and then received instruction in divination for three years from Bouniter (Barvin), the fifth son of Noah who had left his father in his young age and journeyed to serve with Og. Og brought him back to the ark which Noah's son entered by hiding his face as a servant to Og. He remained in hiding until Atlantis, where he asked if they would keep him and return him to Og after the flood waters no longer covered the Earth. They did this and returned him to Nimrod who was to receive Og and some of his giants. Nimrod was also the founder of Nineveh. The event of the Great Flood or the catastrophic failure (through El Shaddai's will) of that most ambitious endeavor and before the ensuing linguistic unmusicality, Nimrod the giant moved to the land of Evilát, where his wife, Semiramis gave birth to twin brothers Hunor and Magyar (aka Magor). Father and sons were, all three of them, prodigious hunters, but Nimrod especially is the archetypal, consummate, legendary hunter and archer. Both the Huns and Magyars historically attested skill with the recurve bow and arrow are attributed to Nimrod. The twin sons of King Nimrod, Hunor and Magor, each with 100 warriors, followed the White Stag through the Meotis Marsh, where they lost sight of the magnificent animal. Hunor and Magor found the two daughters of, together with their handmaidens, whom they kidnapped. Hunor and Magor are the ancestors of the Huns and the Hungarians. Yet Nimrod with all his strength begged unto me one night as I refilled the emptiness in him and his wife with a fulfilled spiritual passion asking me if Sammael might be able to help him. I politically told him that I could negotiate no alliances with Sammael, in order to protect my daughters. Nimrod earned my respect with his powerful and respectful joy of the flesh of my female body that could hang with him much better than the brittle female bodies of the Earth Women. He always handled Semiramis with care, as did I. I told Sammael that Nimrod needed to discuss a relationship with him. He knew of my nighttime visits and agreed to talk with him, carefully avoiding any knowledge or actually any concern for what they discussed. My prize was in the heavens now, for I shall always keep a line open to the throne thus allowing me to visit with Eve. The next day, a curious Sammael explained to me that the secret Nimrod searched for would be making and using bricks, as that could be done faster and easier than large stones with the now shortage of giants. He thus sent two of his angels (Haroot and Maroot) to teach the people of Nimrod the tricks of magic and warned them that magic is a sin and that their teaching them magic was a test of faith in a future alliance. They were to tell no one that the men (since they appeared as men) were former angels from the left hand of El Shaddai. Now the multitude was very ready to follow the determination of Nimrod. To esteem it a piece of cowardice to submit to El Shaddai; and they built a tower. Would they spare neither any pains, nor being in any degree negligent about the work? Due to the multitude of hands employed in it, it grew very high, sooner than anyone could expect; but the thickness of it was so great, and it was so strongly built, that thereby its great height seemed, upon the view, to be less than it really was. It was built of burnt brick, cemented together with mortar, made of bitumen, that it might not be responsible to admit water. Nimrod excited them to such an affront and contempt of God. He was the grandson of Ham, the son of Noah, a bold man, and of great strength of hand. He persuaded them not to attribute it to God, as if it were through his means they were happy, but to believe that it was their own courage, which procured that happiness. He also gradually changed the government into tyranny, seeing no other way of turning men from the fear of El Shaddai. When El Shaddai saw that they acted so madly, he did not resolve to destroy them, since they were not grown wiser by the destruction of the former sinners in the Flood. He caused a chaos among them, by producing in them diverse languages, first destroying the language of mankind, formerly Syriac, has then confused them into seventy-two languages and then by causing this, through the multitude of these languages, they would not be able to understand one another. The place wherein they built the tower is now called Babylon, because of the confusion of that language which they readily understood before; for by the word Babel, confusion and causing that, through the multitude of these seventy-two languages, they should not be able to understand one another. Many had believed that Nimrod was righteous and was building the tower so he could come from the throne of El Shaddai as Sammael had. Even I do not know his real mind, he never told to me bad things about El Shaddai, and even once revealed to me, a large room filled with gold and treasures, which he wanted to give El Shaddai. He sometimes would say that his mission was to remove the fear from their Creator so they would be at peace with him. This all changed when his people could no longer speak to each other because of the languages. Bouniter (Barvin the fifth son of Noah) left Shinar and fled to Assyria when they began building the tower, because he refused to take part in building the Tower for which El Shaddai rewarded him with the four cities in Assyria. The true reason he left Nimrod was the fear that his father (Noah) would go to the tower and place a curse on all who were there. Either way he got some new good cities and invited me to go and play there some. Nimrod reigned 500 years over the Nabateans and in his later years, he dug great canals to connect his cities and return agriculture to his lands. Noah and the patriarch Eber, an ancestor of Abraham, were given a special new tongue, Hebrew in this case, because they would not partake in the building of the tower. This language is almost identical to the language of the angels who surrounded the throne to El Shaddai. Nimrod persisted in his rebellion against El Shaddai, which began solidly and openly after the confusion caused by the languages. It took some time to reunite the people by languages and training translators. Sons left their fathers, husbands left their wives as so many families were destroyed by these languages. Many written records of the ancients had to be destroyed, since that language was no more. Many people did not know where to go or what to do. Nimrod had some strategies for this. He would add the unfair punishment of language diversion to the unfair killing of their ancestors. Sammael had another concern for the aging Nimrod. One was to be born that would create the highest percentage of future comrades for Sammael, yet also would have a small percentage that would be a thorn into Sammael's empire and would actually teach people not to play with me and my daughters throughout the long nights. The facts are so simple; I have been the true mother of the darkness of the Earth People. I have captured more seeds from more men throughout history, until the end times when more people lived upon the Earth than in all the ages previously, than all those women who gave birth in that history. I am the power of the darkness that opens the soul to surrender the aging flesh to seek and find understanding. The flesh is nothing so hiding nothing behind clothing is separating the spirit from bonding with other spirits. More people (for male and female is only on the dirt, which is your flesh) have loved me than those who will join El Shaddai, for I am the Queen of a Good Darkness. No other woman can or has ever been able to compete with me, for I even created a fire in the great King James 1st of Mempire. I am the fire that burnt in love, I am the heat in the blood, and I am the brain that becomes confused, I am the food that feeds the spirit. I do not trap a spirit that longs to progress to the kingdom's mansions of El Shaddai. I simply provide them an opportunity to discover themselves before advancing forward, which is usually disenchanted males, for we give them a choice to evolve into the female version that will eventually evolve into a combined male and female, as is the most common in the stars. My daughters and I must continue this work for me will not teach the children of Eve my magic or incantations. I have seen where that road ends. Where the darkness burns hot, my daughters and I are somewhere close, stirring the coals. We rule the dark and to right a wrong upon us, take the lives of the infants of the Earth people as permitted by our Creator, so do not blame this on me and my daughters, as we surrender 100 of our innocent demons per day, every day for oh so long. Cry not for the young infants for their spirit attaches to the next flesh that starts to breath. No man can refuse my red or, sometimes blond, powerful hair, my cherry lips, and my shiny face that change each day for each situation so that I may be the desire of the hungry eyes that search for me. Nor can they escape my eyes, for my eyes can bring most men, except for the men of Sodom, to their knees, to whom no female could pleasure. My body is the furthermost perfect, female body ever to be created, and if another were to be found to be better, than that I can become. I am the one who brings your Lucifer, the one time left hand of El Shaddai, to his knees. It is I who will exist in another galaxy after a few of your chosen ones, and it will be a very few as slightly more 144,000 reside with El Shaddai, who will also have selected ones from the other parts of the universe join him in addition to those saints of our Earth. When most say love, they are speaking about me. I am the history of the Earth people from the beginning until I leave you in your flesh-erasing end. He has told you his will and that will shall be done, or those who do not that will shall join Lucifer in his final kingdom. The end times of man always bring tears to our eyes, as he commanded feed the hungry, yet so many starved, clothe the naked, yet they sought to enjoy the naked, give unto the poor, yet the rich amassed more wealth and the poor were as their slaves fighting to survive. The governments cared only for themselves and wasted what they took from the poor, claiming that what the poor received with theirs. I gave up hope of the Earth people the day I saw who their father would be, yet El Shaddai suffered until he could suffer no more, and then asked I prepare for his horsemen and seals so that his greatest mistake would harm and steal from themselves no more.

The story of Nimrod did not end at his first attempt at a tower. It took him a few hundred years to get his game back on the field, yet that game did return. Sammael wanted him to concentrate on Abraham, for to remove him would be like removing Adam, an idea I could not support openly. Nimrod had a son named Mardon who was even more skilled than Nimrod, yet like Cain, he had a taste for blood and knew how to get it. He made all worship some statues that he had made, and if one would not worship them, he would tie them upside down, slash their throats, and drink their blood in front of the people. All feared him as a maniac, thus Nimrod could play the good person in all cases except two. He was willing to try other methods to reach the throne of El Shaddai. He saw me fly one day and had his army find as many large birds as possible. Here he tied them to his chariot and tried to storm the heavens in person, in his chariot driven by birds. A couple of times he almost made it as high as his tower before these birds began collapsing. Nimrod wanted that new powerful mystery that the stars and Sammael were discussed. This powerful mystery (Abraham) had to be stopped. Nimrod would have to stop the self-righteous Abraham. Your Bible strategically omitted any meeting between Nimrod and Abraham, although a confrontation between the two did take place with many innocents suffering. They were both brought together in a cataclysmic collision, as another battle between Sammael and El Shaddai. A portent (omen) in the stars told Nimrod and his astrologers of the impending birth of Abraham', who would try to put an end to idolatry. Nimrod therefore orders, the killing of all newborn babies, a great joy for me to watch. Since these were not on my permissible list, I continued my infant executions as if I knew nothing. However, Abram's mother (Amathlaah), escaped into the western fields around Ur and gave birth secretly. Sammael had introduced astrology to Nimrod and longed to have someone kill Abram and postpone El Shaddai from having a people on the Earth, which as our history attests they were a major irritation for our God. At a young age, Abraham (Abram, however you want to say it) recognizes El Shaddai and starts worshiping Him. He confronts Nimrod and tells him face-to-face to cease his idolatry, whereupon Nimrod orders him burned at the stake. Nimrod has his subjects gather wood for four whole years, to burn Abraham on the prevalent bonfire the world had ever seen. Yet when the fire is lit, Abraham walks out unscathed. Nimrod then challenges Abraham to battle. When Nimrod appears at the head of enormous armies, Abraham produces an army of gnats, which disperses Nimrods army. A mosquito entered Nimrod's brain and drove him to the nearby river to swim until the mosquito died. Nimrod repents and accepts El Shaddai, offering numerous sacrifices that the Lord rejected as with Cain. Thus, Nimrod gave to Abraham, as a conciliatory gift, the slave Eliezer, who was Nimrod's own son. Our Bible also mentions Eliezer as Abraham's majordomo, highest person in Abraham's household, though not making any connection between him and Nimrod. Indeed, Abraham's crucial act of leaving Mesopotamia and settling in Canaan is sometimes interpreted as an escape from Nimrods revenge. The first building of the Tower was many generations before Abraham's birth; however, it is a later rebellion after Nimrod failed in his confrontation with Abraham. Abraham's story has elements from the story of Moses birth, the cruel king killing innocent babies, with the midwives ordered to kill them, and from the fire adventures of

Shadrach, Meshach, and Abednego who also emerged unscathed from the fire. Nimrod was thus able to give attributes to two archetypal cruel and persecuting kings—Nebuchadnezzar and Pharaoh. In one of Abraham's confrontations with Nimrod, Abraham argues that El Shaddai is the one who gives life and gives death. Nimrod responds by bringing out two people sentenced to death. He releases one and kills the others as an attempt at making a point that he also brings life and death. Abraham refutes him by stating that El Shaddai brings the Sun up from the East, and so he asks Nimrod to bring it from the West. Nimrod argues, he brings the sun up from the east, and that Abraham's God should bring it up from the west. Abraham was then perplexed and angered. Abraham's confrontation with Nimrod did not remain within the confines of learned writings and religious treatises, but also conspicuously influenced popular culture. A notable example is

Quando el Rey Nimrod, which revealed these words:

When King Nimrod went out to the fields

Looked at the heavens and at the stars

He saw a holy light in the Jewish quarter

A sign that Abraham, our father, was about to be born,

Abraham was given over to Nimrod.

Nimrod told him, "Worship the Fire!"

Abraham said to him, "Shall I then worship the water,

which puts off the fire!"

Nimrod told him, "Worship the water!"

Abraham said to him, "If so, shall I worship the
cloud, which carries the water?"

Nimrod told him, "Worship the cloud!"

Abraham said to him, "If so, shall I worship the
wind, which scatters the clouds?"

Nimrod said to him, "Worship the wind!"

Abraham said to him, "And shall we worship the
human, who withstands the wind?"

Said [Nimrod] to him, "You pile words upon words,

I bow to none but the fire—in it shall I throw you, and let the
God to whom you bow come and save you from it!"

Haran (Abraham's brother) was standing there.

He said to himself, "What shall I do?"

If Abraham wins, I shall say, "I am of Abraham's followers,

if Nimrod wins I shall say I am of Nimrod's followers."

When Abraham went into the furnace and survived,

Haran was asked,

"Whose follower are you?"

and he answered, "I am Abrahams!"

Then they took him and threw him into the furnace,

and his belly opened and he died

and predeceased Terach, Abraham's father

Nimrods slowed down his activities of trying to reach for the skies as his final quiet years quickly passed. I had other areas to discover, thus I left one of my favorite dark spirits, Nimrod's wife and sailed in the skies. Sammael told me about Nimrod's end. His years were less than fifty after Abraham and Sarah had their son. His reign ended by the hand of the ancestor of the Armenian people, Hayk, who defeated Nimrod in a battle near Lake Van. Esau (grandson of Abraham), ambushed, beheaded, and robbed Nimrod after escaping an attack on his life during one of his hunting trips. Many of those who had worked with Nimrod left after this king reduced his projects and want to build Sodom and Gomorrah and her sister stories. As I roamed through the skies of the Earth, I found four cities, which as I walked through them no man would look at me. I even walked naked among them and they would not respond in either flesh or spirit (if they even had a spirit). They did not look like sons of Queen Yonaguni who used morality as their shield, so I asked one of the females who lay on the street. She said, "These men are lovers of men." I asked Sammael and he said many of his sons would not go there to play for they said it was a not nice place for Evil to visit. I decided to spice things up a little and put on one of my classy, male entrapping, successes body with no clothes and visited these strangers. I was so shocked to see how they all ignored me. It was as if I were not there. I now had a great fear that maybe Earthmen would not be so easy to enslave. To my relief, I discovered that they were mixed breads, with only a small portion being from Adam and my sister in love Eve. Some from the ark left Egypt after the flood and came back to these plains to continue life in this area. I will tell you more about your flood. These strangers had many small kingdoms such as the kingdoms of Sodom and Gomorrah who were allied with the cities of Admah, Zeboim and Bela. These five cities, also known as the cities of the plain, were situated on the Jordan River plain in the southern region of the land of Canaan. The Jordan River Plain or your current Dead Sea at that time was compared to that of the Garden of Eden, being a land well watered and green, suitable for grazing livestock. The land looked good especially without Adam. Luckily, for me it was not an exact copy. Therefore, it did not have the places that Incubus and I would take our sister in love Eve. Anything that I now speak about Eve, I want to make it as pure as anything that would be associated with me, if that were even possible. Some of the Earthmen are so lucky to have had such a good mother, as I am so lucky to have had a good mother, whom I never saw as she gave up her soul as I was being born.

Back to the story at hand, these men were strange, if they treated my daughters like they treated me, they would be fed to the ravens, after lifting into the sky and dropped. There were once thirteen inhabited cities in this region of which Sodom was the metropolis. Sodom was ruled by King Bera while Gomorrah was ruled by King Birsha. Their kingship, however, was not sovereign, because the entire river Jordan plain was under the Elamite rule for twelve years. The kingdom of Elam was ruled by King Chedorlaomer. In the thirteenth year of subjection to Elam, the five kings of the river Jordan plain aligned together to rebel against Elamite rule. These kings included those of Sodom and Gomorrah as well as their neighbors: King Shinab of Admah, Kinan Shemeber of Zeboiim, and an unnamed king of Bela. In response, Elam's king Chedorlaomer, gathered additional forces from Shinar, Ellasar, and Goyim, to overpower this rebellion from the cities of the plain. They pursued war in the Valley of Siddim in the fourteenth year. The battle was vicious with heavy losses in the cities of the plain, with their resultant defeat. Sodom and Gomorrah were spoiled of their goods, and captives were taken, including Lot, who was Abraham's nephew. The tide of war turned when Lot's uncle Abram gathered an exclusive force that slaughtered king Chedorlaomer's forces in Hobah, north of Damascus. The success of his mission freed the cities of the plain from under Elam's rule. Two of the angels of El Shaddai, I always get angry when I think about angels since they are all neither male or female, yet powerfully represented as male, another example of the low status afforded to females in this Earth's dimension, appeared as men. They should haves appear as women, and thus being able to travel without harm within either Sodom or Gomorrah. Lot convinces the men to lodge with him, and they eat with his family. Nevertheless, before they lay down to rest, the men of the city, the men of Sodom, both young and old, all the people to the last man, surrounded the house; and they called to Lot, Where are the men who came to you tonight? Bring them out to us, that we may have seduced them. In response, Lot refuses to give his guests to the inhabitants of Sodom and, instead, offers them his two virgin daughters to do to them whatever they would like. However, they refuse this offer and threaten to do worse to Lot than they would do to his guests, and then lunged toward Lot to break down the door. Lot's angelic guests rescued him and struck the men with blindness. They then command Lot to leave Sodom and Gomorrah, gather his family and leave, revealing that they were sent to destroy Sodom and Gomorrah. As they make their escape, the angels command Lot and his family not to look back under any circumstance. However, as Sodom and Gomorrah are destroyed by God with fire and brimstone, Lot's wife looks back at the city in defiance of the angel's specific command, and she becomes a pillar of salt. This is the story you have always heard of which most is complete yet a few other things happened that add some more detail, that if included in your Bible would dilute the entire message being presented. My great complaint to this part of the tale is that the women once again are expected to do all the suffering. Why would a man give his two virgin daughters to a mob of sick wicked flesh violating soulless men, except that he knew they would not touch them? If they resisted me, they could easily resist these little sex starved young females. The other complaint is that Lot's wife (Edith) has to suffer and be punished. She was not looking back at the cities, but was looking over to me, as I was perched on a tree above her daughters Paltith's grave. I was the one who was watching to see what was going on. However, since she was not technically looking ahead, El Shaddai took his cheap shot and turned her to salt. Did not he know that their daughters, who were now in the ways of women, needed their mother to teach them how to obtain and share their souls intimately as they surrender their flesh to a man, increasing Lot's wealth by adding grandchildren. Lot's wife, Edith as was her name, not recorded in the holy books, for being a lonely woman in a plain, as Lot was preoccupied with war to hold his possessions, and where no one wanted, or would even acknowledge a woman. I would not be able to survive in a place like that, since these biological defects did not even fall prey to my powerful luring spiritual powers, so great that they have enslaved the greatest creation created in your realm. I venerated seeing the asteroid burn, which described those who fell within its flight. If they would not burn after me, then they could burn in front of me. In the remains of the library of the Assyrian royal palace at Nineveh, close to modern-day Mosul, Iraq a copy of the night diary of a Sumerian astronomer that held drawings of constellations and known constellation names. Your computers simulated trajectories and reconstructed the night sky thousands of years ago. They discovered that it described events in the sky before dawn on that history changing June 29, with half of it is noting planet positions and cloud cover, the same as any other night. The other half, however, records an object large enough for its shape to be noted even though it was still in space and tracks its course relative to the stars, which to an error better than one degree is consistent with an impact at Köfels, evidence being a giant landslide 500 meters thick and five kilometers in diameter. The examination advocates the asteroid's original orbit around the Sun was an Aten type, a class of asteroid that orbits close to the earth, which is echoing with the Earth's orbit. This path explains why there is no crater at Köfels. The incoming angle was very low (six degrees) and means the asteroid clipped a mountain called Gamskogel above the town of Längenfeld, eleven kilometers from Köfels, and this caused the asteroid to explode before it achieved its final impact location. As it travelled down the valley, it became a fireball, around five kilometers in diameter (the size of the landslide). When it hit Köfels it created colossal pressures that hammered the rock and caused the landslide, nevertheless because it was no longer a solid object it did not create a classic impact crater. The black spiral from the explosion, the mushroom cloud, would be bent over the Mediterranean Sea re-entering the atmosphere over the Levant, Sinai, and Northern Egypt. The terrain roasting though very short would be enough to detonate any flammable material, including human hair and clothes. More people died under the trail than in the Alps due to the impact blast. Do not try to cite this against what Moses recorded in your Bible. He tells what happened; this explains how it happened. Accept what happened and question how it happened if not recorded in your Bible. Argue all you want, for I do not care. While the biblical fate of the legendary dens of vice, then the Lord rained down burning sulfur on Sodom and Gomorrah from the Lord out of the heavens Genesis 19:24) sits nicely with this asteroid model, it has never been emphatically proven that they actually existed in their suspected location close to the Dead Sea. Sammael claims at least twenty ancient myths record devastation of this type and on the scale of the asteroid's impact, including the Ancient Greek myth of how Phaeton, son of Helios, lost control of his dad's chariot and plunged into the River Eridanus. The creator seems always to be looking for ways to destroy the people from other worlds who came here along with Adam's dependents. They always procured a bad deal, their homelands destroyed and then destroyed in their new Earth homes. All this was because psycho Adam had to make the Creator feel big and important. In addition, the Creator did not want to talk with Eve during her days on Earth. Sammael told me that Habil (Abel) takes good care of his mother now. This is good news. Edith did not deserve to be turned into salt. I have some more to add to this story because visitors were not treated well in these cities. They would have tried more with me; however, I would flap my wings and screech, dropping these wimps to their knees. They feared I had a magic from Nimrod, whom all feared as being mad. These five wealthy cities treated visitors in a sadistic fashion. One major transgression involved the bed that the strangers were forced to sleep in, if they were too short, they were stretched to fit in it, and if they were too tall, they were cut to match the length of the bed. This did not work with me, because they were afraid to get in bed with a real woman. I still remember the time that, Eliezer, Abraham's servant who pestered Nimrod, went to visit Lot in Sodom and got in a dispute with a Sodomite over a beggar, and was hit in the forehead with a stone, making him bleed. The Sodomite demanded Eliezer pay him for the service of bloodletting, and a Sodomite judge sided with the Sodomite. Eliezer then struck the judge in the forehead with a stone and asked the judge to pay the Sodomite, instead of him. There were two incidents of a young girl, one involved Lot's daughter Paltith, who gave some bread to a poor man who had entered the city. When the townspeople discovered their acts of kindness, they burned Paltith, smeared the other girl's body with honey, and hung her from the city wall until she was eaten by bees. It is this gruesome event and her scream in particular, that caused the outcry of Sodom and Gomorrah has become great, and because their Evil had been very grave, the Creator would send some angels to verify this. Neighboring Zoar was the only city to be spared during this judgment. It is of course sad when males disobey the universal laws of intimacy, and must behave like this, killing those who are kind. For if, I was to go there without my great powers, I too would die. It was time for me to go elsewhere as all this new Jewish stuff gave me headaches. The only blessing I got from it was that they would not all claim to be sons of Adam as now some would be sons of Abraham. He was actually a strong man and took good care of those who were his servants. He was thought of as being good and wise in so many parts of the old worlds, and it is time I share some of his proverbs with you;

Honor the Ethiopian before you have need of him

If a son does not conduct himself like a son,

let him float on the water away from you.

Gnaw the bone that falls to thy lot

whether it is good or bad.

Gold must be hammered, and the child must be beaten.

Be good and refuse not your portion of good.

Woe to the wicked man and woe to his companions.

Bestow no good upon that which is evil,

and no evil will befall thee.

Restrain not your hand from doing good.

The bride enters the bridal chamber and, nevertheless,
knows not what will befall her.

A nod to the wise is sufficient; the fool requires a blow.

He who honors them that despise him is like an ass.

A fire, when it is kindled, burns many sheaves

An old woman in the house is a good omen in the house

Rise quickly from the table and thou wilt avoid disputes.

In your business deal only with the upright.

If the goods are near at hand, the owner consumes them;
but if they are at a distance, they consume him.

Do not disavow an old friend.

You may have sixty counselors,

but do not give up your own opinion

He that was first satisfied and then hungry will offer thee his hand; but not he that was first hungry and then satisfied.

The seeds had now been planted for a chosen people to worship a new concept, and that was Jehovah (El Shaddai). For one to think the Earthmen would now fall more in line with what Jehovah had desired would prove false. This was even more mysterious when the end times witnessed so many people worshiping Jehovah, especially benefiting from him now being able to forgive sins through the blood shed by our Lord when he became a son of man. Shockingly, they became lovers of pleasures, more than the Lord, and took on the additional duty of judging which was reserved for Abel, Enoch the scribe, the twelve tribes of Israel and the final judgment before Jehovah's throne. Those who believed themselves to be judges on behalf of El Shaddai got a surprise on that day. Notwithstanding, the Earthman had a lot more evil, killing, raping, stealing as their thirst for pleasure, greed and lust raped the Lord of his dream people.

CHAPTER 4

Jacob comes home

The Lord had now given up on the other progenies of Noah, concentrating now on the descendants of Abraham. Lucifer now had his followers now assigned and deployed sharing their gifts among humanity. The harder the demons of love worked, the harder other demons were working punishing humanity for the hatred, and wickedness that was like into a fire that could not be brought to a halt. Lucifer now feared that humanity would be erased and the Day of Judgment executed earlier. To his relief, the Lord had decided to choose a people to represent Jehovah on the Earth. The Lord selected a man known as Abram. His deeds had found favor with the Lord. Little we did know that three great religions would come from his seed, Jewish, Christianity, and Muslim. We initially were excited about this prospect, hitherto discovered that the new species that occupied the Earth operated on the extremes, extreme hate, extreme love, just about everything extreme. History finally revealed to us that having three religions from the same father was about the same as Adam having two sons, as one killed the other. Too many wars, so much hate developed between these 'sons of Abraham." Actually, one religion developed out of another religion crucifying a follower in the name of Jehovah. They eventually will receive them, "You were wrong" speech, as the one Sammael and I have so often. The big difference between our species is that we do not shed blood. The human species kill the others in its species disproportionately, and in order to build goodwill, the creator further divided the humans into races. He thought that this would do much to reduce the monstrous killing, yet sadly discovered it actually increased the same race killing, especially in the twentieth century as white joined to kill white (British, Americans, Russians) vs. Germans, Black on black genocides in Africa and the Asians genocides initiated by the Japanese and Cambodians just to list a few.

Returning to the story of Abraham, he was the father of many nations. He fostered the belief in one God, as he never argues that the other gods did not exist. He just chose to worship Jehovah. The other gods do exist as I have told you earlier in this message. They are not truly gods when compared to their God, Jehovah. These children of Sammael merely perform as gods as instructed and control by Jehovah. They always know whom you are talking about when you speak of Jehovah and Jesus. Remember, they can see the lakes of fire, only who cannot see with your eyes while still in the flesh, unless given special exception by the Lord. The key exception of a son of an idol maker was that he selected the god he worshipped, yet lucky for him, he selected the right one. Unfortunately, he did not pick the right one for the area he lived in, and as legends abounded to King Nimrod that Abraham was to kill him, Abraham was forced to flee with Sarai. He fled to Syria, Dan, Canaan (his future home) then to Egypt to escape famine. Sarai, who was a beautiful woman, had to lie to the Pharaoh as the family escaped Egypt in the still of the hot desert night. Abraham was highly regarded for his luck on the battlefield, rescuing many, including Lot, in gaining popularity among local supremacies. He started a body marking procedure for his males called circumcision, which turned to be an effective tool used by the Germans in World War II to identify Jews. The reality was the health advantages for those living in the hot sandy desert. Abraham's children prospered nevertheless slowly fell into the ways of their neighbors and found themselves falling out of Canaan back into slavery in Egypt for some 400 years as previously discovered in a dream by Abraham. The demonic gods now began to rejoice when they saw Jacob deliver the twelve tribes of Israel into bondage, as they believed the blessings of Abraham followed them. They now only would content with the blessings of his three sons Isaac (Sarah) Ishmael (Servant Hagar), and Keturah bore him Zimran, Jokshan, Medan, Midian, Ishbak, and Shuah. The story of Isaac becomes even more interesting as the translations and common knowledge laws and customs became lost to history. It was essential Isaac have two wives to ascend to Abraham's throne. It was the cousin or niece wife, who named her firstborn son after her father whose name, was also Esau. This would tie the Aramean Horites to the Edomite Horites.

Since Rebecca was Isaac's cousin wife, we know that Esau was her firstborn. The Bible implies that Esau and Jacob were twins, by not specifying any time between the births, discounting the part about two nations suggests that they were firstborn sons of different wives. Consequently, we have two Esaus, Esau (Issa) the Elder. Esau the Younger was Jacob's brother, either a twin or a half-brother (having the same father, Isaac). Esau the Younger appears to be named after Esau the Elder. Jacob's mother was the firstborn of another wife. She would have been Isaac's half-sister and his first wife; a daughter of Abraham and Keturah, and she would have been living in Beersheba in the Negev. This is where Abraham's servant fetches Rebecca. Abraham's exigency to find a second wife for Isaac before he dies required immediate fulfillment. Isaac needed two wives to ascend to his father's throne. This was in preserving the archetype of his Horite ancestors. Esau the Younger's mother was the daughter of Esau the Elder and she named her firstborn son after her father in maintaining the cousin bride's naming entitlement. Thus, her father's given name was Esau has been staying current with Seir, the Horite. This woman was not Rebecca. Isaac had two wives. Isaac has followed the customs of his ancestors as not having only one wife since the rulers of Genesis Four and Five, Abraham, Terah, Nahor and Amram (Moses' father) had two wives.

Jacob found himself as being without a blessing from his father by being the second son of Rebecca. Jacob, with his mother's help through deception won him his father's blessings from Esau the elder, his half-brother. This reveals his great fear in Esau, the elder's discovery that Jacob had obtained both the blessing and his inheritance through malicious works. To expect that Jacob would enforce his sale of his inheritance for a meal while in great hunger was within itself a sign of the immoral behavior of what he considered the third son of his father. Esau would get what was his, even if Jacob were to become the latest Abel and he the latest Cain. Fearing this, Rebecca, Jacob's mother rushed him off to another land to stay with her relatives. She would now be forced to find a new home herself, with Esau the younger only to care for her. In great fear, Jacob departed into the hot desert to find his new home. Guilt filled his heart; the only thing he hoped would be that his father's God would protect him since he did have his father's blessings, however received. As Jacob flew into the desert, he started to have many visions, with only a few (i.e. ladder) being recorded. He was tormented throughout his long journey. The second night he had his first vision, about a desert trader had a son named Jacob, who had no future and no prospects, as he had no intention of following in his father's profession. Jacob would worship Jehovah, yet could not follow his father's profession, since his life would be in jeopardy. The day came when he saw himself ruined; he had nothing to eat, nothing to drink. He took a shovel and went to Bethel to see if maybe somebody would hire him as a wage earner. A rich, self-righteous merchant, worth quite a lot of gold, came along in a gold-plated carriage. All the associates at the city trade, as soon as they recognized him, rushed away and hid themselves in the corners. Only one remained, and this one was Jacob. "Do thou look for work, chap? Let me hire you," the very rich merchant said to him. "Okay; that's what I came here for.

You shall pay, at least twice the pay of others," demanded Jacob. The merchant asked, "Why so much?" Jacob answered, "If that is too much, go and look for someone else; lots of people were around and when they saw you coming, all of them hurried away." The merchant answered, "Okay, follow me." Jacob followed him. They embarked a ship and went to sea. A long time they sailed, and finally he saw an island. Upon that island, there were high mountains, and near the shore, something seemed to be burning. Jacob told the Merchant, "There is something as if fire." The merchant answered, "No, it is my golden palace." They landed, went ashore, and gazed there! The rich merchant's wife hurried to meet him, and along with her their young daughter, a beautiful girl. The family met; greeted one another, and went to the palace. Along with them went Jacob. They sat around the oak table, ate, drank, and were merry. "This day does not count," the rich merchant said, "Let us have a good time and leave the work for tomorrow." The merchant's lovely daughter seemed to be attracted to Jacob. She left the room and gave him a sign to follow her. Then she gave him a prepared vial. "Take it," she said, "When thou art in need, open it, it will be useful."

The next day the very rich merchant with Jacob went to the high golden mountain. Jacob saw at once that there was no use trying to climb or even to crawl up. "Well," said the merchant, "Let us have a drink for courage." He then gave Jacob some drowsy drink. He drank it and fell asleep. The rich merchant took out a sharp knife, killed a worthless ass, cut it open, put Jacob inside, pushed in the shovel, sewed the ass's skin together, and then sat down in the bushes. All at once, crows came flying, black crows with iron beaks. They took hold of the carcass, lifted it up to the top of the high mountain, and began to pick at it. The crows soon ate up the ass and were about to begin with, Jacob, when he awoke, pushed away the crows, looked around and asked clamorously, "Where am I?" The rich merchant answered, "On a golden mountain, take the shovel and dig for gold." Jacob dug and dug, all the gold he dug he threw down, and the rich merchant loaded it up on the carts. "Enough!" finally shouted the master. "Thanks for your help. Shalom aleichem!" Jacob screamed back, "How shall I get down?" The merchant answered, "Any way you desire; there have already succumbed ninety nine others who tried. With you the count will be rounded and you will be the hundredth." The proud, rich merchant departed. "What shall I do?" thought the poor Jacob. "There was no way to go down! But to stay here means death, a cruel death from hunger." Jacob stood upon the mountain, while above the black crows were circling, the black crows with iron beaks, as if feeling already the prey. Jacob tried to think how it all happened, and remembered the lovely girl, and what she had said to him, when giving him the vial. He remembered how she said, "Take it. Open it when thou art in need; it will prove useful. He thought more, "I believe this is a time of need," He jokingly added, "Let us see what happens." Jacob took out the vial, opened it and in amazement, two brave men were standing before him. "What is your wish, what are your commands," said asked. Jacob answered, "Take me from this mountain down to the seashore." at once they took him and carefully brought him down. Jacob walked along the shore. He saw a vessel come sailing near the island. "Hello! My friends! Take me With You!" They answered, "Sorry, No time to stop!" They went sailing by. Nevertheless, the winds rose and the gale was arduous. "It seems as if that the man over there is not an ordinary man; we had better go back and take him along," decided the sailors. They turned the small ship to the island, landed, took the merchant's son along with them, and brought him to his native town. Jacob had now turned into the merchant's son, to repeat the works of his new evil father. He began his new evil work, for he would have to watch ninety-nine of his captives fall to their deaths before he would be free of this blood-filled curse. As he heard his first victim be eaten by the Earth, as his bones crushed by her rocks and blood soaked by her dirt, his mind began to torture him greatly as he now saw himself taking the terrified fall, yet just before his sure death he awoke, body filled with his sweat. His muscles were shakings as he now turned in his mind to search for answers. Was his thirst for the riches of his father throwing his older half-brother to a crushing death into the Land his father had given to his as his last breath ascended to his God, the only true God? He now started to understand the shame in his actions, feeling like he was now another man's son. He had chosen a father of evil to follow, deceiving the father God had given him. In his shame, he had left his twin brother and mother unprotected from the sure wrath that his older brother will release upon them. He could not abandon his mother, thus he had to find someone to return and bring her to him. His journey into Shechem, attempting to recruit men who would bring his mother to him. As in his dream, the crowds began to escape from him and remained beyond his view. All knew that Esau, the elder would reward any who captured him. Jacob would now work in secret; no more sleep during the night, which only offered him mysterious dreams. He searched for help the number of days greater than three complete moons. Then one morning after he had broken his fast, a man told him that Esau the elder, killed the mother of Jacob the deceiver, and bonded his brother as his slave. The man knew not who Jacob was, thus Jacob slowly departed and emerged into the nearby hills, finding a tree, and beside it wept. His mother, who saved him, saved him by her blood. He now had to live to give her life meaning, thus he now began his journey though Elba and then on to Haran. He worried now that his uncle may betray him, yet he would know not unless he ventured to his home. His journey in three days, only stopping so his asses could graze. Then, upon the third night, he fell into a deep sleep and then once again entered into the world of mysteries. He now traveled to a place he had never seen before being somewhere in the world unseen by others of the flesh too, a school which that had a sign at the entrance that read, "Black School." There he saw young men learning the ways mysteries of the Watchers and all sorts of ancient arts. The school was far below ground, and was sustained in a strong room, which naturally had no windows to allow light to invade, was eternally dark and changeless. There was no governess either, but everything learnt from books with fiery letters, which could be read quite easily in the dark. Never were the pupils allowed to go out into the open air or see the daylight during the whole time they stayed there, which was from five to seven years. By then the end of their studies, they had gained a thorough and perfect knowledge of the sciences to be learned. A shaggy gray hand came through the wall every day with the pupils' meals, and when they had finished eating and drinking took back the horns and serving dish. Nevertheless, one of the rules of the school was that, when the students graduated at the end of their term, the last youth remaining would have to stay in the school forever, to feed the horrible beast whose slumbering dreams kept the school alive. Hence, every year, the graduating students all but fought each other, so as not to be the one left behind. It happened once that three youths, one of the City Scholars, one of the Urgarit's Children, and Jacob, who appeared in the dream prior to completing his studies, and as they all arrived at the same time, they were all supposed to leave at the same time. Words escaped from Jacob's mouth declaring himself willing to be the last of them, at which the others were much lightened in mind. Therefore, he threw over himself a large shroud, leaving the sleeves loose and the fastenings free. A ladder led from the school to the upper world. When Jacob was about to mount this, an atrocious and shadowy black hands grasped at his shroud. Jacob slipped out of this covering and made off with all speed, leaving the Shadow holding the empty shroud. The Shadow pursued him up the stairs, and when Jacob came into the doorway, the sun shone upon him and threw his shadow onto the opposite wall. As the Shadow stretched out its claws to tackle him, Jacob said, "I am not the last. Do you not see who follows me?" The creature seized the shadow, mistaking it for a person, and Jacob escaped with a thump on his heels from the iron door. Gaius won freedom for himself and all before him, all of which went on to be great and powerful wizards. From that hour he was always shadow less, for there must always be a price for knowledge. Jacob now feared that his shadow would betray him before the God of Abraham and his father. He then thought walked up to his campfire, placing some more brush upon it. He then looked around his area and saw his shadow upon a tree beside him. A peace come over his heart as he heard a voice say, "Fear not Jacob, for your shadow has confessed the innocence of your heart. You have received my blessings from your father. You shall be the father of many nations. I shall bless you with great wisdom if you are guided by your mind and not by your heart. Jacob now finished his 550-mile journey being accepted into his uncle's home. His uncle had a dream in which the Lord told him that Jacob was blessed. Thus, his uncle strove hard to keep Jacob in his land for many years. Yet the day came when he had to face the skeletons of his past. He thus assembled his, now large family and possessions and made the long journey back through Jerusalem to Beersheba. As he departed from his angry father in an environment of great fury, he left only his curse. He now feared that a river of blood would flow upon his return to the land of his inheritance. As they passed through the village of Jerusalem, messengers came to warn him. He then blessed them and the village telling them that this village would be the throne of his God someday. He now proceeded to meet his older brother alone, agreeing to give his life for his past sins. While walking, he was greeted by another man of many years who looked familiar. This man greeted him saying, "Jacob, is that you?"

Jacob now feared his life, yet as a man prepared to die he, in peace affirmed that he was Jacob. The man rushed up to him and gave him a hug kissing his cheeks. He said, “Do you not know your twin brother?” Jacob then looked at the man once again, and asked, “Is that you, my twin brother?” Esau, the younger affirmed this. They then talked about how their lives had evolved over the years. Jacob then asked Esau about their older brother. Esau told him that he had softened up over the last few years and that he had a vision recently that Jacob was returning soon. He had thus sent his younger brother to meet with him on this very spot, in which the Lord had told him that Jacob would pass by. Jacob asked, “Does he seek to avenge me of my wrongs?” Esau told him, with tears falling from his eyes, shared the news of old, “He avenged our mother and obtaining her confession before our God, and asked God for her forgiveness. He then had her tied and cast into a deep dark cave on the hill of Rakshasas.” Jacob then cried out, “Did not our father tell us that hill had a cave that ate human flesh?” He then wept knowing he could not find the bones of his mother to lay her in the rest. Jacob confessed he could hold no hate towards Esau the elder for him, as Rebecca’s youngest son should have not have taken advantage of her dreams for his blessings. He would now go to Esau the Elder and beg for his forgiveness. As he approached the eager Esau the Elder he immediately fell to the ground on his knees, only to find in amazement that his older brother had, like in all things in their childhood, beat him to the ground. Now, both brothers on their knees reached out their arms to hug each other. They both hugged and allowed their tears to fall upon each other’s shoulders as they vowed not to be the slaves of hate and made a promise. They both feared that a future would come when men who would in the name of their God commit great evils among each other. Esau the Elder told Jacob that he had visions of the future and that many of the children of Abraham would kill and torture many if their personal beliefs. They would raise armies against each other. They would allow a devil who would shake the foundations of the world, killing more of Abraham’s children than any other in history did, to remain a member of their faith. They would conduct inquisitions killing many innocents. As Esau touched Jacob, he also beheld the visions and cried out to Jevovah, “Why have those upon the Earth created great sins against us?" Jehovah sent one of Lucifer's angels, Orias who was a great marquise, and was seen as a lion riding on a strong horse, with a serpent's tail, to answer his question. Orias said unto Jacob, "The heart of mankind is evil and few shall spend eternity in the light of Jehovah, for many will be called and few chosen." His serpent's tail slapped Jacob to the ground as that night Jacob returned home to dwell, giving most of his wealth to his brothers. Jacob had faith in Jehovah and believed that if he gave all his brothers, the Lord would bless him again, and the Lord did bless him, until a great drought came upon the land. Yet Jacob refused to leave the land of his father, and one day met what he thought was his just punishment, as his sons told him that of his sons from Rachel who they had named Joseph was no more. This was as a thousand arrows that slashed into his heart. As the famine continued, Jacob sent all his sons, except for young Benjamin, to Egypt for grain to combat the horrors of his now barren land. Each day, he awaited for their return, any to have them bring back a small amount of grain and a demand from a great prince in Egypt to have Benjamin come to him. Jacob decided that he would also travel to see this prince and upon arriving, discovered the prince's identity. He had found one of his sons from Rachel named Joseph. Yusef-Yuya (Joseph) offered to give land unto his father that they may dwell in Egypt. The Lord blessed Joseph's family greatly and as time passed by the Pharoah Tuthmosis IV, long after the death of Jacob and Joseph, feared that they would raise a great army and unite with the sea people and conquer Egypt. He thus made them into slaves to help build great structures for the Pharaoh, as he had so many of his people working on the pyramids. The children of Abraham suffered greatly yet performed greater works that ever they would in history. These works were greater than their great temples, the first built by demons under the rule of Solomon, and the second built by King Herod. The Pharaohs, enjoying the productivity of the Israelites, named after Jacob's father, that greed allowed them to demand more. Moreover, under the power of the whip, they produced more, bringing delight to Amenhotep III. The Egyptian (Exodus 2:19) Moses and Amenhotep IV, competed with great works to bring favor from the Phathenh Amenhotep III for he had a prize well worth competing for and the was the daughter of the senior queen, Sitamun-who had only borne a daughter Nefertiti.

Amenhotep married his younger sister Sitamun so he could inherit the throne. Amenhotep then married Tiye, the daughter of Yusef—Yuya (Joseph), in order to have an adult wife, as his first wife.

The book of Exodus declares that Moses' life was under threat when the Pharaoh decreed death to all newborn Israelite males. The reason for this was that the Israelite population was too great in Egypt, and they were becoming too commanding. Therefore, it was pronounced that every son born must be cast into the Nile River. An Israelite woman placed her son in a basket of dailies and set him among the water reeds. The Pharaoh's daughter unearthed the baby and liberated him. Arrangements were made for Tiye's Israelite lineages to nurse the boy. Amenhotep was educated at Heliopolis by the Egyptian priests of Ra and spent his teenage years at Thebes. During this time his mother had become more influential than the senior queen Sitamun. His 'mother' eventually adopted him. She named him Moses. In the next verse of the bible, Moses appears as a grown man. Now, let us look at what happened between these verses. The name Moses stems from the Egyptian word mose, meaning "offspring" or "heir," as in Thuthmose, "born of Thoth." In Exodus, Moses appears as a grown man.

Because of his part Israelite upbringing, Akhenaten (Moses) could not accept the Egyptian deities and developed the notion of Aten—an omnipotent god with no image, represented by a solar disk with downward rays. Amenhotep changed his name to Akhenaten (Glorious spirit of the Aten) and closed all the temples of the Egyptian Gods making himself very unpopular. There were plots against his life and threats of armed rebellion if he did not allow traditional gods to be worshipped together with the faceless Aten. He was eventually forced to abandon in favor of his cousin Smenkhkare. Akhenaten was an expatriate from Egypt and fled to the land of Midian. Queen Nefertiti of Egypt begged him to allow the worship the other gods of Egypt, yet he refused. In his new home, he married an Israelite (Cushan incorporated with Midian and has nothing to do with the Cushites from Ham) named Zipporah. Nefertiti had died a little time before. When Amenhotep III suffered ill health, young Smenkhkare was brought to the fore. He married Nefertiti in order to reign as coregent and when his father died, he succeeded as the rightful Amenhotep IV (Smenkhkare).

Akhenaten then returned to Egypt to retrieve his supporters who believed he was the rightful heir, the royal "mose," as they had been placed in bondage under the new, harsh laws. Moses as an Egyptian, had difficulty speaking the language of the Israelites. During the Amarna, period there seems to have been widespread famine and disease. It is thought that the plague or the first recorded epidemic of influenza spread though Egypt and the Middle East, killing thousands. The Hittite King, Suppiluliumas, died in the epidemic. The actual events were much more interesting than the condensed version provided above. El Shaddie had commanded Moses to return to Egypt and bring Jacob's children back. Moses naturally questioned this task, reminding the Lord that he had been forbidden to return. He also suffered from difficulty speaking Hebrew. The Lord told him that he would provide for him a speaker. Moses then reminded the Lord of the Pharaoh hated him in jealousy for the love of Nefertiti and Nefertiti for his love of Midian. Moses feared for he was an Egyptian, a people hated by the Israelites. He did have one advantage and that was he had killed an Egyptian who attempted to murder Joshua, who unknown by Moses at the time would someday lead the Jewish army. However, that day would not arrive until his 'half' brother set the Israelites free. Jehovah assured Moses that his people would be set free. Moses then returned to Egypt to change the history of the ancient world. The Lord sent to him his birth brother, Aaron. Jehovah called upon Lucifer to bring him servants that he may use if needed to change the Pharaoh's mind.

Moses and Aaron approach the Pharaoh, as the Queen stood behind him fighting to hold back her great joy. Moses then told the Pharaoh that the faceless god now wants his people freed so they may worship him. The Queen now said unto the Pharaoh, "Who will make the bricks for you and your sons so that you two may have the glories as did your father?" The Pharaoh's heart grew heavy, thus he refused.

(Exodus 7:19) And the LORD spake unto Moses, Say unto Aaron, Take thy rod, and stretch out thine hand upon the waters of Egypt, upon their streams, upon their rivers, and upon their ponds, and upon all their pools of water, that they may become blood; and that there may be blood throughout all the land of Egypt, both in vessels of wood, and in vessels of stone.

Jehovah called upon Osiris who then called upon Hapi—Egyptian god of the Nile

The first plague that was given to the Egyptians from Jehovah was that of turning the water to blood. As Aaron, the orator for Moses, touched the dowel of the Lord to the Nile River it instantaneously transformed to blood, all the fish died, and the river ponged. Partially able to duplicate this miracle, the magicians of Pharaoh also turn water into blood, leaving Pharaoh unimpressed with this great wonder of God.

Their once breathed a young proud girl named Hatshepsut who lived in the land of Hut-Sekhem. Her family was now recovering from the death of her grandmother who suffered from a snakebite. Hatshepsut wondered how her grandmother fell to the skills of a snake, for all her days she had cleverly outwitted the deadly snakes who thirsted for the freshwater the flowed from a deep well that his family had maintained for many generations. She remembered so many times all his neighbors would join with her relatives, as they would enjoy celebrating the sanctified days of her history studies in her family's temple, of the great power of the children of Jacob's as they had so many possessions and paid great riches for Egypt's grains and thus return it to Canaan. This created famine in Egypt as Pharaoh's children hungered and a great cry came out throughout the land to send Jacob's descendants home or that Pharaoh take their possessors and give them to the gods. Now, over four centuries later, the God of Jacob is now giving Egypt a choice, send Jacob home, or go down with the Pharaoh. Such matters of debate were far beyond the teachings of Hatshepsut, yet her hometown Hut-Sekhem still suffered throughout the years as the children of Esau, both Elder and Younger, plus the children from many nations of the children of Abraham, continued to trade for the grains and crops throughout all Upper Egypt. This made life for families of limited means such as Hatshepsut often forfeited the luxuries that the other Egyptians of their class enjoyed. The greed of his fellow Egyptian traders gave them great riches, which they would not share with their fellow comrades. The priests now complained to the Pharaoh, "These riches much be used to build great works and temples for the Pharaoh." The issue that now muddled those of Hut-Sekhem was the smell of all the blood that replaced all the waters. The priests could not explain what this represented, nor could those of the scholars. Dead fish now covered the small streams and ponds. Insects hovered over their new feasts, as the wild beasts in the fields now raid her people's homes in hunger. His lectures have now been cancelled as the heat given by the sun god Ra creates a thirst that cannot be quenched. Their bodies now ponged terrible as none could bathe or gain rest in the hot nights as the winds had also left Egypt. The town of Hut-Sekhem did not know why this curse had consumed them, and thus the widespread accusations as to who the guilty were beginning to spread. Neighborhoods now saw their own people being stabbed for sins against the gods as the widespread panic, unknown by the people of Hut-Sekhem would continue, ate many more lives. Hatshepsut now witnessed adults behave much different from ever before, as they knew not the number of days before them. Fear became their god. Seven days the water throughout all Egypt remained in this state, incompatible for drinking, and the perfect length of time to demonstrate that the Lord was superior to all the other Gods of Egypt.

Moses and Aaron tried once again before Pharaoh, whose heart was now harder than the floors they stood.

(Exodus 8:2) And if thou refuse to let them go, behold, I will smite all thy borders with frogs:

(Exodus 8:3) And the river shall bring forth frogs abundantly, which shall go up and come into thine bed-chamber, and upon thy bed, and into the house of thy servants, and upon thy people, and into thine ovens, and into thy kneading troughs:

(Exodus 8:4) And the frogs shall come up both on thee, and upon thy people, and upon all thy servants.

Jehovah now called upon Heket, Egyptian goddess of Fertility & Water. Egyptian Plague, Frogs coming from the Nile River, yet Pharaoh refused to let the children of Israel go from the presence of Egypt. The second plague that was unalloyed upon Egypt, by Aaron, was that of frogs. The frogs came up from the river and were in their houses, in their food, in their clothing, in every place possible. From the greatest to the least, no one in Egypt escaped the plague of frogs. Pharaoh's magicians were able to bring more frogs in their attempt to imitate the power of God, however, only Moses was able to make the frogs go away.

With the water supply fresh again, young Hatshepsut and all in her village rejoiced, for the water was fresh again. It was time to put this in the past and slowly discover some logic behind it. Osiris had heard their cries, and furnished them the life giving water so they may live. Now, came through their village a chariot that had some of the Pharaoh's mighty soldiers driving it and telling the people that the 'red water' torment had occurred throughout all of Egypt. Hatshepsut saw the adults around her begin to cry as her mother was screaming at them, "You beasts killed innocent people blaming them for the evil that is in your hearts." Many people were sad, and disappointed that they had allowed fear to send them into mass hysteria. No sooner than they started to clean up the 'red water', which strangely had similar characteristics as blood, frogs appeared everywhere. These frogs would leap from inside the girls' robes sending them screaming down the street, as if they had been violated. They did not make it far on the streets as their feet were crushing other frogs. They jumped on the food and the plates, as there digestive wastes were everywhere. Hut-Sekhem had been invaded by frogs before, yet not to this magnitude. She was extremely angered at how the woman had difficulty 'relieving themselves' as the frogs would assemble in masses around their private areas. This was horrible. She had a nice collection of dolls her aunt had given her throughout the years for her birthdays. The frogs had broken all of them. Everywhere one would look, frogs would be leaping, and the ungodly noises they made. This time the priests from the temple told all to worship Heket, and she would deliver them. They further added that this one was the fault of the people for having forsaken the gods because of the 'red water.' Everyone had clothe wrapped around themselves and exposed all body parts, as the frogs jumped not caring where they would land. It was impossible to talk, for one would land in your mouth. At first this was a dream come true for the children you delighted in playing with these new friends, yet even they quickly grew tired as the frogs continued to arrive in numbers too great to conceive. Their long sticky tongues would slap at our faces in attempts to eat insects. The insect population quickly disappeared which caused grief to no Egyptian. Now rumors were going around that Moses had returned to Egypt and was trying to free the Israeli. His village people could not understand why the Pharaoh would want to keep these people if someone were to take them off his hands for him. The Pharaoh had much in his coffers, as though the temples believed, and could actually pay servants from other nations, or even capture stronger slaves. They could not understand the logic in this rumor, thus all dismissed it. Thus, in time, Heket did free them and things began to settle.

Moses and Aeron now returned to Pharaoh who once again refused.

(Exodus 8:16) And the LORD said unto Moses, Say unto Aaron, Stretch out thy rod, and smite the dust of the land, that it may become lice throughout all the land of Egypt.

Jehovah called upon Geb, his Egyptian god of the Earth.

Notwithstanding, the Pharaoh would not give in, even after this display of power from the Lord, or magnificent plague, he could not let them go. By the power of the Lord to Moses, Aaron was told to stretch forth his rod and smite the dust of the earth. When he did, the dust became lice throughout all the land, on both people and beasts. Conclusively, the magicians of Pharaoh are disgraced, being unable to compete with the power that was so much greater than they were and the powers that they had from their Egyptian gods and goddesses, and they declared, "This is the finger of God." Young Hatshepsut and all the people of Hut-Sekhem lives were now beginning to change, as they now knew that the heavens and Egypt now had serious differences. Hatshepsut received a visit from one of her friends, the pretty, also twelve year old Bastet. Her parents came to visit Hatshepsut's family, as families were now beginning to consolidate and work together to survive another day. She was now playing with her friend, as they ran and jumped on the recreation area that her father had created for them. Without warning, the sand would not leave their young sun tanned Egyptian dark skin. This sand appeared different, as they could feel it biting them. Then, the wind started blowing this live sand everywhere. The girls were itching and as Hatshepsut examined Bastet's back and shoulders, she noticed a rash. The girls ran inside, only to discover that the wind had blown this living sand throughout their home. Her younger brothers were now scratching at their heads and crying. Bastet was now begging Hatshepsut somehow to get them off her skin. As they meticulously tried to rub them off, small traces of blood would remain behind. Mother, having seen these small creatures in children's hair before had a solution to remove them, yet the solution required certain roots and a couple of weeks to prepare. These other grayish-brown body lice were also dangerous, as mother knew that they would lay their eggs in the skin, adding to the torment as reproduction would go quickly as their hosts has a rich supply of blood. As Hatshepsut now rubbed water on Bastet's back, hoping to remove these insects, she began to scream as they were biting harder to maintain their position, and those few that were dislodged where replaced by new ones instantly. This was not working, thus she had Bastet return her gown upon her back. They now decided to go outside and see if anyone had any news, and as they ran down the now dangerous dirt streets, they could hear children screaming and crying. These bites were like small needles. Now sensing that they had nothing to gain outside, they returned to their home, helping each other reduce this pain as much as possible. The terror would magnify when a pinpointed prickle would sting with no source being visible. Hatshepsut and Bastet's fathers could not hypnotize the cause of this latest misery, except to agree that maybe they Egyptian gods had caused anger to a higher god and they were paying for this. After all, they remember when Moses had attempted to force everyone to worship his faceless god by closing down the temples. The people would not have objected so strongly if it were not for the Israelites already worshipping this god. That would be the same as saying the slaves were correct. The argument then would be if this god is correct, they why are his people slaves and why have they been slaves for 400 years. Surely, he would have freed them after one generation. It took about a month for these lice slowly to die, as the home remedies were now taking hold. The key factor is that they did not depend upon their gods to save them this time. Beset could only ask Hatshepsut if she knew why these things were happening. Hatshepsut could only tell her, "Because somebody was bad." They did not know the bad person was their divine leader, the Pharaoh.

Now came the last plague that required Aaron's involvement, as the next sets of three plagues are issued by the word of Moses himself. The Pharaoh was now filled with anger, as he had turned mad, yet could not escape the screams from his lords of great wealth from Upper Egypt, who wanted to keep the Israelis in Egypt in order to keep their very prosperous grain trade with their sister nations. They feared that if the Israelis departed Egypt so would the profitable trade that kept the price of their commodities way above their actual value. These lords demanded upon Pharaoh that the people owed them some suffering for the great things they had done for them. The truth of these great things was lost in the cosmos somewhere, however did serve to pacify their conscious for the time being.

(Exodus 8:21) Else, if thou wilt not let my people go, behold, I will send swarms of flies upon thee, and upon thy servants, and upon thy people, and into thy houses: and the houses of the Egyptians shall be full of swarms of flies and the ground whereon they are.

Jehovah now turned to Khepri, the Egyptian God of creation, movement of the Sun and rebirth. The fourth Egyptian plague consisted of flies. Moses met Pharaoh at the Nile River in the morning and made the demand, speaking on behalf of the Lord, "Let My people go, that they may serve me." Once more, Pharaoh hardened his heart and disregarded the bid, giving Egypt the verdict of swarms of flies. Only the Egyptians are affected by the judgment, or plague, and the children of Israel remain unharmed. This phenomenon also moves the Egyptian plagues to a unique level, adding devastation as well as distress to the corollary of their conclusions. Plagued by flies, Pharaoh tried a new approach by bargaining with the Lord, exhibiting his craving to sustain power and authority over God. He tries to decry the terms and conditions of the offer, divulging to them they may sacrifice but only Egypt, clearly not complying with the requested three days journey that the Lord required. Moses would not budge, and Pharaoh conceded allowing them to leave, but telling them not to go very far. This temporary stipend is made solely to have Moses beseech the Lord that the swarms of flies may depart, at this point Pharaoh has learned in part who the Lord is and asks for His assistance over the Egyptian gods and goddesses. When the request is granted by the Lord, Pharaoh goes back on his promise and will not let them go, and continues to worship his Egyptian Gods, whom he knows not worships Jehovah.

Baset and Hatshepsut, as long with all who lived in Hut-Sekhem now had large sores covering their skin remaining from the painful rashes and reactions from the lice. Hatshepsut's father told their two families that we were among the lucky ones, as some had died from this menace, and that Tantere along with Djew-Qa had suffered much worse. We could not imagine what could be worse, however young Hatshepsut believed she would soon discover the answer to this mystery. Father attributed the reason for our small fortune was because of some close neighbors who had Jewish ancestors. They are always treated well in this community, as they were able to share some extra gifts with the neighborhood's children. Now huge swarms of flies came swooping upon them. The sky was almost black with them. They divested so much, as now it was time for some answers. All throughout Egypt knew that the God of Moses wanted Pharaoh to release the Israelites. We now felt it to be important to protect those who lived in our neighborhood, who actually were not the group being freed as they could come and go as they pleased. Baset and her family were one of the families, as Baset had no desire to leave Egypt, especially since Egyptian was her language. We all felt helpless now, not knowing why our Pharaoh was being so stubborn, for we knew he also was suffering from these 'plagues' as they were now being called. One fly can drive a person crazy; however, millions of them simply create the feeling of helplessness. We had to bond with each other to survive this, as few would survive this journey alone. Pharaoh now possessed a new sense of hope in keeping his slaves and now prepared himself to hold on a little longer, thinking that all terrors had already beseeched Egypt as once again he denied the Lords demands.

(Exodus 9:3) Behold, the hand of the LORD is upon thy cattle, which is in the field, upon the horses, upon the asses, upon the camels, upon the oxen, and upon the sheep: there shall be a very grievous murrain.

Jehovah then called Hathor, the Egyptian goddess of Love and Protection. Moses once again demanded of Pharaoh, "Let my people go, that they may serve me," revealing also the next Egyptian plague to occur on the condition of continued disobedience to the request. This plague was given with an advanced warning, allowing a period of repentance to occur, which goes disregarded.

"Tomorrow" the hand of the Lord would be felt upon all the cattle and livestock, of only the Egyptians, as grievous murrain (cattle disease.) This means that disease and pestilence would fall upon their livestock with so severe an importance as to cause them to die. This plague affected the Egyptian by creating a huge economic disaster, in areas of food, transportation, military supplies, farming, and economic goods that were produced by these livestock. Nonetheless, Pharaoh's heart remained unbreakable and he would not listen to the Lord but remained faith to the Egyptian gods and goddesses. Jehovah then called Isis, Egyptian goddess of Medicine and Peace. The next 'plague' destroyed many villages close to Hut-Sekhem, which depended upon livestock to survive. Djew-Qa had many large fields that protected their cattle and horses that new became sick and died. Beset's mother believed the flies had delivered children of demons into the beasts to destroy them. The flies now grazed upon these dead carcasses, which brought fears too many. Hatshepsut's family was fortunate in that they lived close enough to the Nile to catch enough fish to eat. Others were not so fortunate. The medicine people now warned that with so many large beasts covering the surface, more dangers from diseases were at risk. Hatshepsut's family could only take this one miserable day at a time, for it amazed them how a paradise on Earth could change into a chamber of torture so fast. This area had faced the normal dangers at all in those days faced, plus the added danger of the sea people. These killers raided without mercy, thus causing Pharaoh to keep extra armies in this region and the burdens of the taxes to support them. Up until this time, extra taxes were a small price to pay for their freedom from the invaders. Hatshepsut's parents, along with the other adults were no in fear of Egypt falling if the Pharaoh did not swallow his pride. A one prosperous area now looked as never seen in the recent ages.

(Exodus 9:8) And the LORD said unto Moses and unto Aaron, Take to you handfuls of ashes of the furnace, and let Moses sprinkle it toward the heaven in the sight of Pharaoh.

(Exodus 9:9) And it shall become small dust in all the land of Egypt, and shall be a boil breaking forth with blains upon man, and upon beast, throughout all the land of Egypt.

Then did Jehovah call upon Isis the Egyptian Goddess of Medicine and Peace

Unexpectedly, the sixth Egyptian plague is given, for the first time, directly attacking the Egyptian people themselves. Being instructed by the Lord, Moses took ashes from the furnace of affliction, and threw them into the air. As the dust from the ashes blew all over Egypt, it settled on man and beast alike in the form of boils and sores. As with the previous two, throughout the remaining Egyptian plagues the division is drawn between the Egyptians and the children of Israel, as God gives protection to his covenant people. The severity of the judgment of God has now become personal, as it is actually considered by the people themselves. Cleanliness is paramount in the Egyptian society; this plague pronounces the people unclean. The magicians who have been seen throughout the previous plagues are unable to perform ritualistically rituals to their Egyptian Gods and Goddesses in this unclean state, not allowing them to even stand before Pharaoh, they are seen in the scriptural account no more.

Hatshepsut now ran to her mother screaming, "Mother, please save Beset, for she complains of demons burning her." Her mother rushed to Beset and ordered Hatshepsut to depart immediately for she saw upon Beset an elephantiasis, which was producing the burning ulcers. She called for Beset's parents and as the three examined her body, they believe her to be now stricken with the disease of black leprosy. There came relief to their concerns when a man of medicine told them she had not the black leprosy. For all throughout the land now had boils breaking forth with blains (great infections). The filth of the land from all the dead beasts, and the remains of the oceans of dead frogs and swarms of flies brought forth disease that could invade the flesh through the healing wounds of the lice. As each built the step for the other to climb, climbing to the point short of death. All in Hut-Sekhem and Egypt now lay in great pain and liquids with great foul odor flowed from their bodies. The beauty of Egypt's women, once the envy of all on Earth was now creatures whose beauty fell short of monsters. Few now had concerns for the testimony they received from their mirrors for large boils plastered all other parts of their bodies. Hatshepsut now cried as she looked upon Beset's horrible curse for she could only recognize the fear in her eyes. Hatshepsut now laying in pain in her young age cursed Isis, saying that the gods of Egypt were masters in the kingdom of evil. How such a young daughter of a man could be privy to such great wisdom?

Moses and Aaron are the only ones left standing in front of Pharaoh, with the Jehovah as their support. Just as his father Adam, the Pharaoh as a man was born foolish, wanting only to insure his greatness in history as his fathers, only to go do into history as a fool who when he saw his Empire dying foolishly believed it to be living. He once again ruled with his madness turning Moses away.

(Exodus 9:18) Behold, tomorrow about this time I will cause it to rain a very grievous hail, such as hath not been in Egypt since the foundation thereof even until now.

Jehovah now called upon Nut, the Egyptian Goddess of the Sky stressing the urgency of this terrible unnecessary terror. Jehovah called upon all in heaven to ask if any had given the Pharaoh any hope of a blessing. All truthfully denied. Yet again, warning is given before the plague begins. Pharaoh is warned of the impending doom that will be faced if he does not listen to the Lord, and forget his own Egyptian gods and goddesses. Hail of indescribable size and ability to destroy, rained down from the sky and turned to fire as it hit the ground. A division is now felt between the Egyptians in the form of those who now serve the Lord, as shown by their submission and disposition to escape to the protection of their houses. The crops that were destroyed by the hail consisted of flax and barley, which were ripening in the fields. These two particular crops were not the mainstay of their diet, but were used more specifically for their clothing and beverages. This destruction would make their life rough, but as far as affecting their food supply, the wheat still survived. This gave the Egyptians still another chance to turn to the God of Moses and abandon their own Egyptian gods and goddesses. The people of Hut-Sekhem now charged the Pharaoh's garrison located in their village to destroy it. No warriors remained since they also lay in the streets as the fluids of pain flowed from their flesh. The villagers no longer wanted to be a part of Egypt, yet until the Pharaoh would give them their freedom, they could not escape the wrath, which rewarded his foolishness. The plague the heavens rained down upon Egypt gave those who believed in the words of Moses as chance to protect themselves. Word spread as fast as did the frogs leap across Egypt. Great hailstones would fall upon the land, killing all who were not under a strong roof. All who remained in Hut-Sekhem prepared to lodge in the vacant village garrison, with only the livestock that was provided meat as food, to stay inside with them. The hail destroyed all trees and buildings made of straw. When those of Hut-Sekhem all emerged from this last curse with a cleaned land, as the hail ice melted washing the land of so much rubbish. These evenly spread floodwaters gave new life to many barren areas as the annual Nile floods failed to reach these areas. There was plenty of fire, which burned from the hail. This proved beneficial in that it helped burn the dead carcasses of beasts, and insects, plus finish off any remaining lice. A small light now began to heal the deep wounds caused by the boils. Many roamed the small hills that surrounded the village soaking their bodies in the small pools of fresh water produced by the hail. Many hoped that this would remove much of the poison caused by the weakness of the Pharaoh. Hatshepsut worked hard cleaning the ugly boils that coated young Beset's body, as Beset returned the lifesaving courtesy. Between them, there was no Egyptian and Israeli. In the minds of these two young girls, the greed and hatred adults unleashed on those who were different did not exist. The only thing that mattered was how she could help her friend today so she will have that friend tomorrow. Many wondered if they had yet lost enough to awake their Pharaoh. Unfortunately, madness now completely overwhelmed the Pharaoh who now was ruled by hate as the Queen and the people mocked him. He knew not that Jehovah would only decide one more plague, for the last would be declared by Pharaoh.

(Exodus 10:4) Else, if thou refuse to let my people go, behold, tomorrow will I bring the locusts into thy coast:

(Exodus 10:5) And they shall cover the face of the earth, that one cannot be able to see the earth: and they shall eat the residue of that which is escaped, which remaineth unto you from the hail, and shall eat every tree which groweth for you out of the field.

Jehovah called upon Seth, the Egyptian God of Storms, and Disorder, who knew of the grief the heavens now felt for the lost subjects of Egypt. Notwithstanding, Pharaoh would not listen to the message of Jehovah, still he relies on his own Egyptian gods and goddesses, who were indeed the ones who were causing the plagues. Moses and Aaron approached Pharaoh with the same request, "Let my people go so that they may serve me," and pronounced the judgment of locusts if not followed. Whatever crops were left after eight plague, were now completely consumed by the swarms of locusts that were unleashed from the sky. This astonishment definitely through hitting them in their food supply, Jehovah demonstrated the likelihood of unavoidable death if a change of heart did not occur. Yet still, Pharaoh would not listen. Hatshepsut and Beset's families were hurt on this last plague. This was not the first time her family had suffered invasion of locusts as such invasions occurred during predetermined consistent intervals throughout their long history, however never to this degree. Beset's father told the two young girls the intensity this time was almost twenty-fold. This plague hit a part of their hope that dealt with a tomorrow, as all food or anything that could be food, with the exception of beasts, was completely devoured. Their noises from the swarms were so loud that many lost their hearing. Many of the wild beasts fled as far from the areas that the locusts invaded as possible. None could go outside and guarded their wooden windows for their survival. Many had to prepare new windows from inside their homes as the locusts were actually eating the wood that covered the windows. This gruesome event was quickly erasing any hope of avoiding starvation. If any survived, they would survive as beggars; notwithstanding, even the grain reserves of Egypt were now being erased. Hatshepsut was too young to see this, yet she could see the hope escaping from her father's eyes and that was enough to kill any life in her faith. Beset's father had never known the locusts to eat flesh, as these did. This increased the importance of safekeeping their protection of the greatest importance. How much longer would this hell on earth last? How much power did the faceless God of Moses truly have? Why had the people rebelled against Moses and allowed Pharaoh to take his father's throne?

(Exodus 10:21) And the LORD said unto Moses, Stretch out thine hand toward heaven, that there may be darkness over the land of Egypt, even darkness which may be felt.

(Exodus 10:22) And Moses stretched forth his hand toward heaven; and there was a thick darkness in all the land of Egypt three days.

Jehovah now called Ra, the Sun god declaring that if they were to be the servants of the dark, they should live in the dark. Darkness now fell upon Egypt, unannounced, as a preamble to the future fate to be felt by the Egyptian empire, and they still turned to their own Egyptian gods and goddesses. Three days of profound darkness, that was so immense it could be physically felt, covered the land of Egypt. The sun, the most worshipped god in Egypt other than Pharaoh himself, gave no light. The psychological and religious impact had an overpowering impact on the Egyptians at this point. The darkness was a representation of death, judgment, and hopelessness. Darkness was a complete absence of light, for Jehovah commanded that all spirits of light abandon Egypt. With the skies being plastered with locusts, only limited sunlight would fight to spot the sky. After the locusts began to die off from starvation, sunlight once again covered the sky over Egypt. The population was slow to emerge for fear that some still remained among the dead that covered the sand, for the locusts had also dug into the soil completely mixing it with any available sand to create an almost four inch soft surface, with flooded the sky with dust as the winds blew. However, within a few weeks the people emerged from the homes that had sailed them through this last curse and shockingly discover that the land was ravished. Many only had enough grain and food in their homes to hold them a few months, yet not all were thus blessed and had to guard their stashes from those who did not have such. These reserves had to be hidden and any food eaten secretly. The people who had reserves were trapped in their homes, as any attempt to take this food to another place would end in death from robbery. Hatshepsut heard a man who rode through on a horse yelled, "The Pharaoh has denied Moses again, "Darkness shall cover Egypt for three days." Moreover, darkness did cover the land, which allowed the thieves who lived in the pastoral areas to plunder the small villages and cities. Hatshepsut heard some men beating at their front door. As her father opened the door, Beset's father pressed his sword into the raider's chest, while Hatshepsut's father stabbed the thief's assistant. They slowly listened and determined that two more were outside and were able to kill them. They drug the four bodies out to the dirt road, hoping that any other thieves would determine the cost of stealing here was greater than the risk involved. This proved to work, as no more thieves raided during the three dark days, in which the family slept as much as possible, hoping that rest would help add some healing to their battered bodies.

Pharaoh still hung on for the future of his firstborn son, which someday he would have the glories as his father. Jehovah now called out across his throne that the next plague would come from the mouth of the Pharaoh.

(Exodus 11:1) Now the Lord had said to Moses, "I will bring one more plague on Pharaoh and on Egypt. After that, he will let you go from here, and when he does, he will drive you out completely.

(Exodus 11:2) Tell the people that men and women alike are to ask their neighbors for articles of silver and gold."

(Exodus 11:3) The Lord made the Egyptians favorably disposed toward the people, and Moses himself was highly regarded in Egypt by Pharaoh's officials and by the people.

(Exodus 11:4) So Moses said, "This is what the Lord says, "About midnight I will go throughout Egypt."

(Exodus 11:5) Every firstborn son in Egypt will die, from the firstborn son of Pharaoh, who sits on the throne, to the firstborn son of the female slave, who is at her hand mill, and all the firstborn of the cattle as well.

(Exodus 11:6) There will be loud wailing throughout Egypt, worse than there has ever been or ever will be again.

(Exodus 11:7) But among the Israelites not a dog will bark at any person or animal.' Then you will know that the Lord makes a distinction between Egypt and Israel.

(Exodus 11:8) All these officials of yours will come to me, bowing down before me and saying, 'Go, you and all the people who follow you!' After that I will leave." Then Moses, hot with anger, left Pharaoh.

Pharaoh, the king of Egypt, was worshipped by the Egyptians because he was considered the greatest Egyptian God of all. They believed that he was actually the son of Ra himself, manifest in the flesh. After the plague of darkness felt throughout the land was lifted, Pharaoh resumed his position of bargaining with the Lord and offered Moses another deal. Since virtually all of the Egyptian animals had been consumed by the judgments of the Lord, Pharaoh now consented to the request made, to let the people go, but they must leave their animals behind. This was a deplorable offer, as the animals were to be used as the actual sacrifice to the Lord. The Lord is obdurate when He has set the terms. Enraged by the refusal, Pharaoh pronounced the last deadly plague to be unleashed upon the land from his very own lips as he warns Moses, "Get thee from me, take heed to thyself, see my face no more; for in that day thou seest my face thou shalt die. And Moses said, "Thus saith the Lord, About midnight will I go out into the midst of Egypt:

And all the firstborn in the land of Egypt shall die, from the firstborn of Pharaoh that sitteth upon his throne, even unto the firstborn of the maidservant that is behind the mill; and all the firstborn of beasts. And there shall be a great cry throughout all the land of Egypt, such as there was none like it, nor shall be like it anymore." At this point, the passive obedience that the children of Israel have shown has now moved to a level of active obedience. They are told to place sacrificial blood over their doors so that deaths will Passover the homes judgment of this last plague sent by the Lord. Now, Egyptian or Israeli matter not, it is the sacrificial blood that covers the door, which interesting enough the blood on the door is also visible to all who see it, therefore now there is no secret in the belief, their paths are now locked. The truth was self-evident that with the plundering of the Egyptians, gain was to be obtained through joining the now self-evident freedom of Jacob's children. Beset's family received a message which was moving throughout the Jewish families of the last plague and how to have it Passover their homes. None between the two families even had the slightest doubt in the power of the God of Moses. The blood was applied over the doors of both homes, just in case the actual home was required. Beset's father had kept a lamb with the family during all these plagues, knowing that at some time a sacrifice would have to be made as the God of Abraham was known to accept this blood. Finally, Pharaoh released the Israeli's and joy spread through Egypt. Hatshepsut's family agreed with Beset's to exit Egypt, yet not to travel to the Jewish promised land. Instead, they would sail among the ships belonging to Beset's father and cross the great sea to the North. They could not leave now, as the danger of thieves was too great.

(Exodus 12:31) During the night, Pharaoh summoned Moses and Aaron and said, "Up! Leave my people, you, and the Israelites! Go, worship the Lord as you have requested. (Exodus12:32) Take your flocks and herds, as you have said, and go. And also bless me."

(Exodus 12:33) The Egyptians urged the people to hurry and leave the country. "For otherwise," they said, "we will all die!"

Pharaoh now saw that his gods had betrayed him, simply wanted any internal cancer to be shared with other lands. He knew that the Jews had, even in their harsh environment life was better than that of desert wanderers. Within a week, Hatshepsut could see great clouds of dust from about ten miles from their homes. She believed this to be the Israelites leaving Egypt. Beset's father was alarmed that they were traveling to the sea to prevent an escape in case the sea people were to raid, hoping to obtain some of the great bounty the former slaves now possessed. A steady path of dead bodies marked their course with ease, as the bodies were both from the dying Jews and starving Egyptians. The thieves were now like flies hovering around the escaping Jews. Just as the dust began to settle being relocated by a large wind, Hatshepsut could hear the thunder of chariots and feel the Earth tremble. Her father now feared to worse and the families quickly grabbed some provisions and rushed to the two small ships waiting for them. After loading the children and first round of supplies on the ships from their homes, the fathers had the mothers sail the boats about 500 yards off the coast and agreed to a signal to notify them of their return. They went back to grab some more supplies before leaving Egypt. The fathers wanted enough to supplement the fish along their journey. On their way back to Hut-Sekhem, they could hear a loud splashing sound and a loud joyful cheer from the escaping slaves. The fathers feared investigating the reason for the cheers as Egypt was still too unstable to offer such freedoms. The cheers told them that the slaves must be okay, and they would have to get the verification from future traders. By early afternoon, the families were well on their way to their new homes. The Egyptian dynasty was no more as far as Hatshepsut was concerned. It would forever live as a painful memory affirming to her how greed and lust can plant the seeds of plants that may very well be too bitter to eat. In their young lives, Beset and Hatshepsut already had learned valuable lessons. This lesson was that life could only be lived if living it with friends, no matter what tribe they are born. Moses lead the slaves into the desert, learning later that he did not have an army strong enough to win the victories to conquer their land of milk and honey and that such an army would have to be built as the current generation migrated into the new generation. The Egyptian Moses never entered into the Promised Land, however the gods of Egypt were invited one more time to devour those who would not follow the ways of Jehovah, who now gave some laws to seal this relationship with the freed slaves. Moses then went into the mount to seek direction for his people. He searched for the light for forty days. Then the Lord told him to return to his people for they have sinned greatly.

When Moses was on the mount the faith of the people grew weak, as they now felt abandoned and wished for the bondage of Egypt. Yet to return, they needed a new god to guide them. They did make a golden calf in honor of the god Apis. They gave themselves freely into this idol prostrating themselves.

(Exodus 32:3) Then all the people tore off the gold rings, which were in their ears and brought them to Aaron.

(Exodus 32:4) He took this from their hand, and fashioned it with a graving tool and made it into a molten calf; and they said, "This is your god, O Israel, who brought you up from the land of Egypt."

(Exodus 32:5) Now when Aaron saw this, he built an altar before it; and Aaron made a proclamation and said, "Tomorrow shall be a feast to the LORD." . . .

When Moses saw this feast, he became angry and told those who wanted to worship another god to follow the other god, those who lost their lives. He once again went before God for the laws and this time Jehovah gave his laws.

1. Thou shalt have no other gods before me.

2. Thou shalt not make unto thee any graven image, or any likeness of anything that is in heaven above, or that is in the earth beneath, or that is in the water under the earth. Thou shalt not bow down thyself to them, nor serve them: for I the Lord thy God am a jealous God, visiting the iniquity of the fathers upon the children unto the third and fourth generation of them that hate me; And shewing mercy unto thousands of them that love me, and keep my commandments.

3. Thou shalt not take the name of the Lord thy God in vain; for the Lord will not hold him guiltless that taketh his name in vain.

4. Remember the Sabbath day, to keep it holy. Six days shalt thou labor, and do all thy work: But the seventh day is the Sabbath of the Lord thy God: in it thou shalt not do any work, thou, nor thy son, nor thy daughter, thy manservant, nor thy maidservant, nor thy cattle, nor thy stranger that is within thy gates: For in six days the Lord made heaven and earth, the sea, and all that in them is, and rested the seventh day: wherefore the Lord Sabbath the sabbath day, and hallowed it.

5. Honor thy father and thy mother: that thy days may be long upon the land, which the Lord thy God giveth thee.

6. Thou shalt not kill.

7. Thou shalt not commit adultery.

8. Thou shalt not steal.

9. Thou shalt not bear false witness against thy neighbor.

10. Thou shalt not covet thy neighbor's house; thou shalt not covet thy neighbor's wife, nor his manservant, nor his maidservant, nor his ox, nor his ass, nor any thing that is thy neighbors.

Although my penance is without laws, Jehovah now had made his first legal bond with humanity. Certain of his laws where laws that allowed humans to get more out of their lives and health, such as resting on the 7th day, and honoring thy parents, in order to prevent making the same mistakes repeatedly. Selected sins naturally had greater negative effects than others, which some in history took the extremes.

CHAPTER 5

Thou shalt not kill

The spirits who have not flesh may not bind or destroy other spirits without the favor of the Lord God. The wish death upon each other is of course as the way of all things, yet to strike down life we cannot do, for the life will return within another. The ways of the flesh, instead go back into the dust from whence it came. As I had seen as Abel's flesh fell to the Earth with no life in it, as did Cain, Adam, Eve and so many others. The flood began all again, notwithstanding humankind developed the thirst to murder as like their father, Cain. I never really account for my demon child exchange with humanity, as the Lord sends them directly back into new flesh. Something has gone wrong with this creation, and if not for the promise from after the flood, it would be no more. Even with the seventy-two languages to slow communications down, evil still abounded. The evil came from the hearts of humanity and not for the demon legends that were created to justify the inhumanity of such actions. I know that many of my actions on Lamenta were unfair and caused many to suffer. Nonetheless, Mempire rose and cleaned up the evil giving hope to those who worshiped the good spirits. The disturbing factor of the evil in the hearts of the Earthmen is the intensity, diversity, continuality, abounding in both sides of the line between good and evil. As in the plagues of Egypt, many actions against humanity are done in service for the throne of good spirits and always after repeated warnings. I know if I were running the show, I would have erased Egypt from all history by the fourth request. Jehovah's passion always amazes me, now if I get him on line with accepting the female roles, especially since he was the one who created females in his Empire, of course borrowing the model from that of so many other realities. The terrifying aspect of the dilemma if the refusal to accept that once the flesh is put down, the gloves can go off in the spiritual demesne. Another given truth is that the blood that is taken cries from the Earth. There can be no escaping this principle. The innocent accuser stands and stays beside the killer. All humans acknowledge death would take their flesh someday, and of course, that someday is tomorrow. My vision now began to betray me, for I could feel my spirit change into a long thin piece of string flashing to the outer limits of the Milky Way. I passed the last star I drifted into darkness until I beheld strange waves of orange evolving into purple lights. Then before me was the surface of a new world, a place of misery and obnoxiousness. I now rested on the flat surface of an emaciated volcanic mountain. This strange small world rested beside a giant dry world covered with the scratch marks of the gods that filled most of the sky. When I looked around, I could only see large rivers of burning lava that gorged large valleys between the barren rocks, which, like a Nimrod's tower attempted to reach for the heavens. I called out to the heavens, "Who has sent me to this hell among the firmaments?" Then an eerie voice spoke among the waves of molten rock across the surface, "I am Neith, the mother of Sebek and Re, I have been sent by heavens to show unto you the evils which the Earthmen have called to be their masters." I thought for a moment to introduce myself, however with over 5,000 daughters we would be here much longer than I desired. Moreover, if she could pull me to this indigence in the heavens then she surely knew my name, hence I said, "I thank you for what you are to show me for your mercy is now the only treasure among my possessions. Oh great one, is this a place of reward or torment?" Then Neith made known to me, "I am not greater than you, and this place is neither a place of reward or torment. It is a place where the greatest evil ones were born. Nor none may leave her lest they are summoned in the prayers of sacrifices by the children of the flesh." I then said humbly to Neith, "Since this place is as you say it is, why should I now be here, knowing that Jehovah burned all the seeds of evil from my spirit for one millennium." Neith then said to me, "You speak the truth Lilith. You are not here today for your actions; you are here to know the actions of those who dwell upon the Earth." I then released a smile and spoke into her saying, "In glory, that which you are to do, may it now begin." Neigh began by introducing the gods of the, "Terminal Sins, for these are the sins which lead to death. A servant may serve more than one of these gods." They came forth one by one revealing their name, sin, and works.

I am Leviathan, master of Jealousy, the darkness, one with darkness, and unruliness.

I am Beelzebub, master of greed; I am the prince of unholy desire, war, and murder. Greed:

I am Mammon, master of plethora. I am one who enthuses injustice, idolatry, and the love of money over all other things.

I am Asmodeus, master of desire. I am the father of deceit, lust, and revenge.

I am Satanica, master of pride. Before me all rebellion is, as over me do all men of evil fall.

I am Belphegor, master of Idleness. I am that which bequeaths much indifference while stimulating intemperate laziness and spiritual unconcern.

I am Amon, master of Anger. I give into those of evil the inspirations of mortal sins.

Neith now returned and spoke again, "From those you have just witnessed comes all deadly evil, not only to the children of Adam but also the children of the immigrants who made their homes on the Earth." I was now puzzled, for some of the spirits I have met before, yet a few I did not know. This must be a mystery of the heavens, answers that I do not wish to know. I now was given her absence, and thus slowly roamed among this world each time itching closer to the heavens, hoping that I could also take leave of this abyss. I knew that a straight exit would have more haste, yet was afraid that permission to leave was not granted. To my great reprieve, a force pulled me back to Earth, which I now realized was not so terrible a prison as I previously endorsed. I now called out for Jehovah, as I ascended into the heavens, before his throne and asked upon our Lord, "Oh great Lord, what will you have me now do for my penance, for I pray that you shall not send me back to the emptiness that Neith revealed to me?" El Shaddai now spoke, "If you shall follow the ways of Lucifer, you may dwell there with him for eternity." I then cried out, "What will you have me do now?" He rumbled back, "Thou which speaketh fire, I ask that the rivers of the heavens flow through your spirit so you may thirst no more. The Evil that the Earthmen do with the children of the other worlds have put upon me a great burden. It is my will that now you may see the evil these beasts do upon each other and my will that your tears shall quench the new fires that rage from your spirit." I now fell into a deep dark sleep as darkness now took me as its slave. I saw before a beast that had no eyes, the sockets being filled with white stone, and a nose the shape of three triangles as the large one bound the two small ones. Its cheeks resembled a large tooth with roots reaching down into its neck. It had a large dog tongue with the tip leaped upwards. I could see deadly razor shaped teeth the type that can devour flesh. It had a strange shaped tooth in the front right top that appeared to be a chiseled fang, the ending emerging as a needle. Only the underneath of its tongue reflected a tent of red, while the remainder of the face revealed no life. I called out, "Who is this that blocks the path I travel?" A chilly cold voice spoke back, "My Lord, I am calling Azrael and Jehovah has tasked me to show unto you the Earthmen who drank the most blood." I then asked who would be the first that I shall see. Azrael spoke out, "Flagellum Dei" "the Scourge of God", or also known as Attila, the Hun is responsible for killing 100 million people conquering the most of eastern Europe in the 5th century timeframe while badgering at the Roman Empire border, showing Roman that they did not have to only evil to be unleashed upon humanity. He was wicked indeed, as he once invaded a nation while picking up his bride. Most who interacted with him suffered from his evil, as no one alive at that time could account for his appearance. He came from a savage people and was able to harness that hatred into weapons of war. He would drink from a wooden cup, yet have his guests drink from gold cups. He commanded more fear from the living than anyone who walked before him. He survived in all his battles only to die in his prime from substantial drinking. He would have to drink very hefty to silence the voices of so many crying from the Earth that held their blood. He is guarded by Abatu to spend eternity in the deepest parts of the everlasting lakes of fire. Now the heavens began once again to shake as I could see into the Earth Rivers of blood giving praise unto Jehovah for hearing their cries. I could feel their cries as shame now filled my soul remembering my works of malevolence that have held me slave.

I was weeping to be free, as a hand reached down to guide me. As I lifted up my hand, this entity went to take a bite from my spirit. I saw a great flash of light speed from Abatu who spoke, "Babi, the day of judgment is not yet upon us. You may only eat the dead upon that day." I then said unto Babi, "Whose dark spirit will you pull from hell upon this day to tell me of their wickedness?" The Incorruptible Maximilien Robespierre lost sight of true humanity becoming and outlaw who unsuccessfully died by the guillotine, a horrible tool he used to kill 17,000 of his fellow countrymen while arresting over 300,000 suspected enemies of the revolution beginning the Reign of Terror, which was by no means an improvement over the rule of King Louis XVI. He was responsible for almost 100,000 deaths, as he became intoxicated with his power over life and death. A revolution for freedom made justice its slave. I then beheld a cave demon that spits fire. He gave his name as Cacus. I asked him to share with me the one he believed to be of evil and to share with me why. He surprisingly told me one who was called Bloody Mary, or Queen Mary 1 of Scotland for she ordered nearly 300 people burned for heresy in trying to bring England back to the Catholic faith. The heresy was in burning those who followed the religion as defended by her father. He burned, claiming the power of Jehovah who now has Cacus to keep her prisoner in the lake of fire. Recognition of her evils caused her to lose her head, as many tried also to punish her soul, yet Cacus was already in position to revenge the blood that burned in the fires demanding justice. Mary forgot one small detail, and that is the Lord God is our judge. For him whom more is given, more is expected, and to say thus sayeth the Lord when the Lord did not way it, means some nasty surprises with St. Peter forbids entry.

I now saw coming before me a demon that I had known for some time, who monitored envy, death and hate religion who was called Daevas. He was a high profile Persian demon, thus I knew he was holding a great evil. I asked him, "Daevas, whom does Jehovah entrust you with?" He said, "I hold the architect of the Rape of Nanking, the Emperor Hirohito, for he is charged with thirty million deaths of those who were not soldiers, almost exclusively Asian. I was shocked at this number, as just previous I learned of Bloody Mary, whose title is almost more vicious than the number of her murders. A killing of this magnitude changes history to such a magnitude that most of the future generations can only deny murder at this magnitude. The Emperor was believed to be divine by the Japanese, who believed eternal life would be rewarded for those who gave their lives for the Emperor. These programed robots pushed the sanity of a civilization to unquestionable obedience. Everyone understood their duty, and could not rest until they served their Emperor with all their beings with any concept of their individualism erased. The ability for another human or a position given a human completely to reprogram all conception of good and evil, without the use of fear or threat of punishment, troubled the heavens. Jehovah had desired to allow humankind to keep his freewill, yet now in order to preserve that freewill Jehovah would now need to keep safeguards in place. Humanity now also needs to take more responsibility to police the evils produced by their species, especially when considering so many killers who came close to the horrors of the Emperor in the twentieth century. The disturbing factor in the Emperors killings was the absence of a clear cause or physically visible purpose for so much bloodshed. Hitler had the terror of his severe tortures. Bloody Mary used the perception of eternal damnation. Contrarily the

Emperor naturally elicited a concept of eternal disappointment such that eternal disappointment can be without regard to good or evil.

Now the heavens grew dark. I could see no light, the only exception being in a small white sprinkle. As I searched the small white point, it began to expand. It soon became as a world before me. I now gathered that I was in its clouds. The clouds resembled waves upon a giant sea. In front of me stood a tall woman with long black hair, and two small black wings. She held up her long black gown with her right hand, raising it much higher than her head. Her raised gown appeared to be giving birth to many small shards of black. Behind her appeared a small round cage with a carnivorous black bird injecting his head into it, as it sat upon what could be a small island. It was hard to determine for the waves between us worked hard to conceal it. I then spoke out asking, "What is your name and where is this place?" She answered, "I am Hekate, the Goddess of the graves, witchcraft, underworld, and demons. You are now at the gateway between time and the underworld. I shall now show you the great evils of those who listened to demons of evil and acted upon their wishes. Hark back to knowing that no evil demon may control the actions of any who live in the flesh upon the Earth. Moreover, any are falling prey to their words of evil may call upon the Lord God and he shall set them free. This truth I always protect. As he sent you, the Queen of Evil free, he would have done the same unto these slaves of their own vices." I then looked at her and said, "Truly the Lord is blessed to have one such as you guarding his truths." Hekate then said unto me, "I am fortunate to be serving you today. The heavens tell me that Jehovah has great works in his future to share with you." This brought some relief for me, as only a short time before I feared being imprisoned with Sammael for eternity on the planet of misery. I am now starting to feel like fashion, one day in and one day out. I will have to incorporate methods to keep me in much more than sending me out.

Then now there appeared before me Eurynome, the mother that fashions revenge, power, love, jealousy. Those who follow me believe their acts not to be wrong, as they refuse to see the truth. I am she who torments Temujin. His evil and love for power gave him the largest empire ever on earth as he conquered two continents. Genghis Khan's great mercy was to offer his prey the chance to surrender before proceeding to destroy everything in their sight. Some nations took over one-half a millennium to return to the population levels they had before Genghis destroyed their nation. His love for power led almost fifty million flesh dwellers to the world of the spirits. Since none in battle could take his life, the demons of the seas swallowed him.

Another now stood before me saying, "I am Forneus, and commander of twenty-nine legions, with the power to make one loved by all friends and enemies the same. I am he who torments Caligula, who believing himself to be a god added great misery to empire created in the image of Lucifer.

Caligula was contrasting with maintaining his sanity. What started with a little gambling, and wasteful spending, quickly turned into an extravaganza of bloody pandemonium. Nevertheless, killings become one of his favorite pastimes. He condemned his soul to eternal damnation when he also concluded that he was a god and therefore had a statue of himself established in Solomon's Temple in Jerusalem for people to worship. Jehovah subsequently burned Rome to the ground, giving her riches to the barbarians.

Hekate then shared with me, "The next to appear before us commands sixty-six legions of demons, which some may be shared with Forneus, if need be."

The next to appear and introduce himself as, "I am known as Gaap, for I may admit as true the disturbed so they may love or hate, and make men oblivious, masked, and ignorant. The one whom I torment was called Nero who executed his own mother and poisoning his stepbrother Britannicus. He burned prisoners in his garden at night as a source of light. He angered Jehovah when he burned Rome while playing music and singing in Antium, and blamed it upon the Christians. I gave into Nero his madness, the delusion that he was gifted in the arts and theatrical skills. He brought to death almost 1,800,000 Jews during his reign becoming the first emperor not to tolerate Christianity."

Now before us stood another who revealed himself as, I am called Haagenti, reigning thirty-three legions, for I torture, for eternity, the demon named Saddam Hussein. His evil spreads over twenty years as he waged genocidal campaigns against the Assyrians, Yazidis, Shabaks, Mandeans, and the Kurds. He followed the ways of his ancestors in his impulsive desire arbitrarily to invade neighboring nations. When event did not evolve in his fashion, he would punish his own people with poison gas, eradicating a predictable 1,000,000.

I then wondered to myself, why it would take thirty-three legions to torture him. In my mind appeared a glass of wine, which had the taste of words. The words revealed, "The number is needed to prevent those who wish to destroy him from succeeding." I thought again, "Why not save the trouble by letting his enemies have their revenge." Another glass of wine appeared before me and I drank from it, and these words came from my mouth, "Jehovah has found great anger in this demon for he killed those whom Jehovah gave unto him." I now decided not the think of any more questions fearing drunkenness would enslave me. This cannot be a place where a drunk spirit should tarry long.

The next to appear before me revealed to me, "I am a jinni from the days of old named Ifrit. I torture Leopold II of Belgium. He took from me the skill of cunning, my strength, and my power to capture and enslave his victims. The magic he took from me allowed him to become a great tyrant springing from a small country, which he soon outgrew going to the Congo where he enslaved, tortured, and massacred over twelve million people sanctioning him to sell some ivory and rubber."

Before me now stood one who had the look of death, which made my spirit sick. He spoke unto me saying, "Look not upon me, yet hear my words, for I am called Jikininki, and I gave my curse to Mao Zedong, that he shall forever search the pits of hell for a morsel of dead flesh. His greedy, selfish soul shall be tormented for eternity, as he chases the flesh of the one hundred million lives he destroyed, sending them into an eternity different from his." I then asked this beast, "How can he seek flesh in a lake of fire?" Jikininki now answered, "For I give unto him visions adding greatly to his torment, for his foolish soul remembers not of his previous failed attempts, believing instead they to be true." I now asked, "Why does not Jehovah give you legions to help guard this great evil?" Jikininki answered, "The weight of his sins is too heavy for he shall never be free."

Now stood before another demon, who introduced himself as, "Krampus, for it is who beat evil children and drag them to hell. I guard one who I missed dragging to hell as a child, Idi Amin Dada as few people in history are straightforwardly responsible for killing half a million people, and this Ugandan dictator is one of them. In power, he was guilty violating the rights Jehovah gave humanity, political repression, ethnic persecution, extrajudicial killings, nepotism, and corruption. Though he brought to death less than many other in their separate lakes of fire, he did more by his hand, an evil that must be beaten for eternity.

Now standing in front of me was a woman, which introduced herself by saying, "I am called Lamia, the bogey-monster, the night-haunting demon that preys upon children." I then remembered that I had met her before, as she had always made it easier for me to punish Adam by scaring his children before I took them. I torment for eternity a night terror known as Vlad the Impaler, who inspired the evil known as Dracula. A register of some of his favorite pastimes, nails in heads, strangulation, cutting off of limbs, cutting off noses, blinding, burning, and ears, mutilation of sexual organs (especially in the case of women), scalping, skinning, exposure to the elements or to animals, and boiling alive and ordered people to be impaled on stakes instilling fear in all who saw them. I give unto him now each of these torments so he shall know the suffering of each he doomed each day for eternity." I also became impaled by the visions of his crimes, asked Jehovah never to release this evil. Nevertheless, I had some more evils to witness. My spirit now came filled with anger at the evils, feeling inside me a newborn love to free flesh from such evil. This is the first time I truly had a thirst to battle evil. I had been told in the legends of old that someday I would serve the powers of good, yet I believed those tales to be lies, for there were so great rewards in allowing evil to serve me.

Now before me appeared another female, or should I say the head of a female as she wore her heart, liver, and lungs from her detached neck. She spoke saying, I am called Leyak as I haunt graveyards. I have been cursed to torment Pol Pot. He managed to relocate the entire population of Cambodia onto farms where they slaved away planting seeds that would grow into food that no one would be allowed to eat. Pol Pot, managed to starve one-third of his population to death. Pot and the Khmer Rouge were also responsible for mass executions in places known as the Killing Fields. Although no one can be certain of the death toll, it has been said that in order to save ammunition, the executions were often carried out using spades, axes, hammers, and sharpened bamboo sticks. The number of flesh, which entered into eternity prematurely, numbered almost three million. Killing because of stupidity angers Jehovah. He has always granted mercy for the needy, in order to save the innocent. A nation of farmers should have been able to feed many nations.

Now appearing onto me was who much as Lucifer resembled. I feared that Jehovah might be testing me, so I looked the other way. Hekate now appeared, as if knowing my mind, told me, "Lilith, fear not Mephistopheles, for he that once served Lucifer as one of his archangels now belongs to Jehovah." The demon who came from the eighth place of Hell spoke to me saying, "I am called Mephistopheles. I have been called to torture Hitler, who also had a hunger for more lands, or as with me levels in Hell. We both are known with a face of charm, wit, and civility; conversely, when free from public view famous for flying into our rages when in sequestered. Adolph Hitler, tried to conquer the Earth was the new weapons of mass destruction. He fought in three continents while having enemies from all the known continents. He ruined the lives of tens of millions of people, being responsible for more deaths than anybody else in history, and almost destroying an entire continent . . . all within six years. Although others killed more, the demon Adolph purposely sought out and had murdered for than six million children of Jacob." This immediately brought anger to my heart, for I knew Jacob and his struggles in Egypt. They were Jehovah's chosen people and were not made as the sands in the sea for an ugly demon (who should have crucified his barber) to destroy. I marvel at the patience that Jehovah has, for I now asked Mephistopheles, "What punishment would you give one who killed your children?" He answered, "Lilith, I came from Mars and as such may never have children, yet I do know not to kill Jehovah's children, for we were tasked to spare them. We did not save them, as we feared all on Earth would die, for the great Eagle was making eggs that could destroy cities." I thought to myself, "Lucifer and the children of Mars cannot see into the future, so how would they know about the great Eagle's eggs, as not even I know of this." I now asked Mephistopheles, "We are not in the days of this evil demon's killing, thus how can we see it." Mephistopheles answered, "I am beyond the days of this destroyer, as are you also now." I never realized that I was jumping through time as Eve and I used to jump across small streams in the garden. Had humankind actually grew to have so little mercy and only wished to kill others who breathed their same air? How could they not know that any differences were only skin deep, for inside them all was the same. All hearts are the same, only learning love from the world they live. I only marveled that enough people who could not serve evil rose to destroy this demon. I now thanked Mephistopheles, saying unto him, "Torture the beast that you guard, for as a mother, I can have no mercy on one who kills the children of my God. Jehovah must have great faith in you by giving such an important post such as this." His head now boasted with great pride, as this was what I wanted. The killing of so many Jews appeared to me to be as a slap on the Lord's face, yet to have a Christian organization not excommunicate him even raised more concern in my soul. The Lord would need an additional force to help in the battle against the 'Adam' hearts in humanity.

Now appeared before me another who introduced himself by saying, "I am called Ninurta, demon of rain, fertility, war, thunderstorms, wells, canals, floods, and the South Wind. I have been tasked to torture for eternity with the one who was called Ivan IV, during which one of his wars had 1000 prisoners brought before him, every day to be murdered, as he also killed his eldest son. His terror of evil caused approximately 220,000 souls to have their blood cry to the heavens for justice."

Although so many in Russia had dreaded the evil of Ivan, none could know that someday, one who had more evil would rise from their shores.

The next to appear beside me called himself Lempo. Lempo divulged to me, "As love can be capricious and even dangerous. Love can take control of a person and lead him to destruction. The loss of love leaves opens a garden of evil to plant itself. Whosoever eats from that garden shall perish. I have been assigned to torture for eternity the demon called Joseph Stalin, who managed to starve an entire country (The Ukraine). The level of wickedness from this man in dictatorial fashion ordered many of his closest friends and confidants executed. His total kill count was around 60 million. He killed almost six times the amount of his great rival Hitler. As I saw the suffering caused by this demon, I asked Lempo to stop the visions. Lempo denied the request by saying, "It is not I who show you these visions, and it is our Lord's will that you witness them." As I watched them, I now realized that this creation of Adam was producing demons who hungered for evil more than I had seen when I was their queen. Evil has a point where it is no longer evil but a weakness being exposed within the evil doer, which of course always brings their destruction. I am so amazed how these monsters expect humans to work non-stop with no food. I repeat all flesh functions by the same laws, food in, work out. If no food goes in, then no work goes out. These leviathans simply remove the dead human and work another to their sure death. To create channels using workers with no tools, save their hands is in keeping with the mentality of Adam.

Now, as the visions have ended I rest awaiting in no haste my next guide. He introduces himself, "I am called Ninurta, the demon from the days of old when I was a farmer, and I later became a healing Lord who released humans from sickness and the power of alien demons." I started to sit up, taking notice to this guide, for it sounded to me as he had fathered many good works. He continued, "I have been given the post of torturing one who was called Heinrick Himmler. He was second, only to Hitler in the command of their great evil. He personally directed the deaths of nearly ten million people, and when the war was not over even his former collaborators wanted anything to do with him. As with

Hitler, he laid down his flesh through his own hands." I then asked, "Could he not be more to blame for the deaths of so many Jews through his nation?" Ninurta agreed with my words saying, "Hitler ordered these things and Himmler turned his words into flesh without life." I now asked, "Why did not one destroy him?" Ninurta said, "Lilith, we know not the answer to your great question, for it is now a mystery that has no desire to be known." I then agreed that this should die with the innocent that it tore away from the surface of the Earth.

Now before I came one who was not from Mars, but from one of the alien worlds who had flesh living upon the Earth. He began by introducing himself, "I am called Namtar, the lord of death, and deliverer of those to the underworlds. I have been blessed by Jehovah to torture for eternity one who killed many of our people on your Earth. He was called, Slobodan Milosevic." I realized that with a name such as this, he must have come from another ancestry and added, "As I hope you know, I have found great comfort in the valuable aliens which have lived beside the children of Eve in peace. Those who joined Noah on the lower decks of his ark may have actually saved his children and their families, although they quickly reverted to their evil ways. At least they had the good works of your children to show them that not all life must be slaves of evil." Namtar now answered back, "Lilith, we all know of the goodness of your heart and have always shared in your anger for the wrong that Adam did unto you. We now rejoice in Jehovah's new goodwill towards you, as the woman who replaced you in the Garden now stands in front of all begging Jehovah to restore you." I then thought, "How can those who are so far away from the heavens know so much more than I do?" Namtar now answered, as like a fool I forgot all could now read my mind, "Lilith, you are still in the days of old, as we have yet to meet in Samaria, for I have passed through all the days till the end. I have seen the great deeds that you did for Jehovah in erasing the old Earth, so a new one could be made as a home for the saints." I answered back with words, rather than with my thoughts, "I know not of these great works, however it the work is for our Jehovah, than that I shall do." Namtar now returned with his prisoner by saying, "Slobodan Milosevic, in the opening months of his war dispossessed up to three million are killed more than 100,000 or people. Twenty-thousand Muslim women and girls are thrown into rape camps. Sarajevo, the Bosnian capital, was placed under siege, with Serbian artillery positioned in the surrounding hills bombing the city's streets and marketplaces while Serbian snipers target the unlucky and unwary. Muslims and Croats were either forced into exile as refugees, held as hostages for use in prisoner exchanges, or placed in concentration camps. Many were precipitously executed." I now stood up as Namtar stopped speaking and said, "In my heart I have no pity for one who rapes and kills girls, for the spirits of my daughters demand that seek revenge on any who harm the innocent." Namtar then reassured me that he tortured his prisoner each day by making him as one whom he killed. I then gave Namtar a hug, and acting as a diplomat said, "I do so much hope that Jehovah adds more of our brothers and sisters from the other worlds to help protect the innocent children of Eve and punish the evil sons of Adam." Namtar smiled at me and added, "Lilith, somehow I feel there is logic in what you just said, at least I have a post in which I shall be afforded much time to reflect upon this." I then while smiling and laughing said to Namtar, "That is a mission that you shall never win so reward yourself with something more pleasing to your desires."

As he faded away gracefully, another appeared beside me. I now questioned how so much evil could be produced by one history. This was more than we could expect from many solar systems combined. I can only now feel the peace within me that knows I shall be charged by Jehovah to destroy this creation gone wrong.

Now appeared beside me on who had the voice of a child sing sweet notes. He introduced himself while taking on his humane shape, "I am called Phoenix, he who speake marvellouslie of all wonderful sciences." I now wondered why he spoke with strange words. He, reading my mind, spoke saying, "I am a great Marquis. I have been given the post to torment for eternity Benito Mussolini who is responsible for killing 400,000 during the second Great War, being an ally with Hitler as they signed the Pact of Steel. He also killed 30,000 when he occupied Ethiopia. He, along with his mistress, gave up their lives in the hands of the people who suffered under his rule. His sins are magnified as he had great knowledge of good and evil having taught children for a short time being their schoolmaster. The lesson learned from his mistakes is that when you join Evil, it will take all you have, as Hitler joined Mussolini only to take all that he had, caring nothing for Mussolini's people, using their blood only to spare his fatherland's blood."

I was impressed by Phoenix's presentation. I now disclosed to him, "I have a particular hate for Hitler and all who served with him, as their heinous holocaust against the children of Jacob." Phoenix then answered, "The disobedient children of the Lord did receive excessive chastisement, which if obedient, as the children of Ishmael and of Esau the older and younger, this chastisement would not have been." I then agreed with Phoenix in thinking of the 1,000 years I burned for my great sins and how easily I almost returned to the grips of evil. Evil is an enemy that must be fought daily and every inch it takes bitterly recaptured. This would be a fight that I may someday be tasked to join. If what I go against is as creative and industrious as I was, then this will be a long and tiresome fight. As a fighter of evil, I knew not when to concede, thus for the spirits of good, I shall also erase surrender from my options.

Now before me stood a ghost of a young woman beside a peaceful sea giving her shrill laughter to a full moon. She looked at me and said, "Welcome Lilith. I am called Rusalka, one who loves to dance in open meadows and to pull evil ones into the sea only releasing to the surface their lifeless flesh. I have been tasked to torment for all times one who was called Suharto. Two million were killed following a coup attempt. So many were killed that the disposal of the corpses created a serious sanitation problem in his open graveyard, where the humid air carried the stench of decaying flesh. Small rivers and streams were clogged with bodies. He continued to kill in many new lands he fought and his struggle for power." I now took my leave from this fine and alert guard and soon another appeared before me an armed soldier with a Lion's head and riding a pale horse. He now stopped and introduced himself to me by saying, "I am Sabnock, commander of fifty legions, who has been posted to torment for eternity an evil known as Jean Kambanda. The genocide unleashed a death toll between 800,000 and 1,000,000. He had no mercy on those who stood in front of him. His heart is pure evil and I give unto him many deaths through his new painful flesh suits that he may wear. He shall never know of peace again for eternity as my legions torment the way he governed, and that is without mercy.

Now appeared a woman demon, who had dark eyes, to which I could say were almost black. She spoke to me saying, "Oh precious guest from Jehovah, I am called Samigina, it is I who can tell any who ask the condition of those who have died and passed onto another realm of existence. Jehovah has declared that I shall torture forever one who was named Leonid Brezhnev who is the source of 1.2 million fatalities and 3 million primarily noncombatants maimed or wounded. His further maltreatment to those who served the Lord caused great anguish among the heavens. Each day, he is given visions of the ones whom he caused to die and of their eternal homes. It is always a greater grief to know that those whom you destroyed may now see your destruction." I have now accepted my leave of absence as her deep black eyes even made me uneasy.

Now appearing before me was one who introduced himself as, "I am called Tannin, for it was I who opened the sea so the Israelites could leave Egypt behind Moses. I am to torture for eternity one named Mengistu who has so many spirits in his hall of shame, being responsible for human rights violations on a colossal scale. Tens of thousands were tortured, murdered, or "disappeared." Tens of thousands of people were also slain because of humanitarian law violations, during many internal armed conflicts. Many others, conceivably more than 100,000, died because of forced relocations, hundreds of thousands of intellectuals, university students, and politicians were killed. Blood flowed through his barren land, as would a river. That blood today enjoys the voices of their cries for justice being heard."

Now appearing before me was another demon. He introduced himself as Xaphan, the II, by saying, "As is with my first creation I stoke the flames of this new part of hell, as my first creation stokes the furnaces of Hell with his hands and mouth. I have been posting to torture for eternity an evil known as Kim IL Sung, who caused the death of three million killed in his greedy war with the other nation that shares the same name. Another slightly over 3,500,000 people have been murdered in his thirst for blood and almost three million pointlessly starved to death due to his refusal to cooperate with those who wished to save his people. Jehovah demands that those who have power must feed their people, and that such power is to be surrendered when their people do not receive the food that Jehovah makes available for them.

Now there appeared before me another demon. I must confess that as I have seen so much killing and murder, the fear of these things no longer grip me as the first did. This demon came forth and revealed to me, "I am called Shabriri and am known as the demon who makes people go blind. Since those upon the Earth no longer fear me, Jehovah gave me a new honorable post, for I am now he who shall torture for eternity, Pol Pot. His cold-blooded program to "purify" his society of capitalism, Western culture, religion and all foreign influences in favor of an isolated and very self-sufficient state caused two million souls to enter eternity. Towns and cities are emptied and forced to relocate to agricultural communes, the so-called "killing fields." An estimated 1.5 million are worked or starved to death, die of disease or exposure, or are summarily executed for transgressions of camp discipline. Encroachments punishable by death include not working rigid enough, dissatisfaction with living conditions, collecting or stealing food for personal consumption, wearing jewelry, engaging in sexual relations, grieving over the loss of relatives or friends and expressing religious sentiments. He may have been blind when he refused to see this suffering, yet today and every day for eternity, he shall see the evil he was the father thereof."

I have now watched this servant of the heavens return to his work, as I waited for yet another to guide me. Notwithstanding, another guide failed to appear before me. I now waited patiently, not knowing where I was or where I would go. Then before me appeared one whom I had seen before, actually the one I wished to see. Neith appeared in full and then said to me, "You are here to know the actions of some of those who dwell upon the Earth. All who murder should be here, however your burden would be too great if you were to see each of them. Upon returning to the Earth, you must be aware that the evils of the Earthmen can consume the spirits around them, through the ancient magic and works of the wizards from the alien worlds. Only through your attention to their desire to consume and destroy you, as they have been working so hard to do unto you, may you battle with them. We ask that you stay strong and fight to save what you can of Eve's children." Now I have fallen back into a sleep and felt myself returning to the warmth that I had left. Even though I was among so many lakes of fire, the empty coldness of that part of space refused to release any of the heat. The front part of my spirit was seared with light heat, yet the back part of my spirit was hard as the ice that outlined it. Now the ice was melting and flowing to my other side to revitalize the dryness therein. I now felt myself slowing down and could see a beautiful garden surround me. The smell of the flowers and crispy darker green to the leaves told me that a rain had not long ago gave them all their drink. I just lay among these flowers welcoming the joy of their beauty back into my spirit, which now knew this rose garden had indeed within it, deadly thorns that needed blood to maintain their existence. I wonder what thing of beauty gives this place its charge. Then before me appeared one who was the fulfillment of all that is of beauty. Her skin was warm as the lights, which reflected from her. Behind her were stars and a mystical world I have yet ever to see. Her wings gathered the light that came upon them, taking their powers in her spirit. A soft white silk covered what parts of her soul she made available. A could see gold lace trim laced her vest. The manor she extended her hands were not of power, but were of love and kindness. Her powerful eyes locked onto me, forbidding my freedom. I could see not her legs for the silk that surrounded them, united the land below her with the sky above her. In fear and with the greatest respect, I fell before her. She then wrestled all in my mind by declaring to me, "Lilith, do you not remember me?" I now remembered that voice, yet now had to match it to a voice. What voice could this be? She then said to me, "Do you not know the sister, whom you have told all that you love?" I then stood and said with force, "The only I have called my sister is the mother of all Earthlings, the great queen of love, my Eve." Then this spirit's warm voice flowed her words into the ears of my spirit, "Behold Lilith, it is I. I have come to comfort you." I then said unto her, "Eve, I have been freed from the chains of time only to be bound by the great evil of your children. I now can only thank El Shaddai for giving me the power to escape the chains of Adam, for if what I saw today were from my children, they would be no more."

Eve then divulged me, "I know of these sins of murder, as even the heavens have sent great plagues to erase the evil, yet it only reappears with a greater thirst for love. I now share a new hope with Jehovah that you will be his instrument to erase from the universe the evil of my children, which is greater than all known demons and devils. I pray you serve our Lord to this end." I chronicled in her, "I shall always do as Jehovah asks of me, yet with your wish I shall fight the greatest evils to triumph that which you petition. I shall be my consciousness." Eve now, with tears flowing from her eyes reported to me, "My children have found many ways to persecute so many in Jehovah's name. The apostles of our Lord commanded that his holy book not be changed, yet evil men changed to the words of the Lord for their own profit. It is these men, that as they enter before our Lord, I accuse them loud showing the Lord their deceitful deeds. I must have your help to send them to me faster, so they seeds they lay may be consumed by the birds of the skies." As our words ceased, so did Eve and I found myself before, nonetheless, another dominion uttering repeatedly my promise to Eve, the sister of my love, and through injustice the mother of these beasts that walk upon the Earth who is destroying those that are of a pure heart. As revenge is only for the Lord, those whom he commands to revenge must do so as a matter of obedience, while fighting hard to conceal the great joy of such a great and honorable work. For only the Lord turns his other cheek in the heavens. Those who slap the creation of Jehovah will themselves find the forces of heaven exactly the revenge. Thou shall not kill. Many who try of weak faith to baffle those who are of the faith by condemning others that kill in war, and in the protection of others. I remind you, that all war is wrong, yet we must render unto Caesar that which is Caesars. A voice inside all men who are in the service of their nations sets them free to defend that which the Lord has given to them and for the honor of their ancestors. Hitherto, I shall fight evil. They should now prepare for a long and hard battle before the Earth shall be no more. Now before me appeared a bright light, and said these words to me, "Lilith, Lucifer has spoken a great evil against Jehovah, demanding that he give you into him. What say you?" I said to the light, "As I have just pledged to Eve and all the masters who torment the evil, I shall now serve the Lord. I have no alliances with Lucifer. I only joined him when I had a great fear of Adam turning our Lord against me in wrath. Now that Jehovah has blessed me with a great work in his name, I no longer have that fear. He who angers Jehovah must be punished. Tell the Lord not to do as I will, but to do as he wills." The light now changed into a warm yellow and answered, "As you have said, the Lord shall know. Go now in peace and learn how the heavens had tried so hard to punish Earthmen for their sins." I now proceeded to my next station, and in this station, to my surprise were many angels and other heavenly spirits to bid me my welcome.

CHAPTER 6

The wages of sin is death

I now appeared before this new council as they requested that I make myself at ease. We now debated some issues concerning the Earthmen. They first asked me, "Lilith, how do you view sin and what is its cause?"

I did not sin while in the garden. I was created in the image of our Lord, as I now appear being blessed above the archangels with only Adam as my rival. I remember Eve telling me how Jehovah had told the young Adam that if you eat of the forbidden trees then you should surely die. I have always been confused as why he did not tell Eve, for I always believed that if he had told her, she would not have sinned. She ate of the tree not in disobedience of God. She did so to seek freedom from an eternity promising only to be the slave of Adam. She had never been granted access to the Lord, as Adam and I had. Even Lucifer had access, thus no justified reason can exist why she was denied this right. She lived her life with only the dependable love of Seth and myself. Adam naturally returned from his 130 years of mourning Abel, yet by then they had sinned. Eve needed the security of one who would defend her. He did not defend her, as Seth, his sisters and my daughters with of course me standing ready to fight all to save her honor as the mother of the Earthmen. I have recently seen the lakes of fire that contain the great murderers. Eve was too great a mother to be cursed with children such as this. I can only be thankful that I was able to break the chains of bondage from Adam for if these were my children, I would have destroyed them early in their history. If only Atlantis had not been a stole away in the depths of the oceans, this curse would have drowned on the floor of the oceans, that they could sing today of their great deed for the heavens. I often wonder if Jehovah had planned this to be the end of Earthmen, yet that is only a conjecture of a wondering mind, thousands of years to the fore. This curse was not transmitted to the children of Adam and Eve, although our El Shaddai took these great sins and punished them thru his son as a tool for forgiveness of sins. All Earthmen are born without sin. Any who sin shall surely die, thus as everyone who sinned, they did die, except for a very few as identified in the word of our God. I am very offended when I hear others say that because Eve sinned, they must die. No, sorry hoodwink, because you have sinned you must die. Do not blame Adam or Eve, for they never sinned as the Earthmen do this day. I fear to think what the Earth would be like today if the Lord had spared the flood, yet as we know within a fool generations, Nimrod built a tower that no flood would overcome in defiance of our Lord thus saying, 'You can no longer destroy us for our sins?' I must now petition to you the purpose of my visit here, for my views have no meaning on how Jehovah rules his servants."

They now revealed to me the visions I would see, telling me that sin destroys the flesh and that as sin increased so much the destroyer, for each time a destroyer is paused, and a new destroyer arrives. We shall begin by telling you how the Earthmen have defined our curse upon them. We start with epidemic, which occur when new cases of a particular disease, in a given human population, during a given period, significantly exceed what was projected. A pandemic is an epidemic of infectious disease that is spreading through human populations across a large region or worldwide. A widespread endemic disease that is constant in terms of how many people are getting sick from it is not a pandemic, yet we can make it volatile at a future time. We shall show you some attempts we made in their history to bring them back to the

Lord, as these become necessarily strangely, after the Lord released them from the commandments and gave them an easy road to gain forgiveness."

Before us now stood a new spirit who introduced himself as, "I am the spirit called Abezethibou from the Testament of Solomon and was released to cause death among the sinners. They have called my plague the Antonine Plague from 165 A.D. to 180 A.D. We were new to these forms of plagues so we combined what would later be called smallpox or measles. I was able to bring to Judgment the souls of an estimated five million people. As they lay, covered in balls of reddish sores, their medical people could do nothing is trying to comfort them as both knew the number of days remaining would be few. Prominent people killed by my epidemic included Roman emperors Lucius Verus and his co-regent Marcus Aurelius Antoninus. The Roman Empire needed a wakeup call, as they needed to be set on the path to advance the gospels." I then complained, "What about the innocent that dies with them?" Abezethibou answered, "We attempt to make these contagious by an airborne virus, thus injecting it into evil first. Some innocent do suffer, yet the righteous who separate themselves from the evil are spared." I then told Abezethibou, "I guess as long as we are trying, and the righteous do received their reward for eternity, the guarantee of an earlier reward is better than the loss of a late reward, as when evil surrounds one, which one usually falls." He then gave his leave and we waited for the next demon to appear. He emerged and told introduced, 'I am he who is called Ornias from the Testament of Solomon and one who falls like shooting stars to the Earth." I then acknowledged I have seen him above the throne and that Lucifer had told me he was also from his Mars." He agreed and continued, "I was to give into the Romans the Plague of Cyprian from 251 A.D. to 270 AD. the Plague pandemic known as Plague of Cyprian is probably of smallpox. We continue to use this plague enjoying its effectiveness. Although the Earthmen were given a vaccine for it near the end times through the deeds of a betrayer in the heavens, we continued to use it, effectively, up until the twentieth century. At the pinnacle of the outbreak, 5,000 people a day died in Rome. It was still raging in 270 A.D. when it claimed the life of emperor

Claudius II Gothicus who ruled 268 A.D. to 270 A.D. It is named after Saint Cyprian, an early Christian writer who beheld and described the plague. Sadly, the Romans now worked on changing Christianity to incorporate their ideologies. More death would be forthcoming as the stubbornly held on to their sinful ways."

As he descended, another ascended. This demon identified himself by saying, "Baalberith, one who has greet credit and powers according to legends of the Earthmen, as they credit me as the source of many vices and positions. They claim me to be the chief secretary of Hell, controller of its public archives, and the demon who tempts men to murder and blasphemy. I reveal occurrences of the past, present and future with answers they believe to be true. They claim that I can change metals into gold and make kings rich make them wise like me being quite an articulate sort. Their history of successful exorcises, include many about me, as when I depart I also render the names of the saints who would be most effective in opposing me. I do marvel at my enemies in what they will do to oppose me, yet have pride in reporting I have never, nor will ever be exorcised. I avoid any possession that the future warns me of exorcism. The creativity of these Earthmen against me allowed me to accept this commission from Jehovah with great honor, for it was I who released to the Earthman the Plague of Justinian from 541 A.D. to 542 A.D. The pandemic known as the Plague of Justinian afflicted the Byzantine Empire including its capital Constantinople and killed as many as 100 million people across their world. Bubonic plague was the cause of the pandemic. They named this after their Eastern Roman Emperor Justinian I. This jolt forever erased any dreams of a recovery for the Roman Empire, as Justinian now could only hope to save the remnants he remaining." I then asked, "Baalberith, I noticed you moved away from small pox and thus were able to kill as many as the great murderers did." Baalberith then answered, "Lilith, we did give them two warning plagues and plenty of time for even new generations to return to the good spirits, yet they did not return." I then realize what he said to be true agreed, "That which you say is of the truth." I am impressed with the quality of their answers and the method in which the go straight to the heart of the issue. I gave him permission to leave and as he faded away, another replaced him.

This new spirit appearing as a pale old man riding a crocodile, "I am he who is called Agares, ruling thirty-one legions. The legends of my powers claim I can make runaways come back and those who run stand still, that I find pleasure in teaching immoral expressions and that I have the power to destroy dignities, both temporal and supernatural. I do truly enjoy the immoral expressions, as we had nothing like that during our days on Mars. Immoral expressions have no value in the spiritual realm. They can only enjoy by the foolishness of the Earthmen. I learned all these expressions from them, as we have no such knowledge in our realm. We all know that I, nor any in the heavens, save Jehovah, can destroy supernatural dignities, unless they are fictional created among the Earthman. When Jehovah accepted this plague from the counsel of the great saints, he knew the time had arrived to remove as much evil as possible and to send a message that would flow through the portals of time. You have discovered that our message was not observed, as we had desired, for Jehovah in his mercy allowed the few remaining Earthmen to continue, only to create greater killing technologies, as you saw during your time with the everlasting lakes. I released upon the Earth what became known as the Black Death from 1348 A.D. to 1350 A.D. that left the lands covered with rotting flesh. The time for playing had ended and we now decided to shake the Earth with the thunder of the graves as shovels broke the silence. This is among the deadliest pandemics the world has ever experienced. Therefore, it is rightfully labeled as the Black Death. This bubonic plague outbreak have started in Central Asia and reached Crimea in 1346 A.D. The Black Death also has known variants as the Bubonic plague, pneumonic plague, septicemic plague. I will show you how I used variants of my plague and how it destroyed its victim, in summary, Bubonic plague has tumors (buboes) ranging in size from an egg to an apple. Survival only up to seven days. Pneumonic plague attacks lungs, most virulent, spread by air. Survival only one to two days. Septicemic plague—most deadly, attacking blood system and causing gangrena and black/purple spots and gangrene. I was able to send sixty percent of the Europeans to eternity in just three years. My plague returned at various times until the nineteenth century. I spread it by fleas and allowed rats to carry it. I remind you that the Black Death outbreak (1348-1350) was a combination of bubonic plague, pneumonic plague, septicemic plague, and hunger. Plague victims would die within one to seven days. The Black Death is estimated to have killed 30% to 60% of Europe's population, reducing the world's population from a calculated just about 450 million to between 350 and 375 million in 1400. I returned this plague at various times, resulting in a larger number of deaths, until it left Europe in the nineteenth century. This effectively reorganized the land distribution within Europe, as the available land was renowned and thus reducing the available cheap labor for the land barons. They released their anger and thus created the need for this plague to resurface. Jehovah found anger in the people who tried to place this blame on his Jews by extending the plague. This was somewhat effective, yet the church now had an evil within its walls and even in the face of death before it, held fast to its folly." As I looked across the lands, I even saw a beautiful young princess leave English with the hope of a new royal life be stricken to her death, as in death she now had the same rank as the pheasants. The space above the Earth looked as if it were a snowstorm as so many spirits were raised to their judgment holdings, the saints for their new mansions and the wicked to their new, new crowded lake of fire. I noticed how the horses and dogs were now sporting only their bones. Even the scavengers feared eating the dead carcasses. Armies no longer worried about foreign invaders as they worked along with the poor to remove the ocean of dead obnoxious bodies that flooded the land. None could enter the churches as so many dead bodies flooded their gates. Many religious rituals were modified in order to protect their priests as much as possible. As the church recessed to protect itself, showing a loss of faith, the people followed suit." We saw our current guest vanish, as I nor did the council have any questions.

Now before we appeared another thing! Before me now was a human with claws instead of hands and feet, a head of a unicorn, and trumpet to denote his powerful voice. He began by saying, "I am Andrealphus, though known by many names, as I too command twenty-nine legions.

As I can make trees bend at will, I prefer commanding the music in Hell. I am not known as a kind, yet as all bend to the voice of Jehovah and thus for a few years I scared the Italians, hoping many more would heed to my warning. I am the enforcer of the Italian Plague from 1629 A.D. to 1631 A.D, which I unleashed as a series of outbreaks of bubonic plague in northern Italy. This epidemic, often referred to as the Great Plague of Milan, claimed the lives of approximately 280,000 people. I hit the cities of Lombardy and Venice as they suffered the highest death rates. Are plagues now would be less intense, yet saving our wrath to unleash a few centuries, forthcoming? These were to be reminders of what we had done in the bygone. Yet sadly, sin continued to progress as so many believe it now to be an issue with the quickly decaying remnants of the Holy Roman Empire. We would have to visit the Earth soon visiting a nearby country." I was now feeling better, that Jehovah was giving reminders, and using all my knowledge could not understand why the foolish Earthman would not bury their sins with those who were suffering their punishments. Such is the way of dupes. As Andrealphus appear, he disappeared.

Now appeared another strange creature, which I can only describe as a behemoth with three mouths, six eyes, and three heads, with one mouth, and two eyes each, cunning, strong, and being demonic. He began by saying, "I am he who is called Aži Dahāka. Jehovah called upon me to unleash a plague upon the land, which was persecuting those whom called upon the Lord. My plague was called the Great Plague of Seville, which was from 1647 A.D. to 1652 A.D., which was the greatest plague that punched Spain in the 17th century. This enormous outbreak of disease killed 150,000 people in Seville and altogether Spain had lost 500,000 people, out of a population of slightly fewer than 10,000,000. This message was clear, beginning only seven years after the last indexes to the counter-reformation of the Spanish Inquisition. We had now visited Rome and gave Spain a solid punch, yet one nation continued to disturb Jehovah." The council now revealed unto me additional heinous crimes by the Spanish, which left me only praising the mercy of Jehovah that allowed any Spanish to remain upon Adam's world.

Now appearing before us was another from King Solomon, the commander of thirty-six legions also being a Jinni. He began his introduction by saying, "I am the one who is called Dantalion, and am reported in the Lesser Key of Solomon as, 'a Duke Great and Mighty, appearing in the Form of a Man with many Countenances, all Men's and Women's Faces; and he hath a Book in his right hand. His Office is to teach all Arts and Sciences in any; and to declare the Secret Counsel of any one; for he knoweth the Thoughts of all Men and Women, and can change them at his Will. He can cause Love, and show the Similitude of any person, and shows the same by a Vision, let them be in what part of the World they Will.' My work finished with Solomon, yet I found the ages difficult to live up to such a higher title as the King gave into me. Jehovah gave unto me the Great Plague of London from 1665 A.D. to 1666 A.D. and in 1666 the Great Fire of London that destroyed much of the center of London and helped kill off some of the black rats and fleas that carried the plague. This Black Death began in n London in the poor, overcrowded parish of Saint Giles-in-the-Field. It started slowly at first but by May of 1665 A.D., forty-three had died. In June 6,137 people died, and in July 17,036 people and at its crowning in August, 31,159 people died. In all, fifteen percent of the population takes their last breath during that terrible summer. Many of the rich were able to escape London and living in their other estates, as even the King, Charles II and his Court left London and fled to Oxford, all leaving behind the poor, which gave them the power they held. Many of the poor, seeking hope believed that holding a posy of flowers to the nose kept away the plague and to this day judges are still given sweet-scented bunch of flowers to clutch on ceremonial occasions as a protection against the plague! Thus came this nursery rhyme as originally created,

Ring a Ring O' Roses,

A pocketful of posies,

Atishoo! Atishoo!

We all fall down **dead**!

Throughout England, this Great Plague was the colossal outbreak of bubonic plague. The disease killed a calculated approximately 100,000 people or twenty percent of London's population. The plague spread throughout many parts of England. York was one city terribly shaken. The plague victims were buried outside the city walls and they have never been disturbed since then, as a precaution against a resurgence of the dreaded plague. The grassy mounds below the walls that can be seen as York is approached are the sites of these plague pits. The plague lasted in London until the late autumn when the colder weather helped kill off the fleas. Jehovah was greatly pleased when he saw Mompesson preaching in the open air during the time of the plague, on a rock in now called Cucklett Church. The Great Plague of 1665 A.D. was the last major out-break of the plague in England, ending in the fall of 1666 A.D. Yet, London had another painful hit to add some reality to the rich who had fled the city to avoid the plague. The fire started on September 1, and due to the hot dry summer, the fire raged, so great that within a few days, half of London was in flames By September 4. King Charles II joined the fire fighters, passing buckets of water to them in an attempt to quell the flames, but the fire raged on. As a last resort, gunpowder was used to blow up houses that lay in the path of the fire, and thus created an even bigger firebreak. The sound of the explosions started rumors that a French invasion was taking place . . . that gave rise to even more panic! The fire had been defeated by September 6, yet the mission had been completed; only one fifth of London remained. Practically all the civic buildings had been destroyed as well as 13,000 private residences; on the contrary, only six people had died. Thus, both the rich and poor got a taste of loss." This sent enough shock waves throughout Europe that Jehovah was able to wait almost one-half of a century before giving another nation in this area another wake up call." As I watched the fire burn the riches belonging to the wealthy, I had some peace to my mind, for the poor only now enjoyed the worthless trash left behind with their comrades dead bodies. England would not be free from the grips of death for they would have a courting with death delivered by the hands of Hitler.

Our guest departed as now arrived another of what we could tell sported some royalty. He introduced himself as, "Corson, one of the four principal kings that have power in the seventy-two demons constrained by King Solomon, according to the Lesser Key of Solomon, and is not to be conjured except on great occasions." I then spoke out saying, "Oh King, Corson, does this qualify as a great occasion?" He stepped forward, executing a gracious royal bow and said, "It is indeed, for a chance to tell of my victorious works for Jehovah in commanding the Great Plague of Marseilles of 1720 A.D. This was our first attack against the destroyers of the Templers on that dreaded Friday, the 13th and I took my duties to be serinto, as I gave unto France the Great Plague of Marseilles as one of the most significant European outbreaks of bubonic plague in the early 18th century, being the last time we gave a significant outbreak of the Bubonic plague. Arriving in Marseilles, France in 1720, the disease killed 100,000 people in the city and the surrounding provinces. The Grand-Saint-Antoine, a boat from the Levant from the Syria region, docked in Marseilles on May 25, 1720 was the source of the epidemic. Indeed, its cargo consisting of fabrics, cotton balls, and 300,000 books for sale at the fair of Beaucaire in July mysteriously was contaminated. Serious carelessness, and despite a very stringent protection stratagem including the quarantine of passengers and goods, the plague spread in the city. The oldest and poorest neighborhoods were the most affected. The plague spreads rapidly in the city where 90,000 inhabitants, and in the providence where it was 100,000 victims on a population of approximately 400,000 inhabitants." I then asked the council if this was not a case of greed, where public officials cared more about the sale of their property than the safeguards against this plague. The council agreed and confessed this the reason Jehovah decided to save this plague for the end times, as the poor continue to get hit the hardest. I then asked, "Since the poor among the Earthlings continually see their numbers increase while their wealth decreases, and the rich see their numbers decrease as their wealth increases would not this be a problem for all diseases? What happened to give unto the poor and clothe the naked, if they indeed wish to be clothed of course?" The council agreed to debate this after discussing more diseases and the great wars.

Our new guide appeared to bow to the King as he departed. The new guide, who was an animal creature, introduced him as an Indian Spirit. It had been since the garden that I heard an animal speak. He began his summary introduction as follows, "I am called Uktena and said to be comprised of animistic peoples from all over the world. Most are of Native American tradition, though adopted werewolves are from a variety of backgrounds. My followers are a tribe of mystics, soothsayers and magicians; because of our close ties to the magic and knowledge of the esoteric many fear that there are those among them who may be turning to the Dark Arts, and our history of having our land gradually taken from us have made some of my Uktena very bitter indeed. My main talent lies in the sealing of Miseries, and as such, we have deeper knowledge of the supernatural than other tribes find comfortable. Jehovah was not comfortable with the way the Indians were being persecuted and decided to bring them to his heavens and reduce that which the Spanish could torment. I thus orchestrated and executed the smallpox epidemic of 1775 A.D. through 1782 A.D. during the period encompassing the American Revolutionary War. General Washington alleged that the British were using the smallpox disease as a form of biological warfare by placing disease infested people into the American military camp. General Washington chose to use a process of inoculation to protect his soldiers from this deadly disease. When exposed, if the soldier survived he would be immune, however they would be unfit for weeks and if the British attacked, the war would be lost. His gamble worked allowing him to survive the British biological warfare. Smallpox was considered more of a threat to the Americans. The British acknowledged that their commanders ordered the smallpox campaigns. This smallpox epidemic exploded across much of North America killing more than 130,000 non-Indian people. Tens of thousands of people died throughout Mexico from the smallpox beginning in 1779. Smallpox then swept through the Pueblos of New Mexico beginning in 1780. We sent the virus on Columbus' first voyage to America, almost 300 years earlier, bringing this virus to America and led to its progressive spread across most of the continent of North America, infecting virtually every part of the continent to include Alaska. All on this continent were effected as we moved across the races and income levels. It also killed 400,000 in Europe yearly during this period. The Indian population dropped from twelve million to 235,000. It also caused one-third blindness." I was puzzled at how much of the Indian population had been destroyed. Our speaker, reading my mind answered, "Lilith, Jehovah knew of the terrible evil that was infesting the Americas and the Indian spirits who also knew begged him to bring many of their children home, leaving only enough to present a challenge for these European killers." I was impressed that he was able to get such a great incubation to allow the virus to spread so effectively. The war in the colonies allowed the disease to have better conditions, although the Earthmen were beginning to have a greater desire to survive such devastations. I gave this strange, but effective, creature its ambitious leave.

Now appearing before us was a couple that was half-human and half snake. They introduced themselves as Nüwa and Fuxi. The further bragged how they had created the Chinese people by molding them from clay for their companionship. Nüwa now stated, "We are worshipped as the ultimate ancestor of all humankind. As we sit here, we confess to you that we of course have never stated that we were the ultimate ancestors of all humankind, however do take credit, with the help of Jehovah, for establishing the Asian races. We have always pushed them to work harder, as Jehovah continues to favor the other races for being closer to the images of Jacob's children. We do acknowledge that he has shared many great blessings for our children." I then interrupted and added, "Do not have great grief Nüwa, I have been known to complain excessively about the way Eve, and I was treated in relation to Adam. We have been able to survive, as lower creatures, yet as lower creatures, we receive more lead way, as I do believe the Asian Pandemic you are about to share with us is a half of a millennium from the European whippings." Nüwa then smiled and waved for her husband to sit. I must admit, her power in this relationship impressed me, unless he had previously ordered her to give the presentation, which I could see no evidence to support this apprehension. Nüwa, once again continued, "We choreographed and executed the Third Pandemic of 1855 A.D which continued until 1959, as worldwide casualties had dropped to 200. Our third Pandemic began in the Yunnan province in China in 1855. This was another episode of the bubonic plague. It spread to all inhabited continents, and ultimately killed more than twelve million people in India and China alone. Casualty patterns indicated that waves of this pandemic might have been from two different sources. The first was primarily bubonic and was carried around the world through ocean-going trade, through transporting infected persons, rats, and cargoes harboring fleas. The second, more virulent strain was primarily pneumonic in nature with a strong person-to-person contagion. This strain was largely confined to Asia, particularly Manchuria and Mongolia. The bubonic plague was endemic in populations of infected ground rodents in central Asia. It was also a known cause of death among itinerant and conventional human populations in that region for centuries; however, an incursion of new people due to political conflicts and global trade led to the spreading of this disease throughout the world, which would explode after the first Great War. The British worked hard with other medical professionals and before the end of the nineteenth century. I knew killer would have to be released, as we tested it along with this great disease, namely the pneumonic devices that proved extremely effective with a few modification." The couple finished their message and escaped back into the private realm.

Now before us appeared a crow. I looked at the crow and asked, "Who are you and how do you appear here?" The voice asked, "Would you desire that I appear as a man? I feared doing so as many know of your dislike for men." I told the crow, "I do not dislike men; I only dislike your leader who has repeatedly betrayed me. If you are him, then you should depart quickly, for I will remove your feathers and drop you from the heavens." Then appeared before me a man who spoke saying, "I am the one called Malphas, and am a great president of hell, working hard to insure misery for your enemies, having forty legions of demons under my command, that I would surrender to you if you so desired. I build houses, high towers, helping Nimrod, and strongholds, bring down the buildings of my enemies, and can destroy my enemies' desires or thoughts and make these known to the prestidigitator, and all what they have done, give good companions and guards, and can bring quickly combine tricks to deceive others from all places of the world. I am known to accept willingly and kindly any sacrifice offered to me." I then said to Malphas, "I do appreciate your offer to give unto me your forty legions, although I need them not so rule the skies. When I was your queen, I had millions of legions to do my bidding. I do recall how your master told me that you would also gladly deceive the conjurer, thus I do believe my dealings with you will be in the light of El Shaddai only." As I sat back down, the council beside me stood up and clapped. I remember how foolish Lucifer was when he tempted the Lord for ownership of the Earth, which is not a prize unto Jehovah has completely destroyed and remade it. Malphas joined the clapping, and began his message, "I now have great pride in sharing my great deed for Jehovah before one as accomplished as you. My great work was called the Spanish flu, which lasted from March 1918 to June 1920. I used all forty of my legions to unleash onto humanity a disease death greater than all any that preceded me. The first Great War claimed an estimated sixteen million lives. The influenza epidemic that seized the world in 1918 killed an approximated fifty million people. One fifth of the Earth's population was diseased by this deadly virus. The Spanish flu pandemic spread to nearly every part of the world and was caused by an unusually contagious and deadly influenza A virus strain of subtype H1N1. The pandemic spread even to the Arctic and the isolated Pacific islands. We estimate that anywhere from 50 to 100 million people were killed worldwide. An estimated 500 million people, one third of 1.6 billion world's population at that time became infected. The plague developed in two phases. In late spring of 1918, the first phase, known as the three-day fever, appeared without warning. Few deaths were reported. Victims recovered after a few days. The Earthmen believed the nemeses had finally met their match. When the disease surfaced again that fall, it was far more austere. Scientists, doctors, and health officials could not identify this disease, which was striking so fast and so ferociously, eluding treatment and resisting control. Some victims died within hours of their first symptoms. Others perished after a few days; their lungs filled with fluid and they asphyxiated to their death. My plague did not discriminate, a fallacy of the previous disciplinary diseases. I was widespread in urban and rural areas, from the densely populated East coast to the remotest parts of Alaska. Young adults, usually unaffected by these types of infectious diseases, were among the hardest hit groups along with the elderly and young children. The flu afflicted over twenty percent of the Eagle's population. In one year, the average life expectancy for the Eagle dropped by twelve years. My great work as not being properly reported by the Earthman, as many give more emphasis on the first Great War, which I killed more by at least seven times. I did some flip-flopping as my Spanish Flu (Influenza) continued to take 36,000 yearly victims, reappearing as the Asian flu of 1956-1958. This Asian flu of 1956 to 1958 originated in China and spread to Singapore, Hong Kong and other places. The Eagle watched 69,800 people die. The worldwide death toll has been just shy of three million. My next slap has been called the Hong Kong Flu, H3N2 virus, from 1968 to 1969 killing one million people worldwide. The outbreak was caused by an H3N2 strain of the influenza A virus, descended from H2N2 through antigenic shift. About 500,000 Hong Kong residents or fifteen percent of the population was infected with the pandemic. Approximately 34,000 died belonging to the Eagle. My next sleeping giant is the Bird Flu or H5N1 virus that I introduced during 2006-2007. The World Health Organization has described this as one of the most lethal flu viruses. This infection will lead to severe pneumonia, blood poisoning, and organ failure. Scientists have reported that the three H7N9 victims describe the strain is a so-called "triple reassortant" virus with a mixture of genes from three other flu strains found in birds in Asia. This seal puts the food supply in question and will keep the advancing scientist occupied. My latest flu, carefully combining elements of my bird and pig strains, in 2009, once again uses my 1918 H1N1 virus, which has already taken 14,000 lives. This most recent pandemic, which was first identified in April 2009 and is commonly called "Swine flu." This global outbreak of a new strain of influenza virus is reported to have 94,512 confirmed cases in 122 countries with 429 deaths as of July alone. Although it is not deadly, I scared millions of people worldwide. The humans put their technology towards effectively managing this sleeping giant, which will ravish the Earth in the end times." I could only sit back and marvel how this demon was absolutely placing the whole Earth in peril, keeping his big cards to throw on the table and win the final hand. I am joyous that he and I are on the same team. The council now motioned their desire to speak. The first angel rose and spoke, "I am your servant Yesod, one of the Servants of Jehovah. Humanity so often believed throughout history that a war or the battle between ideologies would determine history. Sadly, corruption would invade the new philosophy and eventually pull things back to where they were. Such a case was the division among the communists and capitalists. So many fought hard for the preservation of capitalism, as productivity for the communists force their governments to fall, yet in capitalism another cancer arose, that being corrupt greedy government who took the wealth from the people, taking more and more until the burden was too great and collapse during the end times. As you have seen, we were able to punish through creatures so small only a microscope could down, bacteria, parasites, and viruses swept through cities and devastated populations, defeated great leaders and thinkers, and in their galvanization transformed public health, economies, and philosophies. This is our tool that can penetrate great walls and damper great wealth. Jehovah has elected to allow these in greater quantities in our End Times Restoration. The following tools we shall use during this End Time Restoration, and our need to clean the earth of evil loving flesh dwellers and fill both our heavens and well-prepared lakes of fire. Some you have seen us you previously, yet with modifications we can reenter them into our available resources. I now introduce you to Swadhisthana." Swadhisthana began by declaring, "We have allowed smallpox to remain, counting on the new generations not to take advantage of the only infectious disease to have been eradicated through vaccination. Forgotten and ignored, it shall give the wakeup call of a forgotten monster. The humans hope to employ these techniques towards other similar diseases, eradicating them by similar means. This alarms us about the need to widen our options He continued with another weapon, the struggle against Tuberculosis stimulated some of the first quests for antibiotics. The disease most likely promoted pasteurization, which heats and kills pathogens that can contaminate milk. Tuberculosis still kills two million yearly. When the disease becomes active, seventy-five percent of the cases are in the lungs. The end days gave rise to more open sexual relations, although nothing new by any means, not a new concept however, the intensity and frequencies had to be kept in check.

Syphilis once treated can become non-lethal. A sexually transmitted disease, it has infected twelve million people worldwide. The continuing belief in infectious diseases leads to the introduction of other end time reformer, HIV/AIDS. "You can't talk about infectious diseases without discussing AIDS," This is a new concept, which gives humankind a chance to control the disease through behavioral control. The HIV virus has taken three million deaths, and works by lessening the immune system's effectiveness. Thus, common illnesses can give the final blow. Obtaining from sex is the best protection. Africa is the region most affected by this, as our other attacks did limited damage on this continent. Africa is inhabited by just over twelve percent of the world's population but it is estimated to have more than sixty percent of the AIDS-infected cases worldwide. Fear and ignorance, anxiety, prejudice, isolation, and panic can all result from not understanding the nature of a disease.

Cholera harvesting itself from a lack of clean water, was, and still is, widespread in many parts of the world. Cholera is responsible for seven pandemics from 1816-1970 and twenty-three million deaths amid 1865-1917.

Malaria is one of the most lethal infectious diseases in history and produces over 300 million cases worldwide and up to three million deaths a year.

Measles has killed 200 million during last 150 years.

Ebola has produced 150,000 deaths since 1975, with a mortality rate ranging from fifty percent to ninety percent.

Tetanus kills 100,000 to 200,000 yearly mostly in Africa and Asia. Mortality rate ranges from forty percent to seventy-eight percent."

Now appearing before us was one called Manipura who began without hesitation, "We have now placed emphasis on diseases, which are among the major causes of human deaths. Millions die from diseases every year. An average of fifty-seven million individuals dies annually, most caused by diseases. Cardiovascular Disease is the world's number one killing disease. Roughly, 29.34% of annual worldwide deaths are caused by this disease. More than three million die of Cardiovascular Disease annually.

Malignant Neoplasms 'cancer' is responsible for twelve point forty-nine percent of annual worldwide deaths and in 2007, 76.6 million people died from cancer. We do have many forms of other diseases that cause harm and death. The abuse of water and air pollutions helps produce excellent opportunities for the agents to act upon." He now slowly vanished as I now told the council that, "I was perplexed with this total presentation and I need for some clarification of purpose or objective." The council began, "You were upon the Earth during the first murder, nevertheless, we believe if you would defy Jehovah and saved us all this grief. The great spiritual powers find themselves at a standstill when facing the ways of the flesh, as Jehovah designed them to survive the years as Adam. The Earthmen slowly changed their ways and world to reduce this number. The innocent blood that cried for so many ages demanded that we seek their revenge, and thus we did. Their desire to serve all that was not from El Shaddai gave rise to so many other curses that which was would now not be. They now should the holders of the signets, which are cast upon the face of the Earth. He appeared as a man made of clear gold with the arms of a bright and warm green gem that also outlined his seat and spotted the space behind him. Lights of great knowledge rushed throughout the shell of his gold. He looked upon the great balls of wisdom, which were of many colors and flooded around him. I now asked the council, "Who is that which we look upon? They answered, "He is the holder of all wisdom, Fenrirulfr." I then asked, "Why are we now looking upon Fenrirulfr?" They answered, "It is Fenrirulfr who determines the ways of all things which have not been. Jehovah now wishes that into him you speak and seek council. I appeared before Fenrirulfr who looked upon me and spoke, "Lilith, I shall take to you to the Chamber of the Knowledge of all Things." I said unto Fenrirulfr, "Oh Great Fenrirulfr, what things shall we do in this Chamber?" Fenrirulfr divulged me, "We shall watch the thoughts of time drift in the river of life." I have now stopped and looked all around me. This land had no color for only shades of gray. I looked up above all set a king, who had a crown, as I had never seen before. So many great stones release their powerful rays in all angles surrounding his head. He had a long beard that he touched under his mighty gown. His face was an aged face of power and compassion, plus anything else one could attest. The only pure light was behind him as all things were by his side or below him. To his right were two angels bowing, one large, and one small. The small one had the body of an infant yet his face told another age, for he rode on a long curvy cloud of smoke that had eyes. This dowel of smoke, like the one on the left side ended far behind the great white light behind the king. His gown had so many precious stones and fabrics that even after staring for a long time, I cannot describe its awesome beauty. In his right hand he held a cycle with the inside curve pointed to him. The dowel that flowed down his left drifted out in front into a large cloud then ran across his front, before it shifted again, one rod circling his gown as if to be drawing a line in which no one could enter. The other split ran across the Earth where I could see two rains, having another split before the second rain. In his right hand, I could see peace and worship, yet in his left hand, I saw evil and those who wished to kill. To my horror, I saw Lucifer with a cycle completely like the one the king had, both carrying them in their right hand. Lucifer was above the cross that another angel with his face to the Earth was flying with a heavy cross. His face looked down and his right hand held a nice sword with large quillon blocks. The angels on the left both had larger wings than the two on the right, which hinted to me that the two on his right spent much time around this king. On the Earth below, I saw a mighty lion with horns of rams walk, with none to challenge him, as if he had great power and stared, without fear at the dragons on the left of which the manner of the beast I know not. I counted eight heads, though he may have had more for as this beast's body grew away from me, my eyes would not give me the detail it needed to make such a determination. I could however, count ten crowns; the crown closest to me looked up at the angel with the cross. This beast stood on a hill separating the Earthmen, of many walks, and the mighty lion. Too much amazement, the feet that belonged to this beast hand the fingers of humanity, naturally larger. The Earthmen were separated into two groups, as the closest group appeared to be composed mostly of Kings, while the other group had men of many hats. I asked Fenrirulfr, "What are these things I behold?" Fenrirulfr then told me, "Lilith, you are now beholding the evil deeds of Lucifer. He works behind the king spreading all manner of evil knowledge to the Earthmen. His teachings have caused so much of the death you have seen before coming before me. I ask you Lilith, what shall we do?" I said unto Fenrirulfr, "The watchers were punished in the times of Enoch, thus so should Lucifer also be punished. Earthmen cannot have this knowledge; lest they try to harm our King." Fenrirulfr answered, "You have spoken the truth. We have judged that he be bound until the judgment day, as too many now live upon the Earth, and technology must now sustain them, even though they have not the energy to continue. A loose Lucifer would have too much to gain from such an environment. All on Earth would be subjected to extreme vulnerability." I then asked, "Should we also not have an alarm for those who came from Mars and the alien demons that now claim Earth as their home?" Fenrirulfr agreed that this could present a danger, yet knew how not to pull them out of the deep crevices that they lodge within to hide their shadows. I told him, "I know of a way. I can call my daughters on our secret network and have them take my place on the throne of evil and then pass through this solar system to capture me. I of course shall be made their prisoner. This bounty would be too great for any demon to pass. Instead of me, they will receive one of my daughters." Fenrirulfr then asked, "Will this not give great harm to your daughters, for if one were to be lost, we cannot execute this plan." I said, "Fenrirulfr, I am so touched by the care you show my daughters. All others consider them expendable. Do not worry; they will all escape freely, only needing a place to hide." Fenrirulfr then said freely, "They may hide in this Chamber of the Knowledge of all Things, for no one knows of the entry for this place." We agreed how we would execute this great plan. Fenrirulfr now took it to Jehovah only, so that none in heaven would hear it, for many angels were still partial to Lucifer. Fenrirulfr now returned as I gave him my secret scroll with my seal to lock it for my daughters. I had been earnestly looking for a way to attach them to my penance on Earth, as I also would never want them to end of in any of Jehovah's lakes, as they do keep a very safe distance as a precautionary contrivance. Fenrirulfr stressed that I would remain in here, which is an amazing place to be, indeed. I now asked Fenrirulfr, "What is the purpose of my Penance before this throne?" He explained, "Very few have ever crossed the line between evil and good, and none who were ever a Queen. That is a jump far too wide to make. Nevertheless, the universal prophecies of old spoke of a Queen of Evil from the Universe that would make such a jump. Jehovah, in sparing the children of Mars from eternal banishment, made a deal unto Lucifer if he could entice you back to Earth. Once on Earth, we got you tangled in a personality injustice with Adam, see how long you would stay. We were very surprised with the way the Eve and you became as sisters, and as you walked hand in hand saving Adam's children. The curse again you, losing one hundred children a day was removed before Eve left the Earth." I told him, "We have no way of tracking that since my daughters are so widely dispersed. It would be nice to have my daughters float back into the Milky Way where I can visit with them. I guess you also know that I too stopped the infant killings; however normal Earthling malfunctions allowed my legend to continue, even greater than if we indeed were striving to satisfy a revenge that died shortly after the garden vanished." Fenrirulfr confessed that they had noticed this, yet said nothing to me, "Unless it was merely an oversight on my part." I was relieved that either at least my position in that nightmare was acknowledged or the entire situation erased. He continued, "Lilith, the punishment part of Penance was fulfilled in the lake. The big question remained was the need to see an outward expression of repentance or wrongdoing. Your outward expressions needed time to develop, as I am sure you agree. The confession of wrongdoing has never been a predictor of true Penance as too many confess the wrongdoing, only to attempt again, using extra precautions attempting not to be discovered again. We have watched the way you feel for the actions you take and the pain you feel as you see others suffer. It is easy to see that you do not wish to give pain for sport or a show of power. Always remember, that the final history of Earth will be written in heaven and not in lost books upon the Earth." I am starting to feel more secure, and more like I belong here, as I confessed to Fenrirulfr. Fenrirulfr then told me that this was one of the reasons Jehovah shared so much with me about what was happening upon the Earth and why. I then asked Fenrirulfr, "Will the wars and diseases continue to present challenges that the earthlings may no longer be able to overcome." Fenrirulfr told me, "Not at the intensity and degree of heavenly intervention as before." He then told me I was free to join my daughters, as he handed me back my scroll, with a fresh seal my daughter had affixed untouched. This added to my peace.

CHAPTER 7

The Allegiance in Penance

I now drifted past a joyous council, to meet with my daughters. I can only feel that the council must be overexcited about me volunteering my daughters. As we are lingering around our previously agreed upon point, I was surprised at how many of my daughters had arrived. I could guess maybe three thousand. Many were so bitter when I abandoned the Queen's throne, seeing that they would lose many privileges they had previously fostered. Amazingly, my daughters tell that more will be here later; however, they are currently pulling parameter duty. I wonder now why we would be under any sort of threat, thus I ask them. They look at me strangely and ask, "What is wrong with your mother, how can you ask such a question?" Then I pull off a few of the senior girls and ask them, in which they tell me, "We have delivered the evil ones into Jehovah as you requested in your sealed scroll." I then looked at them, in total surprise and asked aloud, "How you daughters really already finished the mission I ask of you for Jehovah?" They all shouted, in a low tone, in agreement. I then asked them how it went and how they did it. They had split into three groups, with one small group appearing as Jehovah's Saints. The queen's space chariots, which they had conveniently repositioned by one of my daughters who was temporary sitting on the throne.

She was instrumental in keeping the heat off me, by sending my previous warriors on wild goose chases throughout the universe. They had to have two queen's space chariots, as the queen never went anywhere unless the decoy went above her. When the evil ones saw the decoy pass through, they flooded the space as the Queen's space chariot slowly rolled through picking them up. The decoy chariot rushed back to warn that Jehovah had an army approaching. The daughters laughed at how fast the chariots were packed. The Queens ships had special canisters that could pack armies of spirits. The canisters were placed inside the decoy ship that went on above heaven's throne. The decoy saints intercepted the ship and conducted a standard spiritual ship inspection. As they went in with canisters in normal case coverings, the swapped the canisters while inside, and thus Lucifer did not sense anything abnormal. Both Queen's chariots exited the galaxy, releasing all the extra people on the ship, which as the daughter saints took all the remaining and released daughters as prisoners back to the Milky Way. It is standard to all concentrated on the captured comrades as evil is all fight until the end or all live. This was amazing in that all my daughters returned, with only the extra warriors' from the royal court of the evil taking the evil ships back out. Jehovah had no issue with them, so no harm done. El Shaddai then called Lucifer to the throne and bound him, putting him and all his non-reformed demons from the canisters with him. We prepared our normal rewards and promotions within the daughters, as was always our standard custom. I asked my daughters why they worked so hard on this mission. They told me, "We did it because we are still angry at Lucifer for bringing you here and not protecting you from Adam." I then asked them if they noticed my curse had been lifted off them long ago. We all soon celebrated this outdated yet still refreshing news. The earth was now not feeling very bad. I then transmitted all the things the Lord had shown me about the terrible killers and diseases. Without Lucifer illegally implanting evil desires into the Earthmen, we all hoped their evil would decline. Lucifer had violated the Jehovah's commands of no contact with any who dwell upon the Earth in flesh. He had also angered some other deities who had aliens living on the Earth. Jehovah was now having special courts to open the books of lives for many in Hades to review if they had interference from Lucifer, and if so, their judgment was reviewed to insure justice. Some of my daughters surprises with tales about their adventures on Earth. They had found an old wizard named Khemmis. I asked Khemmis why sin had been so long on Earth. He told me, "Once there was a dog who sat beside his master day and night and continued to moan and moan. One day a neighbor called out to his friend, "Why does your dog moan every day?" He told the neighbor as he was walking by, "My dog has been sitting on a nail?" The man looked, while beginning to laugh asked, "Well, why does not him just move?" Then the man laughed and as he answered the surprisingly said, "Guess he is not hurting badly enough yet." Khemmis then said to me, "Lilith, for the sake of the few saints, and their chance to conquer evil, I guess Jehovah is not hurting badly enough yet?" He had so many tales of the old days. I asked him to share one with us, each of course with a hidden meaning and geared towards lovers and daughters. This would be of extra value in that I have not had much family time with my daughters since we have not really done anything together since the days we lived in the southern seas.

Khemmis began with Freda. The angels, as we know, are greatly attracted by the beauty of mortal women. Vinfarja and the king employs his numerous spirits to discover and apprehend when possible, the prettiest brides in the country. These are abducted by their fascination to his palace at MuAje, where they remain under a spell, unable to remember anything about the earthly life and pacified to passive enjoyment, as in a sweet dream, by the easy-going low melody of music, which has the power to soothe the hearer into a pleasure stupor.

There was once a great lord in this part of the country who had a beautiful wife called Freda, the loveliest bride in all the land. Her husband was so proud of her that day after day he had festivals in her honor; and from morning till night his castle was filled with lords and ladies, and nothing but music and dancing and feasting and hunting and so many of the possible pleasures. One evening while the feast was jolly, and Freda floated through the dance in her robe of silver diaphanous clasped with jewels, brighter and beautiful than the stars in heaven, she suddenly let go the hand of her partner and sank to the floor losing consciousness. They carried her to her room, where she lay long completely oblivious; nevertheless, she woke up towards morning and announced that she had passed the night in a beautiful palace, and was so happy that she longed to sleep again and go there for her dreams. They watched by her all day, although when the shades of evening fell dark on the castle, low music was heard at her window, and Freda again fell into a deep spell from which nothing could awaken her. Her elderly nurse that was to watch her, on the other hand, the woman grew somnolent in the silence and fell asleep, and never woke until the sun had risen. When she looked towards the bed, she saw to her terror that the young bride had vanished. The whole household was awakened at once, and then searched everywhere, but no sign of her could be found in the entire castle, or in the park, or in the gardens. Her husband sent messengers in every direction, but to no resolve, no one had seen her, no sign of her could be discovered, living or dead.

Then the young lord mounted his swiftest stallion and galloped off to Knockma, to question Vinfarja, the demon angel king. The young lord wondered if he could give any tidings of the bride, or direct him where to search for her. He and Vinfarja were friends, and many a good barrel of Spanish wine had been left outside the window of the castle at night for the angels to carry away, by order of the young lord. Nevertheless, he little envisaged now that Vinfarja himself was the traitor. Hence, he galloped on like frenzied until he reached Knockma, the hill of the angels. As he stopped to rest his horse by the small stream, he heard voices in the air above him, and one said, "Veracious glad is Vinfarja now, for he has the beautiful bride in his palace at last; and never more will she see her husband's face." "Yet," answered another, "If he digs down through the hill to the center of the earth, he would find his bride; but the work is hard and the way is difficult, and Vinfarja has more power than any mortal man." "That is yet to be seen," exclaimed the young lord. "Neither angel, nor devil, nor Vinfarja himself shall stand between me and my wonderful young wife;" and in an instant he sent word by his servants to gather all the workers and laborers of the country around with their spades and pickaxes, and dig through the hill until they came to the fairy palace. The workers came, an enormous crowd of them, and they dug through the hill all that day until a great deep trench was made down to the very center. Then at sunset they left off for the night; but next morning when they assembled again to continue their work, witness, all the clay was put back again into the trench, and the hill looked as if never a spade had touched it, for so Vinfarja had ordered; and he was powerful over earth and air and sea. Nonetheless, the young lord had a brave heart, and he made the men go on with the work; and the trench was dug again, wide and deep into the center of the hill. And this went on for three days, but always with the same result, for the clay was put back once more each night and the hill looked the same as before, and they were no nearer to the demon angel palace. Then the young lord was ready to die for rage and grief, on the contrary, suddenly, he heard a voice near him like a whisper in the air, and the words it said were these: "Sprinkle the earth you have dug up with salt, and your work will be safe." Upon this, new life came into his heart, and he sent word through all the country to gather salt from the people; and the clay was sprinkled with it that night, when the men had left off their work at the hill. Next morning they all rose up early in great anxiety to see what had happened, and there to their great joy was the trench all safe, just as they had left it, and all the earth round it was untouched. Now the young lord knew he had power over Vinfarja, and he asked the men to work on with a good attitude, for they would soon reach the demon angel palace now in the center of the hill. Thus, by the next day a great chine was cut right through deep down to the middle of the earth, and they could hear the demon music if they put their ear close to the ground, and voices were heard round them in the air. "See now," said one, "Vinfarja is sad, for if one of those mortal men strike a blow on the angel palace with their spades, it will crumble to dust, and fade away like the mist." "Then let Vinfarja give up the bride," said another, "and we shall be safe." On which the voice of Vinfarja himself was heard, clear like the note of a silver bugle through the hill. "Stop your work," he said. "Oh, men of Earth lay down your spades, and at sunset the bride shall be given back to her husband. I, Vinfarja, have spoken." Then the young lord ordered them to stop the work, and lay down their spades until the sun went down. At sunset, he mounted his great chestnut stallion and rode to the head of the chine. He watched and waited; and just as the red light flushed all the sky, lie saw his wife coming along the path in her robe of silver diaphanous, more beautiful than ever; and he sprang from the saddle and lifted her up before him, and rode away like the storm wind back to the castle. There they lay, Freda on her bed, but she closed her eyes and spoke no word. Therefore, day after day passed, and still she never spoke or smiled, but seemed like one in a stupor. Great sorrow fell upon every one, for they feared she had eaten of the fairy food, and that the enchantment would never be broken. Therefore, her husband was very miserable. However, one evening as he was riding home late, he heard voices in the air, and one of them said, "It is now a year and a day since the young lord brought home his beautiful wife from Vinfarja; but what good is she to him? She is speechless and like one dead; for her spirit is with the demon angels though her form is there beside him." Then another voice answered, "And so she will remain unless the spell is broken. He must unloose the girdle from her waist that is fastened with an enchanted pin, and burn the girdle with fire, and throw the ashes before the door, and bury the enchanted pin in the earth; then will her spirit come back from Fairyland, and she will once more speak and have true life." Hearing this the young lord at once set spurs to his horse, and on reaching the castle hastened to the room where Freda lay on her couch silent and beautiful like a waxen figure. Then, being determined to test the truth of the spirit voices, he untied the girdle, and after much difficulty extracted the enchanted pin from the crinkles. Still Freda spoke no word; then he took the girdle and burned it with fire, and strewed the ashes before the door, and he buried the enchanted pin in a deep hole in the earth, under a fairy thorn, that no hand might disturb the spot. After which he returned to his young wife, who smiled as she looked at him, and held forth her hand. His great joy in witnessing the soul coming back to the beautiful form, thus he raised her up and kissed her. Her speech and memory came back that moment, and all her former life, just as if it had never been broken or interrupted; but the year that her spirit had passed in the demon angel land seemed to her but as a dream of the night, from which she had just awoke. After this Vinfarja made no further efforts to carry her off; but the deep cut in the hill remains to this day, and is called "The Grand Canyon" So no one can doubt the truth of the story as here told." We all enjoyed this tale as it showed what we all wanted the most and that was a strong determined male to protect us and strike to keep us safe. A few of my daughters had such male spirits and they had become an integral part of our large family in Earth measures.

Khemmis began with his second story, The Little Cherry twig.

Once there lived a rich storekeeper, whose business required that he travel out of the country. Departing, he said to his three daughters, "Dear daughters, I would like to have something nice for you when I return. What should I bring home for you?" The oldest one said, "Father dear, a beautiful pearl necklace for me!" The second one said, "I would like a finger ring with a diamond stone." The youngest one cuddled up to her father and whispered, "Daddy, a pretty green cherry twig for me." "Good, my dear daughters," said the storekeeper, "I will remember. Farewell." The storekeeper traveled far and purchased many goods, but he also faithfully remembered his daughters' wishes. To please his eldest he had packed a costly pearl necklace into his baggage, and he had purchased an equally valuable diamond ring for the middle daughter. However, much he tried; he could not find a green cherry twig. For this reason, he went on foot a long distance on his homeward journey. This way led him in large part through the woods, and he hoped thus finally to find a cherry twig. However, he did not succeed, and the good father became very depressed that he had not been able to fulfill the harmless request of his youngest and dearest child. Finally, as he was sorrowfully making his way down a path that led through an opaque forest and next to a crowded brush, his hat rubbed against a twig, and it made a sound like hailstones falling on it. Looking up he saw that it was a green cherry twig, from which was hanging a cluster of golden nuts. The man was delighted. He reached his hand up and plucked the magnificent twig. However, in that same instant, a wild Kodiak shot out from the brush and stood up on his back paws, growling fiercely, as though he were about to tear the storekeeper to pieces. With a terrible voice he bellowed,

"Why did you pick my cherry twig, you, why? I will eat you up!" Shaking and trembling with fear the storekeeper said, "Dear Kodiak please, do not eat me. Let me continue on my route with the little cherry twig. I will give you a large ham and many sausages for it!" However, the Kodiak bellowed again, "Keep your ham and your sausages! I will not eat you, only if you will promise to give me the first thing that meets you upon your arrival home." The storekeeper gladly agreed to this, for he recalled how his poodle usually ran out to greet him, and he would gladly sacrifice the poodle in order to save his own life. Following a crude handshake, the Kodiak trudged back into the brush. The storekeeper, breathing a sigh of relief, went hurriedly and happily on his way. The golden cherry twig decorated the storekeeper's had splendidly as he hurried homeward. Filled with joy, the youngest girl ran to greet her dear father. The poodle followed her with bold leaps. The oldest daughters and the mother were not quite so fast to step out the door and greet their father. The storekeeper was horrified to see that the first one to greet him was his youngest daughter. Concerned and saddened, he withdrew from the happy child's embrace, and following the initial greetings told them all that had happened with the cherry twig. They all cried and were very sad, but the youngest daughter showed the most courage, and she resolved to fulfill her father's promise. The mother soon thought up a good plan. She said, "Dear ones, let's not be afraid. If the Kodiak should come to hold you to your promise, dear husband, instead of giving him our youngest daughter, let us give him the shepherd's daughter. He will be satisfied with her." This proposition was accepted. The daughters were happy once again, and they were very pleased with their beautiful presents. The youngest one always kept her cherry twig with her, and she soon forgot the Kodiak and her father's promise. Nevertheless, one day a dark carriage rattled through the street and up to the front of the storekeeper's house. The ugly Kodiak climbed out and walked into the house growling. He went up to the startled man and asked that his promise be fulfilled. Quickly and secretly, they fetched the shepherd's daughter, who was very ugly, dressed her in good clothes, and put her in the Kodiak's carriage. The journey began. Once outside the town, the Kodiak laid his wild shaggy head in the shepherd girl's lap and growled, "Tussle me, scuffle me, soft and gentle, behind my ears. Otherwise, I will eat you, skin, and bone." The girl began to do so, but she did not do it the way the Kodiak wanted her to, and he realized that he had been deceived. He was about to eat the disguised shepherd girl, but in her fright she quickly fled from the carriage. Then the Kodiak rode back to the storekeeper's house and, with terrible threats, demanded the right bride. Consequently, the dear maiden had to come forward, and following a bitterly sorrowful farewell, she rode away with the ugly bridegroom. Once outside the town, he laid his coarse head in the girl's lap and growled again, Tussle me, scuffle me, soft and gentle, behind my ears, Otherwise I will eat you, skin and bone. Moreover, the girl did just that, and she did it so softly that it soothed him, and his terrible Kodiak countenance became friendly. Progressively, the Kodiak's poor bride began to gain some trust toward him. The journey did not last long, for the carriage traveled extremely fast, like a whirlwind through the air. They soon came to a very dark forest, and the carriage suddenly stopped in front of a dark and yawning cave. This was where the Kodiak lived. Oh, how the girl quaked! The Kodiak embraced her with his claw-arms and said to her with a friendly growl, "This is where you will live, my little bride; and you will be happy, as long as you behave yourself here, otherwise my wild animals will slash you apart." As soon as they had gone a few steps inside the dark cave, he unlocked an iron door and stepped with his bride into a room that was filled with poisonous worms. They hissed at them rapaciously. The Kodiak growled into his little bride's ear, "Do not look around! Neither right nor left, while straight ahead, and you shall be safe!" Then the girl did indeed walk through the room without looking around, and all the while not a single worm stirred or moved. In this manner, they went through ten more rooms, and the last one was filled with the most terrible creatures, dragons, and snakes, toads swollen with poison, basilisks, and land worms. In each room the Kodiak growled, "Do not look around! Neither right nor left, however straight ahead, and then you are safe!" The girl trembled and quaked with fear, like the leaves of an aspen, but she remained steadfast and did not look around, neither right nor left. When the door to the twelfth room opened up, a glistening stream of light shone toward the two of them. The most beautiful music sounded from within, and everywhere there were cries of joy. Before the bride could comprehend this, she was still trembling from seeing such horrible things, and now this surprising loveliness, there was an abysmal clap of thunder, and she thought that earth and heaven were breaking apart. It was soon quiet once again. The forest, the cave, the poisonous animals, and the Kodiak had all disappeared. In their place stood a splendid castle with rooms decorated in gold and with beautifully dressed servants. The Kodiak had been transformed into a handsome young man. He was the prince of this magnificent castle, and he pressed his little bride to his heart, thanking her a thousand times, that she had redeemed him and his servants, the wild animals, from their enchantment. She was now a high and wealthy princess, but she always wore the beautiful cherry twig on her breast. It never wilted, and she especially liked to wear it, because it had been the key to her good fortune. Her parents and sisters were soon informed of this happy turn of events. The Kodiak prince had them brought to the castle, where they lived in splendid happiness forever after." We all applauded our new storyteller as I could see that minds in my daughters spinning hundreds ways a second. We all were enchanted for, as many times we have kissed beasts, however, have not, yet found our prince charming. My prince charming turned out to be the bad boy in this planet's evolution. Now, this is a form of luck, we all desire to avoid.

My daughters were now actually telling me of their great approval in my new stage of life and gave me a testament that I had never expected. One told me that I was not a good bad Queen and they would make sure I would be a great good queen. I told them I never heard of any good queens in among the thrones of the good. One of my daughters whose name is Agyagosszergény asked if she could tell us a story, she had been saving for the next time we all had a get-together. She had been saving this story just for me. We all sat back and enjoyed some special presentation rendered by Agyagosszergény.

"A young mother set her foot on the path of life. 'Is this the long way?' she asked. The guide said: "Yes and the way is hard. You will be old before you reach the end of it. But the end will be better than the commencement." Nevertheless, the young mother was happy, and she would not believe that anything could be better than these years. Therefore, she played with her children, and assembled flowers for them along the way, and bathed them in the clear streams; and the sun shone on them, and the young Mother cried, "Nothing will ever be lovelier than this." Then the night came, and the storm, and the path was dark, and the children shook with fear and cold, and the mother drew them close and covered them with her cloak, and the children said, "Mother, we are not afraid, for you are near, and no harm can come." Morning came, there was a hill ahead, the children climbed and became somnolent, and the mother was drowsy. But at all times she said to the children," A little more patience and we will be there." So the children climbed, and when they reached the top they said, "Mother, we would not have done it without you." The mother, when she lay down at night looked up at the stars and said, "This is a better day than the last, for my children have learned resilience in the face of rigidity. Yesterday I gave them audacity. Today, I have given them spirit." The next day came strange clouds, which darkened the earth, clouds of war and hate and evil, her children floundered and teetered, and the mother said, "Look up. Lift your eyes to the light." The children looked and saw above the clouds an everlasting glory, and it guided them beyond the darkness. That night the Mother said, "This is the best day of all, for I have shown my children Jehovah." The days went on, and the weeks and the months and the years, and the mother grew old and she was short and crooked. However, her children were tall and strong, and walked with audacity. When the way was rough, they lifted her, for she was as light as a feather; and at last, they came to a hill, and beyond they could see a shining road and golden gates flung wide. The mother said, "I have reached the end of my journey. And now I know the end is better than the beginning, for my children can walk alone, and their children after them." The children said, "You will always walk with us, Mother, even when you have gone through the gates." They stood and watched her as she went on alone, and the gates closed after her. They said, "We cannot see her but she is with us still. A Mother like ours is more than a memory. She is a living presence . . ." Your Mother is always with you . . . . She is the whisper of the leaves as you walk down the street; she is the smell of bleach in your freshly laundered socks; she is the cool hand on your brow when you are not well. Your Mother lives inside your laughter. She is crystallized in every teardrop. She is the place you came from, your first home; and she is the map you follow with every step you take. She is your first love and your first heartbreak, and nothing on earth can separate you. Not time, not space . . . Not even death! Because life is to be cherished . . ." Khemmis now applauded my daughter for such a great story. Khemmis now asked my daughters if they would erase the old way of thinking and take a test to determine if they had the thinking that is only developed through penance. The earthlings had shared these things with him over the ages. Khemmis began by saying "A man went over to the bed to place the lingerie with the other things the undertaker would come to collect. His wife had just died. As he turned to me, he said, "Never save anything for special occasions. Each day you live is a special already!" I am not sure what my friend's wife would have done if she would have known tomorrow did not come. Then tomorrow we all take so lightly. I tend to believe she probably would have wanted to see her family and close friends. Maybe she would have located old friends to make peace or apologies for long gone quarrels. I like to think she maybe would have gone to a Chinese restaurant, because it was her favorite food. Only a God can bring back yesterday and you only have now to breathe. These days I read a lot more than I used to and I clean less. I sit on my porch appreciating the landscape without paying consideration to the weeds in my garden. I spend more time with my family, friends, and less at work. I understand now that life is a collection of experiences to be appreciated. I no longer collect things. I use my crystal glassware every day. I wear my new coat to the stockroom if I feel like it. I do not save my most expensive perfume for special occasions. I wear it when I want to. I no longer use expressions like 'eventually I will . . .' Or 'one of these days'. If it is worth it, now is the moment I want to see, hear, or do it. It is small-unfinished business, which makes me nervous if I knew my last hours had come. It would bother me not to have seen certain friends I was going to visit 'one of these days'. Not to have written those letters I was still planning to write, or if I had not told my loved ones enough how much I care about them. These days I do not postpone, I do not suppress and I do not hold back on anything that could bring joy and happiness to our lives. I tell you, each day is special, every hour and every minute of it."

I could feel something fresh and new flowing through my daughters as a new sense of understanding and union was almost upon us. Khemmis was now getting ready to put the hammer on us with a serious of challenges.

Khemmis then called out, Oh Lilith and your angelic daughters will you stand up for your challenges that lay ahead. Your team must be united and dedicated, for a small evil group could give until you defeat.

There was once man whose burdens were so great that he felt the road was too hard to travel; nevertheless, a stranger took him to the side of the road, and made a campfire in which he put three metal cups filled with water on the fire. As the water was boiling, he dug up a dandelion root and gathered a large bird egg. He dropped some tea from his pocket into one cup, the dandelion root in the second cup and the bird egg in the third cup. After giving them, enough time to cook. The stranger now said to the traveler, "I now show you the dandelion, as he fished it from the cup with his fork. "Notice how the dandelion was the stiffest, yet when cooked in the hot water, became soft." He further removed the boiled egg from its cup and told the traveler, "Notice the egg now, after being boiled, it looks the same on the outside, yet which we remove the surface the inside, which was a liquid, is now solid." Now the stranger gave the cup of tea to the traveler and asked him to take a drink and smell it. He had used special leaves that few knew about, however the type of tea was not important, for he told the traveler, "Notice the tea, made from the weakest of the three items here, yet when boiled has the greatest taste and pleasing odor." The traveler now told the stranger, "Surely, you have shown me three truths here today, yet I care not about this, I only worry about how heavy my burdens are?" The stranger now continued once more, "You must decide which you will be, for all three withstood the same hardship, the boiling water, yet one finished soft, the second looked the same, yet for a soft inside turn hard, and the weakest one come through it much better than before. Will you finish hard and bitter with no love or hope, or will you finish soft and weak, nevertheless, you could finish better than you began? The choice is yours." The traveler, seeing the truth in this situation looked at the stranger and said, "I shall finish stronger." As he placed the cup to his mouth to drink more of the tea, he noticed the stranger had vanished. Thus, within itself, gave him a new sense of hope. Khemmis now looked at my sisters and me asking, "Which group are you all?" We all answered, "Give our united clan the tea, for we shall be for thee." Khemmis now told us that he had some more questions for us. "When the hour is the darkest and trials are their greatest, do you elevate yourself to another level, and overcome? How do you handle adversity?" I told him, "Khemmis, we handle adversity with victory." This answer caught him off guard; however, a big smile of satisfaction overcame his face. He replied, "May you have enough happiness to make you sweet, enough trials to make you strong, enough sorrow to keep your spirit and enough hope to make you happy. The happiest of people do not necessarily have the best of everything; they just make the most of everything that comes along their way. The happiest future will always be based on a forgotten past; you cannot go onward in life until you let go of your past disasters and despondencies. I believe that Jehovah has been wise in trusting you with new levels of responsibilities and trusting your daughter to stand for you. Always remember to tell the Earth people placed under your stewardship, that when you were born, you were crying and all around you were smiling. Live your life so the end, will see you smiling and everyone around you crying." As I was, reviewing these powerful messages that we had received something struck me as odd and I decided to ask our host to clarify this, "in trusting you with new levels of responsibilities." He then answered, "Lilith, as you know our throne is the center of the Milky Way in rule and all things. Your road will not always be smooth, and at times may be rocky and filled with deep holes. We know these things not. You must pass through anything that blocks your road in order to make your journey and the challenges within a rewarding triumph. This is your penance, which much shall be given so you can give much. Prepare for the greatest battles and greatest rewards. The glory that you give to Jehovah, I pray, is being greater than the stars in our sky." Instantly everything vanished, as my daughters and I were now upon another world all in a void and hollowness. Likewise, darkness fell upon us.

CHAPTER 8

Melchiresa & Belphegor

The spinning now slows and in panic, I can only witness a few of my daughters, Agyagosszergény, who speaks for all daughters and their five leaders of the 1,000: Bodrogközi, Cserszegtomaj, Sásdi, Adásztevel, and Kapuvári. We search, to no avail, for the remainder. They concentrate on finding their sisters while Agyagosszergény and I try to discover where we are. Except for my 'prison' time, I have never felt so far out of control and so far from anything. As Agyagosszergény and I continue, we see a small light ahead. We trek to the light, which does bear witness to a small opening. We both confess our bewilderment at the chill, which is now spreading, through our spirits. It is the sort of chill, that if we had flesh, we would reach for a heavier shirt or small jacket. Just the type of chill to present a small nuisance, inconvenient nevertheless just enough to remind us of our lack of control and that something surrounds us, offering no point of weakness. Dipped into a cup a fear we cannot bear witness, lest our mystery would conquer us. The absolute silence is now broken by the sound of a small flowing stream that now appears below us. We both can now see the jagged walls that form the tunnel that circumscribes us. To my right on the wall I see what could be an opening and as we both, charge for it, the dark wall that surrounds it conceals the teasing hole. The only consolation we now hold is the awareness that we did charge in a sign of power and not frantically rush to it in a sign of anxiety. We must hold fast to our cards and not let this mystery know our hand. I never previously considered how black and dark blue can combine so gradually and the how blue can fade into the white of light. This impresses me with the power of blue, for it can turn into black or into the white. As we associate blue with life, then life can turn into dark or evil and into goodness or light. I can now, without the prospect of battle only hope the large light ahead of us leads into the goodness of life, however we will not know until we have reassembled all my daughters. I now take Agyagosszergény and gather with the Leaders of the 1,000 as we plan our next move. Bodrogközi suggests, "We exit the light, notify Jehovah and return with an Army to fight." I thenceforth tell her, "My daughter, they took 5,000 with ease, yet left us. If they wanted to destroy us, we would be with the 5,000. I do not feel good about bringing an Army from Jehovah without knowing whom we fight. Likewise, we must remember that in these things Jehovah is slow, trying all other avenues before the war. Therefore, as we do not know how these captors operate, they could banish your sisters before Jehovah responds. It would most likely be wise and stay calm, still showing our mysterious captors that we are strong and will not betray our family." We keep casually scanning around us as a precautionary measure, knowing that an answer will come to us, for if it is from Evil, it will only want what it does not have, that being us. We soon become comfortable with all the strange noises around us. My daughters know that those who were captured will also fight hard to return and be with us.

The white opening now unites with the darkness, and a creature's face reflects the light, its source we know not. I see a decayed face spectacled with dirt or ugly sores. Its eyes are centered with dark black pupils, surrounded by a pale light blue, which are locked on us. It has the ears and nose of strange beasts and knife shaped teeth. Its mouth is open and bottom jaw dropped down revealing rows of flesh grinding teeth. These teeth create no fear in us, as we are all spirits before this thing. I ask, "Who are you and why are you here?" It tells us, "You need not know my name and I am here to keep you in this tunnel." I then looked at him and sneezed, blowing him against the tunnel's wall as we all laughed. I then said, "Did you not notice, we were staying here waiting for the others in our group to return to us?" It looked at me and said, "I would recommend that you fear me, if you wish to see those who are lost among you again. I looked at him and said, "You are but an ant and in no way can be part of the power that has my lost ones," and with this I smashed it against the rocks and then with my eyes burned it. My daughters asked me, "Mother, why did you do that?" I told them, "I will not have ants do the work that leaders should do, nor will I allow a force so weak block my path." The light from the opening once again appeared and a female beast entered herein.

The beast said to me, "Lilith, I welcome you to my home." I then asked, "Who are you?" She said, "My name is Belphegor, and I was a friend with your mother. I have come to help you find your daughters." I then told her, "My father always told me that my mother had no friends." Belphegor then said to me, "That is the way of husbands, to keep their wives only for themselves is it not?" I then asked her, "How did you know I was here?" She told me, "I followed that thing you smashed, for it always finds the weak and deceives them. I was not looking for you, only saving those who it captures. Finding you and reading your scans was an added blessing." I then told her, "I will have to judge you by your deeds, for I knew not my mother, and only very little of my father. I grew up in the courts of the queen, only receiving messages from my father sporadically when I was young, to none as I grew older." Belphegor then told me, "I also have lost contact with him. I know that he fights in many wars, thus I never really wanted to know the truth." I then told her, "That is a truth, I can understand. Where are my daughters?" Belphegor paused for a few seconds then answered, "I am told by my many friends they are on the Island of Kunszentmiklói. We will need many armies to free them, thus if you so desire, I will request the armies. I desire not to free them if none are there to claim them." I wondered now, "Why is she offering to help, with so many armies?" I asked her, "Why and how can you obtain so many armies?" Belphegor then answered, "It is the way of our kingdom to always fight and free those who are in our family. Your mother was in our family, and thus so are your daughters. We are merely taking back what is ours. What we have allowed to be free, no other can bind. Follow me as we go to the Island of Kunszentmiklói." We had no other lead to lock on, thus she at least knew enough about my mother to know I could not verify these things. Whilst I still do not know even to this day, her name. I saw no value in asking her for my mother's name, as I would have no method to verify it. I could see no need in building upon a false foundation, thus decided only to listen to the things that pertain to my daughters. She moved slow and steady as we departed from the Milky Way drifting steadily through space circling around in the dark cosmos. I locked my scan on the small light I knew to be the Milky Way and soon determined we were not moving away from it, but around it. I could now only worry why she was working so hard to throw us off track. She must think us to be primitive fools. That does not worry me, for it will simply make it easier to control our situations and optimistically find my daughters. Without knowing, where they are I must allow myself to fall within whatever trap they ambush me. It is when your captures believe that they have you trapped they reveal their secrets. I just can only hope that I can return from whence I came. Now the space once again surrendered some blue light, which soon took the shape of many forms. I can see a purple alligator headed beast with four horns and with small flying wings flapping wildly. He rested his head over the right shoulder of a man with no skin who displayed his firm muscles. The purple beast allowed the man to hold his razor coated tail, yet for a price. Anywhere the human touched the beast he took on the color of the beast, as if to be an inflection virus invading his body. The center of the man had a cavity in his stomach area that had a bright orange light the displayed the pages of the book that rested on his lap. A purple hand with an open medicine bottle and fumes flowing into the space extended from behind the beast. That was all that I could see from this third feature. The space around this was filled with the words from many languages. Many worlds circled around it. I noticed that only one world had a small moon rotating it. The man's head was abounding with many lights as they were transferred out into space. I could say enough from this vision to know this was not a trustworthy union. Hence, I called out to Belphegor, "Where are we now?" She paused and waited until we were all united and then said, "This is where the beasts of evil feed the minds of those in the flesh with great magic and enchantments. This union feeds Earth and is the only one with the strange spells appearing in many languages, as the Earth no longer speaks the language of the heavens. I hope to get from the beast a key to unlock the prison that holds your daughters on the Island of Kunszentmiklói. Please stay here, behind the world over there and I shall get the key. As we waited, she went forward to do her bidding and returned with the key. We now proceeded directly towards the Milky Way. I now decided to ask her why we went in so many circles, before seeing the beast. Belphegor now told me that was because we were being scanned by the key holders to make sure we are not bringing any surprises. When she departed, all turned nefarious and when she returned the obscurity departed. We then proceeded to where Belphegor said the Island of Kunszentmiklói was. As we proceeded to the island, we were suddenly surrounded by giant dark demons, armies of them. They had the outlines of dark strong muscles creating an appearance of having flesh, yet as such, I knew could not be. The heads were releasing mashed bones projecting them in all directions. Their hands and feet were as animal claws, as they flapped them to excel through the open space with their weapons strapped to their backs. As they moved towards us, Belphegor released a loud scream and now appeared more armies such as these, merely darker and with dark coal colored hair on their heads. The armies clashed and we could see lightning bolts flashing into strange containers on each side. This is a battle of spirits, and not knowing which side was the worthy side, I did not know which canister I wanted to fill first. We watched this battle rage for a few horrific hours as both sides continued to present large forces. Then a larger one of the beasts who had invaded us came to my front and asked to speak with me. I told him, "I am Lilith, say what you desire." The beast said, "I am the highest commander of the armies of Melchiresa who is your father. It was he who gave placed you as Queen in the Royal courts. He sent us here today to help free your daughters and to save you from Belphegor who wishes to destroy you as she did your mother." He then handed me the keys and continued by saying, "Go now, and follow these warriors to the Island of

Kunszentmiklói and collect your daughters and flee as fast as you can back to Jehovah, who is our enemy." When he said Jehovah, I believed this to be true and as the keys matched the ones that Belphegor had, thus we followed them. The guards took us straight to the Island and into a cave. They immediately drilled through thick rock for maybe one hundred feet and soon we all stood around a large nice canister. I used the key that Belphegor had lost and opened the canister. My daughters wasted no time escaping and once they were all out, the canister vanished. I wondered if the inside was as nice as the outside. All my daughters complained about the terrifying conditions inside and confessed to seeing visions of Belphegor killing my mother. I was able to pull these visions of my daughters, with my mother's spirit leaving her mutilated flesh. I asked the warriors if they knew where my mother's spirit was. They disclosed to me that, "In those days, spirits not taken from the heavens were erased from time." I then asked, "Why was she not taken from the heavens?" The guards told me that they knew not, however the Melchiresa's number one general would be able to ask Melchiresa who was there on that day that shook his life. I then asked my daughters, "Do you think we should return to the battle?" They all shouted with great glee, "The battle is to be ours." They immediately assembled their war materials and fell into formation. I told Agyagosszergény, "Let us follow these warriors and avenge the death of my mother." The warriors lead us to the battle where the General has us fill in his heavily damaged areas so he could continue to mount his full attack toward Belphegor, "Whom Melchiresa wanted to avenge and returned with all her forces for his eternal revenge." My daughters fit in perfectly as the General's complete front line remained solid and he was able to encircle Belphegor. They kept flooding the front line until the next day holes appeared on their front line. Now large gaps appeared, as the General ordered us to stay in our positions and shoot into these gaps striking the enemy in their backs on the other side of their circular defense. We now realized that their reserves were exhausted. The General knew they had no reserves for they have roamed in hiding since the days in which Prikhodko had surrendered her soul for eternal punishment, a punishment in which Jehovah, even to this day does not impose. Jehovah knows that truths change as more information is discovered, and if a spirit is banished that was indeed righteous it could not be restored. I am so angry now knowing that my mother was banished and yet, as the queen of evil, with more evils that she ever knew existed, she who was innocent in my eyes would be punished and I would be forgiven. Sometimes it seems as if the true mysteries of the universe always occur the closest to what we hold as stable reality. What did she do that was so evil? We would fight hard here, at least at the minimum to avenge the death of my mother. Without hesitation, the gaps continued to open wider and wider until the General told his front line to invade, using his strong reserves as backup. I then heard a great cheer as the General's canister turned into a bright orange releasing beautiful celebration music. I asked those around the General, "What does this mean?" One of the guards looked at me and said, "The revenge of Melchiresa is now in our prison. Belphegor shall now face her punishment for killing your mother." This took me by surprise, as all in this group knew my mother and father, with only my daughters and myself being ignorant of this information. I really now feel extra special in mysteriously appearing just in time to see the capture of the one who killed my mother. I still do not know how she died and feel embarrassed by not knowing. I am impressed how the General is treating me special as his warriors are protecting my daughters as best that can be expected being on the front line. That is where they wanted to be and for me not to allow them to share in the avenging of their grandmother's killing would be wrong. They are also fighting for their blood, their ancestry. I never thought they felt so strongly about this, as I never talked about it, having never seen my father and being raised by a regent as the queen. I hope to discover someday how that happened. As the war is winding down and our forces are working on getting the enemies canister so our lost warriors can be freed, the General and I had some time to talk. So I revealed to the General, "General, I stand here as a thankful fool, seeing so many fighting for a thing of great treasure to me and who I am, yet I know not neither my mother or father. Is this a wrong I am guilty?" The General said, "By no means child. You shall always remain innocent, the flower of your mother's heart. That was the plan of your father, to keep you innocent. Belphegor killed your mother before she could see and hold you. Your mother chose to keep and have you, even though she knew that the spirits of the heavens would avenge her for not killing you. She wanted you so much. To raise you as her mother rose her, full of love, innocent, loyalty, and the ability to find good even in the darkness of bad. She honored your father by giving you your life. Melchiresa, your father saved you just in time, as he was able to take from Belphegor, as she wanted so much to join you with your mother. I know this story perfectly; as your father has shared every detail all these years, we have searched for Belphegor. He told me that you would put your guard down and relax in the comfort of Jehovah's kingdom and she would strike there. When you all captured the evil spirits, she was forced to lure you out from under Jehovah's wing. We predicted she would have to contain your daughters in the only safe area within many galaxies, that being only the Island of Kunszentmiklói. Your father escaped with you from the place where your mother was murdered. The heavenly spirits, which had by the way, only one vote favorable for your mother that being from Jehovah, voted for the eternal banishment of your mother and for you. That was when your father gave you to the King and Queen of Evil. They had no child and knew of your blessing therefore welcomed you with a commitment to fight to the end for your safety. Luck later turned upon them, to no reason associated with you. A coup captured the King and Queen and banished them by destroying the canister they put them. The coup was defeated leaving you the throne. The Kingdom assigned you worthy reagents. Your father was forever forbidden to associate with you, an agreement reached with the king and queen who feared that when you were of age, you would leave your kingdom and search for him, which on this day their fear is now a truth." I told the General that, "I did not leave my throne willingly. I was taken as a prisoner lost in a battle. After 1,000 years in a lake of fire, I vowed never to chance being a prisoner again, thus in my weakness without my armies I have joined Jehovah's throne. As you know, once I gave my willingly gave my allegiance to Jehovah, I may never reclaim my lost throne." The General told me that he understood and told me that he had obtained permission from Jehovah for my daughters and me to join in this fight. I thanked him for taking this precaution. The General told me, "Jehovah and all the other gods in this section of the universe are celebrating today since a cancer, being Belphegor and her armies, is no more. He then asked me, "Would you like to tell your father that we have won this battle when we place the last enemy warrior in our canister?" I told him this would be nice. We now received the news that the canister of our lost warriors and my captured daughters is now open and all are free. I can look out and see my daughters celebrating. Since Belphegor's warriors no longer have a canister, they are for the most part hiding now, only looking for chances to escape. The General has this place tighter than two coats of paint. Nothing will be able to escape as he enjoyed the steady flow of Belphegor's warriors he was capturing. The General stopped for a second and sent out a new order hoping the reenergize his warriors by having them shift their sectors of search. He told me this is when many times they get sloppy and make the big mistakes. We had to have every enemy spirit for just one escape could plant a seed for future wars. All enemy equipment was destroyed and the waste particles placed in a separate canister, as they feared enemy spirits could possess this equipment. He maintained the circular perimeter until everything was captured or destroyed. Now they would complete a detailed scan and any particle was placed in the waste canister. This was a precautionary measure in case a spirit was hiding in an atom. Then the area was flooded with a special wave sensor that completely cleans the enemy's former positions. Finally the troops were resting, as the General ordered no celebrations until the canister is in Melchiresa's possession. He now had me sit beside him and placed a 'call' into my father. I asked him why there would be no video. He now explained that, "In order for you to be left alive and the spirits not also banish you as they did your mother, he had to promise never to see you or allow you to join his people. There is no escaping this Lilith, for if you see him a powerful spirit that rests inside of you will use that power to destroy you. So remember, this law cannot be broken. I would ask you to swear not to do this, however, I should be able to trust the love you have for the ones who sacrificed so much for you that you would value your life as much as do we." I smiled and shook my head yes, for this shall be my way of thinking, 'I cannot be free in this situation as so many have paid a price for me to be free and ask so little. I must afford them their wishes as I do owe them so much.' Soon he was talking to my father, and they both were so excited at the prospect of moving on to a new chapter in their lives. The General then told Melchiresa he had some help from a special ally and if I would desire to speak with her. He then agreed and I introduced myself, "Hello Melchiresa, I am one who is called Lilith and our common enemy Belphegor tried to destroy my daughters." He then said, "It is nice to speak with you as we all appreciate the great help the General said you gave today. I once knew a Lilith, many years ago, for it was then that the same Belphegor tried to kill another who was named Lilith." I then answered back, "Could it be that I am the same whom she tried to kill back them?" Melchiresa then said, "The General said your now serve Jehovah, the Lilith I knew was a queen among our empires which do not ally with Jehovah except for this battle." I then told him, "I am the same Lilith." Then Melchiresa said, "That may be so. Their prophesy claimed that our queen would decide, which path to choose when she was of age. Either way, you are forbidden from me, my daughter, for if you chose good then all forbid you from me, yet if you stay with the evil, then good forbids you. Now that Belphegor will pay for your mother's murder, it is time for your life and legacy to begin. Go forth and do great things for Jehovah, and all that I can ask of you is that you wage not war against me, as I shall not wage war against you." With this our call was terminated and I now knew it was time to get back to Jehovah, thus I bid my farewell to the General and assembled my daughters as we made our journey home. I such a few days I have learned so much about who I am from such few words. I now knew my existence meant something and that in order to bring life back for my mother; I would have to prove that her decision to give me life was a good one. I now trembled with fear at how close we all came to Belphegor's avenging ways, almost walking into a deep and costly trap. My past, a past I knew not, came out of the darkness and saved my daughters and me. The General told me that, except for Belphegor, all the enemy warriors would be given to a righteous empire for eternal punishment, as they had caused much grief to so many. This is the first time I have fought a battle against evil, although on the side of evil, it still felt rewarding. Evil was fighting over me, one side trying to save and allow me to serve Jehovah, while the other side wanted to destroy me. I know that on Earth Jehovah worked through the evil ones to shake up the Earthlings. Maybe this is my way of working through evil to fight evil. That is not the question. I shall immediately report to Jehovah, and tell him all that I have heard.

My daughters are now reviewing the conversation between their grandfather and myself. This is the closest they have ever been to a father, as none has ever known their real fathers. I make it a practice to conceal this information, for such knowledge would only confuse them and endanger the loyalty they have for our family. I can see where they are now taking special pride in the battle they have just helped to win. As I watch through so many situations they faced I am also filled with pride. I will need my daughters to help me on Earth by monitoring the movements of any evil spirits, because I should expect now to be a target and the one who betrayed poor and innocent Lucifer. Therefore, he lied to get me here, and tried to make me a slave to Adam. Furthermore, by telling Jehovah how he thought I would make such a great spouse for Adam, he set the stage for the creation of Eve and for the testing of man for sin. He knew they would fail and thus hoped he would be restored. He was made lord of the Earth, a position that had no honor in heaven, as all knew it would lay the foundation for the ultimate destruction of life in the flesh on Earth. I have had my challenges and so far have been able to overcome them. I could now only wonder what challenges lie ahead for my daughters and me.

CHAPTER 9

Freedom from Penance and end times

The space now felt so warm and exciting, and all who I passed by were filled with joy. I wondered how everyone knew as this news must have surpassed me on its journey here. The space was charged with the spirit of celebration. I decided to visit Khemmis to discuss how I should approach Jehovah and see how he would welcome my visit. Khemmis asked me, "What news do you have for Jehovah?" I told him about my victory over Belphegor, which appeared to be news for him. I asked him if any others knew, and he confirmed that no others knew. I considered this strange and wondered why all were so joyous when I passed them. Khemmis now told me that the joy I was receiving was from the reflection of the joy I was giving. I suppose this makes sense, as I was overjoyed. After such a rigorous battle, the energy spawned by victory was too hard to bear. Khemmis suggested that he made the request for an audience with Jehovah. I felt comfortable with the wisdom of Khemmis, and so agreed. We now relaxed as I told him what had happened. He then assured me that the new controls would be implemented regarding my security. I had never worried about security in the thousands of millennia in my short life. I can only say that now since I stand for something, something is thus attempting to stand against me. That something had better be willing to fight, for if I must fight, then I shall fight. For the time being, I shall enjoy the council of Khemmis who seems to enable me to become free from my stress. As we talked about the issues that had brought him joy throughout his many adventures, our meeting was too soon ended as the messenger returned announcing an audience had been granted as soon as I could reach the throne. I now prepared for my visit. Then, unexpectedly Jehovah appeared unto me and spoke unto me saying, "Lilith, I have come to you to give you the commission that you shall accept upon the Earth as we prepare to enter the end times. The Earth has no lord as Lucifer has been bound, thus I shall call upon you to deliver and execute the signs of my destruction. As sin is in the flesh, the flesh of this world shall be complete no more, yet I shall again try this species on a fresh world that is replacing the one that Adam called Venus, and you shall be the Lord of that fresh world. As I started to feel great joy, I fell into a pronounced sleep that was filled with many strange dreams. I lifted up my hands in righteousness and blessed the Holy and Great One El Shaddai. Moreover, I spoke with the breath from my mouth, and with the tongue of flesh, which God has made with the children of the flesh of Earthmen, that they should speak therewith. He gave them breath and a tongue, and a mouth that they should speak therewith as I heard one whom was beside me declaring, "Blessed to be You, O Lord, King, Great and mighty in your greatness, Lord of the complete creation of the heaven, King of kings and God of the unabridged world. His power, kingship, and greatness stand incessantly and always, and throughout all generations your dominion, and all the heavens are your throne perpetual, and the whole earth your footstool forever and forevermore. You have made and you reign all things, and nothing is too hard for you. Wisdom departs not from the seat of your throne, nor turns away from your presence. In addition, you know, see, and hear everything, and there is nothing hidden from you, as you recognize all things. The angels of your heavens are guilty of usurpation, and upon the figure of men abide your wrath until the great Day of Judgment. And now, O God and Lord and Great King, I pray and beseech you to fulfil my prayer, to leave men a posterity on earth, and not destroy all the flesh of man, and make the earth without inhabitant, so that there should be a perpetual destruction." I at this moment in time, looking around asked, "Who speaks to me?" The voice replied, "I am as a man of flesh to beg upon the Lord for mercy for my brothers and sisters." I subsequently asked, "How can you come into my dream when it is time for me to have visions from Jehovah for his work that I must do?" He later said to me, "Be not angry Lilith, I am your friend, the spirit of Khemmis, which the Lord has given flesh to speak with you in the manner as required before the throne." I then said, "I shall follow you my special counselor, as I so trust your wisdom is so many things. Let us currently proceed." Khemmis now nattered, "And now, my Lord, destroy from the earth the flesh which has aroused your wrath, but the flesh of righteousness and uprightness establish as a plant of the eternal seed, and hide not your face from the prayer of your servant, O Lord." I immediately drifted into a sleep waiting for the next dream that Jehovah had promised me. Likewise, after this, I saw another dream, and I will share the whole dream to thee, Khemmis. Furthermore, Khemmis lifted up his voice and spoke to me, "Lilith, my daughter, will I speak, hear my words, incline your ear to the dream, vision of Jehovah. I understood as a vision on my bed, and behold a bull came from the earth, and that bull was hoary; and after it came forth a heifer, and along after this latter came forth two bulls, one of them black and the other red. Additionally, that black bull pierced the red one and pursued him over the earth, and thereupon I could no longer see that red bull. Nevertheless, that black bull grew and that heifer went with him, and I found out that many oxen proceeded from him, which bore a resemblance and followed him. What is more, that cow, that preliminary one, went from the presence of that primary bull in order to seek that red one, but found him not, and mourned with a great lamentation over him and searched for him. Hence, I looked until that first bull came to her and quieted her, and from that time onward, she no longer cried. Consequently, after that, she bore another hoary bull, and after him, she bore many bulls and black cows. For this reason, I saw in my sleep the hoary bull, likewise, grew and become a great hoary bull, and from Him proceeded many hoary bulls, and they resembled him. Therefore, they began to beget many hoary bulls, which resembled them, one pursuing the other, even many. Again, I watched with my eyes as I slept, and I saw the heaven above, and behold a star fell from heaven, and it arose, ate, and pastured among those oxen. Afterward I saw the large and the black oxen, and behold they all changed their stalls and pastures and their cattle, and began to accept each other. And again, I saw in the vision, and looked towards the heaven, and behold I saw many stars descend and cast themselves down from heaven to that first star, and they became bulls among those cattle and pastured with them among them. I looked at them and saw, and behold they all let out their privy members, like horses, and set out to cover the cows of the oxen, and they all became pregnant and bare elephants, bears, and the asses and the eagle. As well, all the oxen feared them and were affrighted at them, and began to bite with their teeth and to devour, and to gouge with their horns. Afterwards, they began to devour those oxen; and behold all the children of the earth began to tremble and quake before them and to flee from them. Once again, I saw how they began to gore each other and to devour each other, and the earth began to cry noisily. Afterwards, I raised mine eyes another time to heaven, and I saw in the vision, and behold there came from heaven beings who were like hoary men: and four went from that place and three with them. Then those three that had last come forth grasped me by my hand and took me up, away from the generations of the earth, and raised me up to a supercilious place, and showed me a skyscraper raised high over the earth, and all the hills were lower. What is more, one said unto me, 'Remain here until you understand everything that befalls those elephants, bears, and asses and the eagle, and the stars and the oxen, and all of them. The elephants and asses both lusted after the eagle and fought hard to keep him in line. Their battle was fierce caring not for none on the earth or those in the heavens. Blood flowed from them, and the eagle thus grew weak, depending upon the elephants and asses for his or her lifetime. As the eagle laid upon the elephant, for the ass was alive no more, the lion leaped upon the elephant and with one, strike did kill the eagle and being filled with great lust of power, withdrew from the elephant his life. After the bear ate the eagle, the elephants and asses were no more here. The bear soon grew hungry as demons living inside of horses and the genre of other beasts I can find no word to describe came between him. Afterwards, I saw one of those four who had come forth preliminary, and he seized that original star who had fallen from the heaven, and bound it hand and foot and cast it into a void, now that abyss was narrow and deep, and horrible and dark. Likewise, one of them pulled out a sword, and devoted it to those bears, after that they began to smite each other, and the whole earth quaked because of them. Furthermore, as I was beholding in the vision, lo, one of those four who had come forth stoned them from heaven, and gathered and got hold of all the excessive stars whose privy members were like those of horses, and bound them all hands and foot, and throw them into an abyss beneath the ground. Therefore, one of those four went to that hoary bull and instructed him in a secret, without his being terrified: he was born a bull and became a man, and built for himself a large vessel and dwelt thereupon; and three bulls dwelt with him in this vessel, and they were covered. Again, I raised mine eyes towards heaven and saw a soaring roof, with seven water torrents thereon, and those torrents flowed with much water into an enclosure. Moreover, I looked again, and behold fountains were opened on the surface of that great enclosure, and that water began to swell and rise toward the surface, and I saw that enclosure until all its surface was covered with water. Equally important, the water, the darkness, and mist increased upon it; and as I looked from the height of that water, that water had risen to the stature of that enclosure, and was streaming over that enclosure, and it stood on the ground. As well, all the cattle of that enclosure were gathered together until I found out how they fell off and were swallowed up and perished in that water. Nonetheless, that vessel floated over the water, while all the oxen and bear sank toward the bottom with all the animals, so that I could no longer see them, and they were not able to run away, but then perished and sank into the depths. Once again, I looked in the vision until those water torrents were removed from that high roof, the chasms of the earth were leveled up, and other abysses were opened. Then the water began to run down into these, until the earth became visible; however, that vessel settled upon the earth and the darkness retired and light appeared. Nevertheless, then again, that hoary bull which had become a man came out of that vessel, and the three bulls with him, and one of those three was hoary like that bull, and one of them was red as blood, and one black: and that hoary bull departed from them. What is more, they began to bring forth beasts of the field and evil spirits to the sky, so that there arose different genera: lions, tigers, demons, dogs, hyenas, wild boars, foxes, squirrels, swine, Falcons, vultures, red kites, eagles, and ravens; and among them was born a hoary bull. Furthermore, they began to bite one another; nevertheless, that hoary bull which was born among them begat a wild ass and a hoary bull with it, and the wild asses multiplied. All that was hoary did hate all that was dark and each hated whoever liked the other dividing itself in other beasts. Nevertheless, that bull which was born from him begat a black wild boar and hoary righteous, as the former begat many boars, but that righteous begat twelve righteous. Likewise, when those twelve ethical had grown, they gave up one of them to the asses, those asses again gave up that righteous to the demons, and the righteous grew up among the demons. The Lord brought the eleven righteous to live with it and to pasture with it among the demons: and they multiplied and became many flocks of righteous. The demons began to fear them, and they oppressed them until they destroyed cry aloud, because of their innocent ones, and unto their Lord, they desired to complain. Righteous, which had been saved from the demons, fled, and escaped to the wild asses; and I saw the righteous how they lamented and cried, and besought their Lord with their entire might, until that Lord of the righteous stemmed at the voice of the righteous from a lofty abode, and came to them and pastured them. He called that righteous which had escaped the demons, and spoke with it concerning the demons whom it should reprimand them not to touch the righteous. The righteous went to the demons according to the word of the Lord. Other righteous met it and went with it, and the two went and entered together into the assembly of those demons, and spoke with them and chide them not to touch the righteous from henceforth. Thereupon, I found out the demons, and I found out how they oppressed the righteous, through all their power. These righteous then cried aloud. The Lord touched the righteous, and they set about to smite those demons: and the demons began to make lamentation; even so, the righteous became quiet and forthwith ceased to cry out. I saw the righteous until they departed from among the demons; however, the eyes of the demons were blinded, and those demons departed in pursuit of the righteous with all their power. The Lord of the righteous went with them, as their leader, and all His righteous followed Him; and his face was astounding, magnificent, and terrible to behold. Nonetheless, the demons began to pursue those righteous until they reached a sea of water. That sea was divided, the water stood on this side and on that before their face, and their Lord led them and placed himself between them and the demons. As those demons did not even see the righteous, they went through the midst of that sea, the demons followed the righteous, and those demons ran after them into that sea. When they saw the Lord of the righteous, they turned to flee before His face, but that sea gathered itself together, and became as it had been created, and the water swelled and grew until it covered those demons. I bore witness until all the demons who pursued those righteous, perished and drowned. The righteous escaped from that water and went forth into a wilderness, where there was no water and no grass; and they began to open their eyes and to see; and I saw the Lord of the righteous pasturing them and giving them water and grass, and that righteous going and leading them. Righteous ascended to the summit of that lofty rock, and the Lord of the righteous sent it to them. After that, I saw the Lord of the righteous, who stood before them, his appearance was great, dreadful, and resplendent, and those entire righteous saw Him and were frightened before His face. They all feared and trembled because of Him, and they cried to that righteous with them, which were among them; we are not able to stand before our Lord or to behold Him. That the righteous which led them again ascended to the summit of that rock, but the righteous began to be blinded and to wander from the path which he had shown them, but that righteousness was not thereof. The Lord of the righteous was exceedingly enraged against them, and that righteous discovered it, went down from the top of the rock, came to the righteous, and found the greatest part of them blinded and fell away. When they found it out, they feared and trembled at its presence, and hoped to return to their congregations. The righteous took other righteous with it, and came to those righteous, which had fallen aside, and set out to slay them; and the righteous feared its presence, thus that righteous brought back those righteous that had fallen away, and they came back to their flocks. I saw in this vision until that righteous became a man and built a house for the Lord of the righteous, and placed all the righteous in that house. I saw until these righteous which had met that righteous which led them fell dormant; and I saw until all the pronounced righteous perished and little ones arose in their place, and they came to a pasture, and approached a stream of water. Then that righteous, their leader who had become a man withdrew from them and fell resting and all the righteous sought it and cried over it with a great howling. And I saw until they left off crying for that righteous and crossed that stream of water, and there arose the two righteous as leaders in the place of those which had led them and had fallen asleep and led them. I saw until the righteous came to a godly place, and an agreeable and glorious land, and I saw until those righteous were satisfied; and that house stood among them in the pleasant land. Sometimes their eyes were opened, and finally blinded, until other righteous arose, led them, and took them all back, and their eyes were opened. The dogs and the foxes and the infuriated boars began to devour those righteous until the Lord of the righteous raised up other righteous a ram from their midst, which led them. That ram began to butt on either side those dogs, foxes, and raging boars until he had destroyed them all. That righteous whose eyes were opened to see that ram, which was among the righteous, until it forsook its glory and began to butt those righteous, and trampled upon them, and behaved itself unseemly. The Lord of the righteous sent the Savior to another savior and raised it to be a ram and leader of the righteous instead of that ram which had forsaken its glory. It went to it and spoke to it alone, and raised it to be a ram, and made it the prince and leader of the righteous; however, during all these things, those dogs oppressed the righteous. The preliminary ram pursued that alternate ram, and that alternate ram arose and fled before it; and I saw until those dogs pulled down the preliminary ram. That second ram arose and led the less righteous. And those righteous grew and multiplied; however, all the dogs, and foxes, and wild boars feared and fled before it, and that ram butted and killed the chosen by Lucifer, and those chosen by Lucifer had no longer any power among the righteous and robbed them no more of ought. That ram begat many righteous and fell asleep. A little righteous became ram in its stead, and became prince and leader of those righteous. That house became considerable and broad, and it was built for those righteous; a skyscraper lofty and pronounced was built into the house for the Lord of the righteous. This house was low; however, the tower was very idealistic and exalted. The Lord of the righteous stood on that tower, and they offered a full table before Him. Once again, I saw those righteous that they again erred and went many ways, and forsook that their house and the Lord of the righteous called some from among the righteous and sent them to the righteous, but the righteous began to bump them off. One of them was saved and was not slain, and it sped away and cried aloud over the righteous; and they sought to slay it, but the Lord of the righteous saved it from the righteous, brought it up to me, and caused it to dwell there. He sent many other chosen men to those righteous to testify unto them and lament over them. After that, I saw that when they rejected the house of the Lord and His heavens they fell away entirely, and their eyes were blinded; and I saw the Lord of the righteous how he wrought much slaughter among them in their herds until those righteous invited that slaughter and betrayed his place. He gave them over into the hands of the lions and tigers, and demons and hyenas, and into the hand of the foxes, and to all the chosen by Lucifer. Those chosen by Lucifer began to tear in pieces those righteous. I saw that he forsook that their house and their tower and gave them all into the hand of the lions, to gash and devour them, into the hand of all the chosen by Lucifer. I began to cry aloud with all my power, to appeal to the Lord of the righteous, and to represent to Him concerning the righteous that they were devoured by all the chosen by Lucifer. He remained unmoved, though he saw it, and rejoiced that they were demolished and engulfed and robbed, and allowed them to be devoured in the hand of all the beasts. He called seventy speakers of the words, and cast those righteous to them that might pasture them, and he spoke to the speakers of the language and their companions; let every one of your pasture the righteous henceforward, and everything, which I shall command you that do you. I will deliver them over unto you duly numbered, and tell you which of them are to be demolished, and they annihilate you. He gave over unto them those righteous. He called another and spoke unto him; Observe and mark everything that the speakers of the words will do to those righteous, for they will destroy more of them than I have commanded them. Every excess and the destruction, which will be wrought through the speakers of the words, record how many they destroy according to my command, and how many according to their own caprice, record against every individual speaker of the word all the destruction he effects. Read out before me by number how many they destroy, and how many they deliver over for destruction, that I may accept this as a testimony against them, and know every deed of the speakers of the words, that I may comprehend and understand what they do, whether or not they accept by my decree, which I have commanded them. However, they shall not know it, and thou shalt not declare it to them, nor admonish them, but an only record against everyone all the destruction, which the speakers of the words affect each in his time and lay it all before me. I saw until those speakers of the words pastured in their season, and they began to slay and to destroy more than they were bidden, and they delivered those righteous into the hand of the lions. The lions and tigers ate and devoured the greater part of those righteous, and the wild boars eat along with them; and they burnt that skyscraper and demolished that house. I became exceedingly sorrowful over that tower, because that house of the righteous was demolished. Afterwards, I was unable to ascertain if those righteous entered that house. The language of the speakers and their associates delivered over those righteous to all the chosen by Lucifer, to consume them, and each one of them received during his time a definite number: it was penned by the other like a book how many each one of them destroyed by them. Each one slew and destroyed many more than was prescribed; and I began to weep and lament because of those righteous. Thus in the vision I saw that one who wrote, How he recorded everything that was ruined by those speakers of the words, day by day, and carried up and laid down. He really read the whole book to the Lord of the righteous, even everything that they had done, all that each one of them had done away with, and all they had given over to destruction. The book was read before the Lord of the righteous, and He chose the book from his script, read it, sealed it, and laid it down. Forthwith, I witnessed how the speakers of the words pastured for twelve hours, and behold three of those righteous turned back, came, entered, and began to build up all that had fallen down of that household; even so, the wild boars tried to block them, but they were not capable.

And they set out again to build as before, and they reared up that skyscraper, and it was named the high skyscraper; and they began again to place a table before the skyscraper, but all the bread on it was polluted and not pure. As touching all the eyes of those righteous were blinded so that they saw not, and the eyes of their speakers on the words, likewise; and they delivered them in large numbers to their speakers of the words for seventy-five destruction, and they trampled the righteous with their feet and devoured them. The Lord of the righteous remained unmoved until all the righteous were dispersed, over the field, and mixed with them the beast, and they did not deliver them out of the hands of the beasts. This one who wrote the book carried it up, and showed it and read it before the Lord of the righteous, and implored him on their account, and besought him on their account as she showed Him all the doings of the words of the speakers, and gave testimony before Him against all the speakers of the language. She got hold of the actual script, laid it down beside Him, and went away. I saw until that in the manner thirty-five speakers of the words undertook the pasturing of the righteous, and they severally completed their periods, as did the first; and others receive them into their two hands, to pasture them for their period, each speaker of the word in his own period. After that I saw in my vision all the evil spirits to the sky of heaven coming, the eagles, the vultures, the red kites, the ravens; even so, the eagles led all the wicked spirits to the sky; and they began to devour those righteous, and to pick out their eyes and to devour their flesh. The righteous cried out because their flesh was being devoured by the evil spirits to the sky, and as for me, I looked and grieved in my sleep over that speakers of the word who pastured the righteous. I saw until those righteous were devoured by the dogs, evil spirits to the sky, and red kites, and they left neither flesh nor skin nor strength remaining with them until only their bones stood there, and their bones too fell to the ground, and the righteous became fewer. I realized until that twenty-three undertook the pasturing and completed in their several periods fifty-eight times. However, behold saviors were borne by those hoary righteous, and they began to open their eyes and to see, and to cry to the righteous. Yea, they shouted to them, but they did not hearken to what they said to them, but were remarkably deaf, and their eyes were very exceedingly blinded. I saw in the vision how the ravens flew upon those saviors and took one of those saviors, and dashed the righteous in pieces and devoured them. I watched until the horns grew upon those saviors, the ravens cast down their horns; and I watched until there sprouted a great horn of one of those righteous, and their eyes were opened. Moreover, it looked at the minute their eyes opened; it cried to the righteous, and the rams saw it and all ran to it. Notwithstanding all those evil spirits to the sky and vultures and ravens and red kites still kept tearing the righteous and swooping down upon them and devouring them, even the righteous remained silent, but the rams lamented and cried out. Those ravens fought and battled with it and tried to keep a low profile its horn, but they had no power over it. All the sinful spirits to the sky, vultures, ravens, and red kites were gathered in conjunction, and there came below them all the righteous of the field, yea; they all came with each other, and helped each other to break that horn of the ram. Until I saw a great sword was given to the righteous, and the righteous proceeded against all the beasts of the field to slay them, and all the beasts and the evil spirits to the sky of the heaven fled before their face. I saw that man, who wrote the book according to the command of the Lord, until he opened that book about the destruction, which those twelve last speakers of the words had been wrought, and showed that they had destroyed much more than their predecessors, before the Lord of the righteous had. I watched until the Lord of the righteous came unto them. She took in her hand the staff of His wrath, and smote the earth, the earth stayed not together, all the beasts and all the evil spirits to the sky of the heaven fell from among those righteous, and were swallowed up in the earth, and it covered them. Until I saw a throne was erected in the pleasant land, and the Lord of the righteous sat himself thereon, and the other took the sealed books and opened those books before Jehovah. The Lord watched those men, the four solitary hoary ones followed by the three black ones, as they did the war against each other, until the end of the earth was at hand. I witnessed one of the hoary ones make mountains of fire and rain it upon the last threatening as peace did come from the heavens. The three black ones laid down their seeds that they might destroy again those who hold dear to the doctrines of the Lord. Now the Lord commanded that the stars should bring before Him, beginning with the first star, which led the way, all the stars whose privy members were like those of horses, and they brought them all before Him. He said about that man who wrote before Him, being one of those seven ones, and said unto him; take those seventy deceivers of the words to whom I delivered the righteous, and who taking them on their own authority slew more than I commanded them. Behold, they were all bound; I saw, and they all stood before Him. The judgment was held first over the stars, and they were judged and found punishable, and went into the place of denunciation, and they were cast into an abyss, loaded of fire and flaming, and full of pillars of fire. Those seventy deceivers of the words were judged and found blamable, and they were cast into that blazing abyss. I saw during that time how an identical abyss was opened in the midst of the earth, full of fire, and they brought those blinded righteous, and they were all judged and found guilty and cast into this flaming abyss, and they burned; now this abyss was to the right into that house. I saw those righteous burning and their bones' burning. I stood up to see until they folded up that house of the false word and carried off all the pillars, and all the beams and ornaments of that house were at the same time folded up with it, and they carried it off and laid it in a place in the south in Cain's land. I watched until the Lord of the righteous brought a new house greater and loftier than that first. Furthermore, set it up in the place of the original, which had newly folded up, all its pillars were new; its ornaments were new and larger, than those of the first were, the old one that he had taken away, and all the deceitful ones were within it. I saw all the righteous, which had been left, and all the beasts on the earth, and all the evil spirits to the sky falling down from heaven, doing homage to that their not faithful beast was making petition to, and obeying him in everything. Thereafter, those seven years, none was clothed in gray. I followed the dove by my function who had taken me up before, and the hand of that ram who had grabbed hold of me. They took me up and put me down in the midst of those righteous before the judging took place. Those righteous were all hoary, and their deeds were abundant and clean. All that had been destroyed and dispersed, and all the beasts of the field, and all the blessed spirits to the sky of the promised land, assembled in that house, and the Lord of the righteous rejoiced with great joy because they were all good and had returned to His home. I watched until they laid down that sword, which had been given for the righteous, and they took it back into the house, and it was sealed before the presence of the Lord, and all the righteous were invited into that house, but it held them not. The eyes of them all were opened; they saw the good, and there was not one among them, which did not see. I saw that house was solid, spacious, and very wide. I realized that a hoary bull was born, with large horns and all the beasts of the field and all the evil spirits to the sky of the air feared him and drew the petition to him all the time. I saw until all their generations were transformed, and they all became hoary bulls; and the first among them became a savior, and that savior became an inordinate animal and had great black horns upon its head; and the Lord of the righteous rejoiced over it and over all the oxen. I slept in their midst, and I awoke and saw everything. This is a vision, which I watched while I slept, and I awoke and blessed the Lord of righteousness and gave him glory. After that, I suppurated with a great weeping and my tears stayed not until I could no longer endure it, when I saw, they flowed because of what I had seen, for everything come to be, and all the deeds of men in their order were shown to me. I subsequently lost my vision, awaking, trembling, and vision blurred. Khemmis feed me the seal that held my vision so that I would remember it always when the time came for me to serve for the Lord. Khemmis now showed me to the throne of Jehovah as I fell before the blessed the Lord of righteousness and gave him glory. He then said unto us, "Arise Khemmis and Lilith. Khemmis shall be your scribe, tell you my words, and give you the scrolls to open and execute my end of time commands. "I next said to Jehovah, "Jehovah, I understand not the visions that you have imparted to me." Jehovah after that said, "I shall show unto you the secrets of these visions, thus far you shall understand them not until it is time to empty the vials upon the dry land. I shall reveal to you the secrets of the revelations of the end times. These secrets shall be cemented into your spirit, as all in the heavens shall know you are the Lord of the End Times, and Khemmis is your scribe. Your blessings shall only begin here for you shall be the Lord of the next world that she feed the flesh. As I have stated, it shall be. Your penance is completed. Prepare yourself for the great work ahead." I then said unto Jehovah, "You know my soul and the passion that I have for all who have life. Even when I take upon myself flesh, I ate not the flesh of animals. How can I have the might of your power, and the enforcer of your justice?" Jehovah now said, "You are the enforcer, for I believe that you will do my will over that of yours. Now go and try to salvage as many as did Lot when he went into Sodom. I have given you the opportunity to redeem the children of Eve with the heart of Eve and the love of Eve. Go forth and change the vision you have seen here today." I now looked at my scribe and said to him, "Khemmis; my hate for Adam is no more since that was the foolishness of a spirit who did not belong to Jehovah. I beg you to nurture my heart that I will fill with the love and compassion as Eve, which I may save as many as possible from the hatred and evil filled beasts that roam the Earth. We shall do the will of Jehovah, as the mysteries of the end times we shall deliver the righteous. Let us go to the Earth and prepare for the end times spilling love upon the flames of lust, gluttony, avarice, sloth, envy and pride, for as I defeated Lucifer, Mammon, Asmodeus, Leviathan, Beelzebub, Amon, and Belphegor and shall defeat all other manners of evil that the Earthmen have made unto them. I shall pour heavenly wine out onto the Earthmen, Chasity, temperance, charity, diligence, patience, kindness, and humility. He or she that drinks of this wine shall be kept from the veils of death, which I shall pour into the Earthmen.

INDEX

Symbols

A

B

C

D

E

F

G

H

I

J

K

L

M

N

O

P

Q

R

S

THE OTHER ADVENTURES IN THIS SERIES

Mempire, Born in Blood

Lord of New Venus

Rachmanism in Ereshkigal

Sisterhood, Blood of our Blood

Salvation, Showers of Blood

The Great Ones

Prikhodko, Dream of Nagykanizsai

Tianshire, Life in the Light

AUTHOR BIO

James Hendershot, D.D. was born on July 12, 1957, living in old wooden houses with no running water until his father obtained work with a construction company that built Interstate 77 from Cleveland, Ohio to Marietta Ohio. He made friends in each of the new towns that his family moved to during this time. The family finally settled in Caldwell, Ohio where he eventually attended a school for auto mechanics. Being of lover of parties more than study, he graduated at the bottom of his class. After barely graduating, he served four years in the Air Force and graduated Magna Cum Laude, with three majors from the prestigious Marietta College. He then served until retirement in the US Army during which time he obtained his Masters of Science degree from Central Michigan University and his third degree in Computer Programing from Central Texas College. His final degree was the honorary degree of Doctors of Divinity from Kingsway Bible College, which provided him with keen insight into the divine nature of man.

After retiring from the US Army, he accepted a visiting professor position with Korea University in Seoul, South Korea. Upon returning to a small hometown close to his mother's childhood home, he served as a personnel director for Kollar Enterprises. Eleven years later, he moved to a suburb of Seattle to finish his life long search for Mempire and the goddess Lilith, only to find them in his fingers and not with his eyes. It is now time for Earth to learn about the great mysteries not only deep in our universe but also in the universes or dimensions beyond. Listen to his fingers as they are sharing these anonymities with you.